THE GENTLE REBEL

BOOKS BY GILBERT MORRIS

THE HOUSE OF WINSLOW SERIES

CHENEY DUVALL, M.D.[1]

CHENEY AND SHILOH: THE INHERITANCE[1]

THE SPIRIT OF APPALACHIA[2]

LIONS OF JUDAH

[1]with Lynn Morris   [2]with Aaron McCarver

GILBERT MORRIS

the GENTLE REBEL

Minneapolis, Minnesota

Published by Bethany House Publishers
11400 Hampshire Avenue South
Bloomington, Minnesota 55438
www.bethanyhouse.com

Bethany House Publishers is a division of
Baker Publishing Group, Grand Rapids, Michigan.

Printed in the United States of America

Library of Congress Cataloging-in-Publication Data

Morris, Gilbert.
    The gentle rebel / by Gilbert Morris.
        p.   cm. — (The house of Winslow ; 1775)
    ISBN 0-7642-2947-8 (pbk.)
    1. United States—History—Revolution, ca. 1775-1783—Fiction. 2. Winslow family (Fictitious characters)—Fiction. 3. American loyalists—Fiction. I. Title II. Series: Morris, Gilbert. House of Winslow.

PS3563.08742G46   2004
813'.54—dc22   2004012899

This one is for my redheads—

Alan Blake Morris and
Zachary Alan Morris

POWER IN THE BLOOD

Alan, my son, quite without intent
Wheeled around as I came in and bent
His head to one side grinning crookedly—
And from his eyes, my father looked at me.

A thousand times I'd seen my father twist
His head just so (sort of a starboard list)
Squint-eyed, as though peering through a haze,
Just as he looked at me through my son's gaze.

I saw my father clear in my son's light,
O, there is power in the blood all right!
That father's blood that cools and slows its pace
Will glow again in a grandson's face.

One day, perhaps, when I am gone from here,
I'll come again to look at Alan plain and clear;
Then he will halt, will stand in shocked surprise
To see *me* smile at him—through Zachary's eyes!

GILBERT MORRIS spent ten years as a pastor before becoming Professor of English at Ouachita Baptist University in Arkansas and earning a Ph.D. at the University of Arkansas. A prolific writer, he has had over 25 scholarly articles and 200 poems published in various periodicals, and over the past years has had more than 180 novels published. His family includes three grown children. He and his wife live in Gulf Shores, Alabama.

CONTENTS

PART THREE
GUNS OVER BOSTON

PART ONE

FIRST BLOOD—LEXINGTON

★ ★ ★ ★

THE
🍂 HOUSE OF WINSLOW 🍂

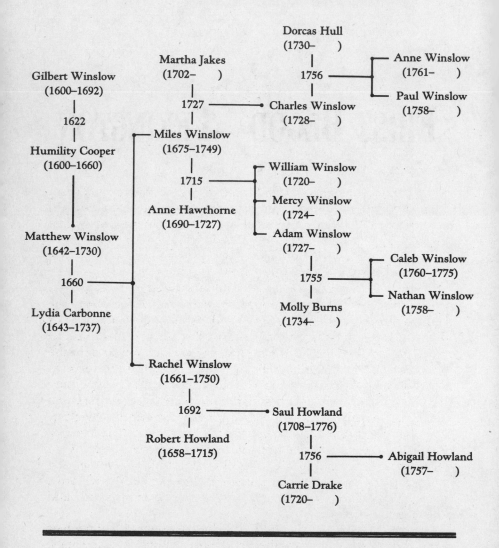

Gilbert Winslow
(1600–1692)
|
1622
|
Humility Cooper
(1600–1660)

Matthew Winslow
(1642–1730)
|
1660
|
Lydia Carbonne
(1643–1737)

Martha Jakes
(1702–   )
|
1727
|
Miles Winslow
(1675–1749)
|
1715
|
Anne Hawthorne
(1690–1727)

Rachel Winslow
(1661–1750)
|
1692
|
Robert Howland
(1658–1715)

Dorcas Hull
(1730–   )
|
1756
|
Charles Winslow
(1728–   )

William Winslow
(1720–   )

Mercy Winslow
(1724–   )

Adam Winslow
(1727–   )
|
1755
|
Molly Burns
(1734–   )

Saul Howland
(1708–1776)
|
1756
|
Carrie Drake
(1720–   )

Anne Winslow
(1761–   )

Paul Winslow
(1758–   )

Caleb Winslow
(1760–1775)

Nathan Winslow
(1758–   )

Abigail Howland
(1757–   )

CHAPTER ONE

ALONE!

★ ★ ★ ★

If Julie Sampson had been born two years earlier or two years later, she would not have been in such a trap—or so she thought as she stood trembling in her small room, her back pressed against the wall.

If I were only twelve or thirteen, he'd leave me alone—or if I were seventeen, I'd be old enough to leave here!

She held her breath as heavy footfalls sounded on the stairs, came down the hall, then stopped abruptly outside her door. She suddenly pressed the back of her hand against her mouth to shut off the cry of terror that rose to her lips. The silence grew thick, so thick that between the solemn tickings of the clock she thought she could hear heavy breathing. Her eyes were riveted on the door as she waited for the pewter knob to turn. When the thought of escape through the small window beside her pierced her mind, she cast a quick glance at the snow that was drifting gently outside the glass.

She edged cautiously to her right. *I wonder if I would break my legs on the cobblestones?* she thought fleetingly, looking down at the walk that ran in front of the shop. She didn't really care—all she wanted to do was escape. She touched the catch on the window; then suddenly the footfalls retreated, going down the hall, and echoing down the stairs.

"Thank God!" she breathed, and then discovered that her legs were trembling so violently she could hardly stand, let alone make the jump to the walkway below. Dropping into the chair beside the small oak table, she hid her face in her hands and tried to think. She struggled to choke back the sobs that rose in her throat; finally, with great effort, she shook her shoulders, rose from the chair and walked to the washbasin at the foot of her bed. Dashing her face with cold water, she dried it with a thick, white cloth that hung at the end of the stand, then began to pace back and forth. Her mind whirled, filled with insistent but ineffective thoughts. She couldn't seem to sort them out, and any prayer she tried to utter seemed meaningless, an empty formula, a ritual learned from childhood.

She walked to the window, looking down over the wooden sign that said SILAS SAMPSON—CARTOGRAPHER in crimson letters, carefully scrolled. The sight of it evoked an image of her father, and as she thought of his slight figure bent over his desk, the tears flooded her eyes, and she dashed them away almost angrily.

I can't cry for him anymore! she thought. And then she looked across the street, resolutely past the sign swinging in the stiff January breeze, and saw a man wearing a heavy fur coat. Her lips grew firm, and snatching a heavy coat and a bonnet from the pegs on the wall, she stepped outside her room, walked down the hall and descended the stairs.

Her hope of passing through the shop without being noticed was dashed as a voice said, "Julie—where you going?"

Aaron Sampson suddenly appeared, interposing his bulk between her and the door, and as always she had to restrain herself to keep from flinching as he put his meaty hand on her shoulder. "I don't want you to go out in this weather," he said, and his grip changed to a caress that made her flesh crawl.

"Rev. Kelly asked me to come by today," she said quickly.

"The preacher? What's he want with you?"

"I—I think he wants some work done on his books."

"Oh, work is it?" Aaron Sampson cared nothing for preachers, but he dearly loved a dollar. Reluctantly, he let his thick hand slide off Julie's shoulder, stepped aside, and a sudden grin pulled the corners of his thick lips up as she slipped by him. "Might ought to tell that preacher that he'll be needed right soon, Julie!"

She closed the door quickly to shut off his words, but his coarse voice penetrated the three-inch oak with ease: "Might have a marrying job, ain't that right, girl?"

The hard lines of Philadelphia had been blurred by soft folds of new snow, and the rough street felt like thick carpet as Julie hurried to catch up with the tall minister. Her feet made no sound, and flakes as big as wafers stung her face. When she called out, "Rev. Kelly!" there was an echo in the icy air, as if her voice were frozen, too.

"Why, Julie!" Rev. Zachariah Kelly's skeletal thinness was disguised by the bulk of the fur coat, but the face that peered out from under a tri-cornered hat seemed even more pale and bony, framed as it was by the black hat and coat. "What are you doing out in this weather?"

"Oh, I—I just thought it would be good to get some fresh air." Julie's face flushed suddenly. She had lied to Aaron, and whatever the man's designs, her lack of truthfulness troubled her. Then she lifted her face and said quickly, "Rev. Kelly, you told my father once that you wanted him to make a map for you—of County Cork, I think it was?"

"Why, bless me, child!" He stared at her with kindly blue eyes, and then nodded. "I'd almost forgotten that—but so I did."

"Could—could I go home with you so we could talk about it? I can make the map—almost as good as Father could have done it if he . . . !"

Kelly's vision was weak, but he did not miss the sudden tears that rose to the girl's eyes at the mention of her father. He reached out, took her hand, and said gently, "It's very hard to lose a dear one, Julie—hard for anyone. But doubly so when we only have the *one* to lose." His mind went back two months when he had tossed the handful of dirt into the ground, hearing it strike the wooden coffin containing Julie's father with a dull *thud*, and he remembered that she had flinched at the sound as if the earth had struck her in the face—or as if a musket ball had smitten her in the heart. "You were very close to your father, Julie," he murmured. Then briskly, he took her arm and said, "Why, I think that's a splendid idea— that map of the old country! We'll just pop along to my study and I'll show you where I came from—and did you know, my dear, that all Irishmen are descended from kings?" He chattered away lightly, and was rewarded to see the lines fade from her smooth brow.

They passed under the shadow of Christ Church, an imposing virgin clothed in winter white, then walked around the path to the small cottage in the rear that almost touched the graveyard. Rev.

Kelly bustled Julie inside, and asked his wife to fix some tea and bring it to the study.

"There's no tea, you mind," Mrs. Kelly said with a mischievous smile. "Don't you remember, Zachariah?"

He stared at her blankly; then a grimace of annoyance swept his thin features. "Blast!" Then he laughed, and a twinkle lit his blue eyes. "When the Crown put that tax on tea, I got carried away with some of Sam Adams' talk—and when the Sons of Liberty dressed up like Indians and threw the King's tea into Boston Harbor, why, I joined the rest of the Bedlamites and threw all my tea in the fire!" He shrugged ruefully, then added as he guided Julie to his study, "That's the way it is with that sort of *repentance*—a man gets carried away with something, then has to live with it after the parade's over!"

Julie followed him into the large study lined with books. "Now, let's see," he muttered, staring at the two large tables against the wall almost buried with papers, drawings, books, and other scholarly material. "Ah! Here we have it!"

The minister extracted a large book from the midst of a stack of papers, opened it, and soon he and Julie were chattering away about longitudes, latitudes and other matters of the business. Rev. Kelly was not thinking of mapmaking, however, but of the young woman who stood beside him. Since the death of her father, Julie had been grappling with a problem that he could not quite identify. She had been a member of his church all her life, as had her father, and the two of them had been inseparable. Since his death, however, she had become more and more silent and her ruddy cheeks had grown pale.

He looked down on her, thinking not for the first time what an attractive girl she was. She was tall, and Kelly guessed that her five feet eight inches came from her mother's side, for her father had been slight—only a little over five six at best. She was no lightweight, and her transformation from childhood to womanhood was obvious—her blossoming figure was revealed by the simple gray gown she wore. Her shoulders were square, her arms rounded and strong. She had very black hair, thick and slightly curly. Her eyebrows, thick and dark, arched over eyes so dark that the pupils were difficult to see—eyes wide and almond shaped with long curling lashes. Her nose was straight and her rather square face and firm chin announced more than a hint of stubbornness.

She looks well enough, Kelly thought, but after they had talked of the map, settled the details of the price, he ventured to ask, "Now, Julie, tell me what's bothering you."

She looked startled; then a flush touched her cheeks. "Why— Rev. Kelly . . . !" Actually she had asked for this visit to try to tell him of her desperation, but now that he stood there, she could not force herself to say it.

"You know, Julie, I promised your father on his deathbed that I'd take care of you. As a matter of fact, if it weren't for your uncle, my wife and I would have had you come to live with us. We talked about it."

"Oh, could I do that, Reverend?" she asked quickly. Her eyes pleaded with him as she said nervously, "I'd do all the work! And I'm a very good cook, you know!"

Her quick response caught Kelly off guard, and looking into her face, he wished he had not mentioned the matter. "Why, my dear, we would love it—but Mr. Sampson is not at all sympathetic to the idea."

"You talked to him?"

"Why, yes, I did. It was only a few days after the funeral. I told him that it might be better for you to stay with us, but—"

"He said he wanted to keep me, didn't he?"

Aaron Sampson had said much more than that, Rev. Kelly remembered grimly. The burly man had cursed, his beefy face red, ending up by saying, "You preachers is all alike—out for all you can get! That milksop of a brother of mine, you pulled the wool over his eyes, but you don't get nothing off me, see? The girl stays here, and I've got the law on my side!"

Kelly's pale, thin face grew red at the memory of how the big man had practically thrown him out of the house, sending him out the door with a shove. "I'm afraid there's little hope that your uncle would permit you to come here, Julie," he said regretfully.

"I—I'm afraid of him, Rev. Kelly!"

"Afraid of him? Has he hurt you, Julie?"

"N-no."

"Mistreated you, has he?"

Her face burned, and she said in a whisper, "He—he won't leave me alone!"

Kelly felt a quick thrill shoot along his nerves—half anger and half fear. There was no mistaking the girl's meaning, but he stood there feeling impotent, having no clue as to how he could help her. *Her father was a fool!* he thought angrily.

Silas Sampson had been a good man, but weak in many ways, Kelly recalled. His wife had died when Julie was only six, and he had never remarried. Some had thought it wonderful the way he had let his daughter fill the place of a wife, but Kelly had thought it abominable, seeing that the child had been robbed of much that all children ought to know. But to be fair, he would have to admit that Silas had been a loving father; nothing had been too good for his Julie!

A year ago, he had fallen ill, very ill, and as his condition worsened, he became almost frantic. Kelly remembered well his visits, when the sick man had cried out, "I'm not afraid to die— but what will happen to my girl when I'm gone?"

The thought had tormented him, and nothing the minister or anyone else could say gave him any peace. Finally, he had surprised them all with a solution. He had sent for Rev. Kelly, and with fever glazing his eyes, he had said, "I—I have one relative, Reverend— a younger brother. We've not been close—in fact, Aaron and I haven't spoken in many years. But now I must call on him! He's all I have left!"

It had been, in Rev. Kelly's judgment, a bad decision. When Aaron Sampson had come to Philadelphia to live with his brother, he had been so unlike the frail cartographer that it was difficult for Kelly to believe they were related. Aaron was overbearing, arrogant, crude—in every respect the opposite of Silas. He had moved in, taken over the affairs of the business, and, with unbelievable callousness, waited for his only brother to die. Indeed, by the time Julie's father had slipped away, Aaron Sampson was spreading his elbows wide on the board.

Now looking down into Julie's pale face, Kelly was appalled. He knew only too well the power of men over women in the courts. No girl of Julie's age would have a chance against a full-grown man like Aaron Sampson. And the minister knew for a fact, having been told by that babbling fool of a lawyer, Will Spelling, that Julie's father had given Aaron Sampson everything! Nothing for the daughter. *The man was a fool!* Kelly thought again, but he only said gently, "Try not to worry, child. God is not unaware of our problems. I'll have another talk with your uncle."

"Please try to get him to let me come here!" Julie whispered, and the fear in her eyes was a living thing as he nodded.

After she left, Kelly walked into the kitchen and sat down at the table with his wife. She was a large woman, as thick as he was thin, a condition that gave rise to some ribald talk from the cruder elements of the town. But she was wise and had lived long enough with the tall preacher to know his thoughts. "You're worried about Julie, aren't you, Zachariah?"

He picked up the glass of cider she placed before him, tasted it, then set it down. "That man is after her, Bess!"

She stared at him, her lips growing white with pressure. "What will you do?"

He suddenly smote the table with his fist and shouted, "Nothing! Not a blasted thing!" Then he stared at her with a hopeless anger in his blue eyes, adding in a whisper, "There's not one blessed thing anyone can do, Bess!" He rose to his feet, and there was misery in every line of his tall body, for he was a true shepherd, and he loved this girl. The thought of Aaron Sampson's gross figure drew his lips together into a grimace, and he said bitterly, "The only hope—and it's a foul thought—is that he'll marry the poor child!" Then he left the kitchen, and went to the church, praying long—partly for the child and partly for himself, for forgiveness. For he was filled with a raging hatred for Sampson, and he well knew that until *that* changed, he could pray for nothing else.

Business was booming, and for the next month Julie was kept so busy (as was her uncle) that her fears subsided. Her father had trained her, and although it had been necessary to hire an assistant to fill the gap her father had left, the shop had prospered. Perhaps it was the constant talk of war with England that created a demand for maps, but whatever the cause, Julie had worked long days and many nights to keep up with the orders.

The new cartographer was a taciturn man named Isaiah Johnson. He was a good workman, but a heavy drinker, so he brought no levity into the shop. Aaron knew a little of the work, and was determined to learn more, and this was, perhaps, the reason why he had left Julie more or less alone. For all his crudeness, he was no fool; a shrewd man, he realized that the girl was profitable.

More to the point, he had gone into details with Will Spelling, and discovered that his grip on the property was not as firm as he had thought.

"Your name is on the paper," Spelling had pointed out, "but so is Julie's. In law, you and Julie are more or less partners—with you being the junior partner." The lawyer was a small man with close-set eyes, a catfish mouth, and no scruples. He smiled now, adding, "That's the way your brother wanted it, Aaron."

"Junior partner?" the huge man snorted, a wicked light in his small eyes. "Well, well—junior partner, is it? Well, there's a way around that!"

"I'm sure you've thought of it," Spelling said with a small smile. "And the girl's a likely looking filly!"

"Aye! And I think she'll make a better wife than a senior partner to me! Yes, indeed, Lawyer Spelling—I think we'll be needing to do a little more of your blasted paper work soon!"

It was nearly midnight when Julie made her way wearily up the steps, her fingers stained with ink and her eyes burning with fatigue. She undressed and washed, and had just donned her heavy nightgown when the door opened suddenly.

"Julie—we've got a little talking to do!"

Sampson stood there filling the. doorway, and Julie's heart leaped with fear as she saw the cruel smile on his thick lips. Quickly she reached for the robe that lay on her bed, but as large as he was, Aaron moved quickly. He stepped forward, caught her by the arm, and the power of his hand was awesome.

"Please—" She swallowed and could only whisper, "Let me go, please—we'll talk in the morning."

He said nothing, but his grip on her arm tightened, and then his eyes glittered. His eyes ran over her, and she struggled vainly to pull away. "You ain't a baby, Julie," he said thickly. "You're a full-growed woman!"

Her ears were ringing, and the rank smell of the man sickened her. There was no one in the house; even if she screamed, no one could hear, and if anyone did, it was unlikely they would come. She stood there trembling and trying to break his grip, but it was hopeless.

He suddenly pulled her closer, putting his massive arms around her, and said, "You need a husband, Julie! And I'm him!"

"No!"

"I say you're going to marry me, girl, and don't make no mistake! The law says I'm your guardian—but we can't live here together alone—why, it wouldn't be decent!"

He leered down at her, grinning at the irony in his own words. "I'll leave!" she cried out. "I'll give up my share of the shop. I'll go live with the minister!"

"No, you'll marry me, Julie, and that's final!" Sampson drew her closer and attempted to speak more lightly. "Why, I know you're young, Julie, and I reckon you're afraid of men—seeing you ain't never had no fellows, that'd be natural. But I aim to treat you right—and Silas, he made me promise to do it."

"No!" Julie tried to pull away, but his arms held her in a powerful vise. "Father never said that!"

"Sure he did!" Aaron laughed, then pulled her face up and kissed her. "That's just a sample, Julie," he said. "I'll have a talk with that preacher tomorrow. Don't think we ought to put this thing off. You don't need no big wedding. Just have the parson come in tomorrow and do the job—or if he won't, I reckon I can find one who will!"

He laughed down at her horror-stricken face, kissed her again, then released her so abruptly that she nearly fell. "You get a good night's sleep now. I want you rested up, 'cause tomorrow you'll have a husband to keep happy!"

The door slammed, and in the silence Julie stood there, tears running down her face. She listened as his footsteps faded, then his door slammed. More than anything she wanted to fall across the bed and weep, but she knew that would be futile.

Finally, she went to the bed, knelt down, and for a long time she was still. The room was cold and quiet, and there was no sound at all except for a muffled word now and then as she prayed. Thirty minutes passed, then an hour. At last the clock in the hall struck one—a ghostly tone in the silence of the night, a round, mellow tone that seemed to touch her, for she suddenly raised her head, tears making crystal tracks down her cheeks.

But there was no fear in her dark eyes, and she slowly got to her feet and stood staring out the window into the darkness. The snow on the rooftops had turned to silver through the alchemy of moonlight, and there was not a soul stirring on the street.

Julie said, "Amen!" and then she knelt again, this time to pull a small traveling bag from underneath her bed. Opening it, she began to throw her clothes into it, her face set like flint. When the valise was packed, she paused, then picked up the Bible from the desk, placed it gently on the top of the clothes, shut the case and fastened it.

At last she walked to the door, pulled it open firmly, and without a backward glance, passed through the dark hall and out of the shop into the blackness of the night.

CHAPTER TWO

RUNAWAY

★　★　★　★

Julie climbed down from the Conestoga wagon and, reaching up, took her small bag from the muscular hand of Matthew Perkins. The big man said as he passed it along, "You better think about going on with us, missy. Be right glad to have you."

"Do come!" his wife Ruth urged. She was a worn, middle-aged woman with still a few remnants of beauty, and she added a smile as she leaned over her husband to make a final plea to Julie. "You're all alone, and we'd be proud to share our home with you."

Julie looked up and for a moment was tempted, but quickly decided that their home was too close to Philadelphia. They had picked her up as she trudged along in the snow three days earlier, and they were such plain, simple people it had never occurred to them to doubt her story. She had told them that she was an orphan who was going to New York to work and live with an aunt. The lie had pained her, but she finally had said to herself, "It's *almost* the truth—I *am* going to live with an aunt."

She had left home with one thin fragment of a plan. Her mother's sister lived in Portsmouth, on the southern coast of England. The sisters had been close, and even though Julie's mother had been dead for years, Mrs. Collingwood had written at rare intervals, expressing some interest in her niece. Silas had spoken at times of a visit, but nothing had ever come of it. As Julie had prayed, the thought had come to her, and she conceived the idea of going to New York, there booking passage to flee the Colonies. She knew that Aaron would have the law looking for her, and the New World was a small place in which to hide—but England!

So she stood there in the snow with the Perkinses, looking very young. But there was a firmness in her voice as she shook her head and said, "I'm so grateful to you both, but—my aunt would be very disappointed if I didn't come! God bless you both!"

They said their farewells; then as the heavy horses pulled the big wagon down the rutted street, Julie turned and looked around at New York for the first time. The Perkinses had brought her to a section of town near the harbor, and she passed by a good many inns with names such as The King's Arms, The Merchant's Coffee House, The Blue Boar, and The Three Pigeons. It was late afternoon and she had eaten a good breakfast at dawn, but now the smell of cooking meat and fresh bread drifting out of the inns drew her, so she looked until she found a small one with the pretentious name of The Spread Eagle.

Going inside, she almost faltered. All the customers were men, except for an elderly couple who sat against the far wall. But hunger nudged her, and she took a small table next to the couple. The innkeeper was a rough-looking man with one eye covered by a black patch, but the meal he produced was good—beef and cheese with plenty of fresh hot bread and yellow butter. She ate hungrily, lingered over the steaming tea as long as possible, then got up and paid for the meal.

"Is it far to the harbor?" she asked.

"No more'n a quarter-mile down that way," he nodded with his head. Then he looked her over and added, "Be dark soon, miss. Best not be on the streets all alone."

"Oh, my brother will meet me, thank you." The words leaped easily to her lips, and she thought wryly, *It's getting easier to lie!* Then she hesitated and asked, "Do you have a room I could have for the night—in case I can't find my brother?"

"Right, miss. Cost yer a shilling with breakfast throwed in."

She gave him a coin. "I'll take it. Give me the key."

"Key was carried off long ago, miss—but I'll see you right. Don't allow no fancy tricks in my place! Not likely!"

It seemed the best thing, as it appeared unlikely that she would find a berth in a ship that evening. The man looked rough, but there was no guarantee that another place would be safer. She nodded and followed him up a small stairway that led to the upper floor. He opened a door, then stepped back, saying, "If you wants hot water later—or a late supper, just you call, miss."

"Thank you."

Julie waited until he left, then put her small bag on the bed. A pitcher of water and a basin on the table beside the bed beckoned, and she washed her face carefully, then put her coat on and started to leave. She reached the door, then paused suddenly, went to the bag and removed a purse containing most of the money she had. She counted out fifty pounds, dividing it into three parts. She put twenty pounds each in two leather bags and wrapped the other ten in a handkerchief and slipped it into a smaller bag with a long drawstring. This one she placed around her neck, allowing the bag to fall inside the front of her dress. She dared not leave any of the cash in an unlocked room, so she put one of the larger bags in her handbag and the other in her deep coat pocket. As she passed through the main dining room, the one-eyed innkeeper said, "Remember, miss, it won't do to be on the streets late."

She nodded, then walked rapidly down the narrow streets, filled with many more people than she was accustomed to. She saw more foreigners than was usual in Philadelphia—French, Spanish-looking men, swarthy fellows she took to be Portuguese, and many, many blacks, usually accompanying their owners on errands.

The harbor was a forest of masts, thicker than stalks in a field of corn—far more than most harbors. She wandered down the wharf, wondering how to find a ship bound for England, but there was no such thing as a passenger ship. She knew enough to realize that she would be fortunate to get a compartment on some sort of cargo ship headed back with a load of tobacco, furs, or lumber.

Twice she stopped men to ask about a ship, but neither of them knew of one. Then a tall man with a wolfish face came up to her, saying, "Hello, darling! Looking for someone?"

"No!" she said abruptly, then wheeled and walked back along the pier as rapidly as she could without breaking into a run. It was almost dark when she got back to the inn. She noted that a smallish woman with red hair was serving the customers their drinks. The smoke was thick and she felt uncomfortable there, so she ascended the stairs to her small room. There was no light, and when she had to go back downstairs to get a light for the candle on the small table, the red-haired woman looked at her in a sharp, peculiar way.

The room was cold, of course, with no heat at all except that which drifted up from the fireplace below, so she pulled the covers back and got under the heavy blankets fully dressed. For over an hour she read the Bible, and finally, putting it on the table, she blew the candle out. Sleep came almost at once, but she woke several times, awakened by the raucous laughter and shouts from the inn below, and more than once by bad dreams.

Finally the noise from downstairs subsided, and she slept an exhausted sleep.

The sound of the door opening brought her instantly awake— a very small sound, but in the silence of the room it seemed very loud. She sat bolt upright, clenching the covers to her breast as a thin line of light outlined the door as it opened, and in an unsteady voice she cried out, "You get out of here!"

Then the door swung open and a burly figure filled the opening as the one-eyed man bearing a brass lantern in his hand stepped inside and shut the door. He put his back to the door and said, "Well—looky whut we got here!"

"You—you better get out of here or I'll—!"

"You'll scream?" he asked with a rough laugh when she could not finish. "Go ahead, see what it gets you."

He pulled himself away from the door, and as he stepped beside her, she threw the covers back, and leaping from the bed started for the door. He caught her easily, and for one moment held her by the arm, looking down at her. There was a greedy look in his one black eye, and his breath came faster; then he said, "You're a pretty little thing, ain't you now?" He reached out with his free hand and with careless strength held her face. She knew it was in his mind to kiss her.

Then he gave her a shove and said, "Yer ain't got no need to fear—not from me. All I wants is the reward."

Julie stepped back suddenly as he released her, breathless with relief that he had no intention of molesting her. "Reward?"

"Aw, you know about that—don't be so innocent!" He reached into his inner pocket, pulled out a folded sheet and shoved it at her. "Soon as I seen you, I knowed you was familiar, but it didn't come to me till I was in bed. So I gets up, goes down to the harbor and finds out that I'm gonna make a pile of money off of you!"

Julie opened the paper and read in large print:

RUNAWAY GIRL—REWARD

The description that followed fit her; the handbill offered a reward of twenty pounds, and it was signed by Aaron Sampson of Philadelphia.

"Easiest twenty guineas I ever made!" the innkeeper laughed. Then he said, "You jes' come with me and we'll get going."

Julie's mind raced like a wild thing, and like a flash an idea leaped into her mind. She stood straight and looked right into the man's face, her voice steely as she said, "You'll get no twenty pounds—but you'll get a thrashing and a holiday in jail—that's what you'll get."

He stopped smiling, surprised at the sudden hardness that had crossed her face. "What's that?"

"You see that name—the man who's offering the reward?"

"Yeah, I see it—Aaron Sampson. What about it?"

"You may think you've seen some hard men here, but you've never run across one as mean as he is."

"Who is he?"

"My father," she lied easily. "I lied about meeting my brother. I'm going to meet my lover and we're going to England together and get married."

"That's a lie—but even if it ain't, your pa, he'll pay twenty pounds to get you back!"

Julie made herself shrug and look careless. "All right, have it your way."

Something about the easy way she gave in disturbed the man, and he hesitated. She caught it, and said, "What will happen is that I'll tell him you abused me, and he'll beat you half to death and then have you put in prison. He's a magistrate and knows the law—he's had people put in jail for less." A shadow of doubt had begun to cloud the single eye of the innkeeper, and Julie said, as though it had just occurred to her, "Of course, there's one way you can have the reward—and stay out of jail."

"How's that?" he asked quickly.

"Why, I'll give you the twenty pounds—if you promise to say nothing. We'll be gone tomorrow—then I don't care what you say to anyone."

"You ain't got no twenty pounds!"

Julie turned and picked up her small bag. Opening it, she plucked out the bag containing twenty pounds and tossed it at the man, who caught it. He pulled the strings opened, poured the coins out in his palm, and counted them. Then he looked up and said with admiration, "You're a shrewd one, you are! Gor!"

Julie feared any delay, for he could change his mind, so she fastened her small case, picked up her coat, which had fallen from the bed to the floor, and said, "Remember—I want nothing said about this—or I'll have a story to tell my father that'll get you drawn and quartered!"

"If you ain't something!" The innkeeper shook his head in admiration. "Blamed if you ain't a bold baggage!"

Julie left him, sweeping down the stairs and out into the street. The stars burned coldly in the dark sky, but rosy lights were breaking the darkness to the east as she hurried blindly down the street. There was no hope now of finding a ship in New York; the posters made capture almost a certainty. She moved quickly away from the waterfront area, and by the time the pale morning light washed across the streets, she was on the outskirts of town. Every time she passed anyone, she turned her face away like a guilty felon. She expected at any second to be stopped and hauled off to jail. Finally she halted, out of breath and shaky from fear. She found herself on a side street with only a few shops.

Some wagons were making their way out of town, and she knew her only hope was to get a ride in one of them, as she had with Matthew Perkins and his wife, but the thought nagged at her that the reward posters would be all along the coast, in every port, probably.

A bench made of a half-log with whittled posts for legs offered a moment's rest, so she sat down, and for half an hour tried to think of a plan. Nothing came to her, and finally she rose, intending to ask for a ride on one of the wagons, hoping for another miracle.

Just as she was about to move away, the door beside the bench swung open and a short man shaped like a barrel stepped outside with a shovel in his hand. He stopped upon seeing her, then smiled and said, "Well, you're here early, miss, but come on inside."

"Why, I was just—" she began; then she got a look at the merchandise inside the shop and stopped suddenly. She moved slowly, a thought coming to her, and she entered the shop followed by the owner.

"I could use a few things," she said, and for the next quarter of an hour she selected a small collection of items.

"This be all?"

"Yes. How much?"

"Well, let's see. . ." He added up the total, and she reached into her coat pocket to get the money.

"Something wrong, miss?"

Julie was searching her pockets frantically, but the leather pouch was gone. With a sickening feeling she remembered that the coat had fallen to the floor, and she knew that the heavy pouch must have slid out.

"I—no!" she said, then turning to one side, she pulled the purse-strings around her neck free, and opening the pouch, paid for the merchandise from its slender store. It took two pounds, and she resolutely put away the fear that touched her as the man wrapped the goods in a paper and handed them to her.

She left the shop so quickly that the shopkeeper came out to watch her disappear around a corner. "Funny sort of things for a young girl to want," he muttered, then started shoveling snow from the walk.

Julie walked down half a dozen streets, looking for some sort of privacy, and at last she found an old barn that was apparently deserted. She looked around furtively, then darted inside, her breath coming quickly. The place, she saw at once, was not being used, and she found a stall with a window that let a shaft of light into the darkness of what had been some sort of small harness room. She put her bag and the package on the floor, then slowly pulled the paper aside. Reaching down, she picked up a pair of scissors and held them up. She stared at them, then removed her bonnet and with a quick motion let her long hair down. It fell down her back, thick, black and lustrous, and she felt a momentary twinge of sadness, but then her lips tightened, and she reached back and awkwardly cut a long, thick tress. She held it up, looked at it for a long moment, then gave a half sob and dropped it to the floor and began snipping steadily.

Thirty minutes later, when the door of the abandoned barn swung open, the figure that stepped outside looked nothing like Julie Sampson!

The test came at once, for just as she slipped outside and was walking toward the main street, a man rounded the corner and walked right by her. Her heart almost stopped, but he only gave her a quick nod, said, "Morning," and without another word or look passed on down the street.

What he had seen was a young fellow, not over fifteen, with a soft cap pulled down over a head of roughly-cut black hair. To be sure, there was a little softness in the lad, something a little girlish in the curve of the cheeks—but no more so than in other city-raised lads.

Julie had deliberately scuffed the gray homespun shirt, the knee breeches and brown stockings in the dirt, as well as the heavy wool coat that hung down to her knees. The garments were too large and so poorly cut that they effectively concealed her developing figure.

She walked down the street carrying the case, which contained a few other masculine garments. All the clothing she had brought with her, along with personal feminine items, she had left in the loft, and the pile of hair she had buried.

It took great courage for Julie to join the growing stream of people on their way to work, but she knew no other way was possible.

I've got a chance! she thought. *If I'm careful and keep to myself, I can do it.*

So she made her way to the outskirts of town, was picked up by an old man with a wagon load of glass windows headed for New Haven. He was a foul-mouthed old man, and the things he said to the young "fellow" beside him made her cheeks burn, but she managed to cover her confusion, and as the wagon rumbled along, she tried to ignore the fact that she had only a few pounds. She had no idea how she would get across the sea to her aunt's, but one thing kept coming to her mind—a verse of scripture that Pastor Kelly seemed to love more than any other. He quoted it every time he preached, usually more than once. Now as the wagon bumped along over the rutted road and the old man told raw stories, Julie let that verse linger in her mind, saying it over and over again: "With God—nothing shall be impossible!"

During the weeks that followed, Julie felt as if she might wear that verse out, and more than once her faith almost failed. The pitifully small stack of coins dwindled rapidly, even though she spent money only for food—and not a great deal of that.

She traveled where the wagons went that picked her up, falling into a kind of aimlessness. Her idea of getting to England she clung to stubbornly, but there was no money for her passage, so she moved steadily up the coast, touching briefly at Newport, only to discover the reward posters there as well.

She had grown more assured with her disguise, discovering that people did not really care much, especially as the clothes she had bought grew dirty and worn. Sometimes she would stay in a barn and cut some wood for a meal with a farmer, but as she moved northward, the weather grew worse, and when she came to Boston on the third of February, a blizzard swept in from the west burying the city under ice and snow.

In desperation, Julie tried to find a ship that would take her in exchange for work, but nothing was available. Few ships made the trip in such weather, and those that did go were usually able to make up a crew of able-bodied seamen.

Her last coins went, and then she had nothing. She shoveled snow for some of the merchants, but most of the shops shut down, waiting for the warm breath of spring to thaw the city out.

On the third day after her money ran out, Julie touched bottom. She had gone up and down the streets asking for work with the few merchants who still opened their businesses, and found none. For two days she had eaten nothing, and her head was aching with fatigue.

Snow began to drift downward late in the afternoon, and with her stomach in a knot, she went to the harbor, stumbling through the falling snow, not really caring a great deal what happened.

The cold paralyzed her hands, and finally she sat down facing the forest of masts, all white and glittering with snow and ice. The sounds of the city were muffled by the thick, fleecy blanket of snow, and she realized that she would have to get up and find shelter in a barn or in an alley, but she had no will to do it.

Closing her eyes, she ignored the snow gathering on her head and whitening her clothing. She thought of her father and of those good times in the past. She remembered the church and Pastor Kelly with his thin face and hearty voice. She even remembered her mother, dead and buried—living only in her memories now.

Julie sat there, dozing and thinking of the sweet warm days of the past—and still the snow fell. Gently it fell, making a soft blanket that was no longer cold, but seemed warm—warm as her memories and her dreams.

Slowly she drifted into a gentle sleep like a little child.

CHAPTER THREE

A FAMILY DIVIDED

★ ★ ★ ★

Caleb Winslow was roused from a sound sleep by the sound of his brother's head hitting the oak headboard with a solid *THUNK!* He turned his head and grinned as a muffled oath broke the morning silence.

"Ministers aren't supposed to swear," Caleb said. By the thin gray light of the January sun he watched as his brother, holding the top of his head, swung his feet to the floor and sat up. "That must be a million times you've banged your head, Nathan. Appears to me you'd figure out a better way to wake up than beating your brains out every morning."

"Like what?" Nathan asked grumpily. "Cut my legs off and be a midget like you?" He stood up cautiously, avoiding the low, rough-hewn beam that dissected the small loft bedroom. He went to the oak washstand and, breaking the skim of ice from the water in the basin, began splashing his face, sputtering and wheezing. He worked up a thin lather and scraped at his cheeks with a razor.

Caleb watched with interest, and when Nathan was finished, he said, "Think I'll start shaving." He had said this since Nathan had started shaving two years earlier and had no real intention of acting on it.

"Shaving *what*?" Nathan grinned as he stripped off a flannel nightshirt and began pulling on his clothes. "Might as well look for whiskers on an egg as on your face. Got to be a man to grow something to shave, boy!"

Caleb's face flushed and he rolled out of bed and thrust his chin forward. "A little hair on your face don't make you a man!" His dark eyes flashed and he put his hands forward in a wrestling stance, adding, "You think you're more of a man than me, Nathan; why, you just come on, and we'll see!"

A sudden grin touched the lips of the older boy, and he regarded the stocky figure of his brother fondly. "You're getting too big to fool with." He rubbed the top of his head and added ruefully, "I keep growing *up* and you keep growing *around*, Caleb—looks like we could sort of *average out* somehow!"

The two did present a stark contrast. Caleb, at fifteen, was short but powerfully built. His chest was deep and pads of muscle swelled his upper body. His legs were thick and solid, and there was a ponderous quality to all his movements. He had a square chin, and even by the feeble morning light that streamed in, his dark coloring and dark eyes were visible.

He stood there, a solid figure, looking up at Nathan, and there was a trace of envy in his dark eyes as he took in his brother's tall form. Nathan was exactly six feet three inches tall, and though at seventeen he was two years older than Caleb, he had not filled out as he would later on. He had shot up like a weed for the past three years, his clothes becoming too short before they wore out. He had discovered his actual height by measuring the bed he shared with Caleb and found it to be exactly six feet and three inches long— which meant that if he got one inch too high in it, he would bash his head against the hard oak as he had done a few moments earlier. The only solution he could find was to sleep at an *angle*—a practice that did not make Caleb happy, since it meant sharing his half of the bed with his brother's long legs.

There was some awkwardness to Nathan's movements as he finished dressing and moved toward the door, for he had grown so fast that his coordination had not yet caught up with his stature. He had the cautious movements of a very tall man—always measuring low beams and door openings. In spite of this coltish awkwardness, there were traces of grace and strength as he moved through the door, and most people who saw him asked themselves, *What will he be like when he gets his full growth?*

But it was not only in height that the two differed; where Caleb had dark skin, blue-black eyes, and black hair, Nathan had auburn hair and the high complexion that frequently goes with that shade. His face was triangular, sloping down from a broad forehead to a pointed chin; his nose was rather short, but flared out at the base. Smallish ears almost hidden behind the hair, a wide mouth, straight eyebrows over a pair of startling light blue eyes—these were all part of the Winslow heritage that had come to him. He was almost delicate in feature, and some said he was pretty enough to be a girl. Yet there was a hint of stubborn strength in his features and a steadiness in his eyes that offset any touch of the feminine, and his long reach and developing strength had enabled him to hold his own in the youthful brawls that had come his way.

"Better get yourself dressed," Nathan called as he left the room. "I think Ma is frying donkers."

The fragrance of baking filled the house as they hurried down from the loft and into the broad hallway toward the kitchen. His mother turned as he entered, greeting him with a smile. "Good morning, Nathan."

"Morning, Mother." His appetite was ferocious, and the smell of cooking meat made his stomach rumble. His mother made donkers from the week's meat leftovers, chopped together with bread, apples, raisins and savory spices—fried and served with boiled pudding. He picked up a wooden spoon, filled it from the heavy black pot and jammed it into his mouth.

"Nathan, you'll burn your tongue off!" She took the spoon away from him, reached up and smoothed his hair down where it rose up in the back, and then pushed him toward the door. "You better get some firewood in before your father sees that empty wood box!"

"That's Caleb's job," he complained.

"Oh? You're too dignified to help around the house now that you're going to college?"

"I didn't say that!"

"You know Caleb does his work—and some of yours as well."

"All right, Mother, all right!"

He stalked outside to the woodpile, and a mixture of righteous indignation and guilt made him make four trips to the house, piling up the short chunks of red oak until the box overflowed. His mother said nothing, but watched him out of the corner of her eye, a furtive smile springing to her lips as he dumped the last load, then slumped into his chair, a picture of wounded innocence.

"You think *that's* enough to do for a spell?"

Molly Winslow's maiden name had been Burns, and she had the type of beauty often seen in women of Scottish blood. She looked ten years younger than her forty-one years, and her ash-blonde hair had no more gray in it than it had when Adam Winslow had first seen her as a child on the streets of London. She had the figure of a young girl, and only a few lines around her eyes revealed her age.

She nodded, but before she could answer, Caleb bustled into the kitchen. He came over to kiss his mother, as he always did, saying, "I'm starved, Ma!"

"After that supper you ate last night," Molly said tartly, "you're not likely to die of hunger." Her tone was sharp, but there was a fond light in her eyes as she looked at the boy. A stab of regret came to Nathan, mixed with envy, for he lacked the easy ways of his younger brother—especially where his parents were concerned. It was not that he loved them less than Caleb, but somewhere along the way an awkwardness had developed. Perhaps it was due to his tremendous height; it was, he recognized, much easier for both of them to see Caleb as a child—after all, who wants to reach up and caress a giant? But that resentful thought passed, and he knew that the wall between himself and his parents was the product of more than a few inches in his spine.

The outer door swung open, and Adam Winslow stepped inside, his dark eyes sweeping the room quickly. His tread was soundless as he came to stand beside his chair. "Morning. Food smells good." He greeted his sons, then sat down in an easy way, and while Molly was putting the food on the table, Adam sat there listening as Caleb chattered on about the trip to Boston. As he ran on, Nathan thought how odd it was that his brother talked so much, and he talked so little. *You'd think he was going to be the minister instead of me!* he thought suddenly.

As Nathan's mother put the hot bread on the table and sat down, suddenly he saw that room as he'd never seen it before—as if it were a painting with the title *Puritan Family at Breakfast*. It was a nice picture, too. They ate in the dining room on the Sabbath, and Mother set the table with china and silver, but on weekdays they ate in the kitchen. So in his mind he saw them sitting around the rough board table with the big fireplace, four of them but with an extra place set for five. His father claimed that the empty chair reminded them that they had an Unseen Guest with them at all times. It was a powerful image, and as a child Nathan had been a little afraid that God would come in and take His seat!

As his father asked the usual blessing, Nathan stole a glance at him, thinking that the Unseen Guest thing was one of the few outer traces of imagination Adam Winslow ever showed. Oh, he was creative enough at the forge, making beautiful rifles or even silver jewelry, but he had little of fancy in him in other ways.

Nathan thought that his father was the most *practical* looking man in the world. He was five feet ten and weighed one hundred eighty-five pounds, and if there was a stronger man in the county, he hadn't shown up to prove it. Adam had a square face with dark skin and darker eyes, and his hair showed only a few gray strands in the midst of the black. His hands were almost square, thick with pads of muscle and scarred from years of work with iron and wood. Nathan took a quick glance at Caleb and almost smiled, for there was something comical in the way his younger brother sat there, a mirror image of the father! They both had the same darkness, the same powerful frame, and despite the fact that Caleb was much more of a talker than his father, they thought in the same way.

"Did you pick up that last load from the warehouse, Nathan?"

"Yes, sir."

"You remember that bale of prime beaver that Louis left up in the loft—the one Dupree brought in last winter?"

"Yes, sir."

There was doubt in the way Nathan's father stared at him. He'd always made the annual trip to Boston to haul the furs, but this year he was so far behind in the forge that Nathan argued him into letting him do it—and somehow he had done even more—he had talked him into letting the two of them stay the rest of the summer with their Uncle Charles!

"I've been with you on the last five trips, Father," he'd pleaded, and then Mother had joined in so that finally a week earlier he'd agreed to let Nathan make the trip. Then Caleb had set up a howl to go, so the two of them were to leave the following day, on their own for the first time in their lives.

Now Nathan saw the questions in his father's eyes, and knew that if he decided his sons weren't to be trusted, he'd just take the furs himself. Right then Caleb jumped in, and for the first time in

Nathan's life he was glad his brother was such a talker!

Caleb knew his father, and he began talking cheerfully about how good it was for young fellows to learn responsibility and how glad he was to have an older brother. As always, he got his way. Nathan saw through it in a second, but he'd learned to accept the fact long ago that his father had a weakness for his younger son.

"It'll be good for them, Adam." Molly came over and put her arm around him, something which always gentled him down. "Charles wants them to come."

"I know. And I suppose the boys can learn something about business from him." His eyes fell on Nathan and there was a peculiar glint in his glance that the older son couldn't read. "But I can't see what good it will do a minister to know about business."

There it was. Nathan felt his face flush, for he resented the fact that his father had never put much stock in his call to the ministry. Ever since that day when Nathan had told his parents that he felt God wanted him to be a minister, the wall between him and his father had grown thicker. Now he said quickly, "Well, Father, I don't think it will do a minister any harm to know something of business."

"I suppose not."

Mother pulled at Father's arm, saying, "We'd better hurry if we don't want to be late for service, Adam." Then she smiled at Nathan and there was a gleam in her gray eyes as she said, "And it wouldn't look very good for you to be late, Nathan. Rev. Patterson might feel your dedication is lacking."

Adam snorted and there was a flash of anger in his dark eyes. "I wish he'd preach the gospel instead of singing the praises of King George!"

"He's not doing that, sir!" Nathan said, and was sorry at once.

Adam stared at the tall young man, his face settling down into an angry look that made Nathan wish he'd kept his mouth shut.

"Nathan, the man is no more than a mouthpiece for the Crown! He has a right to speak his mind, but he uses his pulpit for attacking loyal men in these Colonies—and he has no sense of justice!"

"Sir—I think that's not fair!"

"Not fair!" There was a thick silence in the room, and Nathan saw that they were into another of their arguments over politics. Adam Winslow had fought in the French and Indian War under Colonel Washington and sympathized with the group led by Sam

Adams who were out to challenge English authority. And it saddened Nathan, for his father was not an unreasonable man—quite the contrary. *But he's just as blind as the rest of that crew who want to push us into a war we can't win!* the boy thought.

"You think I'm *unfair*?" Adam demanded, stepping closer to Nathan. "Why, Patterson has branded my friends traitors from his pulpit! And you don't think it's *unfair* for a minister to use his office for a political platform?"

"You don't say that about those ministers who use their pulpits to demand freedom, Father," Nathan shot back, but over his father's head he saw his mother shaking her head violently, and it brought him up short. He realized that if his father got angry, he'd not let them go to Boston, so he said, "Oh, Father, I'm sorry we got into this. Let's drop it and go to service."

Adam was caught off guard with the sudden apology, and Nathan's mother came forward quickly, saying, "Yes, we have to go, Adam."

"All right, Molly."

Nathan and Caleb went quickly to hitch the team and saddle their own mounts. Nathan drove the wagon out of the stable to the front gate, and held the lines until his father helped his mother into the wagon. "Don't race those horses, boys," he said as he took the reins. "Not on the Sabbath."

Nathan said, "No, sir," then went to where Caleb sat on his horse. He mounted easily, and the two of them started down the road. As soon as they were out of hearing, Caleb said, "Why'd you have to start fighting with Father? If you'd kept on, he wouldn't have let us take the trip to Boston."

As they approached the white church just outside the village, Nathan thought of how his father had looked strangely at him when speaking of the founders of their family. Gilbert Winslow, the first of the family to come to America, had been a great and honored man, according to the family tales, as had his son Matthew. But once, in an unguarded moment, Adam had said to his son, "You're too much like Charles, Nathan."

As he pulled his horse down and allowed Caleb to catch up, Nathan thought about his uncle. Charles Winslow was the half brother of Adam, and there'd been some sort of scandal in his life, but Nathan could never find out exactly what it was all about. His uncle was a very successful businessman in Boston, and on the rare occasions when he'd come to Virginia, Nathan had been very impressed. He remembered him as a tall, handsome man with fair hair and bright blue eyes, and that he'd always given generous gifts to him and to Caleb. Slipping from his horse, he tied him to the post, thinking with excitement of the trip. Though he was older than Caleb and had gone to Harvard for one brief term of ten weeks, he was as excited as the younger boy about the trip, and some of it was the expectation of seeing his uncle again.

His parents pulled up fifteen minutes later, and his father said, "I told you not to race those horses, Nathan." There was displeasure in his dark eyes, and he led the way into the white frame building to their customary pew, speaking little to anyone.

Rev. Patterson was a short, broad man with a full, fair face and a strong Bristol accent. Nathan, although he agreed fully with the pastor's political sentiments, hoped fervently that his sermon would stay inside the covers of the Bible. His hopes were dashed, however, for the text was taken from that section of the Scriptures that teaches men to be obedient to those in authority. And those in authority, of course, were of the Royal House of Hanover—King George and his court of ministers.

Rev. Patterson was a man of strong opinions, and his displeasure with those who chose to challenge the authority of the Crown was intense. His eyes lingered longest on Adam Winslow, though there were many others in the congregation who were more adamant in their stand against royal policy than he.

Halfway through the sermon, Nathan heard Caleb snort and say under his breath, "Big jackass!" He dug his elbow into Caleb's ribs, hoping that nobody had heard, but there was a sullen "amen!" that came from his father, and Nathan slumped into his seat, wishing only that the service would end and they could get away.

After the sermon, Rev. Patterson posted himself at the door, and when the Winslows stepped up, he said with an angry light in his eyes, "Mr. Winslow, you should keep your sons in order!"

"Rev. Patterson, you should keep your sermons in order."

There was a sudden hush in the church, the humming of talk stopped abruptly. The position of a minister in the community was an elevated one, and few men would speak so harshly to one of them as Adam Winslow had just done.

"Sir, you are impertinent!" Patterson's face flushed richly, and he added angrily, "It's obvious, sir, that your rebellion against the

Crown has been expanded to include disloyalty against your church!"

Adam Winslow was an even-tempered man, but he had sat through a long line of political harangues masquerading as sermons, all directed at himself and some of his friends. Now the pastor chose to make the thing personal by singling him out, and it stirred him to anger. *There is something dangerous in him,* Nathan thought, and it startled him. He had seen his father aroused only once, years before. A large man had been mistreating a horse, and Nathan never forgot how his father had exploded into wrath, thrashing the bully so quickly and thoroughly that the story still lingered in the town.

"Rev. Patterson, when you preach the gospel, I am a faithful member of your flock. If you choose to depart from your calling and turn your pulpit into a political arena, I cannot respect you."

He might have said more, but Molly suddenly was there. She put her hand on his arm and said, "Adam—please!"

At once, he looked at her, and then said, "This is no place for argument. Excuse us, Pastor."

Nathan followed his parents, but the minister grasped his arms. "Nathan, you must try to talk to your father."

Nathan shook his head. "There is nothing I can say, Pastor. He just gets angry with me."

"I understand you're going to Boston."

"Yes, tomorrow."

"Be careful, Nathan!" Patterson's full face was still angry, and he added as the boy pulled away. "That's where all Sam Adams' gang is, and they'll pull us into a war if something isn't done!"

Nathan hurried away; this time he and Caleb followed the buggy down the road. As he expected, Caleb began to berate the minister. "Why, that preacher ought to be tarred and feathered!" he exclaimed. "I'll bet he gets his pay from ol' King George himself."

"Caleb, you're crazy!"

"No, I'm not!"

"You're just a kid—and not too smart at that!" The anger that had gnawed at Nathan spilled out, and he glared at Caleb, saying loudly, "What do you know? Oh, sure, there have been a few unfair taxes, but what do you think we can do about it?"

"We can fight!"

"Why, you *are* crazy, Caleb!" Nathan snapped. "England's the strongest nation in the world—and you think a few farmers like us can fight her?"

Caleb's dark face was stubborn. "England's thousands of miles away, Nathan, and this is a big country. All of us can shoot, can't we? How long can we stand for being treated like slaves?"

Nathan was shocked, for he had known men put into the stocks for saying less. "Caleb, that's *treason!*"

"It's the same as Father thinks!"

There was so much truth in Caleb's reply that Nathan was speechless. He shook his head in despair, and listened in silence all the way back to the house as Caleb talked endlessly about the matter.

Finally he said as they unsaddled the horses, "You'd better not say any of this to Father, Caleb. He'd never let you go to Boston with me."

"Yes, he would," Caleb argued, but caution kept him quiet, and the house, though filled with a certain restraint that evening, was unbroken by any political talk.

Molly lay quietly as the crowing of a cock broke through the silence of the morning. She felt the tension in Adam's body, and reaching out, touched his cheek. "You didn't sleep much."

"No."

"Neither did I."

He rolled over and peered at her in the dim light, then gave a quick laugh. "We know each other pretty well, don't we?"

"I guess when two people love each other like we do," she smiled, "their moods get all mixed up. When you're happy, so am I. And when you're troubled, I can't rest."

He shook his head, threw back the cover and got out of bed. Pulling on his clothes, he was silent, but when they were both dressed, he turned to her and said, "Should I let them go, Molly?"

"Yes."

He suddenly laughed. "You're always so certain of everything. I wish I were!"

She was almost as tall as he, so she only had to pull his head down a couple of inches to kiss him on the lips. "They'll be all right. They're good boys."

He stared at her, and there was an indecision in him that she had never seen. "Are they? I hope so."

"You're worried about Nathan, aren't you?"

"Yes, I am." He hesitated, then said, "He's too impulsive, Molly. Too much like Charles."

"No, he's not like Charles." Molly half turned to the window, then turned back, a thoughtful look on her face. "Oh, he *looks* like him, of course, and there's some of that wild Winslow blood, but deep down he's like you, Adam. I know you can't see it—but I can."

He struggled with the thought, then finally smiled and said, "You're right, I can't see it. So I'll just have to go on your judgment, Molly." He put his arms around her, and a fond light replaced the anxious look in his face. "It's been a long time since that first time I saw you. I think of that time often. How old were you?"

"Just eleven—and I thought you were the handsomest thing I'd ever seen."

"Will ye buy a handkerchief—only five bob!" He smiled at her, and added, "That's the first thing you ever said to me, wasn't it?"

"And you bought it, didn't you, dear?" Molly laughed and added, "If you'd known what you were getting into that morning, I think you'd have run away like a deer!"

"No. No, I wouldn't have. You've been my life, Molly."

She stood there, surrendering to his quick embrace, thinking of the strange manner of their courtship. She'd been an unfortunate child of eleven on the streets of London, mistreated by a drunken father. He'd been there on his first trip from home, and he'd been so moved by her plight that he'd paid her brute of a father all the money he had, getting her under his care as a bound girl—an indentured servant. She remembered how he'd been in love with Mary Edwards, and how, as the years had rolled by, Molly had been in love with him. And she remembered the shock in his eyes when he at last saw her as a woman—and fell in love. Since that time, they'd been truly man and wife, in spirit as in flesh.

Now she said, "Nathan will be all right. He's your son."

He stared at her, and his face relaxed. "We'll trust God to take care of them."

When they went downstairs, they found Caleb and Nathan had already fixed breakfast, a feat which amused them both. "Well, if I'd known a trip to Boston would produce this sort of thing," Adam smiled, "I'd have let you go long ago!"

Both boys were champing at the bit, anxious to go, so they ate a quick breakfast, and then it was time for them to leave. The wagons were loaded and the teams were in the village ready to go, so there was nothing to do but say goodbye.

But it was hard for Molly. Despite her brave words, it was the first time her boys were leaving to go farther than the small village, and there was a lump in her throat that would not go away.

She took Caleb's quick hug, and kissed him, then Nathan stood before her, a little embarrassed, as always, at showing affection. She pulled his head down, kissed him soundly, and said, "Take care of your brother, Nathan! Take very good care of him!"

"Ah, Mother," Caleb said with a wide grin. "It's me as will take care of him!"

Then the boys stood before Adam, and for once for some reason, Nathan did not feel intimidated. He looked into his father's eyes and saw there for the first time in years, an approval that he had always longed for.

Adam sought for words, but could only say what Molly had said. "Nathan, take care of your brother."

"Yes, sir." Nathan put his hand out awkwardly, but it was ignored and suddenly Adam put his arms around both boys, drawing them in with a powerful hug that took their breath, then released them.

"Get on your way now—and take care of each other."

They left, and all the way to town and for a long time after that, Nathan heard the words that his parents had spoken: "Take care of your brother." And he always remembered the strength of his father's arms in that last powerful embrace.

CHAPTER FOUR

COUNTRY COUSIN

★ ★ ★ ★

Ice glittered on the backs of the horses, and their frosty breath rose like miniature clouds of incense as Nathan pulled them to a halt in front of the two-story building that fronted the harbor with the sign THE WINSLOW COMPANY over the door.

"Wake up, Caleb." He nudged the small mountain of blankets huddled close beside him, and a smile touched his lips as a groan of protest emerged from the depths. "We're here—come out of there, boy."

"What is it?" The blankets parted, and Caleb reluctantly surfaced from the warm cocoon. He wore a black wool knitted cap pulled down to his eyebrows, a red and blue scarf swathed his face, so that all that could be seen of him was a sleepy pair of dark eyes.

"Go see where they want the load," Nathan said. "Looks like they might be closed." He watched with amusement as Caleb climbed down stiffly, then waddled across the snow to the big double doors. He looked like a walking barrel, for he hated cold and wore every garment he'd brought on the trip, in addition to a buffalo coat of Nathan's.

Been a hard trip, Nathan reflected as he watched Caleb disappear into the depths of the warehouse. *Bet not even Father could have done better!* Ice glittered in the short red stubbles of his beard, and he shook his head ruefully at his pride, knowing that his father would have made the trip faster.

But it *had* been a hard journey. Winter had closed like an iron fist, freezing the roads to slick ribbons, and near-blizzard cold had punished the horses terribly. Caleb had begun well, but for the last week he had done nothing but hug the fire at night and swath himself into every garment he could find during the day's trek. They had met with few travelers, and Nathan could not resist a heady gust of pride as he realized that he had brought the furs through when most men had sought the warmth of fire inside snug cabins.

As the big double doors swung open, he glanced down at his large hands, blue from the cold and calloused from handling the lines, and was pleased. There had been doubt in his father's eyes when they had parted, but the good feeling of accomplishing a hard task was a solid feeling in Nathan. "Hup, Babe—Dan!" He guided the team into the dark interior, climbed down and stamped his feet, which had no more feeling than the iron ring he tied up to.

"Mister Winslow didn't look for you." A thick-bodied man with a face blue from cold and red from drink stared at Nathan, and there was some resentment in his clipped New England speech as he added, "Don't have no help this time of day fer unloadin'."

"It'll wait for tomorrow."

"Them horses won't wait!"

If the man had been more civil, Nathan would have helped unhitch, but he was bone-tired and both he and Caleb were half-starved. "We're going to my uncle's house. How far is it?"

The big man's face flushed, but he said, "Three miles back down the old Turnpike—you must'a passed it comin' in—big white house with pillars." He gave them instructions in a grudging voice, then grinned sourly. "You'll have a nice little walk—may get there by dark."

Nathan stared at him, then said, "Caleb, we'll take Babe and Dan." The two brothers unhitched the horses, put a pair of hair hackamores on them, and led them outside. Nathan said tersely to the heavy man, "Get those other two animals unhitched and fed!" He mounted easily, but Caleb had to lead Dan to the watering trough and use it for a platform as he scrambled aboard, not without groaning.

The horses were just about played out, but three more miles would not kill them. As they plodded down the frozen road, the light beginning to fail, Caleb asked, "Uncle Charles won't be looking for us, will he?"

"I guess not, with all this weather. But he'll sure be glad to get the furs."

Caleb beat his hands together, then blew on them for warmth. "I can't remember much about him, Nathan. Is he like Father?"

There was a small interval of silence; then Nathan shook his head, a thoughtful stirring in his eyes. "No, Caleb, he's not like Father." He paused and the sound of the iron shoes on the frozen ground punctuated the cold silence, and a small smile touched his broad lips as he added, "But then, nobody else is like him, either!"

"Well, I sure hope they ain't finished supper yet," Caleb said. "My belly feels like my throat's been cut! I've sure heard a lot, though, about how fancy Aunt Dorcas is. She might bow up over having us at her best table, dirty as we are."

"Might be right," Nathan nodded, then added with a touch of warning in his voice, "Don't think they'll chuck us out for being trail worn—but you keep your revolutionary talk to yourself, Caleb. You mind what Father told us about Uncle Charles."

"Yaaaaa! Makes me sick!" Caleb scowled and gave Dan a hard kick. "Think of Winslows being a bunch of Tories!"

"That's what I mean!" Nathan said sharply, and he reached out and grabbed Caleb's arm strongly. "You keep that talk to yourself while we are here—and stay away from that rabble that calls itself Sons of Liberty, you hear me?"

Caleb turned suddenly, and his customary smile faded. His square face turned stubborn, and for one instant Nathan had the feeling that he was looking into his father's dark eyes. "I'll say what I think, Nathan—here or anywhere else!"

Hot words leaped to Nathan's lips, but he bit them off. He and Caleb had been through this many times, and it always ended with both of them white-lipped with anger. *No use to argue with him,* he thought wearily. *Mother and Father feel the same way, so it's no wonder he's getting to be a fire-eater.* But he only shook his head, saying in a reasonable tone, "Look, just keep your political opinions to yourself, Caleb—while we're here. Because if you don't, we'll get sent home quick, and Father won't ever let us do anything like this again."

The latter warning seemed to have some effect, for Caleb quickly shut off his protests and said only, "Well, guess you're right about that, Nathan—but it goes against the grain!"

Darkness fell quickly, and they managed to get lost inside the city, so that by the time they pulled up in front of a large white house on the outskirts of town, Nathan had to lean down and put his face to the sign. He made out the letters, straightened up, and said, "This is it. Come on."

A long ice-packed drive led to the house, and the rising wind made the frozen branches click overhead as they passed beneath. Tying their horses to an iron fence that set off a flowerbed, they mounted the high steps, and Nathan gave a couple of firm raps with the heavy brass knocker on the massive door.

Caleb shifted nervously as they waited, and finally he said, "Maybe we should have gone to the back door."

Nathan stared at him, then said, "What did that sign say over the door at the warehouse?"

Caleb thought, then answered, "The Winslow Company."

"That's right—and my name is Winslow. You go to the back door if you feel like it." He turned to hide a smile, for his taunt had done exactly what he'd expected—turned Caleb stubborn, which wasn't too hard to do in any case.

The door slowly opened, just a crack, and a black face appeared. "The family is at dinner. Is you expected?"

Nathan shot back, "Not *all* the family's at dinner. Go tell your master his nephews from Virginia are here!"

The steely quality in Nathan's voice must have startled the black man, for he quickly opened the door, and gave a nervous nod, saying, "Oh yas, indeed! You gentlemen come inside, please." He shut the door behind them and gave another nervous nod. "I'll tell Mistuh Winslow you is here!"

He turned to go, but at that moment, a voice called out from down the long hall, "Well—well! What's this? Is it you, Nathan?"

A tall man with bright blue eyes and reddish hair had emerged from a set of double doors and now came forward. He held out his hand, gave Nathan a firm grip, then slapped him on the shoulder, "My word! Are you *ever* going to stop growing, Nathan? And you, Caleb—" He turned to shake hands with the younger boy, and there was a light of amusement in his bright eyes. He laughed in delight, and reached out to give the boy a sudden hug. "Why, you're Adam Winslow!" He looked again and shook his head. "My word, you're the image of your father when he was your age, Caleb!"

"I take that as a compliment, Uncle Charles," Caleb said at once. He did not make quick judgments, and the instant warmth of Charles Winslow had caused him to throw up some sort of a wall. Nathan had seen it often, not only in Caleb, but in his father as well. Both of them were slow to judge, while he himself (often to his own chagrin!) gave his loyalty readily.

"We're a little late, Uncle Charles."

"Late!" Charles stared up at his tall nephew, then shook his head in wonder. "We didn't think you'd make it at all in this storm, Nathan!" Then he clapped their shoulders, saying, "You go get washed up—Benjamin, take my nephews to their room. Get them some hot water to wash with. We'll hold dinner until you can get there, boys."

"Yessuh, Mistuh Winslow!"

"Well, all our clothes are on the wagon, Uncle Charles," Nathan said, looking down at his mud-stained clothes. "We can't come to dinner like this!"

"You come as you are, Nathan," Charles said at once. "I don't think a little honest dirt from hard work will kill us!"

He gave them a smile, then turned and walked quickly back to the dining room off to the left of the wide hallway. It was an enormous room, for one of his demands for a house was that it be able to handle large dinner parties. Two massive fireplaces faced each other, and the heavy logs that popped and roared kept the room warm. The dining table was over twenty feet long, and it was covered with blinding white linen. Two giant chandeliers reflected their myriad candles on the silver that lay beside the five places set at the end next to the door.

"Mary, set two more places," Charles said to the black woman who stood by the wall.

"Two places? For whom?" Dorcas Winslow looked up sharply, her brown eyes reflecting her displeasure. She was an attractive woman, dressed in high fashion, even for a simple family dinner. Her dark brown hair shone in the candlelight, and the diamonds on her fingers winked as she raised a hand to pat it carefully. "I wasn't expecting anyone."

"It's Nathan and Caleb—just got in with the furs."

"Couldn't they wait until tomorrow?" Dorcas murmured. She loved ceremony, and any distractions that broke into the rituals of their affairs displeased her.

"Well, Mother, you couldn't ask them to sleep in the warehouse, could you now?"

The speaker was a young man who sat directly across from Charles, and there was a teasing note in his clear voice as he looked at Dorcas. "After all, they *are* family, aren't they?"

"I suppose, Paul," she said slowly, then added, "But they'll have to learn some manners if they stay here with us."

"I expect they'll have good enough manners," Charles said easily. "Virginians are just about the most hospitable people you'll find, Dorcas."

"Backwoods manners are not exactly what I like to see in my own home, Charles." She sighed and said, "I know you want them here, but it's going to be difficult."

"I do want them here," Charles said, and there was a sudden firmness in his voice. He was too heavy, and his face was marked with the signs of good food and too much liquor, but at times the vigor of his youth flared out, and at times like that the family had learned to avoid argument.

He picked up his wineglass, took a swallow, and looked around, saying, "We need some strong fresh blood in the business. I know you don't like Adam, Mama, but you'll have to admit he's a strong man—and I suspect these boys are just about the same."

"A stubborn man—I never trusted him!" Martha Winslow was seventy-two, but there was no weakness in her. She stared at her son with sharp black eyes, and added, "You were always a fool about Adam—but he never cared a pin for you—nor for any of us!"

Paul Winslow sat back, his quick mind analyzing the scene before him. He knew much of his family history, but he had never understood the hatred his grandmother had for her stepson, Adam Winslow. Once he had asked his father about it, but Charles had shook his head, saying, "She always hated him, Paul—even when he was a child. I think she was jealous of his mother—but she'd never admit it. Just don't think about it."

As the old woman stubbornly said, "You'll regret any dealings you have with that man!" Paul glanced at his mother and saw that she agreed with the sentiment—but for a different reason, he suspected. Suddenly he turned his head and caught the gaze of Anne Winslow, his fourteen-year-old sister. She had been listening quietly, but she missed little, Paul knew, and he winked at her, which made her drop her eyes.

"Adam's all right, Mother," Charles said adamantly, his face flushed as it often did when he was crossed. "He's kept his end of the business going well enough. And we need to keep the fur trade open. It's the most prosperous part of the company."

"Are they wearing Indian clothes, Father?" Anne piped up. She was a thin girl with her father's auburn hair and fair skin. Her bright blue eyes came from him as well.

Charles stared at her, then leaned back and laughed, "Indian clothes? Why, no, sweetheart, of course not!"

He was very partial to Anne, so he carefully explained how that some years ago, he and his brother Adam had divided the family business—with Adam moving to Virginia to handle the fur trade while he himself stayed in Boston to take care of the other aspects and the shipping. But Paul knew there was more to the separation than that; there had been almost no contact between the two families, and there had to be some reason.

He was still pondering on the matter when footsteps sounded and he looked up to see two young men enter. One was tall and fair, and looked so much like his own father it gave him a small shock. The other was short and dark.

"Well, here they are!" Charles stood up and waved a hand toward the two, saying gaily, "This is Nathan and this is his brother Caleb. Let me introduce you to your relatives, nephews. This is my wife, Dorcas; and my mother and your father's stepmother, of course, Mrs. Martha Winslow. This is my son, Paul, and my daughter, Anne."

Paul rose to his feet and walked around the table, saying with a smile, "Strange we haven't met—but better late than never, eh? Come now, you two sit down and eat."

Nathan and Caleb sat down, both feeling awkward, and as the black servant placed food before them, Nathan said, "I apologize for our clothing, but—"

"It's quite all right," Dorcas said in a tone that implied just the opposite.

"Did you see any Indians?"

Everyone laughed, but Anne's question eased the tension, and Nathan said, "No, Anne, it's too cold out for Indians, but I've seen lots of them back home, and I'll tell you some scary stories about them."

"You eat up now, and then you can tell us about Adam and Molly," Charles urged.

The food was good, and after Nathan and Caleb finished, Charles plied them with questions about Virginia—some about the family, but more about business. Nathan answered as well as he could, and his answers pleased their host.

All might have gone well, but suddenly Martha Winslow asked, "And has your father gotten rid of his erroneous ideas about the King?"

Before Nathan could answer, Caleb said loudly, "Why, ma'am, I expect my father's opinions on King George are about what any honest man's are—that he's a fool and not in the least interested in the freedom of his subjects in these Colonies!"

He's done it now! Nathan thought, but even as he tried to come up with some way to smooth the situation over, Paul Winslow took over. He said easily, "Now, Grandmother, we won't have any political arguments!" Getting up with a smile, he walked around and stood behind his mother and grandmother, and placing a hand on each of their shoulders, he said, "My cousins are probably worn out from a hard trip—and we have a lot of things to do in the next few weeks. There's a ball tomorrow night at Uncle Saul's and I want to show off my Virginia kinfolks. We'll have some of these pale Boston maidens falling at your feet, I can assure you!"

He went on easily, and Nathan drew a sigh of relief. *He knows how to handle them!* he thought with envy.

Later that night, when he and Caleb were finally in bed, he said, "You nearly ruined us with that rebel talk, Caleb. Keep quiet, you hear me?"

"You better worry about all those 'pale Boston maidens' Paul is going to throw at you," Caleb muttered faintly, then fell into a sleep so sound that he did not hear Nathan's drowsy reply. "You keep your mouth shut and I'll take care of the pale Boston maidens!"

"Oh, Abby, can't you hurry? The music's already started!"

Abigail Howland looked up from the French mahogany dressing table at Ellen Alden and gave a languid smile. "It will be the same crowd we've had for months, Ellen." She looked back into the mirror; then a thought struck her and she lifted a pair of hazel eyes to the tall girl who was pacing nervously back and forth across the room. "But I suppose you're thinking of Daniel being with Mercy Williams, aren't you? He's been giving her some pretty hot glances lately. If you don't make him propose to you pretty soon, she's going to get him."

Ellen was a slender girl with earnest brown eyes and auburn hair. "I—I wouldn't have a man I had to *force* into a proposal!" she said tightly.

"Mercy isn't as choosy as you, I think." Abby gave her shining brown hair a pat, then rose and led Ellen out of the room. As they went down the curving stairs, she said, "I can tell you how to get a proposal out of Daniel."

She spoke softly for a few moments; then suddenly Ellen's eyes opened wide and she cried, "No! I couldn't do *that!*—and neither could you, Abigail!"

"Men fight for land, for money, for power," Abby said. "But women fight for men!" She suddenly paused and nodded her head toward the milling crowd below. "There's Daniel—and I'll give you one guess as to who's dancing with him!"

"It's her!" Ellen moaned. "Oh, Abby, I love him so!"

"Well, let's see what can be done," Abby smiled. For the next half hour she busied herself with pushing Daniel Mains into the proposal that Ellen wanted to hear. Actually, it meant nothing to her, but Abigail Howland was bored with Boston, and it was a challenge to her. She herself had turned down more proposals than most girls ever had, but then she was beautiful, witty—and her father, Saul Howland, was one of the wealthiest men in Boston.

She enjoyed the only game possible for a woman—men; and it gave her some pleasure to maneuver the hapless Daniel Mains. In the space of thirty minutes she had devalued the character of Ellen's rival, elevated his opinion of Ellen herself, and when she left the two alone it was obvious that if she played her cards right, the tall girl had her fish hooked.

"At it again, Abby?" She turned with a smile to face Maury Simms, come to claim her for a dance. He was a tall, broad-shouldered man of twenty-six, who had been her suitor for a time, but had given up in despair. Now as they danced he said with a grin, "Giving Ellen a little help, are you?"

"I don't know what you mean, Maury," she said, but there was a smile on her red lips and she laughed aloud, saying, "Men are such fools!"

"Yes, we are, aren't we?" Maury had gotten over her, and it was one of her pleasures to be with a man who wasn't stalking her or her father's money. "But not all of us. Paul Winslow's no fool—not like me. I don't think you can maneuver him as you do the rest of us."

"Oh, I don't want to maneuver anyone, Maury."

They finished the dance, then joined a group at the long table crowded with wine and food. Emily Rauter was one of them, and she smiled briefly, saying, "Your dress is beautiful, Abby."

"Thank you, Emily—you look wonderful."

Maury stood there with a broad smile on his face, thinking, *They hate each other so well—both of them would like to tear the other's face to rags with their fingernails.*

But that wasn't true—not so far as Abby was concerned. She knew that Emily wanted Paul Winslow desperately, but it didn't bother her. She had taken more than one man away from Emily.

"Who's that with Paul?"

They all looked across the room to see Paul Winslow coming toward them, accompanied by a very tall young man with red hair. "Oh, that must be Paul's country cousin," Maury said. Then a thought struck him, and he said with a smile, "Better leave that one alone, ladies—he's not available."

As he had suspected this statement made both women raise their eyes for a closer look at the tall man. "What does that mean, Maury?" Emily asked.

"Oh, well, in the first place, according to Paul, he's probably a frightful patriot—which makes him ineligible right off—but even worse, he's a minister. Parson of some sort."

"He may be a minister," Abby smiled, "but he's a man."

"Better leave him alone, Abigail," Emily said smoothly. "Paul might not like your paying attention to his cousin."

"We'll have to see, won't we, dear?" Abby smiled, and moved across the floor to meet the pair.

"Well, we don't need tigers in this country," Maury smiled at Emily. "Not as long as you girls are around to eat each other alive." Emily did not listen, for she was watching carefully as Paul introduced his cousin to Abby.

"And this is the most beautiful woman in Boston, Nathan, Miss Abigail Howland."

"Pay him no heed, Mr. Winslow," Abby smiled and held on to Nathan's hand for a second longer than necessary. "You can't believe a word this man says—but a Virginian like yourself, why, a girl could trust you, I think."

Paul lifted his eyebrows; then a saturnine smile crossed his lips. "Well, I'll leave you two to get acquainted. And I forgot to tell you, Nathan, you two are kinfolks."

"What?" Nathan stared at Paul in confusion.

"Oh, I'll explain all that to you while we dance," Abby smiled up at him brilliantly and drew him into the dance. "My! It's so nice to dance with a really *tall* man!"

"What—what's this about our being kin to each other?" Nathan's thoughts were disjointed, for he had never seen a girl half so lovely. She wore some scent that seemed to paralyze him. As they moved through the dance, from time to time her body would brush against him, and he could not keep his thoughts straight.

"Oh, that's true enough," she said, and she spoke so softly that he had to bend down and put his face close to hers in order to hear. "Paul explained it to me once—he didn't want me to think that there'd be any—problem, with us being close kin." She laughed, and let her hand rest on his arm where it seemed to leave a mark. "Let's see, now—my grandmother was Rachel Winslow. She was your grandfather's sister. His name was Miles Winslow, I think. Oh, Nathan, that was ages ago."

As they floated across the floor, Nathan felt somewhat bewitched. He had spent little time with girls, and never with one this attractive, so he moved like a man in a dream for the next hour.

Paul was standing beside the wall, looking on when Emily came up and claimed him. "There are too few men here for you to be an observer. Dance with me!"

He agreed readily, and soon she had him laughing. She was a witty young woman, and it was not long before he found himself telling her of Nathan. Finally she said, "Well, he's a most attractive man, Paul. I'm surprised you let her dance for so long with him."

"Well, you know Abby, Emily. She'll do what she pleases."

"A woman should do what her *man* pleases, I think!"

He nodded. "I'll vote for that, but look, Nathan may not last long. Abby's taking him over to meet the officers. That's sort of like introducing the sheep to the wolves!"

Nathan did feel intimidated, for he was surrounded by a group of scarlet coated British officers. Miss Howland knew them all well, it seemed, and one by one he shook their hands; then they began shooting questions at him. A fine-looking man of forty, Major John Pitcairn, asked at once, "Well, Mr. Winslow, how blows the wind in the South? I know Mr. Washington. Is he going to get involved in this rebellion that seems to be brewing?"

Before Nathan could answer, a short, fat man with small, squinty eyes grunted, "Nonsense, Pitcairn! There'll be no rebellion! These Colonists are stupid, but not stupid enough to go up against the strongest power in the world—the British Empire!"

"Colonel Smith is correct!" A portly man with a bluff manner and bright brown eyes spoke up. This was General Thomas Gage, commander of the King's forces in Boston. "Washington is a gentleman, and I believe he's a loyal man. It's Sam Adams and Hancock who keep the pot boiling!"

"What do you think, sir?" Major Pitcairn asked Nathan. "Will there be a rebellion?"

Nathan felt every one of the King's officers watching him closely, and he cleared his throat before saying carefully, "As for me, I believe a revolution would be a disaster. I have to add that not all my family thinks in this way—"

"Good man!" Smith said at once, and the others nodded agreement.

"You must come with Paul to our mess, Mr. Winslow," Major Pitcairn said warmly. "He's there often, and we'd like you to join him."

"At your service, Major," Nathan said; then he felt a small hand close on his arm, and turned to find Abby.

"It's time for the refreshments you promised me, Mr. Winslow."

He followed her to the table, and she asked with an arch smile, "I understand you are a clergyman. Does that prevent you from taking a little wine?"

Actually it did, for Adam felt that wine was the first step to being a drunkard, but looking into her eyes, Nathan could not refuse, so he took a glass of wine and she toasted the King.

The one glass was a mistake, for it seemed to have so little effect that soon he was taking another. Dance followed dance, and each was punctuated by sparkling glasses of wine.

Nathan had never felt so wonderful in all his life! He was a fine fellow—a devil of a chap, really! And as the wine went down, his shyness fled, and soon he was laughing and talking with the most beautiful woman in Boston as if he'd done it all his life.

Hours later, he found himself with Abby in some sort of alcove, where she was showing him a picture of their mutual ancestor. He gazed into the strong face of Rachel Winslow, and then when he looked down to comment, Abigail's face was lifted. Her lips were red and she swayed against him. His head was swimming, but he could not stop himself. He took her in his arms, lowered his head, and then he kissed her. It was a powerful moment, for she did not draw back, but shared his kiss.

Then, she pulled away, and her voice seemed to come from afar as she said, "For a minister, you are quite a man, Nathan Winslow!"

Then she vanished into the crowd of dancers, and he suddenly discovered that for the first time in his life, he was drunk. He found that he had difficulty walking, for the floor seemed to shift and tilt under him, and he was acutely conscious of too much wine rolling around in his stomach.

Paul came to his rescue. Seeing his cousin's difficulty, he got him out of the house just in time for him to lose his supper, bundled him into a buggy, and finally helped him stagger upstairs. And it was Paul who said gently to the sleeping giant with the flushed face, "I think, Nathan, that Boston has been a little too much for you—or maybe I should say that Abigail Howland has been too much!"

CHAPTER FIVE

A BOY NAMED LADDIE

★　★　★　★

Despite the severe cold, Nathan had to push his way through heavy traffic that flooded the square. The bright scarlet coats of British soldiers added a dash of color to the somber old buildings, but he was jostled by chimney sweepers, sawyers, merchants, laddies, priests, carts, horses, oxen, and his ears buzzed with the talk that floated over the square.

He arrived at the British Coffeehouse, which occupied the first floor of a four-story, frame building painted a bilious yellow, and as soon as he pushed his way through the door, he heard his name called: "Winslow! Over here!"

Major John Pitcairn, seated at a small round table near the far wall, had to raise his voice to be heard, for the large room was packed with officers and their guests. Nathan threaded his way across the crowded room, nearly reeling from the scent of pipe smoke, stale whiskey, and unwashed male bodies.

Pitcairn pushed a bottle and a pewter cup toward him, saying, "Cold as the devil out there! Take some of that, my boy—it'll warm your insides!"

During the two weeks he'd spent at Boston, Nathan had learned how to handle the problem of drink. To say "No" created an instant problem, for almost everyone in the country drank some sort of liquor. Even ministers frequently received part of their pay in the form of kegs of beer, and *all* British officers drank a great deal. At first Nathan had refused, but that action had created such a discomfort on the part of the soldiers that he had learned to take a glass and simply give the appearance of drinking. He took the glass and sipped at it, but the sharp eyes of Pitcairn caught it, and he smiled. "Haven't done too much drinking since that night at Howlands', have you, Nathan?—or before either, I'd venture."

Nathan scowled and shifted uncomfortably in his chair, and finally he looked straight at the major and said, "I made a fool of myself that night, Major!" A flush touched his high cheekbones, and he shook his head, adding, "Shakespeare said 'God forbid I should put an enemy in my mouth to take away my brain'; I reckon that's what I did that night."

"It wasn't so bad as you remember it, Nathan," Pitcairn said with a sympathetic smile. "As I think on it, you may have been the most sober man in the house that night! At least three that I know of had to be *carried* out."

"That's them and not me!"

"Oh? Well, I wasn't watching you all the time. Maybe it was something you did with Abigail Howland that's got you as sensitive as a man without a skin?"

"I won't listen—!" Nathan half rose from his seat, his face twisted with anger, but looking at Pitcairn's honest face, he swallowed, sat down, and ducked his head. He drew a figure in the moist surface of the oak table, then looked up and there was a weak grin on his wide lips. "You're too sharp for me, Major."

Pitcairn sat there quietly, saying nothing until he refilled his clay pipe. Picking up the candle, he sucked the flame into the bowl until it glowed cherry red, then put it down carefully, a characteristic thing with him. He had learned to like this tall young man with the startling blue eyes, and for the past two weeks had spent several hours with him. He had not pried, but the young man had been open, and he had learned how his family was split by political opinion—Nathan's parents in Virginia strongly behind the patriot cause, while his Uncle Charles and his family were staunch loyalists. He had something to say to Nathan, and was hesitant.

"Well, you must have done *something* right with the young woman. You've been a pretty frequent guest at her house—and poor Paul must be cursing the day he ever took you there!"

"I—I'm sorry for that—about Paul, I mean."

"Oh, they weren't engaged." Pitcairn shook his head and

added, "She's a real catch, my boy—looks *and* money. But I don't know if she'd suit your family."

Nathan shook his head sadly. "You're right about that. She's got little use for the rebel cause."

Pitcairn studied young Winslow, then made a quick decision. "Nathan, I sent for you because there's something you need to know."

Pitcairn's serious air was disturbing. "What is it, Major?"

"It's about your brother. He's getting involved with a radical group, and I think you ought to know it."

"Caleb? But he's just a boy!"

"That may be, but nonetheless he's taken up with a young man who works for your uncle—Moses Tyler, he's called."

"Why, I know Moses," Nathan said at once.

"We've had our eyes on him for some time. He's joined to the Sons of Liberty—perhaps you've heard of them?"

"Yes, but I thought they were harmless enough."

A rare anger touched Major Pitcairn's face, and he said, "Let's get out of here, Nathan. Too many ears to hear in this place."

He laid a coin on the table and Nathan followed him outside, both of them pulling their coats high to protect their faces from the bitter cold. "You ever hear of the Boston Massacre, Nathan?"

"Of course."

"Well, this is where it happened." Pitcairn waved his hand toward the square. "It was most unfortunate, Nathan. A band of unemployed laborers attacked a British sentry right over there, and a mob collected, throwing oyster shells and snowballs. In the confusion, somebody called out 'Fire!' and our men fired. Five men were killed and six were wounded."

"They shouldn't have fired on unarmed men, Major."

"No, certainly not, and a better officer would have prevented that. But it was a great opportunity for Sam Adams and James Otis! They got Paul Revere to do an engraving of the riot—you've probably seen it." A bitter smile touched Pitcairn's lips and he pointed at the Custom House, which was next to the British Coffeehouse. "Revere put a sign in the engraving on that building. Know what it was?"

"It was BUTCHER'S HALL." Nathan remembered the engraving well, for copies of it had been carried all over the Colonies. "But that's not treason, what Adams did."

"No, but it gave Sam Adams a beginning! And the next thing he did was organize the Boston Tea Party—*that* was a criminal act, Nathan."

"I suppose so," Nathan said slowly.

Pitcairn took the arm of the tall young man, his grip like steel, saying, "Nathan, Sam Adams was a business failure, one of those whining, nagging malcontents you want to poke in the nose—but just the sort you'd want on your side in an eye-gouging fight. He's a burr under the saddle, blast him! Such men breed revolutions, and they don't give a hang who has to die for it."

"And you say Caleb's been going to their meetings?"

They had just turned a corner and a blast of cold air struck them so hard that both men gasped. "See that old red brick building—the one with blue shutters?"

"What about it, Major?"

"That's Sam Adams' house—where they meet. The rest are no better, Nathan. Otis was a Massachusetts lawyer who couldn't handle his liquor. He was a Tory once, then switched over to a Whig position because he saw a dollar to be turned. And there's John Hancock—and he may be the worst of the lot—though he's smooth enough!"

"Rich, isn't he?"

"Oh yes, and how did he get that way? By smuggling tea! And that's why he got in on the tea party in the harbor—his profits were in danger. Nathan, the man's a criminal, and sooner or later the Sons of Liberty are all going to dangle from ropes." Major Pitcairn stopped fifty yards away from the red brick house. "I'd hate for your brother to be one to hang with them, Nathan, and that's why I've told you this."

Nathan thrust his hand out impulsively, and grasping the officer's hand, he burst out, "Thank you, Major!"

"Well, well, now you know—but what will you *do* about it, my boy?"

The question struck Nathan hard, for his mind was a total blank as to what could be done. He set his jaw, and there was a fire in his light blue eyes as he said, "I'll do *something*, Major—and you can bet on that!"

Major Pitcairn gave him a clap on the shoulder, but added a final word: "Our informer tells me they'll have a meeting tonight. I should try to keep the boy away if possible—but be a little careful,

Nathan. These men are revolutionaries—they'd think nothing of snuffing you out! Well, let me know if I can do anything."

Pitcairn wheeled and marched down the street, a trim, erect military figure, and Nathan moved to the shelter of a tiny inn across from the brick house. He took a seat and ordered a meal as an excuse for his presence. The food was slow in coming, and was badly cooked, but he never noticed. His brain was racing as he tried to think of some way to get Caleb free from trouble. He thought of sending him home, but knew at once that Caleb would never go. *Maybe if I write father—? But he'd probably be proud of Caleb, feeling as he does.*

He finished his meal, then realizing he couldn't stay in the inn until the group met, paid his bill and returned to the street. Snow lay in white stripes everywhere, and the flakes were getting larger. He looked up into the sky, then turned and walked slowly in the direction of the harbor. *I'll go to the warehouse and stay warm until later—then I'll do something.*

By the time he had covered the distance from the center of town to the waterfront, the snow was coming down as thickly as if some unseen giant were dumping it out of huge baskets. The flakes were huge, almost the size of a tuppence, and lay in drifts several inches deep along the shopfronts. The temperature had plummeted; by the time he turned off High Street and began walking along the docks, his cheeks were numb and his feet had no sensation as they struck the carpet of white that covered the wharfs.

Nathan moved closer to a long tobacco warehouse to avoid the icy blasts that stung his face. He glanced out at the harbor where the ships seemed to be frozen carcasses—their sharp outlines of masts and spars rounded into smooth curves by the blanket of snow.

But as he glanced out at the fleet, his half-frozen feet struck something. He tried to jerk his hands out of his pockets to catch himself, but he failed and his long body fell headlong into the snow!

"What the devil—!"

He yanked his hands out of his pockets and swept the snow from his face with a forearm. He rolled over and saw what appeared to be a bundle of rags under a white mound, and he lifted his heel to give it a savage kick, for the fall had knocked out his breath and one cheek was bleeding, scraped raw against the rough wood of the wharf.

"What—?" he gave a startled look, then lowered his boot, for he thought he saw a tiny movement beneath the mound. Scrambling to his knees he reached out and brushed the snow away and saw at once that the bundle was alive!

Fear struck him in the belly, and with hands that shook more from nervousness than cold, he tugged at the figure, which seemed to be swathed in some sort of ragged blanket. Pulling it to one side, he could barely make out in the gathering darkness a pale white face, eyes shut tight. "Hey! Wake up!" He shook the small figure, but there was no response.

"Got to find help!" he muttered. He got to his feet and looked wildly around, but he knew there was no doctor in the area. *Got to get him out of this cold!* He stooped and lifted the still figure, and was shocked at how light the lad was. Then it came to him what to do, and he plunged along through the snow. *The warehouse*, he thought—*it'll be warm there, and I can send somebody for the doctor!*

It was nearly a quarter of a mile to the company warehouse, and his lungs were on fire by the time he stopped, gasping in front of the door. There was no light inside, and he groaned as he saw the heavy padlock in place. Carefully he placed his burden down, extracted his key, then with numbed fingers managed to open the lock. Picking the boy up, he kicked the door open and stumbled inside. Even inside, the cold was bitter, but he made his way through the high-ceilinged area lit by a single lamp to the office at the rear. It was dark, and he felt his way to a small cot used by the foreman for quick naps. He groped along the desk, found the small candle, then ran back to the lantern in the warehouse area to light it. Cupping a hand around it, he hurried back to the office and stood there looking down at the small form he'd brought out of the storm.

Ought to be doing something! he thought, *but it's Saturday night.* For an instant he stood there in the cold silence, irresolute, still winded from his run through the storm.

Then he did something that was not customary, an involuntary reaction, something that just welled up in him. *"God, don't let this lad die!"* he prayed—then he blinked, surprised at what he'd done. Most of his praying was public, a form of rhetoric that he'd mastered by listening to others pray. Solitary prayer he'd given up on years before, for although he knew some—such as his mother—who spent much time praying, his own prayer life was a matter of form.

Then it came again, involuntarily: *"Oh, God! I didn't bring him here to die! Let him live! Please—let him live!"*

Again he was shocked at the emotion that drove his prayer, and at that instant he saw a flicker of an eyelid on the still pale face, and at the same time a moan passed through the lips turned blue by the cold.

"He's alive! Thank you, God!" Nathan rejoiced, and the pressure of fear lifted. He whirled and quickly built a small fire in the fireplace, set a kettle of water over it, then carefully added larger pieces to the fire until it crackled and began to drive the bitter cold out of his hands.

A small sound came from behind him; he turned from the fire to see the lad's arms moving, and he leaped to the cot. "All right, now, don't be afraid—you're all right!"

A pair of eyes, black as pools, suddenly peered up at him, and the blue lips moved painfully. "What—what—?"

"Don't try to talk, lad," Nathan said quickly. He stripped off the dirty blanket so thin it was no protection at all, and whipped off his own thick wool coat. Wrapping it around the boy, he noted the thin arms and hollow eyes. *Half starved,* he thought, then said, "I don't know much about taking care of frozen people, lad. Not much snow down in Virginia." He smiled as the huge almond-shaped eyes stared at him owlishly, then added, "I heard somewhere that you're supposed to rub snow on people who are just about frozen, so maybe—?"

He got up to go get some snow, but the dark eyes widened, and a thin hand clutched the coat closer. "No! I—I'll be all right."

The voice was weak, but color was coming into the thin cheeks, so Nathan said, "Well, guess we'll just let you thaw out, lad. Maybe pretty soon you can have a sip of tea—that sound all right?" He saw one quick nod, then the eyes closed, but he saw that the thin body was beginning to shake as feeling came back. "I'll see if I can find a doctor."

He got up, but to his surprise a hand flashed out and grabbed his sleeve, and there was fear in the dark eyes. "No—please—don't leave me!"

He hesitated, then said, "Well, I won't leave until we see how you do." The eyes closed, and the hand fell, as if that one effort had drained all strength from the cold flesh.

There was little he could do, then, but keep the fire going. He knew enough not to build up a roaring blaze, but slowly allowed the tiny fire to bring the temperature of the room above freezing. Thirty minutes passed, then an hour, and several times he got up and went to lean over the cot.

He saw a thin face with a set of thick, arching brows black as a crow's wing, the same color as the hair that looked as if it had been crookedly hacked with a blunt knife. He took in the straight nose, the square face and the firm chin, and thought, *A good-looking boy, but just about played out. If I hadn't stumbled over him, he'd have been gone by morning.*

The kettle began singing, and once again the eyes opened. "How about if you try to sit up and have a swallow of tea?" He put his arm around the boy, helped him to sit up, then said, "Might be good to get rid of this coat now—" He paused and asked, "What's your name, lad?"

There was a brief silence; then the boy slowly licked his cracked lips and said in a feeble voice, "Laddie. Laddie—Smith."

Nathan did not miss the hesitation over the last name, but he ignored it, saying, "Let's have the coat, and you try to get down a mite of this tea. I'm Nathan Winslow."

Laddie nodded, slipped out of the coat, and reached a thin hand for the huge cup that Nathan had found. The odor of the tea was rich in the cold room, and he had to use both hands to hold the cup, but when he began to drink, it was not in tiny sips, but in long swallows that made the thin throat contract.

"Hey, you'll founder yourself, Laddie!" Nathan reached out and pulled the cup back, then stared into the black eyes over it. "I found some biscuits and a bit of cheese. Why don't you come over to the desk and have just a little?"

The hunger in the dark eyes flared up, and at once he swung his legs from the cot and stood up—only to sway like a sapling in the wind.

"Easy, now!" Nathan put his arm around the thin shoulders and, guiding him to the chair, eased him down carefully, then put one biscuit and a thin slice of cheese on the top of the desk. "Eat that—real *slow*," he said, and sat down to watch. The boy wanted to thrust the whole morsel in his mouth, but with a struggle, took a tiny bite and sat there chewing it slowly, then washed it down with a swallow of scalding tea.

As Laddie ate, Nathan talked easily, telling how it was that he'd stumbled across what he thought was a sack of clothes. Then as the boy's eyes brightened with the food and tea, Nathan began trying to find out something about the waif. He saw at once, however, that it was not going to be easy, for his probing built an instant wall, and the dark eyes seemed to say "No Trespassing!"

Finally he got up to say, "Well, Laddie, I think I ought to roust a doctor out of his warm bed to have a look at you—and a good one, too!" He looked critically at the thin wrists and the hollow eyes and added, "We better have him strip you to the buff and be sure everything's—"

"No! I'm fine, Mr. Winslow!" Laddie lowered the cup so abruptly that some of the scalding liquid fell on his lap, but he did not seem to notice. "I don't want a doctor! Please, just let me stay until morning and I'll be able to take care of myself. I won't be a bother to you!"

There was fear in the dark eyes, but pride as well, and Nathan stood there perplexed. The lad was on the verge of starvation! Finally he said with a shrug, "Laddie, that storm out there is mighty likely to get worse, not better. You go back outside and you'll freeze." He hesitated, then asked, "You got any family? Anybody I can write to?"

"No. I got no folks."

The barren look in the dark eyes raked against Nathan's nerves, and he wondered if he'd have the nerve to make out as well as this youngster. His life had been easy; he'd never been hungry in his life, and suddenly he knew that he had to do something. The prayer he'd prayed came back to him, and he thought, *Well, if God's done His part, I've got to do mine!*

He looked down and asked quietly, "You need a place to stay, Laddie?"

The thin shoulders squared, and the full lower lip trembled ever so slightly, but the answer was clear: "I need a job, Mr. Winslow. I'll do any kind of work at all."

Nathan looked at the thin arms and said, "Well, guess you won't be loading bales of cotton right away, but I'm wondering if you can write and do sums?"

"Yes, sir!" Hope softened the youth's face, and he swallowed and added, "I'm very good with books."

"Why, that's good, because we need someone around here to help with that." *Which will come as a surprise to Uncle Charles!* he thought with a flash of humor. But he had worked with his uncle at the business for two weeks, and knew that there would be plenty for a clerk to do. Laurence Strake, the manager of the business, had even said something to that effect, hadn't he? *"Got to have a little help with the books, Mr. Winslow."*

"I—I'll work hard!"

"Sure, Laddie, but there's no hurry. We got to get some meat on your bones. Say, how old are you—twelve or thirteen?"

"At least." There was a glint in his eyes as he answered; then he smiled for the first time, and Nathan marveled at the even whiteness of perfect teeth. "Actually, I'm fifteen, Mr. Winslow."

"Pretty young to be alone, Laddie," Nathan said, and he laid his hand on the boy's thin shoulder. It surprised him when the boy drew back instantly, and he thought, *Someone's been mistreating him!* He stepped back and stroked his chin, saying, "Let's see, I'm staying with my Uncle Charles, and in that big old house of his there's got to be a place for one small clerk."

"Couldn't I just stay here? I could fix up something."

"No, no, that won't do," he shook his head. "Well, we'll stay here tonight; then I'll talk to Uncle Charles Monday. Maybe we could find a little room close by the business."

"I'll take anything, Mr. Winslow." Then Laddie stood up and went over to stand by the fire. As the frail figure looked down into the leaping flames, Nathan took in the ragged shirt, dirty, and so torn that he could see the heavy cotton undergarment beneath. He looked at the ancient trousers, so old and worn that they had no color left, and he smiled at how Laddie had to keep them up by a piece of string. The shoes, he saw, were far too large, and one of the soles flapped loosely as the boy moved.

"Tell you what, Laddie, I'll find some blankets somewhere, and we'll stay here until morning." His face lighted up and he added, "First thing, we get us a big hot breakfast; next we find you a room to rest up in for a day or so—then we hit my uncle up for a job. That sound good?"

The small figure did not move at first, then he turned and faced Nathan, dark eyes glittering with tears. It was a struggle to speak, but finally Nathan caught the words that came so softly he had to lean down to hear them.

"You—you saved my life, Mr. Winslow." The lower lip trembled, but the soft voice went on. "I heard a story once about people in some far-off place—I think it was maybe India. It said that when somebody saved a person's life—why, that person was supposed to serve the one that saved them as long as they live."

The fire crackled and spat in the silence that followed, and Nathan said, "Well, Laddie, this isn't India—so you don't have to serve *me* all your life."

He smiled at the earnest face, trying to make a joke out of it, but the boy said quietly and directly, looking right into Nathan's eyes, "I'll always want to serve and honor you, Mr. Winslow—as long as I live!"

It embarrassed Nathan, so he laughed; then a thought came to him, and he spoke before he thought: "I forgot all about Caleb and the Sons of Liberty!" Then he went to get the blankets, and Laddie stood there staring at the door he passed through. A thought came, bringing a strange smile—but whatever it was, there was no mention of it to Nathan when he returned with the blankets.

CHAPTER SIX

SONS OF LIBERTY

★ ★ ★ ★

As soon as a weak gray light came through the small window, Nathan painfully rolled out of his blankets and got to his feet. He had slept fitfully, not being able to get Caleb out of his mind, and the hard floor in the cold room had stiffened his muscles. He had banked the fire, so the water in the basin had a skim of ice on it.

"Laddie?" He walked over to the mound of blankets on the cot and gave one of the protrusions a slap. Instantly there was a muffled cry, and he laughed when the boy's head appeared from the opposite end, eyes startled with fear. "Couldn't tell that was your rump, but guess it's not the first swat you ever got on your backside, is it?"

Laddie stared at him, and finally gave a tiny nod, saying, "No, it's not."

"Well, pile out of there." He picked up Laddie's thin coat and considered it. "This won't do. You better wear mine."

Laddie got up and stood there unsteadily, then with a shake of his head reached for the ragged garment. "No, yours would be way too long. I'll make out."

"Well—we'll try it. There's an inn just down the street. Think you can walk, or you want me to carry you?"

"I can walk—but can we go by where you found me? I've got a sack with my things in it."

"It's on the way." He led the boy outside, locked the door, then put his hand on the thin arm, moving slowly down the empty street. They had not gone over a hundred yards before he felt the boy weaving. "Here, you can't make it like this, Laddie." He swept the small figure up into his arms and picked up his pace.

Once he glanced down and saw that the thin face was red with embarrassment, he gave a short laugh, saying, "Aw, Laddie, don't be so touchy. You're weak, that's all—you don't weigh no more than a bird! Why I've packed deer out of the woods for ten miles that weigh *twice* what you do!"

"I—don't want anyone to see me!"

"Well, they won't. In a couple of hours there'll be lots of folks going to church, but it's too early now—anyway, what if they do see?" Nathan had his left arm under the boy's legs, and with his right hand supported his side, and he gave him a quick grin. "I can feel every rib you got, Laddie—but we'll get you fat and pretty as a suckling pig before long!"

There was no answer, and he saw that the youth had buried his red face against his coat, and felt the thin form tremble both with cold and shame. He shrugged, then walked quickly to the spot where he'd found Laddie, knocked the snow from a mound, and swept up a small, lumpy cotton sack. "Got it! Now, let's get out of this weather."

The Blue Boar was one of the lesser inns of the harbor, a tiny place squeezed between a large tobacco warehouse and a ship repair yard. Laurence Strake, Charles's manager, had taken Nathan there for a meal or two. It was run by James Nelson, a former foretopman in the Royal Navy, before he had turned to innkeeping.

Nathan set Laddie up right, then banged on the door loudly, calling out, "Nelson! Nelson! Open up!"

A window overhead popped open, and a man's red face appeared, "Wot's this?"

"Can you fix us up with a room, Nelson—and some breakfast?"

The burly innkeeper scratched his bald spot, then nodded and said, "We got a place—be right down."

An hour later they were pushing away from the table, having filled up on a kidney pie, hot bread and butter with dollops of jam, and a rasher of bacon, all washed down by draughts of strong, hot India tea. Laddie had begun by eating ravenously, but soon had enough. "Stomach's shrunk, I expect," Nathan said. "Better eat lots of little meals, rather than stuffing yourself."

"I think so—but it was so *good!*" The food had brought color to Laddie's cheeks, and his eyes were much brighter.

Nathan got up and led the way up the crooked, narrow stairs to the room he'd arranged for. He pushed the door open, and Laddie followed him inside. "It's not much, but it won't be for long."

It was a small room, not over ten feet square, and most of that was filled by a massive bed with ropes supporting the shuck ticking. A small pine table with a cracked basin and a pewter pitcher completed the furnishings—but it was warm, for the heat from downstairs moved into it. "Have to keep your door open to keep warm," Nathan said.

"It's—nice." He looked at Laddie quickly and saw that the worn face was pale and beads of perspiration covered the smooth forehead.

"Maybe you ate a little too much," he frowned. "Look, you need to get cleaned up and into bed, Laddie. Why don't I get you out of those old clothes, give you a good wash? You must have something to sleep in, in here!"

He started to empty the bag on the bed, but was surprised when he heard, "Oh no, Mr. Winslow, you—you don't have to do that!"

"Why, it's no bother, lad! You'd do the same for me, I take it?"

Laddie looked at him strangely, then reached out and took the sack from him. "Please, I'm all right, really I am. I'll wash up and get into bed like you say."

He stared at the boy, then shrugged, "Well, be sure you do. I've got to get going. I'll tell Nelson's wife to feed you lots of broth and soup." He cocked his head, looked down with a frown. "I'll be gone all day and all night. But I'll be back first thing Monday morning, and you ought to feel a lot stronger by then."

"Yes, sir, and—thank you again!" Hesitantly, Laddie extended a hand. When Nathan's big paw closed around it, he was very careful not to press hard—it was such a fragile hand—and withdrew it quickly. "God bless you, Mr. Winslow."

Nathan was always embarrassed by gratitude of any form, and the look in the lad's dark eyes made him grunt, "Oh, nonsense!" Then he turned and left quickly. He paused only long enough to say, "Nelson, the boy's not well, so keep an eye out for him, will you?"

"Aye, sir, I'll do that—have me ol' woman make a spot o' fresh chicken broth fer the lad, I will." He rolled his eyes upward and shrugged a set of massive shoulders. "He ain't wot yer'd call a hearty lad, is he, now?"

"I'll make it worth your while, Nelson," Nathan said, then hurried out of the inn and looked around for a carriage. There were none stirring so early, but he managed to catch a ride with a farmer going his way. He washed, dressed in his best clothes and got downstairs just in time to have a quick breakfast with the family.

"You may be a little critical of Rev. Lockyear, Nathan," Charles said later as they got out of the carriage in front of a massive old church on the south side of town. "You're more in the line of Jonathan Edwards—the old school."

"I've heard that Rev. Lockyear is pretty high church," Nathan said.

"Oh, as to that, any Anglican minister would seem rather popish to you." He chuckled and lowered his voice so that the women who'd gone ahead couldn't hear, adding, "Your father went to school with Edwards and was converted under Whitefield, so you've pretty well grown up with a hell-fire and damnation sort of preaching. But it's different with the Church of England."

"They don't believe in hell?"

"Hell's not dignified enough for most of 'em." Charles laughed at the thought, then sobered. "You won't get much theology today, I'm afraid. Lockyear spends most of his pulpit time preaching the gospel of reconciliation—not man to God, but Whigs to Tories. If he *did* believe in a hell, he'd populate it with the likes of Sam Adams and his Sons of Liberty!"

They had reached the door, and once inside Nathan felt intimidated by the rich trappings: the massive altar in the fashion of Catholic churches, the silver and gold of the cups that reflected the glittering chandeliers overhead, and the rich walnut panels and pews carved by a master.

Not much like our plain little church back home. He followed the family down the aisle, noticing that the scarlet coats of British officers were liberally scattered throughout the congregation. He smiled at Major Pitcairn, sitting with General Gage and Colonel Smith, and then found what he was seeking: Abigail sitting with her parents in a pew close to the front. She turned and caught his eye, and the smile that came to her lips made him miss a step—

until he felt Paul beside him, and then was uncertain as to which of them she was smiling at. *Keeping us both running at her heels*, he thought, then sat down and took it all in.

The service was, indeed, strange to him. A trained choir hidden from view in a loft did most of the singing, and much of the service involved a ritual that called for the worshipers to respond, sometimes in Latin, and there was much standing and some kneeling on special pads. But the preaching was what he had come for, and he forgot the exotic surroundings when Rev. Lockyear mounted the pulpit, much in the manner of the captain of a ship of the line taking charge. He was a massive man, well over six feet, with a full face that reeked of authority. His voice was as big as the rest of him, and for the next hour the congregation was informed on the near-divinity of King George the Third, and how that the most powerful evidence of total depravity lay in the traitorous behavior of those who challenged any law of the British Parliament.

After thirty minutes of this, Nathan began to feel that he had been hit on the head once too often with a single idea, but looking around he saw that the congregation was drinking it all in. General Gage was leaning forward, his face intent, but Pitcairn was less intent. He caught Nathan's glance, gave a careful wink and a shrug, as if to say, *He does go on a bit, doesn't he now?*

Finally it was over, and Nathan outmaneuvered Paul neatly. He managed to place himself by Abigail, shook hands warmly with her parents, then drew her off to one side as soon as they were outside. "You've not forgotten about tomorrow night?" She had agreed to attend a lecture with him, a boring affair, but one which he felt safe inviting her to.

"I've thought of nothing else, Nathan." Her words were sweet to his ears, but he thought there was a mocking light in her eyes. She kept him off guard constantly, for she had more experience in courtship than he. She saw his face redden, and put her hand on his arm, saying softly, "I really have, Nathan. Oh, I don't care about the lecture, but it'll be good to have some time with you."

Warmth flooded him, and he opened his mouth to answer, but it was too late. The crowd came flooding out of the church, and Nathan was caught up with the small entourage that surrounded the general. Gage spotted him, nodded vigorously and said, "Well, now, Mr. Winslow, that was a most inspiring address by Rev. Lockyear, was it not?"

"Very powerful, General," Nathan answered dutifully.

Colonel Smith edged slightly between Nathan and Gage, as if the general were his personal property, not to be approached by a mere civilian. His small eyes narrowed, and there was a malevolent expression on his round face. "Not strong enough—not by half!"

"Why, Colonel, the Reverend practically delivered the rebels into hell—what more could you ask?" Pitcairn's handsome face was bland, but there was a glint of humor in his blue eyes. Nathan had noticed that he had no respect for Smith and lost no opportunity to poke fun at the man.

Smith's face grew crimson and his voice rose in real anger. "Ought to hang the lot of them!"

"Take a good deal of rope," Pitcairn answered mildly.

"Let me get them in front of a troop of British soldiers with loaded muskets, and I'd show you what I'd do!"

"Now, now, Colonel," Gage said with a shake of his head, "we must hope it doesn't come to that."

He went on speaking, but Pitcairn caught Nathan's eye, and giving a motion of his head, left the group. Nathan did not want to leave Abigail, but felt impressed to go. The officer made his way to a vacant spot, then said quietly, "There's a meeting of the Sons of Liberty tonight, at the place where I showed you."

"Thanks, Major," Nathan said. "Are you sure?"

"My informant has been accurate so far."

"I'll try to keep Caleb away." He paused, then asked, "You don't think Colonel Smith meant what he said, do you?"

"About shooting the rebels? I think it's possible. Most of us would have more sense, but there are enough like Smith to set the thing off, Nathan." He hesitated, then reached up and put a friendly hand on his shoulder, saying quietly, "You're putting yourself in a very bad place, I fear. You're being pulled in two directions, aren't you? Your family is one thing, and yet you've made some good friends—like me, I trust—on the other side. I hope it won't ever come to the point where you have to choose one way or the other."

Nathan looked down into the eyes of the officer and saw the honesty and simple honor written there. "I—I don't want to lose you as a friend, Major!"

"Nor I you—but I'm about in the same boat as you, Nathan. I've learned to respect Americans, most of them, and yet I'm a commissioned officer in the King's army, and I must obey orders."

"It'll work out, John." Nathan spoke with the optimism of a young man who had never seen his dreams turn to dust. He did not see the sudden compassion in his friend's eyes, for he had turned to go with Charles who was hailing him to the carriage.

Pitcairn turned to his friends, but there was a sadness on his face as he thought about the tall American who had come to mean so much to him.

Moses Tyler was fully satisfied with Caleb's reaction. He had taken his new friend to a simple Congregational church, then out to an inn for a good lunch, and now they were about to start a Sons of Liberty meeting.

Moses was a thin pock-marked boy of fifteen with faded blue eyes, but a strong chin and firm mouth. The eyes glinted out of an angular face, and his whitish hair was so long he brushed it away from his face with a habitual gesture.

He'd had a hard life, so there was an adult quality in him despite his slight form and youthful features. Born out of wedlock, he'd grown up as a bound boy—more a slave than a servant—and had never had a friend, at least not until Caleb Winslow had come to town. Moses was bound to Charles Winslow for another two years, and did the menial work at the company warehouse. He lived in a small room over a shop, and his only pleasures in life were found in his church activities and in the meetings with the Sons of Liberty. He'd been hired by one of the leaders to clean the place they used for a hall, and he'd stayed to listen at the meeting. Nobody paid him any heed, but he'd come back every time the society met, cleaning the place and being of general help, until finally Sam Adams had noticed him. "Boy—you are a patriot?" he asked directly.

"Yes, sir—that is, I wants to be."

"Then you shall be!" Adams had quickly found out that Moses had no family and plenty of free time, so he'd used the boy for chores and let him attend the less important meetings. Moses had never dared to say a word at any of these meetings; indeed, most of the time he had not the faintest notion what they were talking about, but once he said shyly to Adams after the fiery leader had addressed the group, "I liked what you said—about men being free, Mr. Adams."

"Did you now?" Adams was a stern man, slovenly in his personal habits and not given to light talk. He had a harsh way about him that kept most people at a distance, but there was a friendly light in his brown eyes as he looked at the boy. He put a hand on the thin shoulder, a most uncharacteristic gesture for him—and the first time any man had ever done such a thing to Moses. His shoulder seemed to burn under the weight of the hand; then Adams had nodded and said quietly, "When the trouble comes, Moses, it'll be boys like you, not old men like me, who'll have to make it work. Old men can make speeches, but it'll be you who'll have to look down a musket at a British soldier. And I think you'll be up to it!"

From that time on, Adams had always noticed the boy in small ways, and once had encouraged him to keep his eye out for any young fellow who might make a good Son of Liberty.

Looking around the crowded room, Moses leaned over and whispered "That's him, Caleb, that's Mr. Adams! And that's Mr. Revere with him."

"The silversmith? I've heard of him. Who's that coming in?"

"That's Dr. Warren. He's a real big shot in Boston."

Adams had turned from his talk with Revere, and seeing the two, came over and said, "Brought a guest, did you, Moses?"

Moses beamed, proud to be noticed. "Yes, sir! This is my friend Caleb Winslow."

Adams gave Caleb a straight look, then asked directly, "You're interested in our group, Mr. Winslow?"

"Well, I don't live in Boston, Mr. Adams, but I sure would be if I lived here."

"Where's your home?"

"I come from Virginia."

Revere had come up to listen. He was a full-faced man, with a heavy lower lip and sharp black eyes. "Virginia? Well, welcome to Boston!" He shook Caleb's hand and asked idly, "Don't suppose you know Colonel Washington?"

"Well, as a matter of fact, my father knows him pretty well." Caleb tried to keep his tone casual as he said, "My father was a scout with him and Braddock."

"Indeed!" Revere said, and he exchanged a quick glance with Adams, who looked more closely at Caleb. "Your name is Winslow? Any relation to Charles Winslow?"

"My uncle, sir." Caleb saw a dark look cross the faces of both men, and added hastily, "My father is his half brother—but they don't agree on politics."

"I see." Revere was rubbing his chin, a thought nibbling at him. Then he looked up with a smile and said, "Why, I've got it now! It was a few years ago, but I met your father—and your grandfather, as well."

"Really, sir?"

"Yes, I remember it now quite well. Your grandfather had come to Franklin to get a book printed, and I was in the shop. Matter of fact, I did the engraving for the frontispiece. It was quite a book—" He turned to Adams and said, "Here's a *real* American for us, Sam! This boy is a descendant of Gilbert Winslow from the *Mayflower*. You must have read that book of his; it was a bestseller for Franklin."

Adams stared at Caleb. "I am impressed, very much so."

"Wait now!" Revere said, and again struggled to remember; then it came. "Isn't your father a metal worker like myself?"

"He's a fine gunsmith, Mr. Revere."

"Ah, now, that's what I'd like to hear!" Adams' face was alive with interest, and he began to throw questions rapidly. In ten minutes Adams had his life history, the fact that he himself was a good gunsmith and that his family was strong for the cause. Finally he looked around and said, "Well, we must have more of your time, Mr. Winslow. I think you have a place in the Sons of Liberty."

"Why, that's kind of you, Mr. Adams," Caleb said. His heart was beating fast, and he was lightheaded. *Me—a friend of Sam Adams and Paul Revere! Just wait until I tell Father about this! He'll let me stay in Boston, I'll bet!*

The meeting began soon, but Caleb heard little of it. He was too engrossed with the personalities to listen to ideas. One thing he knew—for the first time in his life, he felt more like a man than a boy! "It's just great, Moses!" he said as the last speaker, Dr. Warren, ended and they all stood up. "I want to join with you."

"Let's go tell Mr. Adams."

They started toward the front, but at that instant there was a loud knock at the door. Revere was closest, and he moved to open it; there was caution in his face, and Adams said quietly, "Remember, we're just a group meeting to study history!" A small laugh sounded, but Adams frowned and they took their cue. "Open the door, Mr. Revere."

Caleb was never so surprised in his life, for there in the open door stood his brother Nathan!

"I'm looking for Caleb Winslow," Nathan said loudly, looking like a giant in the doorway, drawn up to his full height. There was a hard look on his face, and he suddenly met Caleb's eyes. "I see he's here."

"Why, yes, he is," Revere said. He smiled and put his hand out. "We're just finished, but won't you come in?"

"I have no business here—and neither does my brother." Nathan's voice was cold, and he ignored the hand, pushing past Revere to come and stand before the two boys. "Let's go, Caleb."

There was a sudden stillness in the place, an ominous and uncomfortable silence, and everyone looked right at Caleb.

He felt the pressure of their eyes, and though most of them were strangers to him, he felt Moses lean slightly against him, and it was enough to make him say, "I'll take care of myself, Nathan!"

"You're not taking care of yourself like this!"

"You have objections to our study group, Mr. Winslow?" Sam Adams did not move, but his deep-set eyes suddenly burned with the anger that always lurked just beneath the surface.

"Study group, you call it?" Nathan scoffed. "I think we all know exactly what it is you *study*! How to overthrow the King's true government!"

Revere said quietly, "I don't think Gilbert Winslow would have looked at it like that, my boy. He left England to make a world where men could be free. And I suspect your father feels that way, as well."

Nathan said angrily, "I will not argue politics with you, sir! Caleb, come with me!"

"No, I won't do it, Nathan."

Nathan stood there towering over the sturdy form of his brother, and he forced himself to say quietly, "Father said for me to take care of you, Caleb. I can't let you stay here with these men. You could end up in jail—or worse!"

"In that your brother may be accurate, young man." Dr. Warren suddenly moved out of the cluster in the rear and came to stand close to the brothers. He was a tall man with a fair complexion and a kind expression in his dark eyes. "It would not be fair to let you stay without knowing this well. All of us in this room are in danger—and it will probably get worse."

Nathan was taken off guard by the tall man's honesty. "Why, that's decent of you, sir."

The doctor glanced at Adams, and seemed to find what he sought. "Caleb, I suggest you go with your brother. Your father seems to have put you in his charge. Think about this, talk to your parents. Then make your decision."

Adams nodded. "Good idea, my boy. You do it."

"All right—but I know I'll be back."

Revere stepped back, but said to Nathan, "Give my regards to your parents for me, Mr. Winslow. I've often thought of them."

"I'll do that," Nathan said, then walked out of the room followed by Caleb, who was close to tears and bit his lips to hide it.

"Those lads are in for trouble," Dr. Warren murmured.

"That they are—and the tall one is in for the most grief," Adams nodded. "Well, there'll be many a family like that before this thing is over—split right down the middle."

"I wonder what Gilbert Winslow would have said about this?" Revere mused. Then he gave a rueful laugh. "He'd probably have whipped out a foil and run King George through! He was a real fighter, that one."

Adams looked toward the door, nodded slowly, then said, "We could do with some hot blood like that in this place. But it seems more likely that the real Winslow blood's in the young fellow—my hope's in him—not the older one."

"Maybe." Revere was rubbing his chin thoughtfully, but then he shook his head. "I remember that Gilbert Winslow, according to his book, got off the track himself when he was about this boy's age—but when he finally got his head pointed in the right direction, why, sir, he just about got the job done!—and this tall one has the same look about him!"

Nathan said nothing all the way back to the house, knowing that there was an iron stubbornness running through his brother. He had seen it many times as they had grown up together, and the one thing that he could not do with Caleb was force him to do something. When they were children, he had always been able to dominate Caleb physically, but no matter how much he was hurt, the boy *never gave up*. Knowing this, he determined to say nothing of the business. But Caleb felt differently.

As soon as they were in their room, he said, "Nathan, don't you ever do that again—not ever!"

Nathan made no attempt to avoid the charge, for his anger had gone, and it was replaced by a fear of what might happen. He shook his head sadly, then said, "Caleb, you don't know what you're getting into."

"I think I do!"

"I know you think so, but will you let me tell you how it looks to me?"

The request caught Caleb off guard. He'd expected hard talk, and now there was a plea on his brother's face that he'd rarely seen. "Well, I'll listen, Nathan."

"All right, here it is. You are forgetting one thing, and that is that we are *Englishmen*. Oh, I know King George is an idiot, probably insane! And I know that he's surrounded himself by men who are *not* fools, but are greedy and unscrupulous. And it doesn't take a smart man to see that we've been treated unfairly."

"Why, if you see that, Nathan," Caleb said in surprise, "why can't you see that we have to stand against them?"

"Say that we do," Nathan said slowly and with great intensity. "Say that we even do what Adams and Revere say we can do—defeat the Crown and set up our own government—which is impossible, but say that a revolution worked, where would we be then?"

"Why, we'd be free!"

"Not for long, Caleb. Have your forgotten Spain? She's already got a foothold in Florida and Louisiana. We'd be a little group of states with nothing in common—no army, no law, nothing to fight with. And if not Spain, it'd be one of the strong European nations like Prussia who'd get us."

"But we could be strong, Nathan, in time—"

"That's just it, Caleb," Nathan interrupted; "wouldn't *have* time! We'd be little and weak, and one of the wolves would pick us off sure as the world. Can't you see that?"

Caleb's face settled into the stubborn lines that Nathan had learned to dread, so he broke off at once. "Well, I'm sorry if I shamed you, Caleb, coming for you, but I—" The words stopped, and silently the tall young man who spoke so well on some things had no way to say what he felt. He wanted to say, *I came because I love you and you're my only brother and I don't want you to be hurt.* But his emotions were too subdued for that, so he merely put his hand on Caleb's shoulder and said, "I just want what's good for you, Caleb, that's all."

Caleb tried for a smile that didn't quite work. He said only, "I wish we thought the same about this thing, Nathan. I—I don't want to be against you." Then he whirled to hide his confusion and began to prepare for bed.

Nathan's heart was full, but there was no more to be said. He sat down at the desk and said, "I've got to write Father and Mother about this, Caleb. You know that?"

"Yes. You go ahead."

By the light of a candle, Nathan began to write. The scratch of his turkey-quill pen echoed in the quietness of the room. He could hear Caleb's steady breathing, but knew that he was not asleep. For over an hour he wrote, first about unimportant things, but finally he had to come to what he hated to put on paper:

> Finally, I have bad news for you about Caleb. He is physically well, but I must tell you he has joined himself to the Sons of Liberty—the radical "patriots" led by Sam Adams and others of that sort.
>
> It will be hard for you to read this, as it is hard for me to write it. Our opinions differ in this matter. But sitting here in the middle of the thing is different from being in the quiet backwaters of our little town. This place is like a powder keg, Father! You know how it is in a powder-making plant, with explosive powder everywhere, how they make people wear soft shoes with no nails that might give off a spark, and how nobody would *ever* think of striking a match? Well, if you can imagine a powder-making plant where wild, irresponsible men run down the aisles with torches and striking flint to steel right over the powder—that's what Boston is like!
>
> The Crown is sick of Boston's smuggling, and sick of the Sons of Liberty, so to protect Royal officials, 4,000 Redcoats have been stationed here under General Gage. That's one soldier for every four citizens, and the people refuse to house these men (which they are bound to do under the Quartering Act passed by Parliament). Many of these ill-fed, ill-paid men hire themselves out at menial jobs for low wages, incurring the bitter wrath of Boston's unemployed. Every day there is a street fight with mobs taunting the troops with cries of "bloody backs!" and all the while it is Sam Adams and his Sons of Liberty maneuvering in the background, fanning flames of revolt!
>
> I beg you, send for Caleb! He is hypnotized by the "romance" of being in a revolution that could well mean his life. As for me, I would like to stay, but will do as you instruct me.
>
> Your loving son,
> Nathan

CHAPTER SEVEN

A NEW CLERK

★ ★ ★ ★

When Laddie opened the door of his room to admit Nathan the next morning, the youth saw at once the marks of sleeplessness on his face. But Winslow smiled, saying, "Well, you look pretty good this morning."

"I'm fine. Mrs. Nelson fed me so much chicken soup, I'm about to sprout pinfeathers!"

"You feel like moving around a bit?" The boy nodded, plucked his ragged jacket from a wooden peg, and followed Winslow down the narrow stairs. "You had breakfast yet?"

"Oh, yes, I'm fine."

"Well, we'll go find you something to wear, then come back for a bite later."

Laddie felt very uncomfortable walking with Nathan down the street. Winslow was wearing buff trousers, a crisp white shirt with ruffles, a dark blue waistcoat and a wool cloak of a lighter hue. His auburn hair escaped here and there from beneath the blue and white tri-cornered hat, and he wore highly polished black boots to the knees. *I look like a beggar he's picked up from the gutter*, the lad thought, and when he led the boy into a shop filled with good clothing, it was worse.

"Yes, sir, may I be of help?" A short fussy-looking man with a prim moustache and a pair of silver-rimmed eyeglasses came up at once. He gave Nathan's figure an approving glance, but seemed not to notice Laddie at all.

"Yes, I want this young fellow suited out," Nathan said. He must have seen the supercilious look the clerk gave the ragged figure beside him, for he spoke with an edge to his voice. "I doubt you've got anything good enough to suit, but you can try."

That challenge seemed to change the man, for he straightened himself to his full five feet five and said indignantly, "You are mistaken, sir, grossly mistaken! We have just what the young gentleman needs!"

"We'll see. Now from the skin out, mind you—breeches, shirts, stockings, waistcoat, overcoat, a good hat, underclothes—anything else that's needed."

The light of pure greed brightened the clerk's narrowly spaced eyes, and he nodded so rapidly that his glasses almost fell off. "To be sure! Clothes make the man! And we'll have a new man here in no time, won't we, young fellow?"

A flash of humor appeared in the youth's dark eyes, but Laddie only nodded briefly, then turned to Nathan. "I can't let you spend all this on me, Mr. Winslow."

"You can pay it back out of your earnings," he shrugged. "You'll have to pass muster for my uncle—and his wife, which will be more difficult. I'll leave you here for an hour, all right?"

He gave an encouraging smile; then as he left the shop, the clerk at once began laying out the articles he had mentioned. It was a trying hour for Laddie, for men's clothing was something she knew little about. But she went at it carefully, choosing items that would be less revealing of the figure underneath. Some of the choices surprised the clerk, and he showed grave displeasure, but when Nathan returned at the appointed time, all the items were in a large bag ready to go.

"Get everything?" he asked, then at the lad's nod, asked the price and paid it without comment. "Let's go back to the Nelsons' place. I could use a bite now."

As they walked along the street, Nathan said, "We'll have to go out to my uncle's house, Laddie. I talked to Strake—he's the general manager—and he says he can use a clerk; you'll have to satisfy him before we get my uncle's approval."

They turned into The Blue Boar, and went upstairs, but Nathan called out as they went through the bar, "Nelson, let's have some battered eggs and some fresh fruit if you've got any—for the two of us."

When they were inside the door, Laddie opened the bag and began laying the items on the bed, saying, "Let me show you what I bought, Mr. Winslow—such nice things!"

He glanced down at the clothing, grinned and said, "Well, I don't want to see how they look with the *bed* wearing them, Laddie! Go on and put them on."

Laddie stared at him, and a red flush began creeping up the slender throat. Nathan looked at the boy in surprise and asked, "What's wrong?"

"N-nothing—but would you—would you mind waiting outside until I—get dressed?"

"Outside?" He could not have been more surprised if Laddie had asked him to jump out the window. Then he suddenly laughed and said, "Why, Laddie, I think you're ashamed because you're so skinny! Well, that's no matter to me—but I'll go on down and hurry Mrs. Nelson up with the breakfast. Quickly now, will you?"

He slammed the door as he left, thinking with a wry smile, *Pretty modest for a beggar!* But he was hungry and sat down, listening to Nelson tell one of his tall tales about how he'd saved his ship in the Indian Sea once.

Finally the breakfast was brought out by Mrs. Nelson, and he looked up at that same instant to see Laddie come down the stairs. He was so surprised at the change in the boy's appearance that for a moment he could only stare.

Nelson, however, was more vocal. He looked up from the mug of ale that he was sipping, and his eyes widened as he said, "Well, now! Lookee wot we got 'ere! A real gentleman is wot we got!"

Laddie crossed to the table, with no little grain of fear that they might see through the disguise. An examination of their faces drew a sigh of relief, however, for there was no indication of that.

Julie, in the guise of Laddie, had given much thought to the matter of concealing her sex, but the old plan of merely covering up with loose fitting, bulky clothes would not serve for this new life. Her quick mind had seen at once that she would have to dress like a clerk—but that meant wearing clothing much tighter and therefore more dangerous. All the time she had been choosing the clothing, this had been in her mind, and she had done well. She had, first of all, bound her upper figure tightly with a broad strip of cotton cloth ripped from her old clothes. Then she had donned the white stockings and a pair of buff knee breeches, the universal garment of young men everywhere. A light brown waistcoat, as loose-fitting as she dared, was buttoned up to where a white ruffle rose and covered her slender throat. Over all this she wore a dark brown broadcloth coat with wide double lapels and white ruffles from a shirt extending past the cuffs. A pair of high-topped brown boots covered her slender legs.

What Nathan saw was a thin young man with eyes perhaps too large and features more delicate than most his age, but looking very well in a suit of new clothes. He smiled and slapped his hand on the table. "Stab me!" he cried out with an approving smile, "I think that idiot of a clerk had *some* sense! Clothes *do* make the man, don't they, Nelson?"

"Why, I could get the lad a post as midshipman on the *Victory* right this day, sir! He's a proper gentleman, he is!"

"Well, and if he's good enough for the Royal Navy, why, he ought to be good enough for the Winslow Company," Nathan grinned. "Eat up, Laddie, then we'll get you gainfully employed!"

The interview with Laurence Strake took little time. Strake, a tall man with a lean face and sharp black eyes, shoved two papers toward Laddie. "Total up the figures on the one—and write a letter on the other," he demanded. He sat there and waited, surprise crossing his face when Laddie totaled the figures faster than he himself could have done and got it right. The letter pleased him even more. "Why, it's a fair hand you have, Smith! You've been well trained." He nodded to Nathan, adding, "I'm satisfied, but you'll have to gain Mr. Charles's approval."

"No problem there, but we'll have to go to the house. Come along, Laddie." They took the carriage and arrived just in time for an early lunch with the family.

"Now don't be nervous, Laddie. My uncle isn't a hard man." The servant admitted them, and he led the boy straight to the dining room. Charles looked up in surprise, as did the others. "Sorry to interrupt your meal," Nathan said hurriedly, "but when you finish, Uncle, could we have a word with you?"

"What is it, Nathan?" Charles asked, looking curiously at Laddie. "Who's this with you?"

"This is Laddie Smith, sir—it's a matter of business, but if you don't mind . . . ?"

Dorcas was staring at the pair, and she gave a quick frown toward her mother-in-law, then said sharply, "Get on with it, Nathan."

"Well, it's just that I remembered you and Mr. Strake spoke of needing a clerk last week, and I'd like to recommend this young man."

"A clerk?" Charles frowned, then nodded absently. "I believe we did have that in mind." He looked at Laddie more carefully, then said, "We'd thought of an older man—what's your age?"

"Oh, I took him by and Mr. Strake gave him a very strict examination," Nathan spoke up quickly. "He'll give you the result himself, but I can say he's ready to employ Smith at once."

"Well, it's Strake who'll have to work with him, so you may consider yourself hired, young fellow."

"Thank you, Mr. Winslow," Laddie said breathlessly. "I'll do my best for you."

"By the way, Uncle, Laddie here has been a little under the weather lately, so would it be all right if he started work in a few days—just until he can get his strength up?"

"He looks frail to me, Charles," Martha said.

"Clerks don't have to lift anything heavier than a pen, Mother," Charles said idly. "Yes, that'll be all right, Nathan. Anything else?"

"Well, as a matter of fact, we haven't spoken of wages, but if we could find a room here, we could count that as part of his wages."

Dorcas suddenly straightened up, her interest piqued. "You are competent with figures—and a fair penman?"

"I trust so, ma'am."

"Charles, Anne is doing very poorly with her studies. I suggest that it might be wise to let Smith have the room over the stable in exchange for lessons for her."

Always ready to do anything for his daughter, Charles gave Laddie a quick look, then asked, "Would this be acceptable with you, Smith?"

"Why, I'm no teacher, Mr. Winslow, but I'll give the young lady what pointers I can."

He put his hand out to Laddie, surprising the boy, and shook his hand warmly. "I'll have the room put in order at once—and this would be a good place for you to recuperate. Nathan, you've done well."

Anne jumped up and ran around the table, "Mama, can I show Mr. Smith his room, please?"

"All right, and tell Else to have it cleaned up." Dorcas was tight with money, and it pleased her to think that she had managed to wring a free service out of the young man. "You can begin your tutoring at once, young man. And I'll expect great improvement in my daughter's work."

"Yes, ma'am." Laddie turned to follow Anne out of the room, but paused to stop and say quietly to Nathan, "I must thank you again, Mr. Winslow."

After the two had gone, Charles said as he headed for the door, "Seems a fine chap—but a bit frail, as Dorcas says. Known him long?"

"Oh, not very—but I feel he'll make you a good clerk."

"You're very like your father, Nathan—the way you help people, I mean," Charles said. He paused and looked into his nephew's face. "I know Adam doesn't think too much of me, but I must tell you, I've long considered him the most honest man I've ever known." He paused; then a cloud crossed his face, and he said with a shrug as he wheeled to leave, "Indeed, perhaps the *only* honest man I've ever run across!"

A warm breeze drifted through the small window of Laddie's room, bringing in the odor of freshly turned earth and the sound of the martins building a nest outside the window. The iron hand of winter had relaxed a few days earlier, and warm spring winds had stirred the land to life.

Laddie looked down at the book before her, reading what she had written. Keeping a journal had never been a thing she cared to do, but in the isolation imposed by her secret, it had come to be a pleasure to be totally honest, even if only in a closely guarded journal. She looked back at the first entry, dated, Feb. 18, 1775, and smiled at the words:

"Here I am, like Jonah out of the whale's belly!"

She shook her head, thinking *I was pretty dramatic about everything then*. But as she slowly turned the pages, it struck her now that there was something dramatic in her life. It was a role she had to play, and unlike real actors who got off the stage and had a life of their own, she was *never* off stage—except for times like this alone in her room. She had a flair for capturing scenes on paper, and knew that she could write fiction if she turned her hand to it. As she read her own rather breathless accounts—how she had managed to keep up the charade of being a man, how in this case she was almost found out, how in that case she learned another useful trick for adding to the illusion of masculinity—she grew sober, and looked out the window, musing. *Sooner or later I'll be found out. A girl can't get by with pretending to be a man forever.*

Then she gave her head a rebellious shake, and read the entry she'd just made:

March 20, 1775

I had a strange thought tonight. Ever since I've been here with the Winslows, I've been so afraid of being found out! But that seems unlikely. I've become a student of masculine behavior—how to walk, for example, which is *nothing* like the same act performed by a woman! How to listen to male profanity without blinking an eye. I even take a night off at times and return boasting of my conquests over some beautiful woman—which Nathan scoffs at, saying I'm too young for such. I've learned to act the role well, but it's a hard thing!

But the thought I had tonight—it wasn't for me. For the first time I found myself worried about someone else. It comes to me now that I'm caught up in the Winslow family—only natural, since these people have become my whole world.

Charles Winslow is not a good man, perhaps, but he's treated me fairly enough. He is the half brother to Nathan's father, and from what I gather the two are not alike.

But Caleb is in trouble. I've seen how he's been cut out of the family here—and it's no wonder, since all these Winslows are Tories to the bone! He can't talk to Nathan, that's clear. So it came as little surprise when he began talking to *me*. I'm his age, and the only "man" he can speak to, so I've learned a lot from what he's said.

Nathan Winslow is the best young man in the world—but he's so in love with that painted flirt Abigail Howland that he can't see his own brother is being pushed outside!

She slammed the journal shut, slipped it into a cloth cover, put that into a box, and then carefully placed it in the false bottom of a small chest packed with her things.

She failed to understand the anger that raced through her when she thought of the problem, but it was, she knew, getting more severe. She closed the door, went across the fresh green grass from the carriage house and into the back door. The cook, a fat black woman named House Betty (to distinguish her from Field Betty), looked up, saying, "Dey's already havin' brekfust, Mistuh Smith."

It had been difficult at first, taking meals with the family, but during her first days, while giving Anne lessons, eating with the Winslows had evolved as the simplest way; now the first part of "Laddie's" work was tutoring the girl after breakfast, then she went into town to the business.

"Laddie, I showed Papa the letter I wrote," Anne said at once, her face beaming, "and he said it was the best he ever read!"

Charles smiled and nodded. "You've done wonders, Laddie—both here with Anne and at the office. I don't see what we ever did without you."

"It's easy to be a good teacher," Laddie said with a fond glance at Anne, "when you have a willing student."

Paul spoke up. "Let me say, Laddie, that the best day's work that Nathan here ever did in the business was to find you."

Nathan smiled, but there was a restraint in his manner. He was subdued, and Laddie wondered if there had been some sort of problem. She asked no questions, but later in the meal, Charles said with a peculiar look in his eye, "I think I mentioned a while back that someone from our office would have to go to New York very soon to learn that new bookkeeping system from Johnson? Well, it's got to be now. I want it set up here as soon as possible."

"Well, *I* can't go," said both Paul and Nathan at the same instant, then paused and looked at each other.

"Neither of you want to go?" Charles said in surprise, but there was a gleam in his blue eyes. "Well, that's too bad." Everyone at the table, except Anne, knew that the rivalry between the cousins for Abigail had grown so heated that they stayed awake nights scheming new ways to edge one another out.

The two of them began to bicker, each trying to shove the trip off on the other, and although they were polite enough, it was obvious that they were both determined to be the one left in Boston to court Abigail.

Finally Charles raised his hand for silence. "All right, I'll have Strake go." He watched as they settled down, then set off his little bombshell. "But it will be a shame—because he'll be wasted on Abigail."

"Abigail?" Paul demanded. "What's she got to do with a trip to New York?"

"Oh, didn't I mention that?" Charles tried to look surprised. "Why, she's gotten Saul and her mother to let her go for some shopping there, so we agreed that since she needed clothes and I needed someone there to learn some business, they might as well make the trip together. But it will be good for Abigail to spend some time in the company of a serious man like Strake, don't you think so, Nathan?"

Laddie gave a sudden grin at the blank expression on Nathan's face, but tried to look sorry when he glared balefully at her. "Why, Uncle Charles, I suppose I've been selfish about this whole thing." He put a look on his face that was revoltingly pious, and added smoothly, "I suppose I *could* make that trip."

Then Paul raised his eyebrows and said defiantly, "I'm going to New York, and that's that!"

The next fifteen minutes were tense, both young men ready to fight in order to go, but in the end Charles wearied of it. He raised his voice over the strident tones of his son, who was speaking much too loudly, and said, "All right! That's enough! I knew when this came up, there'd be no way for *one* of you to go—so *both* of you will go—and you'll have to go along as well, Laddie." He laughed at the surprise that crossed her face, and said, "You'll have to do the real work while these two pound each other over the fair lady."

"Charles, it's not dignified!" Dorcas said.

"Love hardly ever is," he said sourly.

"Please, Uncle Charles, I'd like to go along."

Caleb had said nothing for so long at the table that he was usually forgotten. Now he spoke up clearly, and added, "Will it be all right? Maybe I can learn something, too."

Charles stared at the young man, then slowly nodded, a strange expression on his face. *He looks so much like Adam!* "Well, it can't do any harm. You'll have to take the big carriage to hold all of you, but I have no objections."

"When do we leave, Father?" Paul asked.

"You'll pick Abigail up at ten in the morning." He gave them a sly smile and said, "I told her you'd *both* be going—and that seemed to please her a great deal."

It would! Laddie thought angrily. *She'll have them shooting each other in some fool duel before we get back!* Then she had to try to console

Anne, who felt left out. She took one quick look at Caleb, trying to fathom his motives, for it was one of the last things he'd have wanted to do—be away from the Sons of Liberty—but there was nothing on his face but a slight expression of satisfaction.

CHAPTER EIGHT

"A MAN IN LOVE IS BOUND TO BE A FOOL!"

★ ★ ★ ★

"I don't reckon Uncle Charles's big idea is going to work, is it, Laddie?"

The front wheel of the big wagon struck a pothole just as Laddie turned to look at Caleb, and the unexpected lurch threw her heavily against Caleb, who was driving. She pulled back quickly, took a tight grip on the seat, and asked, "What big idea?"

"Why, he got this whole thing up so's Abigail would have to choose between Nathan and Paul." He turned to face her, a sardonic smile on his lips. "But it sure has turned out different!"

Laddie's shoulders sagged, for the trip had been no pleasure for any of them. They had left Boston three days earlier, and the spring weather had been ideal for traveling. The roads were still heavily rutted from winter travel, but the inns had been fairly clean and the food mostly good. At their first night's stop, however, at a villainous place called The Blue Lion, Paul had spat out what was reported to be tea, and called to the innkeeper: "Sir, if this be tea, bring me coffee. If this be coffee, bring me tea."

And it was later at that same place that the sleeping accommodations almost caught up with Laddie. There were only two rooms; one, of course, was for Abigail, and the other for the rest of the party. All throughout the meal, Laddie's mind was racing, and when Nathan said, "Let's get some sleep—we've got a long trip tomorrow," panic had almost taken over, but the room, they found was so small that after one look, he had said, "This bed's too small for four. Caleb, you and Laddie will have to make out in the wagon tonight."

As she and Caleb had settled down that night, fortified with blankets, Caleb had said, "I like this better than that dirty old room, anyway. Don't you, Laddie? I'd just as soon camp out like this the whole trip." Laddie had quickly agreed, and then for a long time they had lain awake, listening to the spring peepers in a nearby creek and tracing out patterns in the icy points of light the stars made against the velvet sky.

Now as Caleb drove the wagon down the final stretch of road to where the silhouette of New York could be faintly seen, Laddie looked across at his stocky figure, thinking how strange it was that she should know more of him than Nathan. Caleb had spoken wistfully of how close they had been once, and his loneliness was a sharp pain that he exposed, she knew, only to her.

Now, she picked up on his comment, saying, "I guess men in love are generally fools."

"You got that right, Laddie!" Caleb nudged the off leader a touch with his buggy whip, and then gave a short laugh. "Don't know what my hurry is."

"Why'd you want to come along?" she asked.

He gave no direct answer, saying only, "Might as well be here as in Boston, I guess."

Paul took the reins when they got to the outskirts of New York and drove to the branch office, which was located in the center of the harbor. Hiram Johnson, the manager, was a short man with a full black beard and deep-set black eyes. "Won't take more'n two or three days to learn that system." He looked over the party and said innocently, "Reckon they's enough of you to handle the job?"

Paul looked a little foolish, and at that instant Laddie had an idea—an answer to the ever-present problem of where she would sleep. "If you've got a cot here, Mr. Johnson, I could stay here around the clock. That would be quicker, wouldn't it?"

"Sure, we can do that," the manager agreed, and Laddie saw that both Paul and Nathan were relieved.

"I'd like to stay, too."

Nathan stared at Caleb, and he opened his mouth to question

the boy, but at that instant, Abigail said, "I really need to get settled; if you'd be so kind as to take me to the hotel."

As Caleb and Laddie got their bags from the carriage, then watched the party drive off toward the inner city, Caleb said, "Looks like we ain't going to be bothered much with their company, are we, Laddie?"

There was something so childish about the way the two men followed around after Abigail, glaring at each other, that Laddie muttered angrily, "Like I said, men in love are bound to be fools!"

By the third day of the visit, Nathan would have agreed totally with Laddie's statement. He had begun well, showing up early at the office in the morning, but as the day wore on and Paul made no appearance, he grew moody. Finally at noon, he said, "Laddie, do you think you can handle this alone? I mean, I'm no clerk—so I might as well get out of your way." Then almost without waiting for an answer, he had walked quickly out of the office and had not returned.

But he did not better himself, for if he had felt useless at the office, he felt even more out of place following around after Abigail. When the trip had come up, he had thought, *Well, now I'll be able to get her alone—away from family and everyone.* But he never did that; in fact, he saw rather *less* of her than he had in Boston!

New York was a thriving beehive of a town, bursting at the seams, and filled with activities day and night. The streets teemed with people, including many sailors from the Royal Fleet that lay at anchor in the East River. Nathan was acutely aware that the threat of revolution lay always just beneath the surface, exactly as it had at Boston—which disturbed him. But he had little time to think about politics, for he found himself caught up in an almost frantic round of social activities led by Abigail and a group of young socialites.

They began in the mornings with tea in the lovely homes of the city, and Nathan was ill at ease. Paul and Abigail knew everyone, it seemed, and he stood on the outside looking in. He felt himself to be an outsider, a quaint colonial, a backwoodsman from Virginia, which was to some extent quite accurate. More than one pretty girl tried to draw his attention, but he was so single-minded in his pursuit of Abigail that he never noticed.

In the afternoons they prowled the streets of the Battery, took in the waxworks and the gardens, and later probed into the lower side of the city, attending a horse race and the many curiosities, peep shows, and wax museums that abounded on the lower side of Manhattan.

Then in the evenings, Abigail's friends scheduled dances in their large homes. These affairs were like small "balls" and lasted until the early hours of the morning, and Nathan felt out of place at them as well.

On the fourth night he stood with his back against the wall in a large Dutch-style mansion, watching the dancers weave across the polished floor. He had eaten little for the past two days, and his nerves were jangling from the constant frenzied activities and from lack of sleep. He had broken his own rule and had several glasses of wine, so his head was not clear.

He had danced several times, but only once with Abigail, and as he stood there, she danced by with Paul, looking up at him, laughing, and Paul suddenly threw his head back and laughed. Behind him someone said, "Make a lovely couple, don't they?" He glared at the overweight woman who had spoken to her equally overweight husband, then moved away.

For the next hour he grew more morose and he took several more glasses of wine from the refreshment table that groaned under the weight of food and drink. Finally, he thought, *A man's a fool to torment himself like this!* He caught a glimpse of Abigail dancing with a red-coated British officer, and impulsively plunged across the crowded dance floor, bumping into several couples, until he reached them.

"Abigail, I've got to talk to you!" he said urgently. Both Abigail and the officer, a compact young captain with a smooth face and a pair of cold blue eyes, turned to look at him in surprise.

"Why, Nathan!" she said. "What's the matter?"

"Come along; we can't talk here."

He took her arm and pulled at it, but found that the captain had anchored himself to her other arm. "You need better manners, fellow!" he said evenly. "Just you move along now."

Nathan stared at him, but did not release the arm he held. "Soldier, we'll get along very well without you."

The sharp rebuke fired the cold blue eyes of the officer, and he moved toward Nathan, but Abigail said, "Edgar! Please!" She placed her hand on his arm, smiled up and said, "Excuse us, will you, please?"

"Very well—but I'll have a word perhaps with you, sir, before you leave. We don't need your backwoods manners in this place!"

She patted his arm, then turned, pulling Nathan after her, through a door that led into the main hallway. He followed her until she led him through a set of French doors to a small porch that looked out onto a garden.

"Now, Nathan, what's the matter?"

"Well—" Suddenly he could say nothing, but felt foolish over his actions. He stood there in confusion, longing to say so much, yet somehow rendered speechless by her beauty.

She *was* beautiful—more than he had ever known! She stood there bathed in the pale moonlight that washed over her hair, and the night was so clear that he could see the curves of her cheeks, the arch of her lips. Yet coming out of the noisy ballroom into the almost holy quietness of the secluded garden had not cleared Nathan's mind, for now, looking down at her, he felt more confused than ever.

Finally she said, "What is it, Nathan? Tell me." And she leaned against him slightly, then raised her hand to place it on his cheek. "You've been so quiet lately. Are you angry with me?"

"No—but I feel like I'm out of your world, Abigail." He took her shoulders, and the fragrance of lilacs came to him, and he whispered, "You're so lovely, Abigail—and I feel so far away from you."

"Don't feel like that!" She smiled up at him, and then as he stood there, all the confusion of the trip seemed to fade. She was there, and she was lovely—so he simply leaned forward and kissed her. She did not hold back, but pressed herself against him, and the eagerness that he felt in her slim body struck him powerfully, so that he held her even tighter.

He drew back, and there was a softness in her eyes, a gentleness that she had kept hidden, and she said, "Nathan, you are . . ."

What she would have said, he never found out, for at that moment there was the sound of a door creaking, and Paul's voice said, "Quite a pretty scene—but a little public, don't you think?"

Nathan released Abigail and turned quickly to see him standing framed in the door. He waved a hand, and following his gesture, Nathan saw a man and a woman in a gallery across the garden watching them, and then looking to his right, several observers were standing at the large windows laughing and pointing at them.

"Nathan, you ought to have more sense!" Paul said more sharply. Then he took Abigail's arm, saying, "I think we'd better go."

"Take your hand off her!" Nathan said at once.

"Oh, don't be a fool!" Paul retorted.

Nathan's temper was even, as a rule, but once or twice in his life he had discovered that deep inside him there was the capacity for blinding rage—not just anger, much more intense than that. He had felt it once when a boy had smashed his favorite toy, and even at the age of ten he had so completely lost control of himself, bellowing and striking out, that his father had been shaken.

"Nathan, you must never let yourself go like that again!" he had said with a pale face. It had happened again, however, just two years earlier, when a man who'd been half drunk had pulled a pistol and shot Nathan's favorite dog. Nathan had no remembrance of his actions, but he'd finally come to himself with half a dozen men holding him with some difficulty, flat on his back. He had broken the man's jaw in two places, and left his face hopelessly shattered, and the shock of it had been so great that ever since he had been careful to avoid the black rage that he knew lurked deep within him.

Now, to his horror, he felt the thing, black and ugly, rising up again, and as before it seemed to deprive him of speech, to numb his brain and thought. He heard himself give a hoarse roar, felt his hands reach out and grasp Paul, and then he heard Abigail's frightened cry, which seemed to come from far away.

Sanity came sweeping back, and he found himself staring into the wide eyes of Paul, who seemed paralyzed by the awesome wrath that had leaped out of his tall kinsman without warning. Nathan wrenched himself away, whirled, ran headlong off the porch and across the yard, then disappeared down the street.

"I never saw him like that!" Abigail whispered. "He would have killed you!"

Paul's hand was not quite steady as he put it on her elbow and guided her inside. He said nothing, but there was a mixture of anger and wonder in his eyes as they left, and he cast one look down the dark street where Nathan had disappeared. *Yes—he would have killed me—and that's the dark side of the Winslow blood Father's tried to warn me of,* he thought grimly.

Laddie gave a start, coming out of a sound sleep on the couch.

A large hand was shaking her arm, and she opened her eyes to see Nathan, his face pale and angry, looking at her.

"Where's Caleb?"

"Caleb?" She sat up quickly, gave a look at the second cot that had not been used across the room. She threw the light blanket off and stood up. "I guess he hasn't come in yet." She gave him a careful look, then asked quietly, "What's the matter, Mr. Winslow?"

He stared at her, then shook his head. "Never mind, Laddie. I'm leaving here. Do you want to go with me or come with the others?"

"Why—" She stood there confused, knowing that something had happened, but not daring to pursue it. "I'll go with you—but what about Caleb?"

"I want him to go with me." He shook his shoulders, struck his hands together in a sudden burst of impatience, and asked tensely, "Has he been out late like this before?"

"Well—yes, he has. Guess he got bored watching me work on the books. But he's never been later than midnight."

Nathan stood there, a tall, silent shape, and then he said wearily, "Well, I'm not waiting until morning. Get your stuff ready. I'm going to hitch the horses."

He left her then, and she moved quickly to collect her few belongings. She put them into a small bag, then left the room, walking down a short hall to the door that led to the stable. Nathan was busy with the horses, and she said, "I'll help you."

They said nothing, but just as the last horse was harnessed into place the outer door opened, and Caleb walked in.

He was not alone; a tall man wearing high boots and a dark cloak was with him. Both of them paused abruptly, and Laddie saw the shock on Caleb's face as he spotted Nathan.

The tall man said something softly, and Caleb nodded. He walked toward the door to the hall and disappeared. Nathan dropped the lines over a steel ring fixed in the wall and went to stand before the man. "Who are you?" he asked abruptly.

A pair of steady gray eyes looked out at him from under a tri-cornered hat, then after a pause came the answer in a flat voice. "My name is Dawes."

"What's your business here?"

"Nothing with you, I think."

"I disagree. What are you doing with my brother?"

"Your brother? I see." Dawes nodded and said, "I have a little business affair with Caleb. Won't take but a minute."

A sound of footsteps drew Nathan's head around, and he saw Caleb come out the door with a flat leather pouch in his hand. He didn't look at Nathan, but simply walked forward and handed it to Dawes. "There you are."

"Thank you, Caleb." Dawes pushed the pouch into an inner pocket, reached out his hand and said, "You've been a great help to us. I'll be sure and tell—" Then he cut his words off, gave a quick look in Nathan's direction, and nodded as he wheeled and left the stable.

As the door closed softly, Caleb turned to face Nathan, his sturdy shoulders square in the dim light of the lantern. There was a stubborn look on his face, and he said, "I'll tell you before you ask, Nathan. I've brought those papers from Boston to give to Mr. Dawes as a favor to a friend of mine. That's all you need to know."

Nathan stood there, knowing at once that the "friend" was Sam Adams or Revere. He knew that every colony had formed a Committee of Safety—an armed force to be summoned when called—and it was kept alive by a link of messengers. He'd even heard of Dawes as one of the fire-eaters in the organization.

But there was nothing to say. Caleb stood there, daring him to speak, but he could not. He finally said, "I'm going back to Boston tonight. I want you to come with me."

Caleb shot a glance at Laddie, and she nodded, so he shrugged and said, "I'll get my things."

While he was gone, Laddie came up to stand before Nathan, and spoke quietly. "I can see you're in trouble, Mr. Winslow. I'm sorry for whatever it is." She put a light hand on his arm, and added very softly, "I'd help if I could."

He stood there trying to fight back the bitterness that welled up in him. His world seemed to have fallen apart, and he wanted to strike out. But he slowly made himself relax, and then he put his hand on her shoulder, feeling a quick rush of gratitude for the sympathy in Laddie's dark eyes.

"I know you would, Laddie, and that's a help." Then he shook his head. "Man sure does act like a fool sometimes, don't he now?" He gave her an embarrassed smile, then added, "And I guess I'm a bigger fool than most."

She wanted to put her arms around him and comfort him. He was so big—and yet there was something of the hurt child in him, crying out of his eyes.

But she carefully hugged herself and said, "No, you're not a fool, Nathan. You're just a little lost right now."

It was the first time he had ever heard Laddie use his given name, and it warmed him. He gave her a rough hug, then with a sharp laugh said, "Laddie, never get messed up with a woman!"

She looked up at him and smiled, her dark eyes gleaming. "I won't, Nathan," she promised.

CHAPTER NINE

DEATH AT LEXINGTON

★ ★ ★ ★

The earth grew warm in April, and the hot summer winds that thawed the cold ground not only stirred the buried seeds to life, but seemed to kindle the spirits of the men of Boston. The Sons of Liberty, ever-growing flickers of heat lightning that threatened to turn to actual bolts at any minute, were inundated with volunteers, and the Provincial Congress of Massachusetts met illegally but regularly in Cambridge, within sight of General Gage's sentries. Led by John Hancock, the Committee of Safety formed militia units, the Minute Men, subject to instant call.

Gage knew most of this, but hoped for something to bring a halt to the activities of the colonists. Instead, the first two weeks of April brought two developments that the general could not ignore. A group of patriots led by Major John Sullivan swept down on Fort William and Mary at Portsmouth, overpowered the guard, and made off with all the ammunition; the next day seventeen cannon were taken by another militant group in Boston itself.

A week later, on April 14, General Gage and Colonel Smith met to find some solution to the problem.

"General, we can't let this rabble build up their arms at the Crown's expense," Colonel Smith said heatedly to the commanding officer. "We've got to *strike*—we've got to hit hard enough to show them what comes of treason."

General Gage stared at Colonel Smith and bit his lower lip

nervously. He was now backed into a corner; London insisted he take action, not realizing how volatile the situation was. Now his options were gone, and he nodded wearily, "I suppose we must— but it's going to be a nasty affair, Colonel!"

"For *them*, General Gage," Smith grinned, "I'm sure it will. Now, where shall we direct the attack?"

Gage looked at the map on the wall, his mind trying and rejecting possibilities. "We must have an objective, of course," he said. "I have a bit of information that seems valid. The rebels have purchased a store of arms sufficient for fifteen thousand men, and one of our informers has given us the location." He stared at the man, grimaced, and said, "They've been pretty shrewd about it, I'm afraid."

"Shrewd, sir?"

"Yes. If they'd stored these arms in Boston, we'd nip them up in a lightning raid—they've put them far enough away so that a successful raid will be very difficult. You know how they watch our every move—we can't cross a street without every rebel in America knowing about it!"

"We can move at night, sir," Smith said eagerly. "And you haven't forgotten your promise that I am to lead the men in the first action?"

"No, I've not forgotten."

"Well, General Gage, where are these arms? I propose to strike them hard, sir!"

General Gage stared at the short, fat officer, and wished heartily that he had another man with more balance, but he did not. Slowly he raised his hand and placed a finger on the map.

"Concord. That's where we must strike!"

"We will scotch this snake, General!" Smith cried with excitement.

"Secrecy is my hope," Gage said slowly. "The raiding party will be composed of seven hundred men. Every eye in this city will be on them, so we must create a diversion—make them think we're going where we're not. Won't work too well, but I think these militia—what do they call them, Colonel?"

"Minute Men, sir."

"Well, it'll take more than a minute to collect an army! You will leave on the night of the eighteenth—but only you and I and Major Pitcairn will know the exact date."

"Major Pitcairn? But, sir, there are no Royal Marines here for him to command."

"I know, Colonel, but if you go down, there must be a commanding officer."

"Very well, sir, but don't trouble your head about me. *I* won't be the one who goes down if that rag-tag bunch of beggars dares to cross our path!"

Gage had been accurate in his prediction that it would be impossible to raise a sizable force without attracting attention. As the tempo of the British forces quickened, so did the eyes and mouths of a myriad of Colonials. Taverns such as The Green Dragon or The Bunch of Grapes hummed with rumors; Gage's orders detaching the grenadier and light infantry companies for extra maneuvers reached the Colonials almost as quickly as it did the British units. *Why? What were these picked troops, the elite, specially trained and equipped units of each regiment, going to do? You don't create a force of 700 picked men for nothing!*

Warren sent word by Revere to Lexington, where Sam Adams and John Hancock were lodging with the Rev. Jonas Clarke, close to the congress in Concord. Gage might have arrests in mind, and who were better subjects than Adams and Hancock? Lexington passed the word to Concord, and at once the village labored night and day, packing stores and shipping them west to Worcester.

Then came a new rumor of longboats and barges being made ready—perhaps to float Redcoats across the Charles for a quick landing on the Cambridge side where the roads led north to Lexington and Concord.

As the night of the eighteenth fell, few slept well on either side; a silence fell with the darkness, but it was the silence that one expects to be broken with the sharp sound of cannon fire or of marching feet.

Laddie was working late that night, as she had fallen into the habit of doing since the return from New York. Whatever peace she and Nathan had felt in the house of Charles Winslow had since then degenerated. Whenever Paul and Nathan spoke to each other at all, it was with a tight-lipped and sullen sort of formality, and their attitude cast a pall over the others. Laddie watched with disgust as the two of them pursued Abigail with a dogged persistence, and said once to Caleb, "They're all three acting like fools!"

Caleb had nodded, but the friction between him and Nathan had grown worse as the spring wore on. Laddie went for solitary walks, and often worked late—anything to keep out of the house. On this night, however, the constant shifting of men along the waterfront and down the dark streets rasped on her nerves. Several times she lifted her head suddenly, her heart beating faster, and went to peer out the window at the flickering lanterns that bobbed along the streets.

Finally the outer door slammed, and she jumped out of her chair, her fists clenched nervously as she waited for the inner door to open. Quick footfalls then, and when the door opened she saw Major John Pitcairn enter, his face drawn and a frown on his lips.

"Is Mr. Winslow here?" he said quickly. "Nathan, I mean."

"Why, no, sir, he's not. He went home about five o'clock."

The words ruffled Pitcairn's temper, and he struck his hands together sharply, saying, "Blast!" then turned to go, but he paused and turned to give Laddie a searching look. "You work for Mr. Winslow, don't you?"

"I'm Smith, Major. A clerk for Mr. Winslow."

He seemed to be weighing her in the balances of his mind; then finally he asked, "Are you a friend as well as an employee, Smith?"

"Why, yes, sir!"

Pitcairn bit his lips, and there was an agony of frustration in him, but finally he came close, saying in a low voice, "I want you to get word to Nathan. Tell him that Major Pitcairn said for him to get his brother out of Boston!"

"Sir—!"

"That's *all* I can say!" the words came out bitterly, and then he took Laddie's arm and his eyes burned into hers as he said with terrible intensity: "Tell him to get his brother out of Boston if he has to knock the young fool in the head and tie him hand and foot!"

Then he whirled and ran out of the room. As his footsteps echoed down the outer hall, Laddie stood there, her mind spinning. Then she dropped her ledger on the floor and ran toward the stable. She had obtained the use of a gentle mare to make the journey back and forth, and her first impulse was to get to Nathan, but then as she placed her foot in the stirrup, she suddenly halted. *I haven't seen Caleb all day,* she thought abruptly, and slowly she withdrew her foot, thinking hard in the dim lantern light.

He was around all morning—but after that I didn't see him all after-noon. Suddenly she knew he was somehow involved in the seething activities that ran along the nerves of the city. *But—where can he be now?*

Since their return from New York, Caleb had been morose—mostly with Nathan, but with her as well. He did his work, but the minimal camaraderie that she had shared with him had passed, and now he spent his free time with Moses Tyler. *Maybe he's with him now!* she thought, and ran outside and down the street. Moses lived in a single room over a gunsmith shop. *There's a light in his window!* she noted with a feeling of hope. She had to pass through the shop, asking the elderly man who sat at a workbench, "Is Moses here?"

The old man nodded, and she flew up the stairs. At the first knock, the door opened, and Moses stood there. She had shown some friendliness for the boy, but he was surprised at the visit. "Moses," Laddie said quickly, "I've got to find Caleb—it's very important!"

Instantly the boy's lips tightened, and suspicion flared in his eyes. "Don't know where he is," he said tightly.

She knew instantly that he was lying, and she realized that wild horses wouldn't drag information out of him—especially if he thought Nathan was involved. She knew from conversations with Caleb how much Moses distrusted the older brother.

"It's very serious, Moses," she forced herself to say calmly. "His mother is very ill—in fact, she's likely to die—and she's asking for Caleb."

The lie was hard for her, even though she was desperate, but she saw that it changed Moses.

"His ma is dying?" He shook his head and muttered, "Caleb, he sets a heap of store by his ma."

"Yes, and he's got to go to her—soon!"

Moses swayed back and forth, caught by indecision, and she forced herself to say nothing. Finally he said, "Well, he's gone—he ain't here."

"Where is he, Moses?"

He bit his lip, then said, "You can't tell anybody else."

"Where is he?!"

"Well—he's gone with his group—the Minute Men, you know?" Excitement lit his eyes, and he said, "The Redcoats is moving out tonight to raid Concord—and we're all going to see they don't do it! Caleb and me, we're in different groups, and he left nearly an hour ago . . . ! Hey, you keep shut, you hear me?"

But she was gone, down the stairs and out of the shop. Running at full speed, she entered the barn, then leaped into the saddle and drove the surprised animal out into the darkness.

It was a wild ride, for the streets were crowded, and she was by no means an expert rider. More than once the bulk of her mount sent a man spinning to the side, and curses followed her as she plunged on through the streets, but finally she passed out of the city and pounded wildly down the road toward the Winslow house.

She passed other riders on the road, and one of them shouted at her to hold up, but she did not pause, driving the mare until she pulled up in the front yard. Falling off the horse, she flipped the reins over a post and ran around the house, going in the back way. The family usually spent the evenings in the library or the small drawing room in the front of the house; through the back way, she might avoid being seen.

Running up the stairs, she went to the door of Nathan's room and knocked on it rapidly. His footsteps sounded, and when he opened the door and looked down at her, he said at once, "What's wrong, Laddie? Somebody sick?"

"Let me come in!" she whispered. She stepped inside and said at once, "I've got some bad news—Major Pitcairn just came by and he said to tell you to get Caleb out of Boston if you had to tie him up to do it."

"What? Why did he—"

"He couldn't say any more, Nathan, because he's a soldier, I think."

"A soldier? What's that got to do with Caleb?"

"Well, I guess he's not supposed to have anything to do with rebels. I—I started out here to tell you what he said; then I remembered that I hadn't seen Caleb all day. So I went to see Moses and asked him where Caleb was."

Nathan stared at her, beginning to understand. "What did Moses say?"

Laddie stood there, eyes troubled and finally the words came reluctantly, "Mr. Winslow, I know how you feel about the rebels—and I have to have your word that if I tell you what Moses said—you won't use it to hurt him."

"Why, you have my word, Laddie," Nathan said instantly. "I don't want any part of this revolution—I just want my brother safe."

"It's not that easy anymore. Moses said that Caleb is with a bunch of militia on the way to Concord to fight the Redcoats."

"What?" The news was so much worse than Nathan had expected that his mouth flew open, and he couldn't speak for a moment. Then he clenched his teeth and said, "All right, Laddie." He turned to pick up his coat, and headed for the door. She followed him down the stairs and out of the house, and he turned toward the barn. There were always good horses ready, and he started throwing a saddle on a tall bay.

"I'm going with you."

He paused, stared at her, and despite the shock that the news had etched on his lean face, he relaxed and even smiled. "Why, Laddie, I think you've done more than enough. And I thank you— but this is bad and likely to get worse."

"I'm going," she said stubbornly. "Saddle a horse for me while I go bring the mare in."

"But you could get shot!" he called as she left. She paid no attention, and Nathan stared at the door, then shook his head, muttering, "What a strange boy!"

In a few minutes they were on the road to Boston, and Laddie asked only one question as they turned toward Concord: "Aren't you going to take a gun, Mr. Winslow?"

"No, I'm not taking a gun." He made a big dark shape on the big bay, and she caught the gleam in his eyes as the moonlight shown in his face. "I'm not in this war, Laddie. I'll get Caleb out of it, and haul him back to Virginia, and that's all!" Then he drove his heels against the sides of his mount, and Laddie followed him as he raced along the strip of road turned silver by the pale moonlight.

They followed the Charleston road, making good time, but when they came to the spot where the road turned east, Nathan pulled up suddenly. Small groups of men were wandering around the crossroad, and there was an uncertainty about their actions that was disturbing. A tall man with a high-peaked hat was walking by, and Nathan said, "What's going on, Friend?"

"Why, it's the King's troops," the man said in a high nervous voice. He pointed down the Cambridge road, adding, "The hull army jest went down there—not mor'n an hour ago." He scratched his backside and looked around at the confusion, then shrugged and said, "I reckoned to get me a Redcoat—but they ain't no chance, now that they've got in front of us. Guess I'll get home to my woman."

Nathan started to move down the Cambridge road, but Laddie said, "Wait." He pulled back on his bridle, staring at her, but she was thinking of a map of the country. She had missed no chances to look at maps, and the Winslow Company had many. One of them was coming into focus in her mind.

"We can take the old road to Watertown. Then we can cut around in front of them where it joins the Cambridge road. That way we'll get to Concord before they do."

He stared at her in wonder. "How in the world do you know a thing like that?" he asked.

"Never mind—it's the only way."

And it worked exactly as she had said. The old road was overgrown in spots and rutted, but it lay only a quarter mile away from the new road, so they could actually hear the drums of the British as they passed by on their parallel course. Then they cut back two miles farther to the Cambridge road and passed on, coming into Lexington only an hour or so before dawn.

"These horses will never make it, Laddie," Nathan said. Both mounts were blowing and frothing. "Let's ask around. Maybe we can find someone to rent us some fresh mounts."

They tied the horses and walked across the open field where a fairly large number of men were standing around talking. All of them had muskets or rifles, but there didn't seem to be anyone in charge. Nathan moved around, but nobody was interested in renting horses; every eye was fixed on the road that led into Lexington from Boston.

"What are they doing, Nathan?" Laddie asked finally.

"Well, they're trying to get their nerve up to fight the Redcoats. But they'll never do it."

"Why, there's not more than fifty of them—and there must be six or seven hundred soldiers."

"They got more sense than to fight. Look, there's a farmhouse over there to the east. One of the men said we might get some horses there."

The two walked over to the house, but the woman who met

them said, "Have to ask my man 'bout horses. He's down there on the green somewhere. Ask fer Malcom Richards."

"This is no good!" Nathan grunted as they walked back. A pale gray light in the east revealed a line of trees, and he pointed at it. "Be dawn soon. We may have to *steal* some horses, Laddie!"

After searching for Richards unsuccessfully for forty-five minutes, the false dawn had given way to a red glow, and Nathan said, "We'll just have to ride our horses till they break down. Come on."

They had to pass through the field where the men seemed to have drawn together, and suddenly, one of them cried out, "There they are!"

And there was a sound like a bird singing afar off, but it wasn't a bird. It was a fife, and as they all stood there the sound of the drum's rattling came clearly on the dawn air.

"Form a line! Form a line!" One of the men on the green called out, and the men moved awkwardly to put themselves in some sort of order. They widened the line and stood there, muskets in their hands, staring at the red flash of uniforms now visible to the east.

Nathan and Laddie moved toward their mounts, but he said, "Let's rest them as long as we can—maybe we can let them go, then cut around them like we did before."

"I don't think there's a road for that." Laddie was suddenly cold and hot at the same time, for the column of red-clad troops was coming steadily on, and the rosy dawn touched their scarlet coats and their brass buttons with bright tips of light. Neither Nathan nor Laddie had ever seen trained troops, and they looked invincible as they marched inexorably toward the small bunch of farmers standing awkwardly on the green grass.

"They've seen us!" someone in the ranks said, and then two officers on horseback, flanked by two flag-bearers, rode forward. Rank after rank of Redcoats stretched back on the road; they did not quicken their pace but marched up to the edge of the common, stopping about one hundred and fifty paces away from the small group of farmers.

Suddenly Nathan gasped as if he'd been struck in the stomach, and he grabbed Laddie's arm with an iron grip. "Look! There's Caleb!"

He moved away toward the group, and Laddie followed. She saw him, then, at the end of a small group a little apart from the main body. He was staring at the British, his musket clasped in his hands, and he didn't see Nathan until suddenly he stood right in front of him.

"Caleb!" Nathan said with relief. "Thank God we found you!"

The shock of seeing his brother made Caleb's dark eyes widen, but then he said, "Nathan, get out of here!"

"Not without you." Nathan made his mistake then, for he put his hand on the other's arm and tried to pull him out of the line. "Look at that army, Caleb. Don't be a fool!"

Others in Caleb's group were watching with one eye, and Caleb yanked his arm away from Nathan's grip. "This is what I've got to do, Nathan. You don't belong here." Then he looked around Nathan and cried: "Here they come! Get out of here!"

"Fix bayonets!" came a shrill cry, and sunlight flashed on the metal. Then one of the officers spurred his horse, and Nathan turned with a shock to see Colonel Smith, sneering and calling out, "Column right!" The Redcoats wheeled to face the small group.

"Lay down your arms, you traitors!" Smith screamed. "Do you hear me? Get off the King's green!"

Then Nathan saw that the second officer was Major John Pitcairn. In the clear light of dawn their eyes met, and Nathan's lips moved in a prayer: *John! Don't let this happen! You're my friend!*

One of the farmers said, "Steady now. Just hold steady!"

Screaming wildly, Colonel Smith spurred his horse, but the words were not clear. He raised his saber, and Nathan at that instant saw a Redcoat raise his musket and fire. One of the farmers clutched his chest and fell to the ground, coughing. Then as Nathan whirled, the whole British front burst into a roar of sound and flame and smoke, and the ground shook with the fury of it.

Nathan turned in time to see a shot strike Caleb high on the chest. It drove him backward and instantly crimson blood gushed out as he went to the ground.

"Caleb!" Nathan cried out, and then Laddie screamed in his ear, "Look! The soldiers—they're charging!"

Nathan looked up to see the British advancing at a run through a ragged curtain of smoke. There was nothing to stop them, for the militia had turned and fled. Two Redcoats reached one man who was rolling on the ground and one of them drove his bayonet with all his force into the man's back.

Nathan reached down and picked Caleb up as if he were a

child, then raced across the green. Laddie followed, and both of them heard the yells of the Redcoats. Just as they reached the cover of the trees, musket balls sang close to their ears. They ran through a thicket, crashing through thorns and vines that tore their faces, and the only thing that saved them was the fact that the Redcoats were carrying packs that weighed over one hundred pounds.

Nathan ran until he was out of breath, then fell helpless to the ground, and as he looked down into the gray face of his brother, he heard far off, the tinny sound of drum and fife of the British Army.

CHAPTER TEN

THE VOW

★ ★ ★ ★

Time had passed, but Laddie had no idea how long she sat there watching helplessly as Nathan held the limp body of his brother. She had been vaguely aware of the sound of marching troops, but that had passed and now came the sound of voices floating to her, filtered by the woods.

Stiffly she got to her feet and Nathan raised his head to look at her as she came close. "He's dead, Laddie."

"I know."

"He was just a boy, and they killed him—the butchers!"

"Nathan, we have to leave here." Then she looked down and suddenly she cried out, "Nathan—look!" She dropped beside the two and put her hand on Caleb's throat, her eyes wide as she said urgently, "I can feel his pulse—and he's bleeding!"

Nathan stared at the face of his brother, not able to comprehend. It had never occurred to him that Caleb was alive, but now he saw the bright blood welling steadily from the wound, and he began to tremble. "Caleb!" he cried out, then said wildly, "We have to get a doctor!"

He started to rise, but Laddie said, "Nathan, we have to stop that bleeding or he'll die." Seeing that he was helpless with shock, she moved quickly. "Cut a bandage out of your shirt," she commanded, and she took the wounded boy's head, as Nathan ripped a strip from his white shirt. "Make a pad of it," she commanded, and she pulled Caleb's coat and shirt away, her heart nearly stopping at the sight of the bullet wound steadily throbbing, pulsing out the young man's lifeblood. Taking the cloth, she placed it on the wound, saying, "Hold it here—tight enough to stop the bleeding."

"I've got to go for a doctor!"

"No, you stay here. Some of the soldiers might still be there. I'll be back quick as I can."

His eyes pleaded with her, but she did not pause. As she left, she said, "Pray, Nathan!"

Then she was gone and he was alone. He sat there holding the pad, staring down at Caleb's pale face—and he tried to pray. His mind was cold with fear, and all he could say was, *"God!—God!"* over and over again. Time dragged on, and as he tried to pray, he seemed to hear his mother's voice repeating the last thing he'd heard her say: *Take good care of your brother, Nathan!*

The tears flowed and the fear grew worse as time went on, and he prayed aloud, "God—let him live—and I'll do anything you want!" His voice frightened a small gray squirrel that had moved to the ground from the top of a tall pine, and it dashed away, chattering angrily.

Finally, he heard the faint sound of voices coming from the direction of the village, and soon Laddie appeared with several men behind her. "There he is, Doctor!" she cried, and led the way to where Caleb lay.

A tall man gave Nathan a strange glance, then knelt and pulled the bandage back to look at the wound. He laid his head on Caleb's chest, listened, then stood up. "We'll move him to the Lewis place," he said. "Be careful as you can."

Nathan watched as four men gathered around and carefully picked the wounded boy up. As they moved slowly forward, Nathan asked, "How is he?"

"Very bad." The doctor shook his head and added, "I cannot offer you much hope, Mr. Winslow."

"He can't die!" Nathan whispered, but the doctor only shook his head and followed the others. Nathan stood there helplessly until Laddie came to touch his arm; then they followed. In less than half an hour, they had reached a small house located on a slight promontory overlooking Lexington. Silas Lewis, a thin, silver-haired man, and his wife Sarah lived alone there, and the doctor had Caleb placed in their bedroom.

Nathan and Laddie watched as he cleaned the wound, listened to the heart, then put a clean bandage on. He stood, and looked across the bed at Nathan. "I'm afraid the bullet has pierced the lungs."

"Can't you get it out, Doctor?" Laddie pleaded.

He looked at the pair, and there was compassion in his gray eyes. "It would be impossible." He moved toward the door, and paused long enough to say, "I would to God I could offer you hope, but the only hope now is in God."

"You're not leaving?" Nathan exclaimed with a start.

"I must," the doctor said, then asked with a curious look at Nathan, "You don't remember me, do you?"

"Why, no."

"I met you with your brother at a meeting. I'm Dr. Warren." He hesitated, then said, "He may wake up—or he may not. In any case, I cannot help him—and I am needed for other things. God help you, Mr. Winslow—God help us all!"

Then he was gone. Nathan swallowed hard, then slumped in the chair beside the bed. Laddie's throat ached, and she went to stand beside his chair. They could hear a clock ticking in the next room. Bright sunlight, like bars of solid gold, fell across the bright counterpane that covered Caleb, and the smell of freshly broken ground from the field drifted into the room. Slowly the hours passed, and Caleb lay there, his eyes closed, breathing so shallowly that at times there seemed to be no life at all. Once Mrs. Lewis came in and brought fresh water to bathe the dying boy's face, but Nathan did not seem to notice. He was crouched over the chair, his face pinched and thin, his eyes blank.

Laddie went out shortly after noon and stood on the front porch. The yard was filled with men, and their voices were tense and angry. One voice, louder than the rest, came from a powerfully built man with a Kentucky rifle in his hands. ". . . won't be no way for them lobster backs to git back to Boston 'cept on the Menotomy Road—and that's where we'll catch 'em."

"There ain't but a hundred of us—or less!" A thin, angry voice argued. "How we goin' to face all them Redcoats?"

"There's more of us than you think, Wilkins," the big man said slowly, and there was a grim smile on lips. "There's six assembly points spotted along the road, and the Committeemen west of Sudbury River and west of the Concord River will be at the North Bridge—and besides that, the Minute Men are come in from all over! I'd say we'll have maybe five hundred by the time them Redbacks come back down that road!"

A shout went up, and for the next fifteen minutes Laddie stood there trying to comprehend what was happening. She had just decided to go in when she heard someone call out "Laddie! Laddie Smith!" and turned to see Moses Tyler running up the hill.

He pulled up in front of her, his face red. "I—I seen Dr. Warren down on the road. He said that Caleb was shot—and he said . . ."

She saw him swallow hard; then when she said, "He's very bad, Moses," he began to cry. It was not a graceful crying. He dropped his musket and several of the men looked curiously as he slumped down with his back against the wall, sobbing and choking on the tears.

Finally when he grew quiet, he stood up and said, "I gotta see him, Laddie!"

"He won't know you, Moses."

"I gotta see him!"

Laddie looked into the boy's intense face, nodded, and led him inside. They passed into the room, where Nathan was slumped down, staring at Caleb's still face. "Nathan, Moses is here." Laddie was shocked to see hatred leap into Nathan's eyes. He leaped out of the chair and grabbed Moses by the arm, raising his fist to strike, but Laddie stepped between them, pleading, "Nathan—don't!"

He stopped, looked down at the small form of Tyler, and said bitterly, "Well, are you satisfied now? You've got him killed!" He whirled and plunged out of the room blindly, his feet echoing on the floor beyond.

"I better go with him, Moses," Laddie said quickly. "You can sit with Caleb."

She reached the porch in time to see Nathan walking rapidly across the yard, his head down. She moved quickly, catching up with him as he reached a copse of hickory trees. "Nathan—you can't leave!" she said.

He stopped abruptly, glared at her with anger lighting his eyes; then it faded and he seemed to sway from side to side, and he whispered, "I can't stay and watch him die, Laddie! I can't do that!"

"You're his brother, Nathan. What if he wakes up—and none of his people are there?"

He shut his eyes, stood there for a long time, it seemed; then he opened them and said, "All right—let's go back."

They made their way back to the porch, arriving at the same time as Dr. Warren. He looked at Nathan, then explained, "I thought I'd come back to see the boy."

Nathan said nothing, but Laddie replied, "Thank you, Dr. Warren."

They went inside, and Moses looked up with tears in his eyes. "Dr. Warren! He just woke up!"

"Caleb!" Nathan shouldered the doctor aside and knelt beside the bed. "Caleb!"

Laddie could see that Caleb's eyes were open, and he said weakly, "Nathan!"

The doctor had moved to the other side of the bed, his eyes searching the boy's face, and he put a hand on the pulse at Caleb's throat. "Dr.—Warren—" Caleb said, his eyes turning to him. "I knew you'd be in the fight." Then his eyes shifted back to Moses, and he asked in a reedy whisper, "Did we whip 'em, Moses?"

Moses started to speak, but couldn't for the tears that choked him. "What's wrong with Moses?" Caleb turned back to Dr. Warren. "Didn't we—turn the Redcoats back?"

Warren shook his head, his face a mask, then said, "You'd better talk to your brother, son." He gave Nathan a warning look and drew back.

Nathan knelt beside Caleb, and heard the labored breath and the rasp in the chest. But Caleb struggled to speak. "Nathan—I'm sorry—about the way it's been—with us."

"It's all right, Caleb," Nathan said, tears running down his cheeks.

"No—no, it's not all right—for brothers to have bad feelings." He lifted a hand and Nathan took it; then he said, "I know you don't believe in this war—" He paused and his eyes fluttered so that Dr. Warren leaned forward quickly, but then he seemed to grow stronger. "I guess I got shot, didn't I?"

"Yes, Caleb!"

"It hurts bad—Nathan." Then Caleb asked, "Am I going to die?"

Nathan sobbed, and Dr. Warren said quietly, "I'm afraid so, my boy."

The words did not seem to disturb Caleb. He lay there quietly, and the room was still. Finally he said, "Nathan, you tell Mother and Father about how I died—and say that I wasn't afraid!"

His eyes closed then, and Laddie's heart leaped, but he wasn't gone. He lay there, and for the next hour he seemed to float between two worlds. He would lie still for a time; then he would open his eyes and take up where he had left off. His mind was clear; he gave messages for some, and once he said, "Nathan?—it's a good thing I was converted at that meeting two years ago, wasn't it?" He smiled and said, "I'd hate to die if I hadn't found Jesus that time—I sure would be afraid to die . . ."

Finally he said, "What are the Minute Men doing, Moses?"

"Gettin' ready to fight the British, Caleb." Moses said. He had kept back to the wall, but now he came to reach a dirty hand out to his friend. "I—I wisht it was me 'stid of you that got shot!"

"No, you gotta go on and fight, Moses." He lifted his head and his voice grew stronger, his eyes fully open. "Oh, I can't help! I can't help you fight!"

"Caleb!" Nathan caught his brother, and the boy's eyes fixed on him.

"Nathan—they're going to fight the British! I got to help! I got to help!" He began to struggle and Nathan held him fast, and then suddenly he fell back. His chest pumped as he fought for breath; then he reached up and put his arm around Nathan's neck, whispering in a voice that rattled, "Nathan—I can't help!" Then suddenly he looked up at his brother. "You have to do it for me, Nathan!"

Nathan stared into Caleb's eyes and saw the life draining out, but again the arm around his neck tightened, and Caleb pleaded, "Nathan—you're my brother! Please—please, Nathan—go help them! Help them!" And then he opened his eyes and asked: "Will—you help—Nathan? For me . . . ?"

And Nathan cried with a loud voice that shook the room, "Yes! Yes, Caleb, I'll fight! Don't be afraid—I'll fight for you!"

He held the body close, and then he heard the words so faint that he barely caught them: "Nathan! Thank you, brother!"

Then Caleb went limp, and when Nathan laid him back, there was a smile on his lips. Dr. Warren reached out and closed his eyes, then said in a tight voice, "Brave boy! Brave boy!"

Nathan laid his hand on Caleb's hair, brushed it back, then rose and walked out of the room, his face a mask. He turned at the door, saying, "Laddie, stay with him till I get back." Then he was gone.

"They're a'comin'!" the rider shouted as he crested the hill. He was a small man, but he had a big voice, and he pulled his fine horse up with a flourish, filled with self-importance as the militia crowded around him. "I been to Concord, and I been watchin' the Redcoats comin' out of there—and they're shot all to pieces!"

"The Redcoats?" Dr. Warren demanded. He stood there, his gray eyes intense in the midday sun. "Who fought them?"

"Why, the Minute Men, 'course!" the rider said. He begged a drink and after a long pull from a bottle, he wiped his brow and said, "The British can't leave the road, and our men been shootin' them to rags from behind stone walls—must a'killed a hundred of the suckers at least!"

A shout went up, and Warren smiled. He had been hard put to it to hold the men together, for none of them were ready to face the British regulars in open battle on a field. But this was different! He got up on a stone, called for silence; then when it came, he said, "Well, here we are, and none of us thought we'd be fighting a war on a fine spring morning here in Lexington—but we are. It was not of our making. They shot our men down without mercy." A cry of anger followed this and he said, "We'll have the cost of that blood out of the Redcoats, won't we, men?"

"Tell us what to do, Warren!" a single voice yelled, and an echo of consent rose.

"All of you with muskets go over there—" He waited for the group to form, then said, "Mason Bates, you'll be captain of these. Those of you with rifles, I'll be your captain."

"Why don't we stay together?"

Warren smiled patiently at the tall man who asked the question. "Because a musket shoots one hundred paces and a rifle carries four hundred. Now, they're coming, so listen carefully. The Redcoats will have to stay on that road. They're hurt already, and we'll hurt them worse on the next ten miles. At least half that stretch is lined with stone walls. Get behind those walls, let them get twenty feet away, then rise up and cut them down!"

"But they'll fire a volley at us!"

"Fall down as soon as you shoot and let the volley go over your heads—then get up, run down the road and do it again!"

"There they come—just like I said!" the rider yelled. "I gotta ride some more!"

He tore down the road, yelling at the top of his lungs, but nobody watched. They were straining their eyes, trying to see the approaching Redcoats. Warren said, "You musketmen, get going! Riflemen, we'll wait here and give them a welcome."

The men with muskets scurried off, and Warren said, "We'll get behind that pile of logs next to the road." He led them to a pile of walnut logs that had been felled and trimmed, then said, "Keep down until they're in range—" He stopped suddenly and every man in the group turned to see what had stopped him. He was staring at a tall man who carried a fine Kentucky rifle in his hands— a rifle that the doctor had last seen on the wall of Silas Lewis's house. Dr. Warren studied him, then said quietly, "Mr. Winslow, I think you should think before you do this thing."

The men saw the tall man stare at the doctor, and his eyes were like blue ice. "I'll leave if you say so, Dr. Warren. But I'll be fighting whether you take me or not!"

Warren gazed steadily at Nathan, and finally he said, "As God wills then."

"No, as *I* will, Dr. Warren! I'll fight in this thing, but I won't blame it on God."

Warren's eyes flashed, but he only said, "Can you use a rifle?"

Nathan stared at him, and there was no trace of pride in his voice as he said, "I can shoot better than any man in your group." Then he waved the muzzle of the rifle toward the distant figure of a rider who had just appeared on the road. "I intend to prove that right now."

"It's too long a shot!" someone complained.

But Warren said, "If you want to be in this war, Winslow, you can begin right now."

Nathan nodded, and his face was pale. The officer was tearing down the road, and was yelling something. He stopped three hundred feet away, made his horse rear, then swung around and started back the other way. He had not gone twenty feet when Nathan's bullet struck him between the shoulder blades and he fell like a broken doll into the dust.

A yell went up, and one man struck Nathan on the shoulder, shouting, "You got him, Winslow!" But there was no joy on the young man's face, Warren saw, and he commanded, "Take cover!

They'll be here in ten minutes!" As the men scattered, he came to stand beside Nathan and said, "I'm sorry about your brother." He gave a curious stare at the silent young man, then shook his head and moved behind a tree.

Nathan Winslow reloaded and stood there in the fine summer air of April and waited for another target.

Major Pitcairn looked up wearily into the pale face of Charles Winslow. He had not slept all night, and the nightmare he had gone through had drawn deep lines into his face. "What is it, Mr. Winslow? I have to report to General Gage, so I can't—"

"Pitcairn, what *happened* out there?" Charles demanded. "We've heard rumors, but they can't be true!"

"Did you hear that we got shot to pieces?" Pitcairn rasped in anger. "Did you hear we lost over 250 men? Did you hear that some of the King's finest troops were routed by a bunch of farmers?"

Charles stared at him, dumbfounded, then said quickly, "I'm sorry to bother you, Major, but I've had word that my nephew might—"

"Nathan was there," Pitcairn said wearily. He passed a trembling hand over his face, then groaned, "Oh, my God, what have we done? What have we done?"

"You saw him?"

"He was right in front of our troops, Charles—and his brother was with him." He shook his head, whispering, "I pray God they survived!"

Then a voice called out that General Gage was waiting, and he left, saying only, "I can't tell you anything."

Charles wandered around a town gone mad, but could find no word of Nathan, so finally he went home. All that day he waited, but there was no word. The family had supper, and once Martha uttered something about "rebels." Charles snapped instantly, "Mother—shut your mouth or leave my table!" The old woman had stared at him, but he had stared back with an intensity that drove her to silence.

He was walking the floor after midnight when he heard a wagon come across the small bridge, and he threw down his cigar, picked up a lantern and ran outside. He ran to a small wagon that was pulling up in the yard and held the lantern up. He saw the haggard face of Nathan, and then his eyes went to the coffin in the rear, and the words stuck in his throat.

Nathan got down, and Charles saw that Laddie was there, too. There was nothing he could say, so he waited for Nathan to speak.

"I'm taking my brother home—to Virginia." His voice was dead, and so were his eyes, Charles saw. "I had Murchinson take care of him at the funeral parlor."

"Why, Nathan—" Charles began, but he was left alone with Laddie. He asked quickly, "What happened, Laddie?"

The dark eyes looked even darker in the yellow light of the lantern. "Caleb was killed at Lexington." And then she, too, walked away into the house.

Charles did not know what to do, so he stood there in the darkness. But fear touched him, and he retreated quickly inside. He paced the floor, and in a few minutes Nathan came down the stair with a bag. He stared at Charles, then said, "Goodbye."

Charles followed him out to the wagon, trying to reason with him, but it was useless. Nathan pulled himself up into the seat, and turned the team around, but a voice cried out, "Wait, Nathan!"

He pulled the team up, and Laddie, carrying an awkward bundle, pulled herself up into the wagon, sat down and looked full into Nathan's eyes. "I'm going with you to take him home. He was my friend."

Nathan looked at her, and for the first time since the shot had killed his brother, the emptiness that had filled him seemed somehow bearable. Laddie's eyes were huge in the darkness, but there was a stubborn set to the wide lips, so he nodded.

"All right, Laddie. Let's take Caleb home."

PART TWO

BAPTISM OF FIRE

★ ★ ★ ★

CHAPTER ELEVEN

"HE'S A MIGHTY FEARSOME MAN!"

★ ★ ★ ★

Spring washed over Virginia in a way that Laddie had never seen in New England, and after Caleb's funeral it became her habit to spend the cobwebby mornings roaming the open country that lay just over the ridge of Westfield. The columbines and wild violets perfumed the cool paths that wound in aisles beneath the gnarled oaks, and the cold spring-fed brooks, plump with sun perch, were shrill with the cries of peepers in the late afternoons.

Adam Winslow had brought Laddie to one of those swift streams that flung up fingers of white where the smooth green water struck an outcropping of rock. There was an abrupt elbow in the stream where the waters had gouged out a deep still pool under a huge white oak, and he had smiled at her, saying, "There's so many hungry fish in that pool, Laddie, you'll have to get behind that oak tree to bait your hook!"

Laddie thought of that moment as she sat with her back against the scaly trunk of the tree, and paused before putting a grasshopper on her hook, thinking as she often did of Nathan's father. *That was just three days after Caleb's funeral*, she thought, and the memory of that stark moment when the plain pine coffin bearing the body of Caleb had been lowered into the red Virginia clay came back vividly. *Adam Winslow was suffering himself—but he saw how out of place and miserable I felt.*

The grasshopper she held between thumb and forefinger

kicked his powerful hind legs, then registered its protest by spitting what looked like tobacco juice on her thumb. Ignoring this, she placed the point of the tiny hook just inside the hard collar forming the neck and threaded the struggling insect through the soft parts of the body. She took the limber cane pole, lifted it and dropped the bait into the green waters. One tiny round lead bullet was fixed a foot above the bait, which pulled him below the surface in a slow and natural way.

Mr. Winslow showed me that, too. As the thin line drifted down the stream close to a clump of willows, the scene from that time came to her.

"See—you just slip the hook in like this," Adam had said, and she had watched carefully as his thick fingers handled the delicate hook and the tiny grasshopper deftly. She had seen him pound a thick bar of white-hot steel at his forge with a fifteen-pound hammer, and his dexterity amazed her.

"Doesn't it hurt them, Mr. Winslow?" she had asked shyly. She had been uncomfortable in the presence of Nathan's parents since they had arrived. Nathan had been so stricken he had only mentioned that Laddie had been a friend of Caleb's; it had been Molly Winslow who had arranged a place for her to sleep and seen to her meals.

"Got no idea, son," Adam had answered, and he had suddenly paused to look at the struggling insect. He lifted his eyes and looked very much like his dead son at that moment, to Laddie at least, and then he had said very quietly, "Guess we don't ever know how much another creature is hurting, do we?"

"No, sir," she replied, then added, "But I've been wanting to tell you ever since I came how I grieve for you."

Adam Winslow was not a man that hung his emotions out for all to see, but Laddie saw his guard drop, and the pain in his dark eyes was so stark that she had dropped her gaze, unable to endure it.

She sat there watching the line arch into the swift water. As her grip tightened on the pole, she remembered how at that moment, he had gently let his thick hand rest on her shoulder, and he had said, "Molly and I—we appreciate your coming, Laddie. It means a lot to know that Caleb had a good friend who'd come all this way to see him home."

Suddenly the line snapped taut, and she cried out, "Gotcha!"

The lithe pole bent nearly double, and the line sliced wildly through the water as the fish tried to make it to the roots where it could shake off the hook. But she had too much skill. Slowly she played it, until finally she led it exhausted to the smooth bank. Carefully she reached into the water, slipped her hand inside its gaping gill, then lifted it out. "Oh, what a beauty!"

She admired the brilliant colors of the sun perch—deep blue, with green and red scales that glittered in the sunlight. "Must weigh a pound, at least," she said happily, then with a deft motion removed the hook before adding it to a string of at least fifteen others about the same size.

Plenty for all of us, she nodded; quickly she untied the stringer and tossed the few remaining grasshoppers into the stream. As they disappeared, snapped up by hungry fish, she picked up her Bible, stuffed it into a small canvas sack with the remains of a lunch, then quickly made her way up the creek. Twenty minutes later she was walking into the backyard of the Winslow house, and seeing Nathan's parents standing outside the forge, she held the stringer up with a whoop.

"Looks like Laddie fished the creek out again, Molly," Adam said, and a smile touched his broad lips. "Reminds me of how much Caleb liked to fish in that spot."

"Yes. He did."

Adam glanced quickly at Molly, and the look in her eyes made him move to her side and put his arm around her. "Sorry. I don't mean to keep mentioning him."

"No, that's as it should be," she said, and though her eyes half-filled with tears, she nodded and forced a smile. Patting his hand, she said, "He's still our son, even though he's with the Lord Jesus now. I won't let grief destroy my son for me—the way I've seen some do." She dashed the tears from her eyes, and two elements of her Scottish blood—the quiet beauty and the rock-ribbed faith—were very real to Adam as he stepped back, an approving light filling his eyes.

Passing through the gate, Laddie caught a glimpse of this fragment of drama, and felt as though she were intruding. She hesitated, but Adam moved toward her, saying, "That's a good mess of fish." He took them from her, admired them, then said, "Molly, Laddie and I will clean these if you'll cook them for us."

"Fish would be good," Molly smiled, then added, "Maybe Nathan will be back in time to eat supper with us." She turned and disappeared into the house.

"I'll clean the fish, Mr. Winslow," Laddie said quickly.

"All right." He walked alongside her toward the side of the forge, and as she stripped the fish from the stringer and put them on a rough slab nailed to a stump, he sat down, saying, "I always did like to watch another man work."

She looked nervously at him, for his dark eyes were so sharp that at times she was sure he would see through her masquerade, but there was no guile in his broad face. Unsheathing her knife, she began cleaning the fish—a job which she'd hated at first, but Adam had taught her how to do it easily. Holding the fish with one hand, she raked the scales off with a few quick strokes of the blunt side of the knife. Putting the knife down, she took the head, broke the backbone with a twist, then pulled head and entrails free with a quick jerk.

"You learn quick, Laddie," Adam remarked as she tossed the cleaned fish down and reached for another. "Can't believe a young fellow like you never cleaned a fish." He looked idly across the fields, then asked, "Where'd you say you were raised?"

"Philadelphia—" Laddie said, then realized with dismay that she'd given away too much. "Well—not really Philadelphia. We just lived there a little while, and then . . ." She invented a likely history for a young man, complete with parents dying conveniently early, and embroidered the tale with hard times and struggles to stay alive.

"Nathan tells me you're a good hand with books and figures."

"Oh—I learned a little here and there, Mr. Winslow—not so much as Nathan thinks."

He shifted, looked across the fields again, and as she cleaned the fish, she noticed that there was something restive in his manner. Finally he said quietly, "Nathan's unhappy."

"Well, yes, sir—but that's natural."

"No, it's not." Adam bit his lip, then shook his head, saying, "He's got something eating him up inside, Laddie—and it's not just his brother's death—though that's part of it." He sat there thinking; then suddenly he asked, "What is it, Laddie? What's wrong with him?"

"Why—" Laddie put the last fish on the stack, then picked up a rag and began to wipe her hands. "I've only known him for a few weeks," she said hesitantly.

"He won't talk to me—or to his mother," Adam said, and it was not a plea, just a statement of fact. "But it's plain that something happened in Boston."

"I—I can tell you a little, Mr. Winslow. Maybe I shouldn't, but I hate to see your family split." She bit her lip, then said, "Nathan's been seeing a young woman, Abigail Howland. I think he's in love with her."

"My brother Charles mentioned that in a letter."

"Did he tell you that Paul and Nathan have been fighting over her for weeks?"

"No."

"Well, they have. And the thing is—her people are Tory, and Nathan knows how you and Mrs. Winslow feel about such things."

"We don't agree, for a fact," Adam said painfully. He got up and said, "I guess Nathan's at Caleb's grave again. He goes there every day about this time. Somehow, it don't seem right, Laddie, for him to be grieving so hard over his brother."

"Don't you see, Mr. Winslow? He feels guilty. He thinks he should have gotten Caleb out of Boston before—"

She didn't finish, but he nodded. "He thinks I blame him, Laddie—but he's wrong on that. Caleb was only a boy, but he had a strong will. I doubt if I could have made him leave myself."

Laddie hesitated, then said, "Why don't you say that to him, sir? I think he needs to hear it."

"You think that?" Adam let the thought run through him, then said, "Thanks, Laddie." He turned and left the yard, walking in the direction of the village's small cemetery.

Laddie gathered up the fish and took them into the kitchen where Molly was rolling out a pie crust. Looking up, she asked, "Got them cleaned already, Laddie? Put them in that pot. Where's Adam?"

"He—went to get Nathan."

The hesitation in her voice caused Molly to look up quickly, and she studied Laddie's face carefully. "Oh?" she said finally. Then she looked down, saying quietly, "I hope Nathan will come to himself."

"So do I." Laddie knew that the death of Caleb had brought tremendous pain to this woman, and there was a desire to give some sort of comfort. There was a reticence in Molly Winslow that would never bring her to ask favors, but she needed someone to talk to. Laddie had learned during the weeks she had spent with the family that Molly Winslow was a woman of genuine Christian faith. It was not just that she was faithful in her duties to her church; there was an unmistakable spirit of love and joy in her that even the pangs of grief could not dim.

Laddie stood there, longing to say something. She looked at the pie crust taking shape. Suddenly she said, "Mrs. Winslow, if I wash my hands real good, maybe you'll let me help you fix supper?"

"Why—can you cook, Laddie?"

"I'm not really a cook," Laddie shrugged, "but anybody can fry fish, can't they? And somebody's got to peel those potatoes."

"I'd be pleased with your help." A smile touched Molly's lips. "Most men would die before they'd do a thing like peeling potatoes or cooking supper."

Laddie picked up a potato, drew her knife, and sitting down on a stool, she smiled and answered, "Except out camping—then all of us cook." She began paring thin strips from the potato, speaking of nothing important, but ten minutes later she had touched on the subject of Caleb. Then for the next half hour she told Molly Winslow of her son, how she had known him and admired him. She had not known him well, but thanked God for those times when Caleb had spoken with her for long hours, for now she had those times to share with the quiet-eyed woman who sat across from her, drinking in every word.

The pendulum clock ticked slowly, and as the meal took shape, the older woman began to speak. Grief had been so sharp within her heart that she had turned from every thought of Caleb, stifling memories as they rose within her, but now she began to speak of him—of simple things he had done as a child, of his quick mind and how it had often led him into mischief. And she laughed—for the first time since the funeral—as she told some of his pranks.

Finally the meal was ready, hidden beneath white napkins on the table, and suddenly Molly Winslow walked to stand beside Laddie, who was looking out the window. "You've been a blessing, Laddie," she said quietly; then she asked, "Are you a Christian?"

"Well, yes, Mrs. Winslow, though not a very good one . . ."

"I knew that you were. You have a gentle spirit, Laddie, and you've given my boy back to me somehow. I praise the Lord for sending you to me."

Laddie felt very awkward, but was spared having to respond, for there were footsteps on the porch, and looking up she said, "Here they are."

Molly turned quickly to see Nathan and Adam enter, and she said quickly, "Just in time, you two! Sit down before it gets cold!"

Laddie never knew exactly what Adam had said to his son at the cemetery, but Nathan, she saw at once, was not the same. He had been under a rigid constraint ever since he had come home, but now the bitter lines that had scored his lean face were softened. A new light shone in his eyes as he came across to give his mother a squeeze, saying, "Smells good, Mother. Hope you cooked enough."

Molly looked up with a startled expression, and gladness leaped into her gray eyes. She reached up and touched his cheek, saying, "There's plenty."

They all sat down and ate—especially Nathan. He had picked at his food for weeks, but now he attacked the fish and potatoes so avidly that Adam commented, "Laddie, you may have to go back to the creek and get another mess of fish for this boy."

Nathan said little, but finally after he put down the last of his pie, he leaned back and said, "Best meal I ever had."

"You need it, Nathan," Molly said. "You've lost weight."

He nodded and then said suddenly, "I've got something to say to you."

Adam looked up quickly, glanced at Molly, then said, "What is it, Nathan?"

A quiet settled over the small group, and suddenly, Laddie, feeling that this was family business, rose to leave. But Nathan said, "Sit down, Laddie. You've got a right to hear what I have to say." He clasped his fingers together, then began to review those last few weeks in Boston. He spoke evenly, without emotion, telling of his feeling for Abigail, his rivalry with Paul. He spoke of his friendship with Major Pitcairn and his admiration for some of the King's officers. Molly and Adam sat motionless as he spoke of how he had tried to get Caleb to stay out of politics.

"I should have tried harder with him—I see that now," he said quietly. The candle sputtered in the holder, and its flickering flames threw his wedge-shaped face into high relief, deepening the caverns of his eye sockets. "God knows I should have done *something*!" And here he paused and stared down at the table.

"Nathan," Molly returned, and she leaned over and put a hand on his. "You can't blame yourself for your brother's death. We always think of things we might have done—when we lose someone. But we know you tried."

"He was a strong-minded lad, you know that, son," Adam stated. "He would do what he thought was right. You can remember a time or two when there wasn't a thing *I* could do with him. He was a Winslow, right enough, and I never heard of any of that breed being very easily led. Don't blame yourself."

Nathan looked up with a smile trembling on his broad lips. "I—I know that, sir, but it's not going to be easy to live with."

"Life goes on, dear," Molly said. "You know we'll see Caleb again."

Nathan suddenly gave her a peculiar look. "This thing has changed me in more ways than one. For one thing—I'm not going to be a minister."

If he expected to shock his parents, Laddie observed, he was due for a disappointment, for neither of them were upset. Molly said only, "Nathan, I've always felt that you took up the calling too suddenly."

He stared at her, then laughed shortly, saying, "I've always known you felt that way, Mother—and it just made me more stubborn."

Adam was staring at his son, and a thought arose in him. "The Winslow men—most of 'em—have had this kind of a battle with God. You remember reading about Gilbert Winslow—how he wrestled with God from Europe to Plymouth Rock, vowing he'd never preach. But he did—and that's happened over several times."

"Well, that's out of my system."

"God will have His way with you, Nathan," Molly said firmly. "I promised you to God the night you were born—and God agreed to take you!"

Nathan gave an impatient shake of his head, but said only, "I don't have much faith—but all this is not what I wanted to tell you."

He got up and stood behind his chair. Silently he stared at them; then he told them about Caleb's death, and how he'd promised to fight for the cause. He went on quietly. "I don't feel as you do about all this—as a matter of fact, I think we'll all wind up either in jail or on a gallows." Then his lips grew firm, and he squared his shoulders in a way that Molly and Adam had seen a thousand times, and he said, "I don't believe very much in this fight that's coming—but Caleb did—and I'll do what I can for him, for my brother."

A silence fell on the room, which was broken when Adam said quietly, "That's not a real good reason for joining a revolution, Nathan—but I'll not try to change your mind. There'll be men fighting in this war for every cause under heaven—and not all of them will be good and pure." Pausing, he took a deep breath and went on slowly. "I guess going to war to keep your word to a brother is a reason that will do—until you get a better one!" Then he asked suddenly, "How you figure to get into this war, son?"

"Why—I have no idea, Father." Nathan suddenly was struck with a thought, musing quietly. "Can't just ride out and take potshots at the lobsterbacks from behind a tree, I suppose."

"No, I think there'll be a little better way than that," Adam said. He looked up and added, "I haven't told you, but Colonel Washington has sent for me."

"Colonel Washington? Do you know why?"

"Only one thing I can think of. Over the years he's asked me several times to join the Virginia militia—and I reckon he's going to ask a little harder."

"Will you do it?" Nathan asked.

"Well, I've told you some about the time I was a scout for him with Braddock." Adam shook his head, then said slowly, "He's a mighty fearsome man! If there's any man in this world I'd follow blind, I guess it'd have to be George Washington!"

"Colonel Washington—they's two gentlemen heah—name is Winslow."

The man at the writing desk looked up and studied the black man's intense face. "Send them in, Billy."

He stood up, a tall man with big bones, wide in the shoulder and wide at the hips. He brushed his hand across his pock-marked face in a gesture of weariness. His nose was large, his chin an ungainly wedge, and his reddish hair was thin in the back. He studied the door, then when it opened and the two men entered, he said, "Winslow, come in." Stepping forward, he extended his hand, and a smile softened the hard lines of his mouth. "Took a revolution to get you here, didn't it, Adam?"

"Yes, Colonel." Adam studied the tall man, noting that the years had aged him too much, but said only, "This is my son, Nathan. I thought you might like to hear firsthand about Lexington."

Washington's eyes did not leave Adam's face. "I heard about your boy. It was a hard thing."

"Yes, sir."

Washington stood there, something rock-like in his expression; then without warning his manner turned gentle. "I have no sons— but I can feel your grief, Winslow." The gentleness retreated again, and he said, "God only knows how many other young men will pay for this thing." Then he turned to Nathan and offered his hand. "You were there, Mr. Winslow?"

"Yes, sir."

"Tell me."

At first Nathan felt uncomfortable, for he was acutely aware that this was the richest man in Virginia, the top of the social heap. The most famous son of Virginia, his fame from his part in the French and Indian Wars had reached even Europe. But that passed, for Washington listened with such an intensity that Nathan lost himself in his tale.

Finally he finished, and the tall man sat there silently. *You can almost hear him thinking—putting it all together,* Nathan thought.

"It sounds like Braddock's last fight, Adam," he said finally. "You remember how they pinned us down and caught us in that murderous cross-fire?"

"If General Braddock had listened to you, sir, we'd have beaten them. He wanted to fight a European war—but the Indians wouldn't line up and let him shoot at them."

"That's what General Gage wants, I expect." Washington stood up and began pacing the floor. Finally he came and sat down again, and he asked at once, "Will you help with the militia?"

Adam shrugged. "I'll do whatever you want, Colonel. It's going to be a bad war, though."

"There is no good war," Washington murmured. "I've prayed that it would not come . . ." He fixed his eyes on Adam. "You'll be needed," he added quietly. He turned to Nathan. "You were in Boston on business?"

"Yes, Colonel. With my uncle."

"Do you intend to return, may I ask?"

Nathan swallowed, and shook his head. "I'd like to go into the militia with my father."

Washington stared at him, and Nathan grew uncomfortable under his eyes. "I would take it as a favor, Mr. Winslow, if you would go back to Boston—at least for a time."

"Sir?"

"The Congress will meet soon, and I have no doubt that it will declare hostilities. An army will have to be raised and arms collected. In the meantime, the British are in Boston. What will they do while our Colonies are trying to get ready to fight?"

"Why—I don't know, sir!"

"Neither do I, Nathan—but I would very much like to know." A gleam of humor touched Washington's cold gray eyes, and he said, "We are the fox—and the fox needs to know a great deal about the pack that's on his trail."

Nathan glanced at his father, then shook his head. "You want me to be a *spy*? I don't care for that at all. I want to be in the army."

"There *is* no army!" Nathan had heard of how Washington's temper could explode, and the evidence rose up before him. "As for being a spy, every man and woman in the Colonies will have to be a 'spy' if we are to win!"

"Sir," Nathan asked quickly, "just what *exactly* would you like me to do?"

The calm question seemed to please Washington. He lifted his hands and answered, "Rumors are worthless, Nathan. I will need to know *exactly* what the British are doing." His face grew suddenly glum, and he said, "It's asking a lot—but it's the job that needs doing right now. Later on, there'll be a place for you in the army."

Nathan looked at the tall man and replied quickly, "Yes, sir. I'll go back to Boston, if that's what you want." He had heard his father say many times that Washington could make men do what he wanted, and now he knew what that meant!

Washington smiled. "It will be most helpful."

An hour later, Adam and Nathan were on their horses headed home, each thinking of what was to come. Nathan finally broke the silence. "He didn't ask me if I believed in the cause, Father."

"No, he didn't." Adam thought back over the years, then shook his head. "Well, the colonel, he's got a way of taking men the way they are—and more times than not, he manages to use up whatever's in them to get what he wants done." Then he said, as he had before: "He's a mighty fearsome man, that big Virginian!"

CHAPTER TWELVE

A MAN'S LOYALTY

★ ★ ★ ★

"I hate to see him go back to Boston, Adam," Molly said. "He's all we have left now—and if half what we hear is true, fighting will break out there soon." It was two days after the meeting with Washington, and Nathan was leaving for Boston as soon as the team was hitched.

"That's right enough," Adam agreed. "The thing is spreading like wildfire. Don't guess there's a man who's not got wind of what happened in Lexington."

This was partly due, he realized, to a veteran postrider named Israel Bissel, who took a bulletin from Colonel Joseph Palmer of the news of Lexington. Bissel was not content with riding to Connecticut; he pushed on to the Sound, then west along its sandy borders, showing his news to all committeemen, shouting his news on greens and in taverns. April 23, Sabbath or no Sabbath, found him pelting into New York, where people clawed at his stirrups, demanding news and more news. Then he was off again, across the Hudson, across the Jersey flats. The last of his message was terse: "For the good of our country, and the welfare of our lives, and liberties, and fortunes, you will not lose a moment's time!"

Adam had been there when the Virginia militia companies came out, buzzing furiously over the seizure of Virginia powder and stores by Lord Dunmore, Royal Governor. By sundown of the twenty-eighth, all realized that the trouble was national, not local.

Colonel Washington dismissed the militia, but not without the passing of a resolution:

> We do now pledge ourselves to each other to be in readiness, at a moment's warning, to reassemble, and by force of arms, to defend the law, the liberty and rights of this *or any sister colony* from unjust and wicked invasion.

Adam turned his head to watch as Nathan drove the buggy out of the barn, Laddie beside him. "He has to go, Molly." There was nothing else to say, and Molly put a smile on as Nathan got down and came to stand before them. He stood tall in the bright morning sunshine, a steadiness in his smile, as he said cheerfully, "I don't know when I'll be back, but I'll think of you every day— both of you." He leaned down and kissed his mother, and she had to fight to keep from holding him and weeping. Then he shook hands with Adam, saying, "Father, you'll write from Philadelphia?"

"Yes." Adam stood there clasping his hand and could have cursed his close-mouthed ways. He had never been demonstrative—except with Molly, who had taught him better—and now he could do no more than hold on to Nathan's hand and finally clap him on the shoulder, saying, "I think you may want to go there— to give a word to—some of the leaders." He had not told Molly of the dangerous assignment; she thought he was going back to take up his duties with Charles.

Nathan turned and climbed back in, but Molly cried out, "Laddie, get yourself down and give an old woman a goodbye kiss!" Laddie hopped down sheepishly, and would have leaned over and given Nathan's mother a peck, but Molly grabbed her with a laugh, saying, "A good-looking boy like you has got to learn to take his kisses whenever he can—even from an old lady!" She was a strong woman, and she grabbed Laddie and gave her a hearty squeeze, then a resounding kiss on the cheek. "There!" she laughed as Laddie struggled and got free with a red face. "Now you know how it's done."

"Goodbye! God bless you," Laddie called after she regained her seat, and both of them looked back more than once and waved to the pair who stood at the gate until the buggy dropped over a hill and out of their line of view.

"They'll be lonesome with you gone," Laddie said.

"They'll miss you, too, Laddie. I never saw them take to anyone like they did to you." He gave the horses a touch with the whip and said, "I wish to God I didn't have to go back!"

They made the trip quickly, camping out beside small streams the first two nights, and Nathan's spirits seemed to lift. On the third night, one of the heaviest spring rains of the season caught them at dusk, and Nathan pulled up at a small inn, saying, "We can't camp out in this toad-strangler, Laddie. I'm ready for a home-cooked meal and a warm soft bed!"

The meal was good, but after they were finished, Nathan said, "You have a room for us?"

"That I have, sir!" The innkeeper was a barrel-shaped man with merry blue eyes, and he led them to an upstairs room with a large bed. He cracked the shutter, saying, "This will let some air in, sir, but you'd flood the place if you opened it full. Good night to you both."

Nathan stretched, yawned, and said, "I'm tired, Laddie. You must be, too. Let's go to bed."

Let's go to bed!

Laddie stood there, her heart pounding as Nathan stripped off his shirt; then as he started to remove his boots before taking off his trousers, she said with a gasp, "Nathan—I'm not really very sleepy right now."

He had yanked off one boot, and he sat there holding it as he stared at her. "Why not? You've not slept any more than I have."

"Oh, I don't sleep much," she said as he pulled off his other boot and stood to unbuckle his belt. She turned blindly and started for the door, but his voice caught her.

"Where you going?"

"I—I think I'll get my Bible and read." She caught a glimpse of him in his underwear slipping into bed, and she went on in a rush: "I—I don't want to keep you awake, Nathan. Maybe I'll just stay downstairs and read—until I get sleepy." She snatched up her Bible, which was in the top of her canvas bag, and started for the door.

"Oh, come on back, Laddie!" came the sleepy answer, and she heard the bed creak as he settled down. "The light won't bother me. Come on to bed when you feel like it—we need to get an early start tomorrow."

"All right, Nathan." With unsteady hands Laddie drew the single chair in the room next to a weathered oak table that held a single candle and sat down, her eyes fixed on the worn Bible feebly illuminated by the single candle.

Nathan sleepily looked across the room at the small figure. "You read that book a lot, Laddie," he observed. "Almost as much as my mother, I think." When there was only a nod for an answer, he asked, "What's your favorite book?"

"I think—Hebrews," Laddie answered.

"Hebrews?" Nathan yawned, then said sleepily, "Don't think I ever knew anyone who had that for a favorite. Why do you like it?"

"I don't know, Nathan—maybe because it's about Jesus being better than anything—better than Moses or angels or Aaron." She gave him a glance, then said quietly, "My favorite is this verse: 'For we have not a high priest who cannot be touched with the feeling of our infirmities, but was in all points tempted like as we are, yet without sin.' "

"Why do you like that?" Nathan was almost gone, his voice slurred with sleep.

"Because—I—I feel so *bad* sometimes, and I need someone who understands why I'm like I am. Have you ever felt like that, Nathan?"

But there was no answer, and she saw that he was sound asleep. Her own eyes were heavy, but she settled down in the chair and began to read. Hour after hour went by, and her eyes watered so that the letters swam together. She grew cold, and quietly pulled a coat out of her sack and covered up as best she could. She dozed as the clock downstairs sounded throughout the night, marking the leaden hours.

Finally, as a gray light touched the room, she painfully got to her feet and stretched her aching muscles. Glancing at the bed, she saw that Nathan was rolled over to one side, but his tossings had rumpled the covers and pillows on both sides.

A thought came to her, and she quietly put the coat back in her sack, removed her shoes and then rumpled her hair wildly. Holding her breath, she slipped into the bed, feeling the warmth of his body; then she gathered up her courage and gave his broad back a vigorous slap, at the same time saying, "Nathan! It's time to get up!"

She sat up and swung out of bed just as he rolled over and stared at her through half-open, sleep-drugged eyes. "Wha—wha's goin' on?" he muttered, still not awake.

Laddie was pulling on her boots as he sat up, and she gave him another slap on the bare shoulder. "I'll go down and get some hot water for you to shave with," she said. She stood up, stamped her feet, then made a show out of stretching, adding, "I never saw a man who kicks and talks in his sleep like you do! I'll never sleep in the same bed with you again!" *That'll take care of that little problem!* she thought with satisfaction.

"What? I don't talk in my sleep," he muttered, and then he called after her as she left, "See if you can round up some eggs—and some bacon, if they've got it, Laddie!"

While Nathan shaved, Laddie hitched up the team, and after a fine breakfast, they were on their way. The rains had stopped, and they camped out again for the rest of the trip, but they were both tired as they drew close to Boston.

"I don't understand all this," Nathan said suddenly. They were driving along at a rapid clip trying to make the city before dark, but in the dusk something was different as they topped the heights of Menotomy. "What in the world is *that?*"

Laddie looked down on the vast, darkening bowl and saw an immense, glowing horseshoe of scattered lights forming an arc about Charlestown and Boston. "It looks like a terrible lot of camp-fires," she answered.

He stared at the glowing dots that thickened in the central and western parts of the province, and nodded. "That's the army, Laddie, come from all over the Colonies." He touched the horse with his whip, and they moved along the road, passing several groups of armed men who seemed to be leaderless.

Laddie expected him to turn down the pike that led to the Winslow house, but he spun the rig around and made straight for the business district. "Aren't we going to the house?" she asked.

"No. I've got to talk to Sam Adams," he answered tersely, then added, "It won't be possible for me to see him during the day—and I've got a message from Colonel Washington for him."

The dark had closed across the sky as they pulled up a hundred feet from Adams' house. "We'll walk the rest of the way—and if you see anyone keeping an eye on the place, we'll walk right by the door."

"Why, Nathan?" she asked, keeping up with his long strides.

He thought for a moment, then shrugged as he answered, "I

guess you'll have to know a little about this business, Laddie. I'm doing a job for Colonel Washington."

When he explained briefly what he would be doing, Laddie said instantly, "Why, you'll be a spy, Nathan! They'll hang you for that if you get caught."

"Better not get caught, then," he grinned at her. "This is it." He knocked at the door, and it opened almost as if Adams had been waiting for a signal. "Mr. Adams, you may not remember me—"

"I remember you very well, Mr. Winslow," Adams said stonily. "What's your business here?"

The tone of Adams' reply revealed his dislike of the elder Winslow brother, and his face was forbidding in the lamplight. Realizing that words would not serve, Nathan plucked a pouch out of his pocket and handed it to him. "I think you'll recognize this gentleman's handwriting, sir."

"What's this?" Adams scowled, but he took the pouch and backed into the light, growling reluctantly, "Come in—come in!"

He broke the seal, pulled out a single sheet of paper, and as soon as his eyes fell on the paper, he gave an involuntary grunt, lifted his eyes to the pair with a new interest, then read the message.

"You know what's in this letter?" he asked.

"Not really, sir. I could guess that it describes the service I'm asked to carry out."

"Come into the study." Adams led them into the same room where Nathan had last seen him, at the meeting of the Sons of Liberty, and he winced as the image of Caleb's face came to him. "I know about your brother, Mr. Winslow," Adams said as he motioned to a couple of chairs. "I'm sorry. He was a fine boy." He sat down and asked, his intense eyes locking on Nathan's, "Is that why you've changed your politics—because of him?"

Nathan moved uneasily, for the question had no easy answer. He was silent so long that Adams grew impatient; then Nathan shrugged and replied, "I'll do what I can for the cause, Mr. Adams. To be perfectly frank with you, I'm not satisfied that this country can ever be independent." He lifted his chin and said steadily, "I made a vow to my brother as he was dying that I'd do the fighting he'd never be able to do—and that's what I will do, sir. If that's not enough for you, I'll trouble you no more!"

The anger that had leaped into Nathan's eyes seemed to please

Adams, and he said quickly, "It will be enough, Winslow. Others have less determination, I fear." Then his glance shifted to Laddie. "But who is this? Nothing in the message about two men."

"This is Laddie Smith, Mr. Adams. He was Caleb's friend, and he knows what the situation is. You can trust him—and since we can't be seen together, he'll be our point of contact."

"That sounds very well." Adams leaned back in his chair and grew silent. His face was lined with fatigue, and his voice was raspy as if he had been using it too much. Finally he said, "It's a good plan, Winslow. The Congress will authorize the army, and the commander in chief's first problem will be to make it work. Did you see the militia as you came through the heights?"

"Yes, sir. It looks like a heap of men," Nathan nodded.

"Lexington brought them here," Adams nodded. "It's the beginning. What matters is that a call went out, and men by the thousands from all walks of life answered it. Your brother's blood on the green of Lexington's grass isn't just marked by a day on a calendar, Nathan—it's a turning point for a whole continent!"

Adams spoke as if he were before a crowd of five thousand people, and both Laddie and Nathan saw clearly that this man had no reason for living but liberty for America. They sat there while he spoke of the terrible task that lay ahead, and finally he outlined the military situation.

"Artemas Ward, the senior general of Massachusetts, has been given command. He's an old man, heavy and with a bad case of kidney stones, but he's the best we've got until Congress appoints a man. And what a job he'll have!" Adams sighed, and added, "The men are there—thousands of them, but they're not an army— not yet."

"What's the problem, sir?"

"Why, most of them have strong local ties. A company from Sturbridge may march beside one from Barre, but they look with suspicion at each other. There are huge problems over rations, rank, pay, and most of these groups elect their own officers." Adams got up and said sourly, "Whoever the Congress appoints will have to turn all these fragments into an *American* army!"

"Who do you think will be commander?" Nathan asked.

"John Hancock wants it so bad he can taste it. He's got tons of money—but no military experience. How my cousin John Adams would love the office—but he can't wear a uniform!" He smiled dryly at this, then added, "I'll be at that meeting—and I've told a few others that choosing a commander in chief may be a harder fight that any battle in the field! But if we get the wrong man, we're doomed, Winslow." He shook his head; then for the next ten minutes they spoke of how information should be channeled.

"I welcome you, Winslow," Adams said as he led them to the door, "to the revolution." He shook hands with Nathan, then with Laddie. They made their way back to the carriage, and Nathan headed it toward the outskirts of town.

They spoke of the affair briefly; then Nathan gave a smile and put his arm across Laddie's shoulders, saying, "They'll hang you as well as me, Laddie, if they catch you. You sure you want to be in this thing?" The pressure of his arm gave Laddie a peculiar sensation, and she said quickly, "Yes! I don't know much about politics, Nathan, but I believe men ought to be free."

He seemed to forget that his arm was there, but let it rest on her shoulder for a few moments. Then he moved it, adding, "I guess freedom is a pretty scarce commodity in this world, Laddie— but if it's to be had, I guess it's worth fighting for."

"What's the matter with you, Major? You're sober as a Puritan preacher tonight!"

Major Pitcairn looked up to see Paul Winslow with Abigail Howland on his arm. He stood up at once, saying quickly, "I deny the charge, Winslow! But you've kept the most attractive woman at the ball captive all night long, so the fault is yours if I've been moping and feeling sorry for myself."

The truth was that the officer really was not enjoying the evening. The food and drinks had been excellent, the company drawn from the best in Boston, and there were, in fact, several attractive young women who had put themselves in his way. He was in a bad frame of mind and he knew it, but now he denied all, saying, "I say, Miss Howland, if you can tear yourself away from this fellow, put a poor soldier down for a dance, will you?"

"I've been waiting for you to ask me, Major," Abigail smiled. She had a way of making trivial remarks sound true.

The baggage can no more help flirting than she can help having hazel eyes! Pitcairn thought. It was common knowledge in Boston—at least in the upper levels of society—that Abigail was having quite a game with the Winslow cousins. *Looks like Paul has won by default,* he thought sardonically.

"I haven't congratulated you on your gallant conduct, Major," Abigail said. "Now, I demand that you tell me all the gory details."

The words raked across Pitcairn's memory, and he said a little sharply, "There was no gallantry that day—not on my part, at least."

"Why, you defeated the rebels, didn't you, John?" Paul asked in surprise.

"If General Percy hadn't gotten to us with a rescue party," he said with a tight-lipped grimness, "not a man of us would have lived to see Boston again!"

"But—I heard that the marksmanship of the rebels was terrible," Paul put in.

"It was good enough to beat the King's troops," Pitcairn said. "You have to remember, Winslow, these men were farmers and tradesmen, not professional soldiers or frontiersmen." He shuddered briefly, adding, "They cut us to pieces as it was—what will it be like if they get organized into a regular army?"

"Oh, they're a rabble in arms, Major!" Abigail insisted. "It's unthinkable that England could be defeated by a bunch of shopkeepers and farmers. Why, our armies have defeated Spain, France, and the best of Europe's trained might."

"That's true," Pitcairn nodded, "but it's just as true that these wars have so sapped our strength and scattered us all over the globe to keep the empire together that we have precious little in the way of troops to spare on this little theatre. And I don't think you realize how far this matter has gone."

"What do you mean, Major?" Paul asked.

"I mean that we are caught in this city, Paul. We are a good force here, but our scouts tell us that we are surrounded by thousands of men from all 13 Colonies. New Hampshire has sent a force under Colonel John Stark—and I can tell you now, he's a good soldier! Then there's Israel Putnam with 3,000 men from Connecticut, as well as Benedict Arnold and Nathan Greene, just to mention a few. South Carolina has voted to raise 2 infantry regiments of 750 men each and a squadron of 450 mounted rangers—and the list goes on and on!"

"Oh, Major, these troops aren't trained!"

"No, thank God—but all that it takes is *one* man who knows

how to whip an army together—and when *that* happens, we're in for a fight!"

"Come, Major!" Abigail said, and she smiled at him, adding, "What you need is more wine and some fun."

She pulled him away, leaving Paul alone. For the next half hour, Pitcairn did enjoy himself, for with such a beautiful woman, how could it be otherwise? Then she left him, and he moved back into the secluded area, taking a chair and watching the dancers sail by across the polished floor.

He was about to rouse himself and leave when a voice said, "Hello, John."

"Nathan!" Pitcairn rose at once as he looked up to see Nathan Winslow in front of him. "I didn't know you were in Boston."

"Just got back."

Pitcairn felt more uncomfortable than he ever had in his life. There was nothing of anger in Nathan's face, but neither was there the open friendliness that had been there before Lexington. There was a stubborn streak of honesty in the officer, and he went right to the issue. "Nathan, it does so little good—but I've grieved over the death of your brother. It was a foolish thing—so useless!"

Nathan gave Pitcairn a steady look, then shook his head, "I know it wasn't your fault, John. I bear you no ill will."

"That's like you, Nathan," Pitcairn said with some relief. Then he asked, "What will you do?"

"Go back to work, I suppose." The question, Nathan realized, meant more than that. *So it begins*, he thought suddenly. *A spy can never forget what he is—not for one second!* He added idly, "I suppose you've been busy?"

"Too true!" Pitcairn said ruefully. "I can't say that I understand General Gage!"

"How's that, John?"

"Why, a child can see what's happening! We're living in a state of siege, and it's just a matter of time until we have to do something about that army that's taking shape out there!" The major shook his head sadly, then added, "But the general just sits there, hoping it will all go away!"

Washington needs to know that! Nathan thought, then was saddened by the knowledge that John Pitcairn had spoken freely, as he would to a trusted friend. *Didn't take me long to learn how to use my friends—guess that's what a spy's life is like!*

"Nathan!" He turned quickly and found Abigail coming toward him, her hands outstretched. "You're back!"

"Just this minute, Abigail," he said, and taking her hands he kissed one of them, which brought a smile to her full lips. She appeared to have no memory of the scene at New York, or more likely she had chosen to forget it. "I've missed you."

"And I've been forlorn without you, Nathan," she pouted. "Now, come and dance with me! I've got so much to talk to you about!"

As they moved onto the floor, Paul Winslow came up to stand beside Pitcairn. He watched them silently, then said, "I'm surprised he came back."

"Are you? Why is that?"

"Because he's a Winslow!" The words were spoken with bitterness, and Paul smiled as Major Pitcairn stared at him in surprise. "Don't let him fool you, Major."

"Fool me? In what way, Paul?"

"He may smile and seem to be your friend—but he'll never forget that it was you who killed his brother."

"Why, I—!"

"Oh, I realize you didn't fire the shot," Paul shrugged. "But Nathan won't be able to make that distinction. It was a British bullet that killed Caleb, and he'll never forget it."

"But he's always been very unsympathetic to the rebel cause."

"That was because the conflict hadn't hurt *him*—but that's not true now."

"Oh, I think Nathan will show good judgment," Pitcairn protested uneasily.

"No, he won't!" The words leaped out, and Paul shook his head as he went on: "My father says that his brother Adam—that's Nathan's father—is the most stubborn man in the world, that he always was. And I think Nathan is his father all over again. You've hurt him—and I tell you flat out, John, you'd better not trust him!"

Pitcairn shook his head. "You're just saying all this because of Abigail, Paul. You're jealous and the girl has blinded you. Nathan Winslow is an honorable man."

"Oh, he is! And he thinks right now that his honor demands satisfaction for the blood of his brother. You can say what you please, Major, but I tell you that Nathan Winslow will never forget that day at Lexington!"

Pitcairn looked across the room, taking in the tall form of Nathan and the open face. Then he shook his head, saying, "He'll grieve for his brother—but in the end he'll do the wise thing."

"Winslows don't do the *wise* thing," Paul said as he turned to leave. "That's our record, I'm afraid."

It's all so different! Nathan thought. Abigail's face was framed in his vision, and the soft pressure of her body made his senses tingle, but he thought grimly: *She's so beautiful—but if she knew what was in my heart, she'd leave me right now!*

The music played on, and he held Abigail, danced, and smiled. But the thought came to him, clear as print on the page: *Sooner or later, this will end—all of it!*

CHAPTER THIRTEEN

A NEW COMMANDER

★ ★ ★ ★

The Boston Grenadier Corps, Laddie decided, was not particularly expert in drill; on the contrary, they handled their muskets rather clumsily, and the command "To the rear, march" on the part of the large drill master produced instant confusion. Several of the men wheeled at once—and ran head-on into those behind them, who plowed ahead heedless of the command.

"You clumsy dolts!" The drill master was over six feet tall, and he thrust his imposing bulk through the confusion, shoving men around as if they were made of straw. He lashed at them with a high tenor voice that carried like a trumpet, leaving no doubt as to his opinion of their parentage. At last he thrust his chin toward a man standing to one side. "Williams, keep them at it for an hour!"

Laddie followed him as he stomped away from the small field where the drill continued. "Mr. Knox?" He stopped abruptly and peered down impatiently. "Mr. Adams asked me to give you this."

"Adams?" Knox opened the envelope, and while he scanned the note, Laddie examined him curiously. He wore a splendid uniform, consisting of snowy white breeches, an emerald green coat with golden epaulets, and high-topped black boots that glistened in the sun. His face was full; a double chin lapped over the white scarf, and his bulk filled out the uniform like a sausage in its skin. He weighed almost three hundred pounds, but like many fat men, he was graceful and very quick in his movements. His heavy face was not dull, but dominated by a pair of sparkling blue-green eyes and a mobile mouth. He wore a white silk scarf around his left hand, which was apparently crippled in some way.

Laddie found herself the target of a penetrating gaze, and remembered what Sam Adams had said of the man: *He's a fat man and a bookworm—but don't let him fool you. Henry Knox has got a mind like a steel trap, and if any man in the Colonies knows more about cannon and ordnance, nobody's found out about it.*

"Come along, Smith. Got to wash the taste of that drill out of my mouth." He proceeded along the narrow streets so rapidly that Laddie had to practically run to keep up with him, and he kept up a lively conversation. "You ever see such clumsy cows? Can't walk across the street without falling down! They look good, though, don't they now? Every man of 'em's got to be five feet ten—that's the rule. Got a bunch of pretty uniforms, but my Lord, if they had to fight, they'd probably kill as many of each other as they would of the enemy!"

He led the way down twisting streets lined with tiny shops, and Laddie caught a glimpse of a sign that said METALWORK— PAUL REVERE over a large white building. "In here!" Knox said, and wheeled to pass under a sign that read NEW LONDON BOOK- STORE—HENRY KNOX, OWNER. He waded past a jumble of shelves and tables stuffed with flutes, wallpaper, telescopes, bread baskets, patent medicines—and books crammed into every inch of space.

"Go get your supper, Mullins," he said, sending an elderly clerk shuffling through the shop and out the door. "Now, young fellow," he said, shoving a chair toward Laddie, and settling down at a large desk, "you're going to Philadelphia, Adams says?"

"Yes, sir," Laddie answered. "Mr. Adams sent word for me to come and bring him some—information." She hesitated slightly, for she was still uncomfortable with the task that had been thrust upon her. Adams had gone to the Second Continental Congress in Philadelphia suddenly, but in a message to Nathan he had instructed: *Send Smith here with all information. Don't come yourself. See Henry Knox for what he may have.*

Nathan had stared at the brief note, then after reading it to Laddie, said, "He's a foxy one! Blasted note could fall into the hands of Gage himself and he'd be no wiser! So, I stay here, and you go with what we've got so far." To all protests, he had said, "I think

they're watching me pretty close, Laddie, but no one would suspect
you. And we won't put anything in writing; we'll put it in that
sharp brain of yours!"

He had tousled her hair, flashed a quick smile, then begun
drilling her on what information he had gleaned. Finally he had
given her some money, saying, "Go see Knox—and be careful,
Laddie! Wouldn't want anything to happen to you." She had thrust
her hand out, and he had taken it, then instead of releasing it, had
held it, opening it to look at her palm. "Mighty small hand you've
got—like a scholar's hand should be." He had looked at her and
she'd known instinctively he was thinking of Caleb, for he said,
"I've lost too much, Laddie—you take care!"

Now she sat there as Knox stared at her, pondering her with
a sharp glance. "Now, we're alone—what's this about?" He sat
there and listened while Laddie haltingly explained what she was
to do.

Finally when she had finished, he pulled the silk scarf from
his left hand, and Laddie saw it was missing two fingers. "Shot
them off while I was hunting," he said idly, then looked up and
said, "Well, my boy, you're young for such a job, but if Adams
vouches for you, I'll not say nay. I'll write out what I'd like to pass
along, and—"

"Sir, it might be best if you just *tell* me instead of writing it
down. That's the way Mr. Winslow's sending his information."

He stared at her, then commented skeptically, "Some of what
Adams needs to know is technical. You might forget it."

"I don't think so, Mr. Knox."

He laughed, slapped his meaty thigh with his good hand, then
got up and as he walked to a map on a large table, said, "By Harry,
I like a man who knows what he can do! Come here." He waited
until Laddie stood beside him, then pointed down at the map.
"Here's Boston, and here's where the Redcoats are massed, and
right *here* is where the Rhode Islanders are located, and here . . ."

He talked steadily for ten minutes, identifying the location of
various units and then he turned and fixed his bright eyes on her.
"Now, let's have that, Laddie Smith!"

Laddie easily rattled off the locations of units, and Knox's face
glowed with pleasure. "Why, by Harry, that's one hundred per-
cent!" He paused, and seeing something in Laddie's face, asked
quickly, "What's the matter?"

"Well, sir, this map—it's not accurate."

"What?"

"It's out of proportion, Mr. Knox—and look, here, it doesn't show the road leading to Dorchester Heights—and this area is *not* flat, but is the highest point in the vicinity." Laddie had done a great deal of work on maps of that area before her father had died, and now she moved quickly, pointing out flaw after flaw in the map. She was so intent on what she was saying that she didn't see the glint of interest in Knox's moon face; finally she said, "Really, sir, you ought to get a better map."

She looked up into the blue-green eyes of the fat man, and flushed, but he said, "I take it you know quite a bit about maps, Laddie?"

"Oh—not really . . . !" Laddie grew flustered, but it was too late.

"Is it possible you've done some map-making yourself?"

"Just—just a bit, sir."

"I see." He sat there looking at her, then suddenly heaved his bulk up and said, "Sit down here, if you will, Laddie—I want you to write something for me."

She was surprised, but obeyed, and he dictated a few lines having to do with a book that he wished to order from London. He waited until she had finished, then reached out and took the paper. He glanced at it, then nodded and said, "Fine penmanship. My own writing is worse than you can imagine." He suddenly got up, and after rummaging through several shelves, came back and handed her three books. "Something for you to read in your spare time in Philadelphia."

Laddie sat there confused, looking at the books, all of which were dull-looking texts on military matters. Knox gave a hearty laugh. "All booksellers are a little odd, Laddie Smith. Pay me no mind. Well, let me give you a written note for Sam Adams. Lord, I'd like to be in Philadelphia! There's going to be fireworks there for sure! When you get back, will you drop by and give me a report, young fellow?"

"Yes, sir, I will." Laddie got up, and after Knox gave her a sealed packet, she left and hurried to catch the post carriage that made the trip to Philadelphia.

The Second Continental Congress had degenerated into something of a dogfight, and Laddie, who expected to see solemn and dignified proceedings from the cream of American life, sat through several days of the turmoil in shocked silence. She had made a quick trip, and had found Sam Adams with little trouble, but he had been up to his ears in the raging debate and had time only to get a brief report. He read the note from Knox, then hurriedly said, "Stick close, Smith. There'll be a time for what you've brought— and I don't want to have to waste time looking for you when that time comes. Knox says you write a good hand—I need a clerk, so stay handy." He had rushed off, but in the days that followed, often he had her write messages, sometimes delivering them to other committeemen.

She found a tiny room, and spent her nights reading the books Knox had given her. They were all on the use of cannon and artillery, and she waded through them dutifully, becoming mildly interested in the one that discussed the difficulties of moving guns from one place to another; she liked this one, for it had to do with maps and terrains, but she would much have preferred some lighter reading.

The days stretched out, became a week, and still the debate raged, it seemed nothing would ever be settled. One evening, just as dusk was falling, she walked to her old neighborhood and stood in the gathering darkness staring at the old shop. The sign that had read SILAS SAMPSON—CARTOGRAPHER was gone, and the new one said AARON SAMPSON—MAPS. Her heart leaped into her throat when, as she stood watching, a bulky form emerged and she recognized her uncle. The fear that swept over her grew as he crossed the street, and she almost ran in a blind panic when she realized that he would pass right by her!

It was dusk, but there was still light enough for him to see her face, and as he came close, he did give her a searching glance— and with a voice that shook a little, Laddie said, "Good evening to you."

Sampson didn't answer, but his small eyes met hers, and for one terrible second she thought that all was over, that he had seen through her disguise—but relief flooded her as he gave a grunt and passed on down the street.

Thank God! she breathed, and turned to enter the small inn down the street. She was apprehensive, for she had been slightly acquainted with the owners, and there was some risk. But as she took a seat, Mrs. Cowens merely glanced at her and said, "Yes, sir, what'll you be having?"

Laddie ordered a meal, then lingered over a pot of tea, and as she had hoped, Mrs. Cowens proved to be as loquacious as ever. She was a bright-eyed woman, big in bulk and a notorious gossip. It was not difficult for Laddie to get her started, and soon she led her into the area that most interested her. "I need a map of the area—don't suppose there's a cartographer close by?"

Mrs. Cowens soon gave a complete history of the Sampsons, including a detailed account of the disappearance of Miss Julie Sampson. "Ah—now there's something odd about that!

"I make no accusations, mind you—" She winked lewdly at Laddie, and went on to describe how the girl's father had died, and the brother had come to take over. "He's not as pleasant as the old man! But it was clear he'd got it in his head to marry the girl—'cause it was a good business, and she was a pretty little thing."

"You say she disappeared?" Laddie took a sip of tea and said in a disinterested fashion, "Maybe she just wanted to live somewhere else."

"Not likely, mister!" Mrs. Cowens sniffed. "She run off—that's wot she done! Why, didn't 'e offer a reward and didn't 'e have posters sent all over the country offerin' a reward for the gal?"

"Well, I guess he's given up by now."

"That 'e ain't, sir, for as Emily Shultz—she does Sampson's cleanin'—Emily says he's got to get hold of the girl 'cause he's in some kind of legal trouble over the business, and 'e needs her name on some sort of paper. Emily, she says Sampson raves like a crazy man and swears he'll get that gal if 'e has to turn every colony upside down!"

Laddie had heard enough, so she made her escape, and for long hours she walked the streets filled with a black despair. She finally went to her room, but slept fitfully, and the next day her eyes were gritty as she sat through the meeting.

Late that afternoon, however, the drama picked up. Washington had sat in the meeting day after day, dressed in a buff and blue uniform. Laddie had stared at him curiously, a tall, tall man, long-faced and wrapped in a deep mantle of silence. His silence was something almost physical and alive, while others raved and John Adams roared, "Oh, the imbeciles! The fools, with all their talk!"

One of the delegates sitting in front of Laddie asked another sitting beside him, "Who is he?"

"Well, nobody important. Name's Washington. He's a farmer from Virginia."

"Well, he *looks* important," the other said.

"He's rich—maybe as rich as Hancock."

"He never speaks?"

"No."

"Maybe he's got nothing to say?"

Later in the day, Sam Adams motioned to Laddie. He was talking to his cousin John, and he paused long enough to dictate a note; then as Laddie was writing it, Sam Adams asked, "How much is this Washington worth?"

"Got as much money as any man in America," John Adams said.

Sam gave him a sharp look, then said, "He's the one I want."

"Commander in chief? Hancock wants it like he wants heaven!"

Sam grinned at his cousin. "You want it, too, don't you, John?"

"Yes—but I can't wear a uniform."

"We've got to have somebody from the South, John—you know that!"

They both knew it, for the New England delegations were safe, but southerners would not follow a leader from that area. The two men talked about it at length; then Laddie heard John Adams say, "All right, Sam, I'll nominate him."

"Hancock will blow up!"

"He'll have to go along."

Late that afternoon, John Adams rose and talked about qualifications needed for a commander in chief. Most of the delegates thought he was speaking for Hancock, and Hancock himself was flushed and looked around the room with a smile.

Then Adams said, "Gentlemen, the qualifications are high, but we must not make a mistake in this matter. Do we have such a man? I say that we do, and I nominate George Washington of Virginia!"

Hancock's face turned pale, and Washington got up and left the room without a word.

And that had been it.

Washington was elected, and the country had a new leader.

Laddie was anxious to return to Boston, for there had been a flock of rumors about the wire-tight tensions of that city, but Adams had said, "I want Washington to hear your report." Two days later Laddie was startled as Sam Adams grabbed her arm and whispered, "Come along—Washington wants to hear what you've brought."

She followed him, her nervousness rising, and then she entered the large room where Washington sat at a desk flanked by two men. She recognized them as General Charles Lee and General Philip Schuyler.

"General, this is Laddie Smith," Adams said, then stepped back.

Washington looked up, and Laddie saw lines of fatigue on his craggy face, and his voice was raspy as he said, "What's the situation there, Mr. Smith?"

Laddie gave him the information from Nathan, and he looked interested at once. He said nothing, but when she had finished, he nodded and said, "Tell Mr. Winslow we appreciate his help."

The interview was over, but Laddie swallowed and said quickly, "General, Mr. Knox gave me some information on the location of troops around Boston."

"Henry Knox?" Washington's face broke into a smile, and he said, "I might have expected it." He looked at the thin, ugly man who was half-listening to the report, and said, "You must get to know Henry Knox, General Lee."

"Who is he?" Lee was an Englishman, had served in Europe and was reputed to be an excellent soldier.

"A bookseller from Boston," Washington smiled. "But he's studied gunnery out of his books—knows more about cannon than any man in America, I'd guess. I'm going to commission him and put him in charge of our artillery." Then he reached his hand out and said, "I'll take the report, Mr. Smith."

"Well, it's not in writing, General. Mr. Knox thought it might be safer that way. But I can give it to you orally."

"Sloppy work!" Lee sighed in disgust.

Washington said quickly, "Give me your report," and Laddie quickly outlined the position of the British, their numbers and their officers. Then she did the same with the American troops, and as she finished, Washington shot a knowing look at Schuyler, saying evenly, "We must hurry, General. I can't for the life of me imagine why General Gage hasn't hit our people!"

"He won't wait much longer—and our men there need you,"

Schuyler nodded. "We've got to make an army out of them quickly."

Washington turned to Laddie and said, "That's very complete, Mr. Smith. We are in your debt."

Adams motioned to Laddie, and when they were outside, he said, "Get back to Boston. Tell Knox what's happened, and tell Winslow to try to find out something about what Gage may do!" Then he put his hand out, a rare smile on his face. "You did well, my boy—very well!"

Laddie hurried away and was on the coach out of Philadelphia three hours later, pleased that it was over and she could go back to Boston. It shocked her to realize how the simple thought of seeing Nathan sent such a thrill of pleasure through her, and she shook her head angrily as the coach rolled along. *Don't think like that—you're nothing to him!*

Washington assembled a staff hurriedly, and on June 21 he set forth, accompanied by Lee and Schuyler and a brilliant escort. Crowds cheered them in every village as they passed through, but they had not ridden over twenty miles when they were met by a messenger on a lathered, wind-blown horse, who cried out his news: "General—there's been a battle!"

"Where?" Washington rose in his stirrups, and his face grew flushed.

"Place called Bunker Hill outside of Boston!"

Washington was a huge figure on his white horse, and he asked in an intense voice: "Did the militia fight?"

"Yes, General—like wildcats!"

Washington abruptly looked up to the blue sky, and half raised his hands. Suddenly he clapped them together in a vigorous gesture and cried out in a voice packed with emotion:

"Then the liberties of the country are safe!"

CHAPTER FOURTEEN

"THE WHITES OF THEIR EYES!"

★ ★ ★ ★

When Laddie returned to Boston, she found the reports of activity had not been exaggerated—for the city swarmed with British regulars. The newly landed generals—Sir William Howe, Henry Clinton, and handsome John Burgoyne—had come to settle the business of rebellion.

Nathan had picked her up in a bear hug when she had come into the warehouse to find him, saying, "Laddie! Bless God! you're back!" When he put her down, he laughed at her rosy face. "Sorry, Laddie. I guess no young fellow likes to be hugged by a big ugly chap like me, does he now?"

Laddie gave a shake of her head, pulled shut the coat that had popped open, and then smiled. "I guess once won't hurt, Nathan. I missed you, too."

He grabbed her arm, pulling her to The Blue Boar, and when Nelson saw Laddie, he called out, "Wife, 'ere's yer old tenant back again," and he gave Laddie a swipe on the shoulder.

"Bring us the best you've got, Nelson," Nathan smiled; then he turned to Laddie and his eyes, blue as cornflowers, shone as he said, "Lord, I've missed you, boy! Now, tell me everything."

Laddie told it all, and finally Nathan sat back and stared at her. "So Washington is our commander! By heaven, that's what we'll have to have if we're to get out of this thing with our necks whole."

"What's wrong? I thought our men had Boston surrounded? That's the word we got."

Nathan shook his head sadly, lines of worry creasing his smooth brow. "I've been spending a lot of time with the British officers. Guess it pays to court a Tory girl who moves in their circles," he added wryly, not heeding the sudden frown on Laddie's face. "And they know about what *we* know about those units around the city."

"They're good men, aren't they, Nathan?"

"Yes, but untrained and unequipped—and worst of all, they've got no leadership."

Nathan had been so glad to see Laddie that it warmed her to think of it, but in the next few days, he grew sober, and she knew he was fearful of a British attack.

When the attack came, it caught Nathan off guard. On the morning of the seventeenth, he was working at the warehouse, and Laddie looked up to see Henry Knox come in, his face tight with anxiety. She had introduced the two men, and there had been a mutual trust almost instantly.

"What's wrong, Henry?" Nathan asked, moving to meet him.

"There's the devil to pay, that's what!" Knox looked around to be sure they were alone, then said with great agitation, "General Ward's made a bad mistake—and the British are going to cash in on it. Haven't you noticed all the troops moving to the ships?"

"Why, I didn't think anything about it," Nathan said in surprise. "Howe's always got them doing some sort of training."

"Well, this is no drill! They're moving in force to attack!"

"Where?"

Knox shook his head and there was desperation on his round face. "I tried to get Ward to fortify Dorchester. It's high enough to command the neck of Boston peninsula—but he picked Charlestown across the James River."

"Why, that won't do!" Laddie said at once, a clear picture of the map of Boston springing to her mind.

"You see it, too?" Knox nodded with a grim smile. "Nathan is puzzled. Show him what the problem is."

Laddie took a sheet of paper, drew a rough map, saying, "See this thing that looks like a polliwog? Well, that's Charleston—there's Breed's Hill and Bunker Hill."

When Nathan still looked puzzled, she said, "Look, this thing sticks out into the water like a polliwog—it's attached by this little tail." She pointed to the thin narrow tail that tied the peninsula to the mainland. If our men are on these heights, all the British have to do is put men ashore at this neck—and our men'll be trapped like rats."

"Right!" Knox nodded savagely. "*You* see it—and *I* see it—why can't General Ward see it? By Harry, I wish General Washington were here!"

Nathan stared at him, then said, "What are you going to do, Henry?"

"Going to get myself killed, I suppose," Knox shrugged. "We've got no cannon, not much ammunition, not much of anything—but the fight's here! It's time to quit talking and fight, Nathan!"

He wheeled and Nathan caught up with him, his face tense. "I'm going with you."

Knox stopped, his eyes growing large. "Why, Nathan, you'll do more good where you are—getting information—"

"Perdition take it all! I'll not be a spy another day!" His eyes were electric, and stubbornness set his jaw. "I can find my way to Bunker Hill with or without you, Henry—but I'm *going*!"

Knox clapped him on the shoulder and said, "All right—but you need a musket."

"Right here!" Nathan ran to the small storeroom and came back with his Kentucky rifle, a small bore rifle, and a shotgun.

Knox stared at the weapons, then threw back his head and laughed. "By Harry, we'll get them far or near, eh, Winslow? Let's go."

"I'll take the shotgun." Laddie was holding out her hand, and Nathan was taken off guard.

"Why, Laddie," he said quickly, "you can't fight!"

"Why can't I?" There was a stubbornness on Laddie's full lips that matched Nathan's own, and there was determination in the dark eyes of the youth.

Knox stood to one side, his blue-green eyes quizzical. He had grown attached to these young people, and he had heard enough of Caleb's death from Laddie to know that Nathan Winslow was not ready to suffer another loss. *Nathan's taken Laddie for the brother he lost*, he thought. *Look at him! He can't bear to think of losing another one.* He said nothing, knowing that it was between the two of them, but he saw that Laddie was determined.

"I can find Bunker Hill, Nathan, just as well without you!"

Knox saw that Nathan was helpless, and he said, "Let the boy come, Nathan. Better with us where we can keep an eye on him, eh?"

Nathan nodded slowly, handing the shotgun to Laddie and the musket to Knox. "I'll get the powder and balls," he said quietly, and left Knox and Laddie alone.

"He's afraid for you, Laddie," Knox said gently.

"Well, so what?" The dark eyes flashed at him suddenly and Laddie added with just a trace of a quiver: "I'm afraid for *him*—but he can't see that."

Knox put his good hand on her shoulder and said quietly, "God will have to take care of you both, Laddie!"

"There's a lot of them, Nathan." Laddie looked down from the top of Breed's Hill, the barrel of the shotgun burning her hands. General Ward's orders had been to fortify Bunker Hill, the higher peak—but the order was misunderstood and Breed's Hill had been occupied instead. It was closer to the water, to the guns of the Royal Navy, and to the beaches where hostile troops would be landed.

The perfection of a June day wore on, and there was a moving blaze of color as the barges and longboats filled with scarlet-clad regulars unloaded one after another. Drums pounded, fifes cut shrill into the warm air, and a floating pageant lurched out across the Charles River to the silver splash of oars. Men in red and blue—the Royal Regiment of Artillery—trundled field-pieces into crafts, and H.M.S. *Lively* and *Falcon* increased their rate of fire.

"There's the Royal Marines," Nathan said. And although it was too far to recognize individuals, he knew that John Pitcairn would be leading his troops up the hill. *God! Don't let him get in front of my gun!* he breathed; then he saw Dr. Warren approaching to speak to Colonel Prescott, who was in charge. They were so close that Nathan heard Prescott say, "General Warren, you're senior in rank."

"No, I'm here as a volunteer, Colonel. I'll take my place with the others." He had a musket in his hand, and turning he saw Nathan and paused. A light touched his handsome face, and he smiled. "Might I join you, Mr. Winslow?"

"Certainly!" Nathan smiled grimly and said, "I'm in somewhat of a different frame of mind than when we first met at Sam Adams' home, Doctor."

"Sam's talked to me of you, Mr. Winslow. I'm proud to see you here." He nodded, then glanced down at the troops forming for a charge. "I think Gage must be senile, Nathan. He's going to make a frontal attack against men in fortified positions."

"I wonder why?"

"He has a contempt for us," Warren said, and then he added with a smile, "I think he'll not feel quite that way later on this afternoon!"

"There they come!" Prescott's voice cut across the air, and he cried out, "Don't shoot until you see the whites of their eyes, men!"

The forces on the beaches shifted, reshuffled, and the assault began—long scarlet-and-white lines, three deep, climbing like a slow surf toward the redoubt. On they came under the hot sun, each man carrying a load reckoned at 120 pounds.

Laddie heard a voice, and turned to see an elderly farmer, his musket steadily aimed at the Redcoats. "I thank thee, Lord, for sparing me to fight this day. Blessed be the name of the Lord." There was an incredible patience on his face, and Laddie said softly, "Amen!"

Sweat poured down Laddie's face as the lines came on. She counted ten companies across the broad British front, and ten more right behind—hundreds of red-coated men laboring in slow steps up the hill.

Slowly, inexorably, the grenadiers and Royal Marines came on. A voice said, "No firing—hold your fire!" Laddie's finger was on the trigger, and there was a taste of fear in her mouth—but it was fear of killing rather than of being killed. She could see their faces clearly now—some of them fat and some thin; some sunburned and some pale, and the whites of nervous eyes were in all the faces.

"Fire!" came a sudden command, and a ragged sheet of flame belched out from the hundreds of rifles and muskets in the hands of the Americans. As the smoke cleared, Laddie saw that entire ranks were down, men thrashing and screaming, while their comrades stepped over them. She heard balls whistling over her head, and ten feet to her right a man suddenly stood up, shot in the throat. He was trying to speak but only spewed out a ragged stream of bright scarlet blood, fell down, kicked the ground twice, then died.

"They're retreating!" Dr. Warren cried out, and it was so. The British were scrambling wildly down the hill, leaving their wounded behind.

"They won't try that again!" someone cried out.

But they were mistaken.

The second attack came with more power than the first, and the first man that Nathan identified was John Pitcairn. Nathan was firing and reloading like a machine, but as he straightened up to fire, he hesitated, for there, right in his sights was the major. He carried only a saber, and he held it high in the air, crying out encouragement to his men. His face was red with strain, but there was no fear on it, and Nathan found that he could not pull the trigger!

But even as he hesitated, a ball struck Pitcairn in the side, and he fell to the ground, clutching the sudden blossom of blood that appeared on his blue coat.

Men were dropping all along the line, but the toll on the charging Redcoats was terrible. The hill was covered with bodies—some still, and some feebly trying to crawl away, many writhing like cutworms. Time seemed to stand still, and Nathan could not remember a time other than this. He seemed to have been on the hill firing and taking fire forever, and it came as a shock when he heard Laddie crying out, "Nathan! They're leaving!"

He came out of the red haze of battle to see for the second time the British retreat. Then he heard Dr. Warren say, "I'm out of powder." Men up and down the line were saying the same, and Warren said, "If they try again, we're in trouble."

"They can't come up that hill again!" Nathan whispered. "It's like a slaughter pen!" Then he stood, grabbed a water bottle, and suddenly stepped out from the fortifications. Ignoring the startled cry of Warren and Laddie, he moved across the field of broken bodies until he came to where Pitcairn lay. He stopped and saw that the major's eyes were closed. "John—John!" he whispered, and as he knelt, the eyes suddenly opened, filled with pain.

"Nathan—is that you?" he whispered. He gave a slight cry as Nathan lifted his head and held the water bottle to his lips; then he drank deeply. There was a pale ivory cast to his fine face, and he tried to smile.

"John—I'm sorry!" The tears were running down Nathan's face, and he held the man as he would have held a child, closely as if to heal the terrible wound that was killing him.

Pitcairn looked up and his smile was gentle. "You must not grieve over this, Nathan. You must not."

"I can't help it!"

"You must not!" Then Pitcairn's body grew tense, and he said in a faint whisper, "The lights are going out—goodbye, my boy . . ." He coughed once, drew a strangled breath, and then relaxed.

Nathan sat there holding the shattered body of his friend, his mind blank and his heart crying out for grief. Finally, he felt a hand on his arm, and looked up to see Dr. Warren, his face stern. "Nathan—they're coming again!"

He followed Warren back and took his place beside Laddie, and slowly he began to see the field come into focus. He checked his powder, saw that he had only enough for one shot. Then he heard Prescott saying, "We'll fall back!"

And as the enemy charged, it became a nightmare! Men with no powder and no shot were defenseless against the bright bayonets of the grenadiers. They tried to use their muskets for clubs and took the bright blades in their stomachs; they tried to run, and the marines rammed the thin slivers of steel into their backs.

Nathan had pushed Laddie to the rear and had smashed the skull of one Redcoat when he saw Dr. Warren caught by two soldiers. The doctor raised his musket to use as a club, and both of them drove bayonets through his body. Warren fell to the ground and they plunged the bayonets into him again and again.

The sun was dropping, and the cool air washed over Laddie's face. "It's hard to believe we're alive, Nathan," she said, taking a deep breath.

"A lot of us aren't," he answered. They were sitting beside a small creek on a hill that overlooked Boston, and the paths were crowded with men who were going back to their homes.

They had rejoined Knox, and he looked at the dim forms of men filtering through the woods, many of them wounded. "There goes our army," he said slowly.

"You think it's over, Mr. Knox?" Laddie asked quietly. She had never seen the big man discouraged, and it troubled her.

He roused himself, and in the fading darkness, they saw him smile grimly. "They won't go far, Laddie."

"We lost, didn't we?" Nathan said.

Knox swore and said loudly, "No, we didn't lose! Howe bought that hill at the price of a thousand men, and we can't have lost more than two hundred. I'd like to sell him another worthless hill at the same price!"

"What's next?" Nathan asked, getting to his feet.

"We wait for Washington," Knox answered, heaving his bulk from the ground. Then he touched Nathan on the shoulder, saying, "You'd better be careful. The British aren't going to go easy on anybody who was on that hill today."

"I'm not going back," Nathan said. His face looked grim in the pale light, and he added, "I'll wait for General Washington."

Knox laughed and said, "Well, we'd all better stay together then. They'd have to find a pretty thick rope to hang Henry Knox, but they'd love to try it. I'm joining Washington as a staff officer. I'd like for you to come with me as part of my command—artillery."

"I know a little about rifles—but not much about cannon."

"We don't have any," Knox said dryly. "So you'll have time to learn until we get some." Then he said suddenly, "And I'll have you, too, Mr. Laddie Smith."

"Me, sir?"

"Yes, you." Knox moved to stand before Laddie, and his voice was gentle as he asked, "I don't think you'll stay in Boston either, will you? Not if Nathan goes."

"I—I don't want to be left behind." Laddie did not look at Nathan, but she felt his eyes on her.

"Knox, what will Laddie do in the army?" Nathan asked.

"I'd say make maps," Knox shot back. "We're going to need someone who can keep us from getting lost—and as far as I know there's not a qualified cartographer on hand." Then he shot a look at Nathan, saying mildly, "Laddie will be one of my aides, Nathan, not in the infantry. Safest place in a war is with the generals!"

Nathan saw that Knox was sincere, and he said to Laddie, "You won't stay out of this?"

"No—not if you don't, Nathan."

An owl sailed over, silhouetted against the darkening sky, and Nathan looked up as it dropped silently like a ghost into a small clump of bushes. There was the sound of a muffled struggle, then silence.

Nathan looked at the dark eyes of Laddie Smith and said with a smile, "I should have left you to freeze, boy! You're nothing but an aggravation to me." Then he laughed and ruffled Laddie's soft, dark hair, saying, "You're bound and determined to be a rebel, I see that plain."

Looking down at Laddie from his great height, Knox noted the soft eyes and the smooth-planed features. He smiled, saying as they turned to leave the grove:

"A rebel, yes—but, by Harry—*a gentle rebel!*"

CHAPTER FIFTEEN

LADDIE IN LOVE

★　★　★　★

July 2, 1775, was a rainy Sunday in Cambridge. As the weather cleared, General George Washington rode into the rain-soaked college town and received from General Artemas Ward command of the entire military force of America. James Steven, a soldier on duty that day made a single bored notation: "Nothing hebbeng extroderly."

Nathan and Laddie had made one quick trip to the Winslow house to pick up their things. Charles had been the only one up as they entered, and there had been a heated argument, for he felt that Nathan was throwing his life away. "Why, you young fool, can't you see the end of this thing?" he'd cried out passionately, and in his agitation he'd seized Nathan by the arm and shaken him. "The King and Parliament *can't* let this rebellion succeed! It would give an invitation to every royal colony to rebel against England!"

"Uncle Charles, there's no point in discussing it." Nathan had pulled away from his uncle and said in a tone of utter finality, "I'm in this thing to the end, and Father is, too."

Charles had stood there, a sad look in his eyes. "It's the death of you, boy! Everything—everything will go. Abigail—have you thought about her?"

"Yes, I have."

"You know she's for the Crown, and she won't change?"

Laddie shot a glance at Nathan, noting the look of pain in his eyes, and then he had straightened up and said firmly, "I'm sorry, Uncle Charles, but it's what I have to do."

They had gathered their belongings and gone back to the rebel lines that night, and in the weeks that passed, both of them struggled to find their niche in the army that was being birthed in the hills around Boston.

Nathan wrote of this in a letter to his father:

August 2, 1775
Dear Father,

I write this hastily, for the post is leaving in ten minutes. I am now a private in Henry Knox's command. General Knox is scraping up every firearm larger than a musket, and I have been given a tiny three-pounder, which barely qualifies!

Laddie has been in the thick of things—for it turns out he has had some training in mapmaking and is a fine clerk. He is an aide of General Knox and has been made a sergeant! He is quite unbearable with his new rank! When he had the gall to try to give *me* an order this morning—grinning like a possum!—I threatened to turn him over my knee, and he faced up to me and said that would be mutiny and he'd have me flogged for it!

Seriously, I am quite relieved to have him in that duty, for it will be much safer than being in the line. He's such a fragile youngster, and I would grieve to see him harmed.

I understand that you will bring a troop of Virginia riflemen to the siege soon, so we will meet. Will Mother come with you? It would be impossible for her to stay with Uncle Charles, I think, but I hate for her to be alone. I will try to find a place in some small village where we can see her often.

Your devoted son,
Nathan Winslow

The troops around Boston lived in shelters made of whatever materials they could lay their hands on, and Laddie quickly realized that if she had not been made an aide to an officer, she would have been in bad shape. Some of the men knocked together rough shacks, a few had tents, but the majority simply lived on the ground between constantly soggy blankets.

All the staff officers had places in houses, and fear of discovery had clawed at Laddie until Knox had taken her to a small bungalow not far from the heights of Dorchester. "Lieutenant Mason and I will take the bedroom, Laddie, and you can bunk in the loft." Relief had flooded her; she would still be able to keep her sex a secret—at least for the time being.

Knox was a dynamo of activity, and he kept her close most of the time, roaring out memos, dictating reports, and spawning letters constantly. She learned to move through the confusion in his wake, and in a week had made herself indispensable to the huge man. To add to the confusion, it was often impossible to tell officers from enlisted men, for despite the efforts of General Washington to outfit the men in some semblance of a uniform, the Congress took no action. Washington finally authorized officers to adopt scarves, cockades, secondhand epaulets—whatever they could find to identify themselves.

As the weeks dragged on and the first American army took shape slowly under Washington's hand, Gage and his troops remained oddly passive in Boston. "I guess he thinks our army will give up and go home," Knox said once to Nathan; then he had added with a grimace, "And he could be partly right—with this eight-months Army of ours. By the end of the year, many of these units will be at the end of their agreed term of service, and will be free to go home."

But it never happened. When some of the men went home, short-term militia were called up to man the lines, while recruiting officers beat their drums in distant towns and hamlets. Many did stay past their time, and Nathan said once to Laddie, "It's Washington they stay for. He's not a man that troops will run after cheering and tossing their hats, but you just notice—when he passes by, men stand straighter and grip their muskets a little tighter—and they wind up writing letters back home trying to explain why it seems fitting for them to stay on after all."

September came, then October, and the hills put on their fall colors of yellow, red, and gold. Men who had been sleeping on the ground suddenly fell into a building frenzy, putting up shacks, and the sound of axes rang constantly as firewood parties fell on the hardwood groves.

On one of those days in late October, Laddie and Nathan went on a day's hunt at General Knox's suggestion. "By Harry, if I have to eat another plate of this stew, I'll give up food," he had groaned. "Winslow, you've mastered your drill with your gun, so take that rifle of yours and get us a buck—even if you have to mistake a nice cow for one! And Sergeant Smith, you go along to be sure he doesn't shoot himself." His smallish eyes had gleamed, for despite his ferocious words, he had noted that both Nathan and Laddie were worn thin with the efforts to put together some sort of artillery unit. "Both of you have done well," he said with a sudden warm smile. "Take a couple of days and forget about trying to kill the British."

Neither Nathan nor Laddie argued, and in less than two hours they were making their way out of the camp, headed toward the thick forests northeast of Boston, mounted on two large mules that would carry back the game. All day long they pushed deeper and deeper into the wilderness, and by dusk they were camped beside a large brook beneath a tremendous hemlock. Nathan had passed up several chances to knock down deer, choosing instead to knock down enough quail to feed them for the night. Laddie could scarcely believe how he could usually take their heads off with a single rifle shot, and as they were roasting them over a small fragrant fire that night, she finally said, "Nathan, if you can hit a tiny thing like that, a man wouldn't have a chance, would he?"

"Well, Laddie," he answered with a quick smile, "one big difference between shooting quail and men—the quail don't shoot back!" He was wearing a fringed hunting jacket, and his high-planed face was thrown into even sharper lines by the flickering of the fire. The trip had relaxed him, and the ease in tension made him look younger. He added thoughtfully, "Lots of men can hit a nailhead at a hundred yards, but nailheads aren't men, and it's a hard thing to take a human life." He looked at her across the fire and asked curiously, "Did you have any trouble pulling the trigger on Breed's Hill?"

"I—I don't think I could have done it," she said in her husky voice, "but the shotgun was loaded with bird shot. I guess that's all we had. It couldn't have killed anybody. I just aimed at the crowd and pulled the trigger, and I know it stung a few men." She thought about it, and when she looked at him, her strange almond-shaped eyes reflected golden glints from the sparks that rose from the fire. "I still don't know if I could shoot—if I *knew* I was going to kill a man."

He didn't answer at once, but her words troubled him, and he gave his attention to the bird he was roasting. "Hey, this is just about right." He pulled off a fragment of the toasted meat, juggled it in his hands to cool it, then tasted it, saying, "Laddie, this is *good!*" The two of them ate the quail, along with some biscuits and a couple of boiled potatoes they'd brought. They made tea in a small pot, and later Laddie brought out the plump wild blueberries she'd picked as they walked through the woods.

"I don't care if it takes a week to get some game," Laddie said finally. The sharp autumn air had brought a rich color to her face, and she pulled her short wool coat snugly around her, lay down on her blanket, and stared into the leaping flames of the fire. Sleepily, she murmured, "Nathan—how long will this war take?"

"How long?" Nathan laughed quietly and poked the fire with a stick, sending the tiny sparks upward to mingle in the tops of the trees with the real stars that glittered overhead. "Why, boy, it's not even *started* and you're already thinking about the end! But I guess you're thinking like lots of the fellows are—we'll spend the winter running the British out of our country; then we'll go home in time for spring planting and be done with King George."

She looked up, caught by the doubt that threaded his words, and asked, "You don't think it'll be like that?"

"No way it can happen. In the first place, we're probably going to *lose*, not win. Laddie, we got a bunch of farmers and shopkeepers with few guns—most of 'em never even *saw* a battle. We have no factories, no navy, no professional soldiers. And England has it all. Why, they got a hundred thousand men of their own troops, and if they're not enough they can hire that many more Germans or Hessians! You saw 'em march up that hill, like machines! What would have happened if we'd been in front of them without any protection—or if *we* had to charge up a hill like that against those trained troops?"

He took a sip of his tea, and there was a silence, broken only by the cry of some night bird—a lonesome sound that made her shiver and draw her blanket closer. She had been in the middle of such activity and such optimism for the past few weeks that defeat had not even been a thought in her mind. Now Nathan's face was so bleak in the firelight that she longed to put her hand on his, but said only, "Nathan, if you don't think we can win, why . . . ?"

"What am I doing here?" He finished the tea, put the cup away, then punched his blanket roll into shape and prepared to lie down. "I made a promise to Caleb, Laddie. I'll keep it. As long as there's a fight, I'll stay with it." A sudden cry in the woods startled them both, and he got to his feet, in one smooth movement seized his rifle and stood there, alert and waiting.

"Just a panther," he finally grunted. "Those critters sound like a woman screaming, don't they?" He laid the rifle down, threw a thick log on the fire, and seeing that she was still sitting, staring rigidly into the dark woods, he stepped closer. Reaching out, he grabbed her thick hair and pulled her startled face up; then giving her head a shake, he laughed and said, "Not scared of a little ol' panther, are you, Laddie?"

The gentle grasp he kept on her hair did not hurt, but his touch sent a shock along her nerves. Looking up into the wide blue eyes that laughed down at her, she could not control the sudden tremor that seemed to make her weak and vulnerable. For months she had kept a constant effort to erase all traces of her femininity from her speech, her movements—and now in one explosive instant the touch of Nathan's hand on her head sent everything crumbling!

I love you, Nathan Winslow! The words leaped to her lips, seemed to fill her breast, and she knew that if she lived to be an old woman, this scene would be fresh in her heart—his face framed by the naked branches of the hemlock, his smile gleaming brightly against his tanned face, the smell of leather and woodsmoke, along with the crackling fire and the gentle bubbling of the brook, and the touch of his hand on her hair—all would be there for her when she thought of this time. *I'll never have him—but I'll always remember this night—when I first knew I loved him!*

He had pulled her head up to smile at her, but he saw something leap into her eyes, and he thought it was fear. He crouched suddenly, and put his free hand on her shoulder, saying, "Laddie, don't be afraid! Panthers never attack men." The dark eyes he looked into blinked rapidly, and just a trace of a tremor touched the full lower lip. What he saw bothered him. Time ran on, and Laddie remained silent. Finally, Nathan said, "Laddie, ever since Caleb died, I've felt rotten—and it's mostly because I—I never really told him how much I cared for him. It's always been hard for me to tell people I care for them. Seems like some families are real good at that—kissing and hugging and always saying how they love each other. But I've not been that way."

The light touch of his hand was a torment to Laddie, but a delicious pain, and she was hypnotized by his closeness. She knew that she ought to move away, but she sat very still, unwilling to lose the slight pressure of his hands.

"What I mean," Nathan said gently, "is that I don't ever want to let that happen again—so that's why I want to tell you right now—I love you, Laddie—hard as it is for me to say such things—I do love you, boy!"

Laddie knew that he wanted her to speak, to say something of her feelings, but she was too full to trust herself. She waited until he released her, saying, "Well, I just wanted you to know."

He rolled up in his blankets, and she did the same, but she was biting her fist fiercely to keep back the choking sobs.

The fire burned on, sending ghostly shadows against the trees, and the wind sighed faintly through the bare treetops. Overhead the stars moved across the ebony sky, rank on rank, doing their great dance.

Finally, much later, the log that he had put on burned in two, snapped, and fell on the coals beneath, sending a shower of sparks upward. And in a voice that Nathan never heard, Julie Sampson—not Laddie Smith!—whispered faintly:

"And I love you—Nathan Winslow!"

The tall form under the blanket did not stir, but far off a lone wolf lifted his muzzle to the stars; his nocturnal cry echoed the sadness that filled the girl's heart.

Two days later they returned to camp, the mules loaded with the dressed carcasses of four deer and a canvas bag stuffed with wild turkey—enough to feed the whole unit! Neither of them had referred to that first night, and Laddie sensed that Nathan felt that her response had been too cold. She had tried to make it up, but the moment had passed, and by the time they returned to camp, Nathan was depressed. Although he had said only a little, Laddie had a suspicion that he was thinking of Abigail Howland. He had said once, "Guess Paul has been having it pretty well his own way with Abigail—with me stuck out here for months."

Knox greeted them with a shout of joy at the sight of the small mountain of game. "Roust that cook out!" he roared. Then he had thrown his arms around the two of them, practically picking Laddie off the ground in his massive arms. "Bless you both! I don't care right now if you never do another blessed thing right—I forgive you for the sake of that fresh meat!"

"Anything happen while we were gone?" Nathan asked.

"No, but something's *going* to happen!" Knox said. "There's a meeting of staff officers tonight, and I've got a plan to save our bacon—if I can get the His Excellency to buy it!"

"What kind of plan, sir?" Laddie asked.

"You'll find out, because I want you there with every map you can lay your hands on, Sergeant Smith!"

Nathan said suddenly, "You won't need me around for a little while, will you, sir?"

"Why, no, Nathan—" He paused, then said quickly, "I won't need you tonight—but if they like my plan, I want you handy."

"I'll be back day after tomorrow."

Knox stared at him, started to say something, but then shut it off. When he walked away, Laddie stared at him, then said quietly, "Don't do it, Nathan."

"Do what?"

"Oh, don't be so innocent!" She lifted her head and said scornfully, "You think I don't know what it is? You're going to sneak into Boston and see that woman!"

He stared at her; then a grin touched his lips. "Guess you know me too well, Laddie. But it's no risk. I'll go in after dark so the patrols won't get me."

She stared at him, then begged, "Nathan, please don't go! You know what they say—that they've already *shot* two men they caught spying!"

"I'm not spying."

"You think they'll believe that? Nathan, wait a while—please!"

He sobered, then said, "I'm sorry, Laddie. I know you're too young to understand this—but love makes you do crazy things."

He wheeled suddenly and walked away, and she stood there helplessly watching until he disappeared behind a line of tents.

She knew that he was gone at supper, for he did not appear to take part in the feast. Many hands were clapped on her shoulder, with a "Good job, Laddie!" and "Thanks for the meal, Sergeant!" but she could not swallow more than a few bites.

Later, she went with Schuyler and Knox to a large house where Washington was staying. His wife was there, a small woman with bright eyes and a quick word of welcome for all, but she soon disappeared, and the council began at once.

Washington spoke briefly, thanking each of his officers for their labors, then said in a tired voice, "Gentlemen, we have the British trapped, but we can't do anything with them."

"Your Excellency," Nathanael Greene, a tall, handsome officer, said, "I'm a Quaker, as you call us, and we are, in principle, opposed to fighting; but I can't see that waiting is getting us any closer to freedom. Can't we hit them head-on?"

Washington would have liked to do exactly that. Waiting was not his idea of war, but he shook his head, saying, "No, we're not yet ready for that sort of head-on fight. The answer, of course, would be to blast them out with heavy guns—but we have none. Until we can get some, we'll just have to pray that General Gage doesn't get inspired to move."

Knox stood up, the tallest man in the room except for Washington. "May I have your permission to offer a solution, sir?"

Washington had a deep affection for the officer, and he said with courtesy but little hope, "Certainly, Captain Knox."

Washington sat down, and Knox looked around the table at cynical Charles Lee, hot-tempered John Sullivan, the old Indian fighter Israel Putnam, John Grover of the 21st Massachusetts Regiment, Greene, and Schuyler. "Gentlemen, guns are the answer, as the general points out. I propose to get some heavy guns, to place them on Dorchester Heights and blow the Redcoats out of their shirts!"

A look of disgust crossed the thin face of General Charles Lee. "Knox, it's impossible! We've tried to get guns from every possible source." Lee was always negative, and now he yawned and dismissed Knox's proposal with a wave of his manicured hand.

"Where do you propose to get the guns, Henry?" Washington asked, a trace of hope illuminating his face.

"Sergeant, hold up map Fourteen-C," Knox said, and Laddie quickly held it up with both hands. She felt Knox's heavy hand punching it, and he said one word:

"Ticonderoga!"

Washington stared blankly at Knox; then the idea brought a light to his gray eyes. "There *are* heavy cannon there—I'd forgotten!"

All of them were thinking of the wild raid under the command of Ethan Allen and his Green Mountain Boys and Benedict Arnold. The two of them had captured Fort Ticonderoga the previous May. The fort itself was falling in, and of no great use to anyone, but there were many cannon there.

"Henry!" Washington was visibly excited, a sight rarely seen. He stood to his feet and stared at the map. "Can it be done? Winter will catch you, and the roads are terrible."

Knox said at once, "General Washington, I will get those guns or die in the attempt!"

Washington slammed his fist down on the table. "We must have those weapons! Take any men you need—do what you have to!"

Lee said languidly, "Oh, it can't be done—not until spring, at least!"

But Knox was staring straight into his commander's eyes, and he said in a steady voice, "You shall have them, sir!"

The meeting went on for some time, but Laddie was dismissed, and went to bed. The next day, Knox moved through the camp like a whirlwind, picking men, choosing only the best and toughest. He stopped long enough to ask Laddie, "Where's Nathan?"

"I—I haven't seen him, sir—but you said he could have two days."

"All right, but as soon as you lay eyes on him, tell him I want him to go on this mission!"

All day Laddie looked for him, but Nathan didn't come. That night after supper, Knox came to her with an angry look on his round face. "I've got bad news, Smith." He stared at her, then said plainly, "Nathan's been captured."

"No!"

"Yes. One of our informers just brought word. There's no doubt of it."

"But, what will they do to him?"

He stared at the stricken countenance before him, then said, "They'll hang him, I'm afraid. He's been tried by a military court and sentenced to death."

"I've got to go to him!"

He shook his head. "It would not do, Laddie. You can't help him—and you might be taken as well."

She looked straight at him and said, "Sir, I've got to go. If you don't lock me up, I'll go."

He stared at her, then said, "By heaven, I'm sorry to hear it, Laddie! You know how fond I am of Winslow—" Then he groaned and said, "Go on then. I'll give you a pass—but it would be better if you didn't go."

Laddie said quietly, "He saved my life, Captain Knox. I've got to go—to do what I can!"

She turned and walked away, shoulders held square, and Knox suddenly swore, whirled and walked quickly away. *It would have been better if he'd been killed at Breed's Hill!* he thought grimly.

CHAPTER SIXTEEN

ESCAPE!

★ ★ ★ ★

"Miss Abigail—dat man, he heah *agin*!"

The black girl entered the room reluctantly, keeping a respectful distance from the young woman who sat up in the bed and glared at her. "I *told* you to say I wouldn't see him! Why can't you ever do a single thing *right*, Susie?"

The slave blinked, then rolled her large eyes upward. "I done tole him 'zactly whut you said—but he jes' set there and say he ain't gonna move till you sees him." She shook her head with exasperation, adding, "It sho' is a shame yo poppa and momma both gone—I bet *dey* get shut of 'im!"

Abigail got up from the bed, smoothed her dressing gown, and walked across the room to stare out into the falling darkness. Her face was puffy with sleep, and she asked idly, "What sort of man did you say he was?"

"Oh, jes' a young man—sort of plain. He ain't no quality folks, Miss."

"I don't know anybody named Smith." Abigail went over to the mirror, sat down and began to brush her hair. Finally she said, "Oh, well, show him up, Susie. You can say I've been ill and can't come down."

"Yas, Miss Abigail." When the slave left, Abigail carefully brushed her hair, then moved to a plush couch, put her feet up and covered them with a brightly colored quilt. When the knock sounded on the door, she said, "Come in," and looked up to see Susie admit a young man.

"Yes, what is it?"

"You don't remember me, Miss Howland?"

Abigail stared in the failing light at the youth, but said, "I don't think we've met." Curiosity had caused her to let him in, but he was merely a plainly dressed youth in his late teens. The oval-shaped face and large eyes reminded her of someone, but she said, "I'm not well, Mr. Smith. I'll ask you to come back tomorrow and see my parents."

She blinked nervously as the man called Smith did not turn to leave, but stepped up so close that she could see determination in a pair of inky black eyes and a firm mouth. Fear rose in her, and she opened her mouth to call for the slave, but he said, "I'm here about Nathan Winslow."

"What! Who are you?" She threw back the quilt and stood to her feet, staring at her visitor. "I don't know you, and I'll ask you to leave!"

"You've seen me, Miss Howland," Laddie said. "I once worked for Mr. Charles Winslow. You saw me there when you came to visit his son—and I was at the warehouse when you came to go for rides with Nathan."

Abigail stared at her, then nodded slowly. "Yes—I think I do remember you—but what do you want?"

"I want to save Nathan's life," Laddie said evenly. "And you've got to help."

"It's impossible!" Abigail cried at once, and she walked to the small French desk and picked up a handkerchief. She dabbed at her eyes, and then twisted the kerchief into a knot. "Do you think we haven't tried? If you work for Charles Winslow, you must know he's talked to General Gage for *hours*—but the general says it's out of his hands."

Laddie did know that to be true, for she had gone straight to the Winslow house and asked Charles point blank what he was doing to get Nathan out of jail. He had stared at her, a haggard look in his eyes, and said wearily, "I've not slept a wink since he was taken—and I've used all the influence I have to get him out—but they're determined to make an example of him, Laddie. I've done all I can!"

She had left, and all day she had haunted the large building where the second story was used for a jail. In desperation she had gone inside and asked to see Nathan, claiming to be his brother, but the burly corporal had shaken his massive head, saying, "Not a bit of it! We got 'im clean, and we're gonna 'ang the blighter at dawn! And we don't mean 'e should cheat us by doin' away with 'imself, either! So it's no visitors 'cept them wot's got a pass signed by the general his own self!" A tall officer in shirt sleeves, his red coat hanging on a peg, looked up from across the room, where he sat idly reading a newspaper, then shrugged and looked back at the paper.

Laddie had left, noting carefully the details of the building. The room below was large, with several desks, but besides the corporal only two privates were on duty. *That's four in here—at least at night*, she thought, then glanced at the stairs at the back of the room. *No way to tell how many up there*, she thought as she left.

All night she walked the streets, and the next day she listened to the talk in the taverns, and found out that Nathan's hanging was to be a celebration of sorts. The Tories looked on it as an example for other traitors, and she heard bets made as to whether he would break his neck in the fall or die of strangulation, kicking wildly.

Her mind raced madly, and fear was a metallic taste in her mouth. *If only his father were here!* she thought. But there was no time. Finally in the early afternoon she passed by a church, and some impulse drove her to enter and take a seat in the dark recesses. A few candles burned on a table in the front, and a few people sat quietly with their heads bowed. She didn't even know what sort of church it was, but that didn't seem to matter.

The quiet soaked into her, and her fear lost some of its piercing sting as she began to pray. It was a strange time for her, for like most, she had always prayed calmly, rather routinely. But desperation numbed her now, and she began to weep, her chest heaving and great choking sobs racking her body. There was no eloquence, no fine phrase. *Help, O Lord! Oh, God, have mercy!* Over and over she cried out, as if she were dying herself. Never had she experienced such a paroxysm of grief and terror, and she remembered once what Rev. Zachariah Kelly had said in a sermon: "Men only seek God out of desperation." Now she knew it was so.

Finally her sobs ceased; suddenly a strange peace seemed to fill her mind, and the exhaustion and fear faded. She heard no voices and there was no mystic vision, but a passage of Scripture quietly drifted into her mind. At first she ignored it, thinking only of Nathan, but it came back, not once but several times:

The Lord is my light and my salvation; whom shall I fear? The Lord is the strength of my life; of whom shall I be afraid? When the wicked, even my enemies and my foes, came upon me to eat up my flesh, they stumbled and fell. Though an host should encamp against me, my heart shall not fear; though war should rise against me, in this will I be confident.

The words were very familiar, for they had been the favorite verses of her pastor, Rev. Kelly. Many times he had quoted the entire twenty-seventh psalm from the pulpit, and she seemed to hear his voice as the words continued to flow through her spirit:

Teach me thy way, O Lord, and lead me in a plain path because of mine enemies. Wait on the Lord; be of good courage, and he shall strengthen thine heart: wait, I say, on the Lord.

She got to her feet and left the church, and there was no trace of fear in her. As she made her way through the streets, she repeated the words: *"Teach me thy way, O Lord, and lead me in a plain path because of mine enemies."*

And there was still no fear in Laddie as she stood before Abigail and said, "There's not much time. They're going to hang him in the morning." She had come to the Howland residence because no other course had occurred to her. She had never been a believer in visions and dreams, but as she walked the streets after leaving the church, she somehow took the impulse to go to see Abigail as part of the "way" that she felt God was going to show her.

Abigail was trembling, and she collapsed on the sofa, moaning. "I've *tried* to help! Can't you understand that? I've had my father practically on his *knees* begging General Gage—and it's no use."

"Have you seen him?"

"I—wanted to. I even had Father get me a pass from General Gage!" She leaped up and ran to the desk. Picking up a sealed envelope, she held it up, then threw it back on the desk with a groan. "But Mother won't hear of it!"

"So it's no visitors 'cept them wot's got a pass signed by the general his own self!"

The words of the corporal echoed in her ears, and in that instant she knew what she had to do! There was no dreary planning, no wrestling with details; it sprang into her mind fully formed, and with a leap of her heart she remembered the words ". . . lead me in a *plain* path."

Carefully Laddie moved to stand in front of the desk, and asked quietly, "How did he get taken?"

"We don't know," Abigail whispered. She looked with a tremulous mouth at Laddie, adding, "He came to see me, of course." And despite the trembling lips, there was a flash of fire in her eyes, pride that a man would risk his life for her! "And I was so afraid! I tried to get him to leave—but he wouldn't listen!" She gave a small smile and shrugged, "Love makes people do strange things, don't you agree?"

Laddie thought of the plan she was determined on; there was a strange smile on her lips as she answered quietly, "Yes, a man will do strange things for love—and so will a woman." Then she demanded, "And why can't you use the pass—go see him, Miss Howland? If he's going to die for you, the least you could do is go say goodbye!"

Abigail dropped her head in confusion (exactly as Laddie had hoped!), and in one smooth motion, Laddie turned, picked up the pass and shoved it into her shirt. It took less than three seconds, and she said quickly, "I'm sorry to have bothered you, Miss Howland. I'll be going now."

Abigail looked up with a startled expression as Laddie reached the door, and she cried out loudly, "*I* can't go to him! Can't you see that?"

But the door closed, and in a matter of seconds Laddie was walking as fast as she could in the direction of the business district.

Two hours later she was opening the door of the Winslow warehouse. Quickly she moved to hitch the team of bays to the buggy—the same one, she noted with a slight shock, that they'd gone to New York in. She was thankful the guard had gone for the night, and even more grateful that she had kept her key!

Dark had fallen by the time the team stood stamping in the cold of the stable, and Laddie picked up the bulky package she'd brought with her. The office was still warm, and she pulled a small box out of the large sack, opened it, and withdrew two small flintlock pistols. Carefully she primed them with black powder and then, wrapping two balls in small fragments of cloth, shoved them home with the small ramrod. Carefully she put them aside, then turned to the large bag.

From it she pulled a fashionable dark blue dress, then one by one all the other garments that a young woman of fashion would be likely to wear. The clerk, she remembered suddenly, had been bewildered by a young man buying such garments, but he had not argued, for the price was high—taking Laddie's meager store of cash nearly to the last farthing.

She stared at the dress, stroking the fine material, and then she faltered—but in the silence as her fears rose, she seemed to hear Rev. Kelly's voice whispering: *Though an host should encamp against me, my heart shall not fear!* She tossed the dress down, stripped out of her male attire quickly, and in a few minutes she stood there, dressed in women's clothes for the first time in months. The freedom and looseness of the dress seemed strange to her, and she whirled and laughed as the skirt rose gracefully. There was no mirror except for the small one fixed over the washstand that some of the men used at times for shaving, but she donned the small bonnet with the flowing veil and stared into the mirror.

Several curls escaped the bonnet, ringing her face, and she had not trimmed her eyelashes in weeks, so they curled up over her large eyes. "I must say, Miss Sampson—you look quite ravishing!" Then she laughed shortly and threw her old clothes into the bag. The two pistols she carefully placed in the belt of the dress, far back at her sides so that they were covered by the short stylish red jacket which she put on.

She ran to the door, opened it, and after driving the team out, shut and locked it. Then she drove toward the jail, her jaw set and her heart steady with purpose.

The dropping temperature bit into her, even through the thick clothing, but she was glad, for the weather had driven most of the citizens indoors, and the streets were practically empty. She drove boldly up to the very door of the red brick building, got down quickly and tied the team to a hitching post. She retrieved the purse she had bought and, conscious of abandoning the masculine swagger she had picked up in past months, walked through the front door, her heart beating evenly.

"Why—wot's this?" The same burly corporal rose up from his chair as she entered, and he looked at her so hard that she was sure for one heartbeat that he remembered her. But he merely looked baffled and said, "You shouldn't be here, Miss!"

"Oh, that's quite all right, Corporal," she said sweetly, in the most feminine voice she could muster, "I have a pass to see Nathan Winslow." She smiled at him through the veil and took the sealed envelope out of the handbag.

He stared at her, then shook his beefy face from side to side. "I can't do that!" He looked nervously to his right and called out, "Lieutenant Fitzwilliam!"

The officer had been lying down on a cot, and he came to his feet slowly; then as he saw Laddie, straightened up and retrieved his coat from the peg on the wall. "What's this, Corporal?"

"Lady says she's got a pass to see Winslow."

Fitzwilliam had been buttoning his tunic—but he paused and stared at her, then shook his head. "That's quite impossible!"

Laddie held it out and said, "You refuse to honor an order from General Gage?"

The name seemed to shock the officer, for he suddenly arched his back and his pale face flushed red in lamplight. "Why—uh—I mean, certainly *not!*" He gingerly took the envelope, broke the seal, then extracted the paper inside. His mobile features revealed the shock that the note gave him, and he said at once in a conciliatory voice, "My apologies, Miss Howland. Of course, you may see the prisoner. I'll take you up myself."

"Thank you, Lieutenant," Laddie said, and took his arm. He said, "Corporal, I'll remain upstairs until this lady is ready to leave."

"Yes, sir!"

As she followed the officer up the stairs, she noted that the two privates, who had been playing cards, were watching with covert eyes, and she knew as soon as the officer was out of sight, the three of them would buzz with talk, but she put the thought of them from her mind.

"We have to keep a close watch, Miss Howland," Lieutenant Fitzwilliam said. He was burning with curiosity, and said carefully, "The prisoner—he's . . . ?"

"We—were to be married!" Laddie brought a sob into her voice and covered her face with her handkerchief.

"Oh—I—I'm sorry . . . !" Fitzwilliams muttered, then took a key as he paused before a heavy oak door fastened with a huge padlock and chain. As he inserted the key, he said apologetically, "You may see the prisoner alone—I'll be right here, so call when you're ready to leave. I'm afraid I must examine your handbag."

He looked through the bag, then pulled the lock free, swung the door open, saying, "Winslow! Miss Howland is here to see you!"

Laddie was behind the officer, who was a very tall man, and her first glimpse of Nathan came when he shifted and moved around her to the door. Nathan's face when she saw it was filled with joy, and then he looked full at her, and instantly there was a change. Laddie knew that the officer was watching, and she said, "Nathan!" and threw herself into his arms, so that he had to catch her. She clung fiercely to him until she heard Fitzwilliam sigh, and then the ponderous door swung to with a bang and the padlock rattled noisily.

Instantly Laddie pulled back and looked up into Nathan's bewildered eyes. He said harshly, "What sort of game is this? Who are you?"

Laddie reached up, yanked her hat off and grinned up at him. "Laddie Smith at your service!" She saw his mouth spring open and his eyes opened wide.

"Laddie!" he gasped. "I can't believe—!"

She shook her head and whispered fiercely, "That Redcoat is out there with his ear glued to the door, so don't talk so loud." He was still staring at her in unbelief, so she said with a smile, "I make a pretty good-looking girl in all this, don't I, Nathan? I think that fool lieutenant wanted to *kiss* me!" She pulled at the dress, adding, "This rig and all this padding is killing me! I don't see how women can stand to wear such clothes!"

"Laddie—you shouldn't be here!" Nathan came out of the shock that held him, and shook his head sternly. "I know you want to help, but there's no way. They'll hang you right beside me if—!"

"Nathan, I didn't come to get hanged!" Laddie snapped. "Now, listen to me—there's an officer out there, and downstairs there's a corporal and two privates. I've got the buggy right outside, and when we get out of here, we jump in and I'd like to see them catch us till we get through the lines!"

He stared at the fire in the dark eyes and said, "But they're all armed, Laddie."

"So are we!" Laddie reached inside the coat and pulled the two pistols out with a flourish. "Primed and ready to shoot!"

For the first time a light of hope leaped to his eyes, and he reached out and took one. Examining the load, he said with excitement, "By the good Lord—we just might make it!"

She nodded and said quietly, "That's right, Nathan—by the good Lord."

He shot a quick look at her, then suddenly dropped his head. He stood there struggling for a long moment, then lifted his face and sorrow was in his eyes. "I—I'd given up on God, Laddie."

"But He hasn't given up on you!" Laddie smiled. "Now, we've got to wait a few minutes; then we'll call the lieutenant in. Let me tell you what we're going to do . . ."

She spoke rapidly, and when she finished he said quickly, "I think we can do it!"

"All right, but we'd better wait a few minutes."

In the pause that followed, he looked at her and said, "Laddie, I—I've thought a lot about you these last few hours."

"You mean about Abigail!" she shot back instantly, then was sorry for it.

"Of her, too, of course, but that's different. I mean, I've thought of you, and of all I hated to leave, why, I guess my family was first and by the Lord, I hated to leave you!"

"Did you, Nathan?"

"Yes." He reached out and grabbed her by the hair as he had at the creek in the woods, and he grinned suddenly, saying, "You're too pretty to be a boy, Laddie!" He laughed and gave her hair a harder tug as a thought struck him. "Why couldn't you have been a girl? Then we could have fallen in love and I wouldn't have gotten in all this mess!"

She gasped and pulled away, her face flaming. "Will you keep your hands off me!" She turned her back, and her breathing was shallow as she said, "Tell me how you got caught."

He told her how he had gone to Charles first, and had stayed there all day to keep out of sight of the patrols. Then, after dark, he'd gone to Abigail's; he ended by saying "So when I came out of the Howlands' a patrol was there and they picked me up."

"They were waiting for you?"

She turned to see a pain cross his face. "Yes," he said, and then said, "I think a servant at the Howlands' must have seen me."

She studied him, but said only, "Best to think that." Then she picked up her bonnet, tied it on, and arranged the veil. "I think you can call Lieutenant Fitzwilliam in now."

"All right." He walked to the door, and banging on it called out, "Lieutenant! Miss Howland is ready to go!"

He positioned himself to the side of the door, while holding one of the pistols in his left hand. When the door swung open, he did not wait, but reached out with a long arm, grabbed the officer by the jacket and pulled him inside in one smooth motion. Fitzwilliam found himself looking directly into the muzzle of a pistol, and the blue eyes that peered over it seemed no less threatening than the firearm held in the man's hand!

"Redcoat, you've got a very, very small chance to live," Nathan said quietly. "I'm a dead man, so I've got nothing to lose. Now, do you want to live—or not?"

Fitzwilliam's throat gave a convulsive swallow, and sweat popped out on his brow. He stared into Nathan's eyes and saw death, so he nodded quickly. "I'll do—anything! Just don't kill me!" he pleaded.

"All right, I promise you, if you do exactly what I tell you, you'll not be harmed. Now, you and I are going to the top of the stairs, and you're going to call the corporal. Tell him the lady is ill, and you want him to come upstairs."

"All right!"

The officer moved nervously as Nathan prodded him with the pistol, and when they got to the top of the stairs, Nathan opened the door, then placed the muzzle right under Fitzwilliam's ear, At once he called out loudly, "Corporal Dietz! The lady is ill! Come up and help me with her!"

"Now, back to the cell," Nathan said, and they moved back inside. Nathan said, "Put that pistol to his ear, Laddie, and shoot him if he blinks!"

They waited as Corporal Dietz dashed into the room—straight into the muzzle of Nathan's weapon. His mouth dropped open, but Nathan gave him no chance to think. He said, "Soldier, you want to live?"

Dietz hesitated, and there was a loud CLICK as Nathan pulled the hammer back, and the muzzle suddenly seemed very large to the corporal. He gasped, "Don't shoot!"

Nathan stared at him, then said harshly, "I'll tell you what I've told the lieutenant—if you do as you're told, you'll live. They can only hang me once, so I'll put a bullet in your brain if you even blink!"

The corporal nodded quickly, and Nathan moved back. "Lieutenant, take off your clothes."

"What?"

CLICK. The pistol that Laddie held to the officer's head cocked, and he at once cried out, "No!" and then began stripping off his uniform.

"Against the wall, both of you—Laddie, shoot them down if they move!" Nathan quickly undressed and put on the uniform of Fitzwilliam. When he buttoned up the tunic, he said, "All right, on your belly, Lieutenant!" Ignoring the officer's protests, he took the cords that Laddie had brought in the purse, then gagged him with a piece of cloth.

When Dietz stared stupidly at the officer, Laddie moved in front of him. "Pick me up, you stupid ox!" He blinked, but obeyed. As soon as she was in his arms, she pressed the muzzle of her flintlock directly over his heart and covered it with her coat. "Be pretty messy if this goes off, won't it?"

"And I'll be right behind you, Corporal," Nathan said. He picked up the purse Laddie had brought and shoved his weapon inside, then pointed the invisible flintlock at Dietz. "We're going down, and you're going to say to the guards, 'Both of you, go up quickly and guard the prisoner! The Lieutenant and I have to get the lady to a doctor!' You got that?"

"And tell them to keep that door locked tight until the two of you get back," Laddie added. She pressed the pistol hard against the thick chest and said, "I think the corporal is going to say his piece real well."

"Let's go," Nathan stated hurriedly, and he followed Dietz out of the door, then locked it carefully, putting the key in his pocket. "All right, we'll go down. Do it quick, and you've got a fair chance of staying out of hell for a little longer!"

They went down the stair in a rush, and Nathan kept his face turned away from the end of the room where he caught a glimpse of the two privates. Dietz performed as if his life depended upon it! He gave a stentorian yell that rattled the windows: "Get up to the prisoner, you two! Me and the lieutenant gotta get the lady to a doctor!" He dove for the door, screaming, "And don't open that cell for nobody till we get back!"

Nathan followed on his heels, and slammed the door, but not before he heard the soldiers running across the room and up the stairs. "Get in the back—on your face!" he commanded Dietz as Laddie unhitched the team and sprang to the seat.

"You gonna kill me!" Dietz protested, but Nathan forced him into the coach, face down in the back.

"We'll let you go if you keep your mouth shut! Drive on, Laddie!"

The horses leaped at the touch of Laddie's whip, and those few people who had braved the cold were surprised to see a carriage driving so fast along the icy streets.

Three hours later, Corporal Dietz found himself afoot and unharmed, but he could curse only in a whisper, for he was so close to the enemy lines he knew he'd be picked up. He slogged wearily back toward town, trying to make up a story that would satisfy the officers, but halfway there, decided that there *was* no such story. He thought better of returning, decided to become an ex-member of the King's forces, and went to the harbor where a certain ship was leaving at dawn for Calcutta.

As soon as they dumped Dietz and he disappeared down the road, Laddie said, "Nathan, I've got to get out of these clothes!"

"Well, you won't be near so pretty—but I guess you got a right to do just about anything you please." She grabbed the sack and sprinted into the woods behind a large oak tree, out of Nathan's line of vision. Her teeth were chattering as she changed back to her customary garb. Then she stuffed the feminine clothing in the sack and climbed back into the seat.

"That's better."

He didn't move, but sat there in the moonlight, staring out at the hills. The silence ran on, making her nervous, and finally he turned to her and said in an odd voice, "Sun's coming up pretty soon." He cleared his throat, then looked at her. "Thought it'd be my last one. Would have been, Laddie, except for you."

She shifted slightly, then met his eyes. "Well, that makes us even, doesn't it?"

"No, it doesn't." When she stared at him, he smiled and said, "I didn't risk anything when I got you out of the snow—but you stuck your neck in a noose for me tonight."

Laddie looked at him, then said quietly, "We better go, Nathan."

He stared at her. "You don't want thanks, do you, Laddie? But

I'll never forget it. Remember what you said once, the old Indian custom—If somebody saves your life, you belong to that person always?" His eyes held hers, and he said huskily, "So, I guess we kind of belong to each other somehow, don't we, Laddie?"

She couldn't speak for the lump in her throat until they had moved along for a few hundred yards, then she whispered, "I guess if you say so, Nathan, we must!"

He put his hand out, and her small hand was swallowed in his. "That's the way it is, then," he said as he released her. "Now, where you think we better go?"

"Why, I forgot to tell you, Nathan, we're on our way to catch up with General Knox. He's on his way to Fort Ticonderoga to get enough cannon to run the Redcoats out of Boston!"

He grinned at her, and said, "Guess I better change clothes, too, Laddie, or he'll shoot me for a lobsterback!" Then he laughed and said, "Ticonderoga, here we come!"

CHAPTER SEVENTEEN

CRISIS AT HALF MOON

★ ★ ★ ★

Laddie and Nathan caught up with General Knox three days later, and after he had listened to their story, he had stared at Laddie, finally saying, "I'm glad you're going to be along on this trip, Sergeant Smith. Getting this character out of jail took courage and initiative—but I've got the feeling this job we've got now is going to be *worse!*"

They pushed on as fast as the men could go, and at first the journey had been a joy to Laddie. She had reveled in the unexpected vistas of mountainous country, the vast, silent forests of New York State blanketed with fluffy, fast-melting snow. Nathan was never far from her side, and the two of them shared the campfire at night. He said little about Abigail; his close brush with death seemed to have freed him from the heaviness that he had carried, and at the same time made him more thoughtful. Often they would read Laddie's Bible long into the night, and Knox sometimes would stalk by, stare down at them, a puzzled light in his sharp eyes. He cared for nothing but guns and his idol, General Washington, so he was fascinated at the pleasure they seemed to get out of the old book.

The trip was uneventful until just outside of Albany. As they crossed a stream, a section of thin ice gave way, and Laddie plunged into the freezing waters up to her waist. Nathan had helped her out, saying, "We better build a fire and get you into some dry clothes."

"Oh, we'll camp in an hour," she had said. "I can wait until then."

It had been a poor decision, and all night she shivered, unable to shake off the biting cold that gripped her bones. The next day she had a slight fever and by night had begun to cough. Nathan watched her silently, unable to help, and on the second day, her temperature jumped and she couldn't eat. By late that afternoon, when they arrived in a small village called Half Moon, where the Mohawk and the Hudson met, she was so weak that Nathan practically carried her the last two miles. He wrapped her in blankets beside a fire that some of the men made, and sought out Knox.

"Sir, Laddie's got to have a doctor."

Knox shook his head, and gave a dubious look at the small settlement consisting of no more then twenty houses. "Not likely there'll be one here—but go see what you can find."

Nathan went into the village and asked a tall man who was chopping wood, "Is there a doctor in this town?"

"Doctor? No—nearest one is up river at Saratoga." He looked carefully at Nathan and asked, "You an army man?"

"Yes. This is Captain Knox's company." He studied the man carefully, for they had encountered quite a few ardent loyalists who hated them on sight. "We're going to Ticonderoga to get guns for General Washington."

The level gaze of the tall man did not waver; then he smiled and said, "Is that a fact? Wal, I hope you git enough to blow them lobsterbacks clean back to England! I'm Ezra Parker."

Nathan shook the hard hand that was offered. "Nathan Winslow. Most of the village feel like you do?"

"For a fact. We had a few Tories, but they felt so out of place they moved out. Whut's this about a doctor? You sick?"

"No, but we got a sick sergeant. Needs help bad."

Parker said slowly, "Wal, now, most of us use Sister Greene when we get hurt or sick."

"Sister Greene?"

"She's the preacher's ma." Parker laughed at Nathan's doubtful look, then said, "Don't blame you much for lookin' like that, Winslow, but I tell you true I'd trust Sister Greene's doctorin' a heap more'n I would most o' these sawbones! I got a wagon here, if you want a hand."

Nathan warmed to the man and said, "That'd be a kindness, Ezra."

Parker hitched his team and called to his wife, "Martha—I'm goin' to take a sick soldier to Sister Greene's house!" On the way to the camp, he listened avidly to the news about the war. "Some of our young fellows went when we got word about Lexington. I thought to go myself, but then Martha said to let them as had no children take care of the fighting."

They pulled up beside the fire, and Nathan said, "Stay where you are, Ezra. I'll get the boy." Then he reached down and picked Laddie up in his arms and carried her to the wagon. "Got to get you out of this weather, Laddie," he said, then added cheerfully, "This is Ezra Parker—he says they got a lady in this town that's good as a doctor."

Laddie smiled weakly, but her face was flushed and there was a hoarse rasping in her voice when she said faintly, "Glad to meet you."

Parker glanced at her, then whipped the horses up. "Young feller does look right peaked—but I got a heap of faith in Sister Greene." A thought struck him, and he exclaimed, "It just come to me, Nathan, Miz Greene, she's got a brother who's a general in the army."

"Nathanael Greene from Rhode Island?"

"That's the one. He's one of them Quakers, you know? And so is Sister Greene, and so is her boy, Dan."

"They don't believe in war, I hear?" Nathan said, and cast a doubtful look at Ezra. "They might not favor doing anything for a soldier."

"Ha! You don't know much 'bout them folks! They won't pull no trigger, but I guess Sister Greene would doctor ol' Slewfoot if he turned up at her door sick!"

"You a Quaker, Ezra?"

"Me? No, I'm a varmint!" Parker grinned. "They ain't many Quakers here—maybe thirty. But lots of the rest of us sort of look at Friend Daniel as our preacher. He don't stand fer being called *Reverend* nor no fancy name, so we just call him Friend Dan, even us sinners—of which we got a overabundance in Half Moon."

He drove into the village, down the main street, then turned off into a lane, pointing at a half-timbered house sitting back under a small grove of tall firs. He jumped down, nodded to Nathan as he tied up the team. "Bring 'im on in."

Nathan picked up Laddie, and as he walked up the path, the door opened and a woman came out. "Got a sick man fer you, Sister," Parker said. "This here is Nathan Winslow, and his sergeant has got the ague."

"Bring him in, Friend Nathan," the woman said. She was a tall woman in her fifties, straight and well-formed. Her hair was auburn with just a trace of silver, and there was a calmness in her brown eyes that Nathan liked at once. "We'll put him in the spare room." Nathan walked behind her down a short hall, turned into a small room, and then set Laddie down.

"Get into that bed, young man," Sister Greene said. "I'll come back in a spell with something that'll do thee good." She stared at Laddie and asked in that same even tone, "Thou art a man of God?"

Laddie looked quickly at her, nodded and said, "I'm a Christian."

"Good. Then we both know where thy healing's got to come from." Sister Green turned and opened a drawer, pulled a night shirt out, and handed it to Laddie. "Get into that."

As the woman left, Nathan said, "I'll be back tonight, Laddie, after roll call. You mind Sister Greene, now!"

He turned and left. As he passed Sister Greene, he said, "I don't like the way he looks, Sister."

"I should think not—he's got pneumonia."

Nathan swallowed and stared hard at the woman. "You—you real sure about that?"

"Yes. How long is thy unit staying here?"

"We'll pull out at dawn, but—!"

"Well, thee can leave the young man here."

"I can't do that!"

"He'll die if he's moved." Then in the same calm, even voice, she asked him exactly the same question she had asked Laddie: "Art thou a man of God?"

Nathan turned red and threw an awkward glance at Ezra, who seemed to be enjoying the scene. Finally he shook his head. "I thought I was once, Sister—but now, I guess I'm just kind of a seeker."

The door opened and Nathan was relieved at the interruption.

The man who walked in had the same chiseled features as Sister Greene—the same warm brown eyes and generous lips.

"Friend Dan," Ezra said, "this here is Nathan Winslow. He's done come to dump a sick soldier on you while he goes to play army."

Dan Greene glanced at Parker, and humor lit his eyes and drew a smile to his wide mouth. "Friend Ezra, when thee gets right with God, thee will have a little more tact." He had a deep baritone voice, and there was a solidness in his shoulders, a thickness in his chest that most ministers lacked. He shook hands with Nathan, his grip like a vise, and said, "I trust the sickness is not too bad."

"Pneumonia, Daniel," his mother said. "We'll keep him until Friend Nathan can come back for him."

"It's a lot to ask . . ." Nathan said uneasily. "I know you folks don't hold with armies and fighting—"

"We hold with helping those who need it, Friend Nathan," the man interrupted. "Thee can be assured your friend will get good care." His eyes studied Nathan, and he asked, "Is he your kin?"

Nathan quickly explained how he'd found Laddie, trying to soften the part he'd played, then said, "I lost a brother at Lexington—and Laddie Smith is . . . !"

He paused, and seeing how disturbed he was, Dan said, "Easy to see thee does care for the young man. But even if I say so, he's in the best hands for a man who's bad sick."

Nathan nodded, unable to speak, so he whirled and said, "I'll come back tonight."

Ezra followed him to the wagon, and said little on the way back to camp, for he saw that his new friend was tormented with doubts. When he stopped to let Nathan get out, he said with a plaintive note in his voice, "Guess it's times like this that sinners like you and me wisht we wuz Christians, Nathan. But reckon you got the boy in to folks who know how to get hold of God."

Nathan was worried and depressed all day, and finally when he came back after visiting the Greenes' house that night, he went straight to Knox. "Captain, Laddie's got pneumonia."

"Is it bad, Nathan?"

"I just came from there." His lips were tight and his eyes were miserable in the lamplight. "He was delirious, General—didn't even know me!"

Knox stared at him silently. "I'd like to let you stay with him,

Nathan—but I need every good man I've got."

"I know—I'll be leaving with you in the morning. But it'll be so hard—not knowing if he's dead or alive."

He had left then, and the next morning as the brigade filed through the town in the gray dawn, Nathan cast one last desperate look down the lane to the small house just barely visible in first light, and prayed fervently, *God—help Sister Greene!*

Even as he prayed that prayer, Daniel Greene was looking down the street at the troop. He turned and said to his mother, who was sitting at the table with a Bible open before her, "They're leaving. Don't think they'll be back for weeks, if what I heard is true. With this weather and these roads, those men are in trouble."

Sister Greene looked up at him and said, "I think we're in trouble, too, Daniel."

He gave her a quick look, for he could not remember many times when his mother had admitted having a problem. Her faith was unchanging, like a rock, and he went over to sit down across from her. "What is it, Mother?"

"That young man in there, Daniel."

"Thee thinks he'll die?"

"No. The sickness won't be unto death—but Sergeant Smith has a worse problem than ague or pneumonia." She paused and he waited. Waiting came easy for him, for the Quakers did much of it. Sometimes they would sit for two hours on hard, backless benches waiting until one of the Friends had the Inner Light touch his soul and a message was delivered.

Finally she lifted her eyes and said, "Sergeant Laddie Smith is living a lie, Dan."

"A lie? What sort of lie?"

"About an hour ago I went in, and the fever was so bad I knew I had to use cold packs to bring it down. That's when I found out—when I took his nightshirt off. Sergeant Smith is not a man, Dan. We've got a sick young woman to care for."

He stared at her, unable to believe what he heard. Finally he said, "That's bad! A woman with all those men!"

He got up and walked to look out the window as the last of the troops passed over the hill and disappeared; then he turned and said quietly, "I was mistaken about Winslow. He didn't seem like the sort to do this sort of thing—keep a loose woman."

"Loose or not—we've got to seek God, Daniel, or she'll be a

dead woman. I'll get the body healed—but thee must see to her soul."

Friend Daniel Greene said nothing, but doubt filled his brown eyes. Finally he said heavily, "God help her—poor child!" Then he got up and left the warmth of the fire, walking for the rest of the morning in the freezing cold.

PART THREE

GUNS OVER BOSTON

★ ★ ★ ★

CHAPTER EIGHTEEN

FRIEND DANIEL AND LADDIE

★   ★   ★   ★

Sometimes the cold gripped so fiercely that she shook in every joint, trying to burrow deeper into the warmth of blankets; then the heat would rise like a tide of fire and she would struggle feebly to throw off the covers. She was down in a cold, dark hole sometimes, being pulled deeper and deeper into an even blacker depth, and she wanted to sink into it—to escape the alternating agony of fire and ice that racked her body.

But every time she began to sink into a welcome oblivion, an insistent voice would come to her, just when she seemed about to slip into the utter depths; it would grow loud and the sound of it would draw her back to the light.

Time was not for her a stream that moved from one point to the other, but a vast ocean with no beginning and no end. Seconds, days, years had no meaning; the only things that marked time were the hands that touched her, bathing her with cool water and holding her head to put a cup of water to her parched lips. And even the voice and the hands were confusing, for in her delirium she somehow came to distinguish between one voice that was soft and quiet and another that was deep and powerful—and sometimes the touch of hands had that same difference.

At last she came out of the darkness, and the bright sunlight streaming in from a window across the room hurt her eyes. She closed them quickly, having glimpsed only a white ceiling and a wall covered with paper ornamented by yellow flowers. Lying there with her eyes shut, her other senses were flooded with signals— cool sheets against her body, the pressure of cool dampness on her forehead, a sour taste in her mouth, the smell of fresh bread baking, the acrid scent of camphor—and the sound of a man's voice.

The voice was very close but so quiet that she thought at first he was speaking with someone else in the room, but suddenly she realized with a faint shock that he was praying. Accustomed as she was to elevated language from ministers in pulpits (which she unconsciously imitated in her own prayers, to some degree), she was caught by the fact that whoever it was spoke with God on most familiar terms!

" . . . and so, Lord, it's been a hard fight, hasn't it?" The deep voice suddenly chuckled, and added, "I came pretty close to doubting Thee a time or two—but Thee never fails. Well, now, it's clear that Thee has pulled this young woman out of the pit as a brand plucked from the burning, and I thank Thee for keeping her alive— but Lord, we've got to do something about her soul! Lord, I'm not much of a preacher, but nothing is too difficult for Thee—so now that Thou has taken away the disease, I'm going to believe that the soul of this sinner will be made whole. And, Lord, when there's— well, friend, so thee is awake?"

He broke off suddenly as he found himself looking directly into a pair of black eyes that had opened and were regarding him intently. He had been holding a damp cloth on her head, and the position had brought his face within inches of hers, so always after that when she thought of him, she saw him this way, framed in her vision, his square face brown and tan. He had thick brown hair and heavy eyebrows the same color over deep-set brown eyes, and she could see clearly the dent in his straight nose and wonder what had broken it. He was a handsome man with very regular features, and a serene expression characterized both his face and his manner.

"I'd guess thee's a little dry," he said when she tried to speak and found her mouth parched. He removed the cloth from her head, picked up a cup, then put his arm under her shoulders and pulled her into a sitting position. "Drink as much of this as thee can."

She was so thirsty that she put both her hands on his, and in her eagerness spilled water down the white gown she was wearing. When it was gone, he gave her more; then she said in a voice rusty with disuse, "Thank you."

"Well, how does thee feel?"

She considered the question, then nodded. "I—feel weak." She looked around the room, then turned her eyes back on him. "How long have I been here?"

"How long? Well, they brought thee here five days ago. Does thee remember that?"

She suddenly remembered the room and nodded. "It's not clear—wasn't there a woman here?"

"My mother. She'll be back soon. Are thee hungry?"

The question hit her like a blow, activating her appetite, and she said urgently, "Yes!"

He laughed and got up. "I'll fix some eggs. It'll be nice not to have to pour broth down thee with a spoon for a change." He got up, adding as he left, "Don't try to get up yet. Thee would probably fall and break thy neck!"

He was gone for some time, and Laddie tried once to get out of bed. The room seemed to tilt, and she fell back and lay with her eyes closed, appalled at her weakness. He came back with a wooden tray containing a plate of scrambled eggs and a large glass of milk. "Can thee sit up and eat, or shall I feed thee?" he asked.

"Oh, I can eat!" she said quickly, and tore into the delicious eggs. She ate it all, and almost licked the plate, but felt his eyes on her. "I'm so hungry," she said as he took the tray away and set it down on the nightstand.

"Thee can have something more solid in a few hours." He sat down and gazed at her with a quizzical look in his eyes. "It's God's own mercy thee didn't die, young woman."

Young woman!

Laddie gave a gasp, and involuntarily she cried out, "You know . . . !" He took her meaning at once, and his mouth tightened as he nodded slowly. Something in his direct stare disturbed her, and she felt a flush creeping up her throat. *He thinks I'm a loose woman, living with the soldiers!* she thought instantly. There were in the young army, camp followers—low women who moved from man to man with no shame.

Her hand rose to her cheek, and Daniel Greene looked at her. *She looks so innocent!* he thought. The sickness had thinned her face, making her large eyes seem enormous. He found himself admiring the girl's beauty—which startled him considerably! He was the most eligible bachelor in the county, and had long ago grown in-

different to the charms of young women; so many had smiled at
him.

*I think I've gotten attached to her—like I did to the sick kitten I nursed
back to health,* he thought. *But she is a fetching girl—and she looks so
young and innocent!* His experience with loose women was practically nonexistent, there being none in Half Moon—at least of the
professional type—but he had always thought of them as being
painted and lewd in manner. The girl he stared at had a dewy
expression in her eyes, and a rosy flush that colored her slender
neck and rose to give color to her smooth cheeks. He had seen a
painting of the Madonna once in a museum in Philadelphia, and
she looked more like that portrait of the Virgin Mary than a Jezebel!

She was twisting the sheet nervously, and suddenly she looked
at him and whispered, "Does—everyone know—about me, I
mean?"

"No. Just my mother and myself." He saw the relief in her eyes
and was puzzled. *Why should a woman who lives with soldiers even care
what people think? Maybe the officers wouldn't let her go with the troops
if they knew her sex.*

"I'm sorry to be so much trouble," she said quietly. "Maybe I'll
be well enough to leave soon."

"The soldiers won't be back for at least three weeks, maybe
more," Greene said. He saw the distress that crossed her face and
took it to mean she was longing for the private that had brought
her. He searched for his name, found it, and said, "I promised
Winslow we'd care for thee until the army comes back through with
the guns."

Greene paused, and there was a change in his face. "Of course,
we didn't know then—" He broke off, not knowing how to end his
statement, and to his annoyance found that his own face was beginning to glow. He got up hastily, took the tray, and said, "I'll
bring thee some hot water and towels. I'm sure thee must want to
clean up."

Two hours later, his mother came in. "Well, she woke up," he
said tersely.

There was a shortness in his words that drew her attention.
"What's wrong, Daniel? Something bothers thee about the girl?"

Running his fingers through his crisp brown hair, he shook his
head, then gave her an odd look. "There's something strange about
her, Mother," he said. "She looks so—*innocent!* But she can't be—
not living as she does."

Carrie Greene was Quaker to the bone, and if she had ever felt that God was moving in her spirit, she felt it now as she stood there staring at her son. He was the joy of her life—strong, as his father had been; from his boyhood, she had seen the fierce desire to serve God grow stronger until now he was, if anything, *too* single-minded. She had wondered once if he was so otherworldly that he gave too little thought to simple earthly things. She longed for grandchildren, but he had never shown an interest in any of the young women who practically announced their willingness to share his life. He was a fine farmer, but he performed those duties routinely, and he cared nothing for the prosperity that had come as a result of his skills.

I've not seen him so troubled, she thought suddenly, watching him pace the floor, and his agitation disturbed her. "I'll see if she needs anything." Anything that touched this son of hers touched her, and she could see that the young woman who lay in their house had managed to break through the tough shell of independence that her son had built around himself.

Slipping into the room, she found the girl asleep, but bathed and with her hair brushed. *She looks so young—and so beautiful*, the woman thought, and then: *No wonder Daniel was shaken by her*. She had lived long enough to know that there was something about a bad woman that drew men, and when one of them was as lovely as this one . . . !

Then the eyes opened, and the girl sat up, pulling the covers up to her chin. "Oh—I must have fallen asleep!"

"Well, thee'll sleep a lot for a few days." Sister Greene walked over and put her hand on the smooth forehead, then nodded. "Fever's gone. Thee'll get stronger now." She stared at the square face and into the almond-shaped eyes, trying to see into the spirit of the girl. "I'm Sister Greene. Thee has met my son, Daniel. What's thy name?"

"They—call me Laddie Smith—" She hesitated; then almost involuntarily she said, "But my real name is Julie Sampson." She gasped, shocked to find herself telling this, but there was something in the countenance of the woman who looked down at her that demanded honesty. She said hurriedly, "Please—don't tell anyone my real name. I—I'd be in trouble."

"I believe thee is already in trouble, child," Sister Greene said quietly. "But it will be as thee wishes. My son and I will keep thy secret."

"Thank you, Sister Greene!" Laddie bit her lip, then said, "I'll try not to be a bother until Nathan gets back."

"It'll be no bother." Sister Greene said, and her eyes suddenly seemed distant to Laddie, and for a long moment she appeared to be listening to some unheard voice. Then she looked into Laddie's eyes and said evenly, "I believe God sent thee to us. For what purpose, I have no word yet—but I will pray that the Light will be given." She suddenly stooped and kissed Laddie on the cheek, and a smile parted her lips. "Rest, now, and we'll talk later."

She left the room, and while Laddie wiped away the tears that had leaped to her eyes over the unexpected caress—the first she'd had from a woman since her mother had died—Sister Greene went back to find her son staring moodily out the window.

"I can see why the child disturbed thee, Daniel," she said at once, and there was a furrow on her smooth forehead. "There's something bound up in her heart."

"She's no child!"

"Well, not physically, I know, but there's a childlike quality in her—and I've had just a tiny word about her in my spirit. We must be very careful with this little one, son."

The two looked at each other, and finally Dan said, "I agree. We spend too much time on the ninety and nine—but this lost sheep has been put in our house for a purpose." He glanced toward the room where she lay, and added, "She's in love with Nathan Winslow—that's plain enough." The thought disturbed him somehow, and he got up and walked out of the room without bidding her farewell.

He's never done that before! she thought, and she too looked toward the room, wondering what changes could be thrust into her small world by the visitor who lay there.

In the days that followed, Laddie was glad that Nathan had left her pack, for it contained her journal—and she found it a relief to pour her heart out on the pages, saying those things that she dared not say aloud. One morning she sat at the table in her room, writing as the first rays of the sun peeped over the eastern hill and cast rosy gleams across her face:

December 27, 1775
It seems impossible that I've been here more than three

weeks! I remember how weak I was when I first came out of the fever, how Friend Daniel had to *carry* me to the table to eat; then later he would let me lean on his arm, practically carrying me on short walks across the floor. But yesterday, I outran him as we walked through the woods! He had a worried look on his face, and he called out, "Thee must be careful!" But I just laughed and called him a slowpoke!

They are so different! All the time I've been here, and they've never asked why I came here dressed like a man. Sometimes Friend Daniel will *almost* ask—but then he draws back—almost like he's *afraid* to know why I do it.

And it hurts me a lot not to tell them. Maybe I will soon. I guess I've been waiting for them to ask, and they've been waiting until *I* was ready—but it's been a strain despite their kindness.

They love God—both of them. Everything in their lives is based on that. They read the Bible all the time, it seems, and they pray more than I thought anybody *could* pray! They make me feel so worthless!

And they think I'm bad. That hurts so much! Before I leave here, I must tell them the whole story—I love them so much—and I can't bear to think they believe such things of me—though I can't blame them, for I know how it looks.

I went to church with them—only they call it "meeting." Everyone thinks I'm a man, so I had to sit with Dan and the men, while Sister Greene sat with the women. They both said later that it bothered them, so I don't think I'll go back.

We sat there for an hour and nobody said a word! Then a woman got up and said that God had spoken to her, and she gave a talk. Then there was another long silence; then Dan got up and preached. He is a real preacher! He's so quiet, usually, but he gets louder when he's preaching, and I felt the presence of the Lord like I never have in church!

I have to write this down. Several times I almost put it in this journal, but it sounded—funny. But now I'm sure.

Friend Daniel is in love with me.

That looks so—so *crazy* as I read the words, but it's so!

He doesn't know it himself—but I think his mother does. She's worried, and no wonder—her minister son falling in love with a wild girl who runs around with soldiers!

I don't know when I first noticed this—but I think it started because he took care of me when I was weak. He'd get attached to anything that was helpless! And as little as I know about men, he knows even *less* about women!

I remember the first time I saw how he was seeing me as a woman. I was staggering along beside him, weak as a cat, and he was guiding me. His mother was gone, and we were both laughing as my rubber legs kept bending and then I nearly fell, and he picked me up like I was a little girl, saying, "Enough of that!" and he carried me to a chair, but just before he put me down, he suddenly stopped and looked down at me, and I saw it come to him—I mean, that I *wasn't* a little girl! I was a woman wearing only a very thin robe, and I had my arms around his neck, and both of us stopped laughing. It was so quiet that I could hear my own heart pounding, and my silly face started burning like it always does when I get flustered! And his did, too! He put me down quick—like I was made of white-hot steel— and almost ran out of the room!

Since then, he's been—different. He talks to me a lot— mostly about the Bible, but he acts so awkward! Seems terrified to touch me!

And I have to put this down, too—I feel strange about him! I've loved Nathan so long, and then this Quaker minister holds me one time—and I have to put it down, that I'm just as nervous about *him* as he is about *me*!

I wish Nathan would come back! I'm so confused about *everything*.

Suddenly Laddie dropped her journal, ran to the bed and threw herself across it, her body shaken with sobs. She lay there weeping for a long time, not knowing why, unable to account for the sudden grief and fear that racked her. Finally, she got up, washed her face, and put the journal safely away.

"Laddie? Time to eat breakfast!"

The sound of Dan's voice came through the door, and her hands trembled as she reached out to open it. *Don't be a fool, Julie Sampson!* she thought fiercely. Then, lifting her head, she put a smile on her lips and left the room.

CHAPTER NINETEEN

NEW YEAR

★ ★ ★ ★

The last day of the year brought no relief from the numbing cold that had frozen the rivers and weighed the trees down with loads of glittering ice, but that did not deter those who had decided to see the new year in with a New Year's party.

"Thee missed Christmas," Dan said at breakfast, "which is what happens when thee takes up with Quakers—but I think we can safely go to the party tonight."

"Why, Daniel, thee has never gone to one of those parties before!" Sister Greene stopped pouring maple syrup over a pancake to stare at him in astonishment. "Some of the men will be drinking."

"Be a good chance to bear witness against it. I don't care for such things, but Julie would like it."

"Please—don't call me that!" Laddie said instantly, and then she was sorry for her sharpness and added, "It's just that if you use it to address me, Friend Daniel, you might let it slip in front of someone."

"Sorry." He shrugged and said, "Would thee like to go? I understand there's music and games."

"Wouldn't it be boring for you?"

"Oh, it won't hurt me—Laddie." He smiled and glanced at his mother. "Maybe thee should go as well, Sister Greene. Taste the fleshpots—see what they're like. No telling what thee has been missing all these years!"

"I believe I'll let thee do the tasting, son," his mother smiled. "One of us needs to keep in good standing with the Lord!"

Laddie had been bored, and as they walked over the snowy crust to the party, they laughed at a deer who scared itself by coming out of the woods face-to-face with them. It had jumped straight into the air, whirled and gone bounding away in that amazing graceful motion that is half run and half flight.

"Oh, beautiful!" Laddie cried out.

"It is. I can't shoot one to save my life." Dan gave her a smile and said, "Funny, I can kill a steer that I've raised quick enough—but I just can't shoot a deer."

"You would if you got hungry enough, I guess."

He nodded, then said, "This war—it's a bad thing for Friends."

"Bad for everyone."

"Yes—but some men—" he glanced at her and mentioned the name idly—"men like Nathan, why, they don't worry about killing in war."

She shook her head, and there was sadness in her voice. "Yes, he worries about it."

He considered that, then shrugged. "I suppose thee knows him—but with us, it's different. We don't believe in killing."

"Even to stay free, Friend Daniel?" She stopped and looked strangely at him. "You and your mother are the finest Christians I've ever known—but a lot of men are going to die for this new country. And—please don't be angry with me, Daniel—" She put her hand lightly on his arm, and despite her male garb and short hair, he thought he had never seen anything more lovely than her face framed against the snow. "You will enjoy the liberty that other men died to win for you."

"I'm not asking them to do it!" He was angry and turned away, but she caught up with him, again pulling at his arm.

"I don't fault you, Friend Daniel," she said, and then she smiled in the growing darkness, and added gently, "You and your mother are closer to God than anyone I've ever met. No matter what, I'll never forget you after we leave here."

He walked along beside her, shocked at the way her words had rocked him. *After we leave here.* She spoke no more of the war, and he only half heard what she said. He was thinking how empty the house would be without her. *Only a month—and she's the first thing I look for when I go into the house after being away!*

The party was in progress when they got to the schoolhouse. The desks were moved, and a line of tables along one wall was loaded with food and drinks. Over forty people were there, almost all of them young people, and over to one side several musicians were tuning up fiddles and dulcimers.

"Why, Friend Daniel!" A small well-formed girl in a pale blue dress left a group by the refreshment tables and came over to greet them. She had sparkling blue eyes and the most beautiful complexion Laddie had ever seen. "I can't *believe* you've actually come to a party—but it's about time." She turned to Laddie, her bright eyes taking in the neat uniform and the clearcut features. "And this is the soldier you've been keeping from all of us?"

"If thee would come to meeting, thee would have met our visitor. Laddie Smith, this is Faith Thomas. Faith, Sergeant Laddie Smith."

"You come with me, Sergeant," the girl said with a bewitching grin. She took Laddie's arm, saying with a toss of her head, "Friend Daniel, you go sit with the elders—Sergeant Smith is mine for the night."

Laddie had no choice, then, but to follow, and casting one helpless look at the minister, she soon found herself being introduced to a wide-eyed group of young people. The names came too fast for her, but she noted with a streak of humor, that the girls were impressed with the uniform; any presentable-looking young "male" creates a stir among the girls of a small community.

The young men were interested in the war, and they pressed close, asking about the army and the battles, but that stopped when the musicians struck up a tune, and Faith Thomas said, "You'll have to excuse us. Sergeant Smith has the first dance with me."

Laddie was stunned, but there was no time to protest, for the girl had stepped close, held out her hands, and suddenly they were dancing. Laddie had danced little, but she had observed much, and a strong natural sense of rhythm came to her aid, so that soon the two of them were moving easily across the floor.

What a flirt! Laddie thought as the young woman smiled and moved closer, whispering softly. Laddie was tall for a girl, and Faith had to look up, which gave her a chance to display her smile and her beautiful eyes to good effect. She said, "You're so young to be a soldier! And—I must say it, even if you think I'm too bold—you look so handsome in your uniform!"

Laddie said what the girl wanted to hear, and as they danced another dance, then a third, she began to be amused. They went to the table several times, and one tall young man attempted to claim Faith, but she said, "Oh, later, Hawk."

"Who is he?" Laddie asked. She looked over the girl's shoulder and got an angry stare from the young man that sobered her. "Is that your young man, Miss Thomas?"

"Oh, he thinks he is," she said with a smile; then she shrugged and said, "He's jealous—but he doesn't own me."

Dan had moved to one of the chairs by the wall, taking a seat by Ezra Parker, who had stared at him in amazement. "Preacher! I never thought I'd see the day."

Dan had grinned at him. "Thee won't come to meeting, Friend Ezra, so I've come to convert thee at a party."

"Well, fly right at it!" Ezra had a fondness for the young minister, and a deep respect that he gave to few men. He made no claims to be religious, but he had said often, *If I ever go get religion—it'll be the brand that young feller's got!* He sat there, and the two of them talked as the party went on. Several times Ezra excused himself, left the room and came back smelling strongly of alcohol, and most of the young men in the room did the same. As it grew late, Ezra brought Dan some apple cider, saying, "Don't reckon that'll hurt yore conscience, will it?"

"No. It's fine."

He spoke quietly, and Ezra followed his gaze to the couples on the floor. Then he said gently, "That young soldier—he was right sick, I hear?"

"Very ill, Friend Ezra."

The light blue eyes of Parker gleamed, and he said gently, "Well, he's apt to be a heap sicker 'fore long, Friend Daniel."

"What's that?" The Quaker stared at the tall, lanky man. "What does thee mean, Friend Ezra?"

"Wal, you know lots of Bible, Reverend, but you ain't too swift on young folks and partyin'—'course, you ain't had no practice. You ain't seen what's been shapin' up, have you?"

"I don't understand."

"Why, look at that!" Ezra pointed across the room and there was a wicked grin on his lips. "See my boy Hawk? You know he's been keeping company with Faith Thomas. He's already busted up two or three pretty strong young bucks when they come a'sniffin' around her! And looks like that leetle soldier is 'bout to have a dose of the same!"

Dan looked up with a startled expression, and one glimpse of what was happening across the room brought him to his feet, but quickly as he moved, he saw with dismay that it was too late.

Laddie had been amused by the situation, but after an hour of it, suddenly it had seemed silly. As the music ended, she moved with Faith to the table, and started to excuse herself so that she could go sit with Dan, but a rough hand suddenly seized her shoulder, whirling her about, and she found herself staring into the icy eyes of Hawk Parker. He had been drinking, and there was a raw rage in his sharp features.

Laddie struggled to free herself, but there was steel in the grip. "I guess you think that uniform makes you something special?" he said loudly.

"You're drunk, Hawk!" Faith said angrily.

"No, I ain't drunk—just want to let this here pretty boy of a soldier know he can't come around here and steal my girl!"

"Let go of me," Laddie said, struggling to free herself, and she caught a glimpse of Daniel hurrying across the room with alarm on his face. "I don't want . . . !"

"I don't gave a hoot *what* you want!" Hawk yelled, and with the speed of a striking snake he whipped his fist around and struck Laddie in the temple!

Laddie never saw the blow; bright lights flashed suddenly; then she sank into blackness, never feeling the hard floor that she fell back on.

Hawk stared at her with confusion in his eyes. He was very strong and accustomed to fighting strong men, so when his fist sent Laddie sailing back unconscious, he stood there confused by the cries of the women.

Daniel got there too late to stop the blow, but the sight of Laddie lying loosely on the floor with her face reddened by the blow triggered a black rage that he had not thought possible. His hand shot out, and he caught young Parker by the arm, whirling him around.

The liquor had befuddled the young man, and he was glad to see a strong man in front of him. He struck out at the minister wickedly, catching Daniel in the mouth with a tremendous blow, yelling loudly, "You keep out of this, preacher!"

He expected Greene to go down, for he had hit him as hard as he had ever hit any man, but the blow seemed to have no effect! The Quaker simply ignored it, and then he sent a terrible blow that smashed young Parker between the eyes. It drove the light out of his eyes, sent him hurtling back, and when he struck the wall, he was already unconscious.

The sound of Parker crashing into the wall brought sanity back to Greene, and he stood there horrified at the way the young man fell to the floor as if he were boneless.

There was a sudden silence, and then Ezra was beside him, looking down at the still form of his son. There was something like awe in his light blue eyes as he stared at the minister, and then he whistled softly and said, "Well—reckon you done the necessary, Friend Daniel—but I shore never thought any one feller could put the lights out on Hawk with one lick!"

"Is he—all right?" Daniel asked faintly. He felt sick and wanted to leave, for the shame of his violence seared his spirit.

"Oh, he'll have a sore head—but I would have whopped him with an axe handle anyway—for hittin' the soldier when he wasn't ready. He wasn't raised like that!"

Dan whirled and moved to where Laddie lay. He picked her up and carried her out of the room. Not one word was said until he passed through the door; then he heard the room humming wildly.

He was so shaken by the incident that he walked blindly down the lane. He had never struck another man in anger, and his mind swirled with the scene: he saw Parker's face as he reeled backward and hit the wall.

"Let me down!"

"What?" He realized that Laddie was struggling, trying to free herself. He set her down at once, and she swayed and held on to him for support. "I'd better carry thee."

"No! I—I'm just a little dizzy." She stood there, holding lightly to his arm, and they could hear a faint sound of music as the fiddles struck up again. She gave a rueful smile and touched her temple. "Never brought the New Year in like this," she said.

He looked soberly at her and shook his head. "Neither did I."

"What happened—after he hit me?"

He stood there silently, and the silver light of the moon highlighted his features, painting his cheeks and throwing the hollows of his eyes into shadows. "I hit him," he said slowly, and he added after a moment, "I didn't know I had such capacity for hate in me."

She didn't move, but stood there looking up into his face, and what she saw was sorrow. She had heard enough of the Quaker faith to know how important it was for a man never to strike out, and she saw the raw pain in his eyes. "Dan—" she said softly, using his first name unconsciously, "don't feel bad. It was all my fault! I made a fool of myself!"

He didn't answer, and the silence grew heavy, broken only by the sound of a dog barking sharply at some unknown foe. Finally he shook his head and his shoulders drooped. "It's not your fault. I've been tried out before, Julie. All the time I was growing up there were boys who heard that Quakers would never fight—and more than once I've taken a blow in the face—and never hit back. Not until tonight."

She was shocked to see his firm lips tremble, and she whispered, "Dan—Dan, you were just trying to help me!" The pain he felt was so palpable it seemed to be ripping him apart, and she knew that the ugly incident had shaken his faith. She hated herself for provoking this doubt, and she reached up, not conscious of what she was doing, and put her hands on his cheeks. It was the gesture she would have used to comfort a child that had been terribly hurt, and she whispered, "Please don't grieve, Dan! I can't stand to see you hurt like this!"

Her eyes, he saw, were filled with tears, and her closeness suddenly shook him. He had long since mastered his emotions, never allowing them to rule any part of his life—but his guard was down. The raw rage that had exploded had left him empty, and now he was aware only that she was lovely in the moonlight, and that she cared for him.

There was no thought in what he did then. Her hands were warm on his cheeks, her lips half open, and she looked up with pleading in her luminous eyes. He put his arms around her, and she gave him one startled look, but she did not draw back. And when he slowly lowered his head and kissed her, there was a trembling innocence in her lips that shook him. Her hands on his cheeks were suddenly still, but as he held her closer, filled suddenly by a hunger, she put her hands behind his head pulling him close.

When he lifted his lips, she whispered, "Dan . . . !" and then she gave a sob and moved away from him.

The kiss had shaken him worse than the fight, and he stood there struggling with his thoughts. Finally he said, "We'd better get on."

"Yes!" She gave a half gasp, and they walked without speaking. The only sound was the crunch of snow under their feet.

Finally they got to the house, and he stopped her before they went inside. "I'm sorry—that I kissed thee."

She shook her head, and when she lifted her face, he saw the tears had made silver tracks down her cheeks. "I'm ashamed . . ." she whispered, and then she felt the deep sobs rising in her, and she whirled and dashed into the house.

He stood there, staring into the house, and finally he went to bed. But not to sleep. All night he lay there with his eyes open wide, staring blindly at the ceiling. He lived out the scene over and over, and the thought rose to torment him: *But she's another man's woman!* He tried to pray, but the heavens were brass. He cried out in agony to God, but his heart felt dead in his breast.

Laddie wept until there were no tears left, and then she sat staring vacantly out the window at the moonlit landscape. The very peaceful look of the fields and trees were a contrast to the storm that went on inside her.

When morning came, it was a relief to leave the bed, but breakfast was a quiet, strained affair. They looked at one another over the table, and though they smiled and spoke, Sister Greene went still, for she sensed that something had changed, and it brought fear into her heart for the first time she could remember.

They were almost finished with breakfast when there was the sound of a wagon stopping outside. Boots sounded on the steps; then a knock came. "I'll get it, Mother," Daniel said quickly. "I asked Edward Rollins to come by this morning." He moved to the door and opened it, but the greeting that was on his lips failed as he stared at the man who filled the doorway.

"Where's Laddie?"

Nathan's voice was sharp, and then he saw Laddie over Greene's shoulder, and shoved past the minister, his face breaking out into a wild grin. "Laddie! You're all right!" He reached out and grabbed her with a wild hug, not noticing her pale face. "I've been about crazy, Laddie, thinking you might be dead, and here you are, healthy as a bear!"

Laddie swayed as he shook her, and with a smile said, "Nathan—I'm so glad you're back!" Then she turned and looked straight into the eyes of Friend Daniel Greene, and said quietly, "Now I won't have to be a burden to these good people any more!"

CHAPTER TWENTY

THE GUNS OF TICONDEROGA

★ ★ ★ ★

Henry Knox had not lost a pound, insofar as Laddie could tell. She had gone out with Nathan to the camp, and to her surprise, Daniel had accepted Nathan's invitation to go along. As they approached the site, Nathan pointed to where a group of soldiers were working on an enormous gun on a sled. "Look at the general, Laddie," Nathan grinned. "This trip has worn all the rest of us down to skin and bone—but Henry Knox stays fat as a seal!"

"Well, I see you didn't die, Sergeant!" Knox spotted them, and came to smile down at her. His cheeks were red and he was bristling with enormous energy. "By Harry, if I'd known you were going to live, I'd have had you at work rounding up oxen for me!" He gave a look at the worn animals that stood with lowered heads, eating listlessly.

"They're not going to make it, General," Nathan commented. "We've got to have some fresh animals. Maybe General Schuyler can help some more."

General Philip Schuyler, a wealthy New York State patrician, had secured eighty specially built sledges and eighty yoke of oxen. But thawed, mushy ground had hindered the caravan, and finally the snow came. The drivers had had to lash their beasts forward, the sledges slipping and sliding on runners. The capricious weather had tormented them, and now many of the oxen were useless.

"You've been here a month, Sergeant," Knox said. "We need

some patriots to help us get these guns to General Washington. Who would that be?"

Laddie said impulsively, "Captain Knox, I guess you're looking at him. This is Daniel Greene. I think he could get you some help—and he's a nephew of General Nathanael Greene."

"Well! Let me shake your hand, sir!" Knox beamed broadly and pumped Greene's hand vigorously. "Your relative is, in my opinion, the best of our young generals—I know that His Excellency shares that belief. Now, Mr. Greene, we must have oxen!" He gave the minister no chance to speak, but pulled him along the line of sleds, pointing out their virtues as if they were his beloved children. "We have fifty-eight pieces—four-pounders to twenty-four pounders. Beautiful, aren't they? And here is my favorite—" He rested his hand tenderly on one giant and said lovingly, "The men call this one The Old Sow—not a pretty name, but she'll do to shell the Redcoats out of Boston!"

"Sir—" Dan tried to speak, but Knox was a hard man to stop.

"We've brought this ordnance two hundred miles through the worst weather and over the worst roads in America! Everyone said it couldn't be done! And we have twenty-three crates of shot and one barrel of fine-quality British flints—all of which had to be freighted down Lake George in a collection of pirogues and batteaux."

"General Knox," Dan interrupted, "I—I must tell you—that I cannot help in this work." He gave Laddie a reproachful glance, then added, "I am one of the Friends—a Quaker, as you say. And it is against our doctrine to engage in war."

Knox stared at him steadily, then said, "General Greene is a Quaker, but he has thrown himself into the cause."

"I cannot answer for him—only for myself."

Knox's good-natured faced reddened. "I'm not asking you to *fight*—just to help with freighting equipment." He had spoken harshly, but he caught himself, and said reasonably, "Two groups have suffered much at the hands of the English—the Baptists and the Quakers. The Baptists have thrown themselves into this struggle, for they well know that if we do not free this land from English tyranny, they'll be crushed. Your own sect has been persecuted in England and in this country as well. If you will not fight, I call upon you to at least help in this way."

"I cannot do it." Daniel turned and walked away, his back stiff and unyielding.

Knox stared at him, then turned to Laddie. "I don't know what to make of such men!" Then he shrugged and said, "You two do the best you can. I've already sent to the villages close by, but we've *got* to have those oxen! If the British decide to attack, it may all be over!"

He stalked away, shouting furiously at a private who had let one of the cannon shift, then called back, "We'll take two days— have all the oxen you can ready by then. Promise them anything— but get them here!"

"I'll get my things," Laddie said, turning to go, but Nathan stopped her. There was a gleam in his light blue eyes and a quirk of humor turned the corners of his generous mouth upward.

"No, you stay there, Laddie. I'll scout around by myself—but you can do more good where you are. I want you to make that Quaker fight! Somehow there's got to be a way to make a patriot out of Friend Daniel Greene, and I want you to find it!"

January 2, 1776
I've tried to talk to Dan about helping us get the guns to Boston, but he won't do it. Nathan says that the people here won't volunteer, but he said if Dan would help, others would follow. Dan's such a good man—but stubborn!

Laddie stared at the words she'd just written despondently; then she gritted her teeth and began to write again, and there was a grim determination in her face.

I think I know why Dan won't help, and it has nothing to do with his religion. Ever since Nathan came back, Dan's hated me! He thinks that Nathan and I are lovers, and he's jealous! I've suspected for weeks that he has feelings for me, and when he kissed me after the fight, he almost came out and said he loved me. But he thinks I'm bad!
I'm going to tell him the truth! And I have to be honest about this, hard as it is—I think it might make Dan change his mind about helping with the guns if he knew the truth—but it's more than that. When he kissed me, I felt—oh, I don't know *how* I felt! But I do know that if I wasn't in love with Nathan, I'd never find a man that I'd be more likely to love than Dan!

She laid down the pen, carefully closed the journal, and put it away. It was early, but she knew that Dan and his mother took that time of the day to read the Bible and pray. She found them both in the small kitchen and said abruptly, "I have something to tell you both." They looked up, startled, and Laddie felt her face flush, but plunged ahead, "Last year my father died and left me in the charge of my uncle, Aaron Sampson . . ."

They sat there staring at her as she narrated her history, including the parts about Caleb's death, as well as revealing Nathan's love for Abigail Howland. Finally she said, "It's been hard, and I should have told you this a long time ago. You've been so good to me—even though you both thought I was a lewd woman living with soldiers."

It was Dan's turn to grow red, and he glanced at his mother. "I—I can't deny it," he said quietly. Then he looked up with a sudden smile that lighted his face, and the load that had burdened him seemed to roll away. "Thank thee for telling us, Laddie," he said.

"I knew in my spirit thee were not evil," Sister Greene said, and she rose to come over and embrace Laddie. She held her for a long moment, and when she drew back there were tears in her eyes. "I don't fault thee for anything, daughter. God has preserved thee in this strange way."

She turned and left the room abruptly, and Dan said in surprise, "Mother doesn't show her feelings much. She's been more concerned about thee than I thought. Even more than—"

"More than thee?" Laddie smiled quietly.

"That's what I was going to say." He had risen and came to stand beside her. Looking into her clear eyes, he seemed to have no words, and she saw the struggle that was going on inside him.

I must not hurt this man, she thought instantly, and as if he had discerned that thought, he said, "I've always been a pretty easygoing chap, Laddie—never had much to do with women. Matter of fact, I've had an idea that God wanted me to give my life completely to Him—and that was fine with me. But thee has changed all that," he finished with a light of wonder coming to his warm brown eyes, and he reached out and took her hand, looking at it as if he had found some strange and wonderful thing.

"Dan . . . !"

She spoke with a breathless quality in her voice, but he paid no heed. He looked directly at her and said evenly, as if he were commenting on the weather: "I love thee, Julie Sampson."

"You—you mustn't say that!" she whispered. His words set up an agitation in her heart, and she tried to turn away to hide her face, but he held her fast.

"I know thee love Nathan Winslow," he said quietly. "But he doesn't love thee, does he?"

"No! But he doesn't know I'm a woman!"

"And we both know why thee won't tell him, don't we?"

"I—don't know what you mean!"

"Thee won't tell him because thee knows thee'll lose him, Julie," he said remorselessly. "Thee know he'll hate thee for what thee've done to him. No man likes to be deceived, and even though thee *had* to do it, it'll make him feel like a fool!"

She pulled away from him, and the truth of his words stabbed her. She had said the same thing to herself a hundred times, had felt blind rage when she thought of Abigail in Nathan's arms—but as long as the words were unspoken, somehow she could still dream that he was hers.

Now she nodded slowly, and she looked at him steadily, saying, "I—I know all that—but I'll never let him know."

"Thee should," he insisted. Then he shrugged; suddenly a surprising grin touched his lips. "Well, one good thing will come out of all this."

"What's that?" she asked in surprise.

"I'll help with the guns." He smiled more broadly at her expression and said, "Thee is not the only one who is self-deceived, Julie. I've been saying that I wouldn't help because it went against my doctrine, but I knew all the time, it was really because I was jealous of Winslow."

"Oh, Dan, we're a couple of fools!" She looked at him and the grief in her face was replaced by an anxiety, and she put her hand lightly on his arm. "I—don't want to hurt you. I'm in love with Nathan."

He shook his head, a stubbornness in his face as he answered, "Thee thinks so, Julie—and no wonder. A young girl is rescued by a tall handsome young man in a romantic fairy-tale sort of affair— why, it would be more surprising if thee *didn't* have an infatuation for him!" Then he reached out and before she could stop him, he kissed her lightly, and smiled as her eyes widened. "But when thee kissed me that night, Julie, thee was not thinking of Nathan Winslow—but of Daniel Greene!"

"Why . . . !"

"Just give a little time, Julie," he said, and though there was a smile on his lips, she saw that he was deadly serious. "I'm coming with thee to Boston, and I'm staying so close that one of these days thee will fall in love with me."

She shook her head, but there was only wonder in her voice as she said quietly, "I don't think it will work—but Knox will be happy about the oxen."

She was right about that, for when the morning dawned for the caravan to leave, Knox was beaming with admiration at the fine array of animals that had been secured.

"By Harry, Friend Greene . . . !" he exclaimed as he looked at the train, all ready to pull out, manned by fresh, strong animals, "You may be a Quaker, but you've done more for this war by helping get these guns to Boston than you'll ever know!"

"I've had to bend my doctrine, Captain Knox," Greene admitted with a shrug.

"What will your fellow Quakers say about this?" Knox asked.

"They've already said it, I'm afraid." He reached into his pocket and pulled a paper out. Unfolding it, he said, "This is an affirmation of the traditional Quaker stand on war. It's just been sent out to all Friends." He read from the paper, his voice steady:

> It is our judgment that such who make religious profession with us, and do either openly or by connivance, pay any fine, penalty, or tax, in lieu of their personal services for carrying on war; or who do consent to, and allow their children, apprentices, or servants to act therein, do thereby violate our Christian testimony, and by so doing manifest that they are not in religious fellowship with us.

Knox stared at him. "Does that mean they're kicking you out?"

"That's about it, to put the matter bluntly."

Nathan had been listening to all this, and he suddenly grinned, saying, "Well, Friend Greene, you can always find a bunk with us! We can use a good man, eh, Laddie?"

Laddie smiled and nodded, but then Nathan added, "Laddie claims I snore too loud, so I reckon you two will have to share the blankets on the way to Boston. That all right with you?"

"I think it would be fine, Friend Nathan," Dan said with a smooth expression. What does *thee* think, Friend Laddie?"

But Sergeant Smith had turned and walked away abruptly with a scowl.

Nathan apologized for Laddie's behavior. "He's a strange

youngster, Dan," he said regretfully. "I've tried to toughen him up, but he's so blasted *sensitive!*" He clapped the other on the shoulder and grinned. "Well, we'll make a man out of Laddie Smith, won't we, Friend?"

The broad-shouldered Quaker looked at Nathan with a gleam in his eyes.

"Such a task may be harder than thee thinks, Friend Winslow!"

CHAPTER TWENTY-ONE

MESSAGE FROM BOSTON

★ ★ ★ ★

General Gage, out of favor in England because of the massacre at Bunker Hill, had been replaced by Sir William Howe, a man who fought and wenched doggedly. In November he had received orders from London to give up Boston and move south to New York, but he could not obtain the shipping to evacuate his men, so he settled back to stay until spring, occupying his time with a certain Mrs. Loring, the wife of his Commissary of Prisoners.

Washington created a small navy of privateers who darted in and out of the rocky harbors they knew so well. They nipped at the slow British merchantmen who came with supplies, and much of the food that did arrive was rotten. Captain John Manley of the schooner *Lee* scored a major coup when he took the British brigantine *Nancy* with her cargo of 2,000 muskets, 7,000 cannon balls, 10,500 flints, and a huge 13-inch mortar, which Israel Putnam christened "The Congress" by smashing a bottle of rum over its gaping muzzle.

Cut off by land and throttled by sea, the British made do with what they had. The Old North Church came down for firewood, as did the Liberty Tree, an arching elm under which Sam Adams and his rowdies had often met. Governor Winthrop's 100-year-old home in the middle of town went to the flames.

To fight boredom, if not the revolution, the British held elegant balls, and Abigail missed none of them. She was usually accompanied by Nathan's old rival, Paul Winslow, and the two of them arrived at Faneuel Hall one evening to attend a farce written by General John Burgoyne. Known to most as Gentleman Johnnie, Burgoyne had arrived in March with Howe and General Henry Clinton and declared, "What! Ten thousand peasants keeping five thousand of the King's men captive? Well, let *us* in and we'll soon make elbow room!" He was later to be called "General Elbow Room" by the troops for this remark.

But now Howe was gambling and gamboling with Mrs. Loring, so Burgoyne, a man of great concern for his men, had concocted the play for their entertainment. Paul led Abigail through the shouting ribald crowd, composed mostly of soldiers accompanied by many painted women, to a seat down close to the front.

"Noisy, aren't they?" He had to speak loudly to make himself heard, and added, "If they can fight like they can play, the rebels are doomed."

Abigail looked around and then smiled at Paul. "So far they haven't done much but get butchered at Bunker Hill and tear our town up. If Father hadn't been a faithful subject, they would have burned our house down."

"Ours too, I suppose," Paul shrugged. The British troops, frustrated with the remaining Bostonians who were thought to be signaling the rebels with burning gunpowder, had burned and pillaged the property of any American who could not prove his loyalty to the Crown.

Paul thought about it, then said, "It would be bad for us if the rebels came back. Some of the patriots who'd had their houses burned would be sure to come calling on every one of us who've stayed loyal to the King."

She stared at him with troubled eyes. "But—there's no chance of that, surely? They're just a rabble!"

"I hope you're right, sweetheart," Paul said. He had a dark streak of fatalism running through him, and he added as the curtain went up, "I'd hate to be at the mercy of our rebel 'neighbors.' I really think they'd be more dangerous to us than the soldiers in the army."

She turned to watch the play, but he saw that she had been shaken by the idea that she and her family might be on the losing side. The farce was taken from a play called *Maid of Oaks*, written by Burgoyne and produced in London by David Garrick. This humbler Boston production starred a caricature of Washington in a huge wig and rusty sword. The soldiers and their women roared with laughter at the farce, calling out lewd suggestions loudly, but as the play was nearly over, a sentry burst into the room crying out: "Turn out! Turn out! They are hard at it, hammer and tongs!"

The audience, thinking this was part of the play, clapped prodigiously, but the sentry yelled, "What the devil are ye about? The rebels are raiding Charles Town Neck, I tell you!"

There was a wild scramble then, as the officers and men saw that the threat was genuine, and Paul led Abigail through an almost empty hall to the carriage. On the way home, she said in a frightened voice, "Paul, can we lose?"

"No, not the war," he said moodily. "But we can lose here. If the rebels ever find out how weak we are—or if they ever get any cannon on those hills up there, it's all over."

"But—what will we do?"

"Get away, if we can, to England. But we'll lose everything. I talked with Father about it last week. He says there's no hope except maybe in Adam."

"Adam?"

"Nathan's father," he said with a strange smile at her. "Didn't Nathan ever tell you our family history?"

"No."

"He's more noble than I would have been. I didn't think your father would say anything, but I thought Nathan might."

"What's my father got to do with it?"

He chuckled and said, "Why your father and mine made a valiant stab at diddling Nathan's father out of his share of the family business years ago. Adam found out about it and just about shook my father's teeth out until Dad repented."

"My father never said a word!"

"Not too proud of that part of his life, I should think." Suddenly he laughed and clapped his thigh. "By George, it's funny now that I think of it! Here we've thrown our lots in with the British—sure that these rebels were going to lose. If the British win, Nathan and his father would be paupers and we'd be rich. Now, if Washington comes back with his army, Nathan and his family will be on top, and if we're not hanged for being traitors, we'll be poor as church mice." He laughed again, then gave her a sudden hard glance. "I think about this time you're having second thoughts about choosing me instead of Nathan, aren't you, sweetheart?"

"Don't be silly," she said quickly. But she was quiet on the ride home, and when he kissed her good night, she was preoccupied.

"May I come up?"

"Not tonight, Paul. I'm tired."

He looked at her cynically, then left immediately, but she tossed and turned long that night, unable to sleep. Finally she thought, *Nathan wouldn't let me suffer. He may be hurt, but he still loves me!* Then she smiled, stretched luxuriously, and felt much better.

Adam and Molly made their way through Cambridge, noting that most of the soldiers who filled the town had little in the way of uniforms. There were some exceptions, of course. The Rhode Islanders were there with their neat tents, each equipped with its own awning. The Twenty-first Massachusetts, men from Marblehead, had given up their occupations as shipwrights and fishermen, but not their seafaring heritage. Molly said quietly as they passed by, "How neat they look!"

Adam glanced at the troops, dressed in trim blue seacloth jackets and loose white sailor's trousers. "Look funny off a ship, don't they now? Make our boys look pretty sloppy."

He was now Captain Winslow of the Virginia Rangers—a rank which he had not wanted, but which General Washington had insisted on, and Molly was proud of him. She said as they approached the house that Washington used for a headquarters, "Our men are so different from the others!"

That was true. The Virginia riflemen had little in common with the other troops. They were tall, violent men with skins the color of tanned leather, and under Adam's command, they had marched seven hundred miles in three weeks, arriving in Boston with no one ill and no deserters.

The Virginians wore voluminous white hunting shirts and round, broad-brimmed caps with dangling fur tails. Their garb alone would have made them a target for attention, but their behavior provoked the other troops even more. They automatically pushed aside anyone who got in their way, and their height and obvious toughness awed most of the troops. They carried guns much longer and narrower than the familiar smoothbore muskets— and they won most of the loose money in camp by challenging all comers to shooting contests and winning every time—shattering bottles at three hundred yards. The Brown Bess would not even *carry* half that distance!

They fought anyone—kicking, biting, gouging out eyes—and if no stranger offered himself, they fought each other. Washington had said when giving Adam his commission, "It'll have to be you, Winslow. The officer of these men will have to be as tough as they are!"

They reached the house, and while the guard went inside to give his name, Adam said, "I'm glad you're here, Molly. This would be a lonesome place for me without you."

She smiled at him, a coquettish look in her eyes as she pinched his arm. "You think I'd let a good-looking thing like you loose in a place like this?"

"Not much danger," he grinned. "I wonder what General Washington wants?"

They did not have to wait long, for the door opened and Washington himself stepped outside, wearing a spotless uniform. Adam noted instantly that the air of expectancy he had come to know in this leader was obviously missing. The pressure had been enormous, and only a few days earlier he had written to his aide Joseph Reed:

> I have often thought how much happier I should have been if, instead of accepting a command under such circumstances, I had taken my musket on my shoulder and entered the ranks; or if I could have justified the measure to posterity and my own conscience, had retired to the back country and lived in a wigwam.

But now the tall Virginian had a buoyancy in his walk, and his eyes shone as he said, "Captain Winslow—Mrs. Winslow, you are prompt."

"Yes, sir," Adam nodded. "I thought the matter might be urgent from the sound of your message."

"So it is," Washington smiled. "Mrs. Winslow, would you be pleased to ride in my carriage while I ride with your husband? It's only a short journey, but this weather is still sharp."

Adam put Molly into the carriage, then mounted a horse provided by an aide. As Washington wheeled his own horse, a magnificent white stallion, Adam thought, *How this man can ride a horse!* As they made their way out of Cambridge, heading for Boston, Washington chatted about small things, which left Adam mystified.

He didn't need me to go for a ride with him!

Then when they reached the turnpike, Washington pulled up and waved toward a small camp set off the road. "I think you'll be interested in this, Captain."

Adam knew at once what it was and exclaimed, "Knox made it with the guns!"

"Thank God, he did!" Washington said, and then he spurred his horse forward. They reached the camp, and as Adam swung down and helped Molly out of the carriage, Knox came out of a tent and almost ran to meet his commander.

Knox had a dramatic streak in him, and he drew himself up to his full height, saluted and said in a full voice, "Your Excellency— the mission is accomplished! Now the cause of liberty is safe!"

Washington laughed delightedly and said, "Henry, you are a little premature, but you have my thanks—indeed, the whole country owes you much, *Colonel* Knox!"

Knox's eyes flew open at his sudden promotion, and for once the huge bookseller was speechless. Then Washington said, "Now, you and I will have a talk on how to best use these little beauties of yours—and Captain and Mrs. Winslow here would like to see their son."

"Of course, General!" Knox said, and looking around he saw Nathan waiting at a respectful distance. "Come here at once—*Sergeant* Winslow!" He turned to Adam and Molly and said with a broad smile, "I'd make him a lieutenant if I could, sir! He and that young friend of his saved our necks on this trip!"

He turned to lead Washington into the tent, and Nathan came up to be embraced by his mother. "You're so *thin!*" she exclaimed.

"Been eating the bark off the trees," he said, looking down at her; then with a smile, he said, "Do I salute you, Captain Winslow?"

Adam looked up at his tall son and thought of the dark moods he'd had in the months since the war had started. There had been a wall between the two of them, and he hated it worse than he'd hated anything in his life. So in full view of the camp, he stepped forward and opened his arms. "Later, you can salute—but I'm so glad to see you—my son!"

Nathan found himself being held tightly by his father's iron-hard blacksmith arms, and as he returned the embrace, his eyes burned and he said, "I—I'm glad . . . !" and then he could say no more.

When Adam stepped back, there was a suspicious moisture in his own eyes and he said briskly, "Well, Sergeant, I believe I have it in my authority to take you into town and buy you a meal."

"And I want Laddie, too," Molly said. "I've thought about him so often."

Nathan's face changed, and Molly thought, *They've had a fight*, but he said, "He'll be glad to see you both. Talks about you a lot— but you'll probably have to take his buddy along. We picked him up on the trail and he and Laddie have been thick as thieves."

"Bring him along, son," Adam said quickly, and when Nathan went along the line of wagons to find Laddie, he said, "You notice something there?"

"Yes. Nathan could never hide his feelings—like you can."

"Me? You read me like a big-print Bible," Adam grinned. "But this new friend of Laddie's—I don't think Nathan cares much for him."

"Well, it may be some rough soldier leading the boy astray," Molly said. "But Nathan was always pretty possessive—like me." She gave him a swift look and said quietly, "I'm glad you did that— hugged him. He needs you, Adam."

"I guess I'm not very loving, Molly."

"Oh—you have your moments, Captain Winslow!" She laughed in delight as his face suddenly grew red, and said gently, "Let's not mention this girl he was seeing, Adam. Let him bring it up if he wants to."

Nathan returned with Laddie, and she was delighted to see them both. "And this is Friend Daniel Greene," she said, and Molly did not miss the admiration in Laddie's clear eyes as she introduced the handsome man in plain black clothes.

The five of them rode back to Cambridge crowded into the carriage, and the full story of the heroic trip after the guns poured out. The Quaker said almost nothing, but Laddie finally added, "If Friend Daniel hadn't rounded up all those oxen, I guess we'd still be perched on the bank of the Hudson River!"

"I didn't do all that much." He had a deep musical voice, Molly noted, and later when they got to the hotel where she and Adam had a room, they left the three long enough to go and clean up before meeting them for a meal.

"Well, what did you think of Friend Greene?" Adam asked at once.

"It's a good thing I'm an old married woman," she answered as she brushed her glossy hair back. "That Quaker is too handsome! What a shame it's all wasted on a preacher who doesn't need all those good looks."

"He *is* fine looking," Adam admitted. "And a husky fellow as well." He stared at her, admiring her long hair, then said, "I thought Quakers were against war and all that. Surprises me that he helped Knox out. But—he's not what we thought, is he? I mean, he's not a drinking or wenching man—likely to corrupt Laddie?"

"No, he'll not do that, I think." She said in a slow voice, then rose and said, "Let's go eat. I want to hear more about the trip."

For the next three days, Washington and Knox had their heads together, and the men were given permission to go into town often. There was little for Adam to do, and he said, "I know Washington— he's up to something. When it breaks, I don't reckon any of us will have any time for fun—so we better enjoy it."

It was a good time for Molly; she had seen little of Adam when he'd been so busy getting the Rangers organized, and the two of them spent a great deal of time with Nathan. They ate together every night, and Laddie was always included, as was the young Quaker.

They laughed a great deal, but Molly saw that beneath the surface, all three of the young people were somehow ill at ease. She said nothing to Adam, but finally on the third night, something happened that interrupted their holiday.

They were eating at an inn, and Adam was debating some theological point with Greene. The two had become good friends, differing on small matters of doctrine, but each sensing the goodness of the other. A young man in civilian clothes came in and asked, "Mr. Nathan Winslow?"

Nathan nodded, took the note he presented, and read it. The messenger, a tall young man still in his teens, waited, and finally Nathan looked up and asked, "Can you take an answer?"

"Yes, sir."

Nathan got up and went to the proprietor, and borrowing a quill, scratched a note on the back of the one he'd just received. He returned to the table, gave it to the messenger, who said, "I'll see she gets it, sir," and left.

The rest of them had tried not to appear curious, but Laddie blurted out, "It's Abigail, isn't it?"

Nathan flushed and said, "I'll have to be gone for a little while. Father, could you get me a pass for two days?"

Laddie stared at him, her face pale, and she turned to Adam. "Don't do it! He nearly got hanged last time he went to see that woman!"

"Nathan, it's too dangerous to go into Boston," Adam said quietly. "If you'll just wait a few days, I suspect you can walk in with the rest of us."

"I can't wait, sir," Nathan replied, his lips pale. "I have to go."

Adam stared at him, then nodded heavily. "I'll get you a pass. Come along."

"You are a bloody fool, Nathan Winslow!" Laddie cried out, and there was such anger in her that the words were blurred.

Molly watched as Nathan stared at Laddie. "I have to do it, Laddie." Then he turned and followed his father out of the room.

Molly got up and said abruptly, "Laddie, would you come with me? Excuse us please, Mr. Greene."

"Of course." Greene rose and watched Laddie follow Mrs. Winslow out of the inn, then sat there for a long time, staring at the table. He was thinking, *Winslow's a fool!—but then, so am I!*

Laddie followed Nathan's mother blindly out of the inn and down the street. She wanted to scream, but bit her lips, and by the time she and Molly entered the hotel room, Laddie was in control.

Molly took off her coat and went to look out the window. She stood there so long that Laddie grew nervous, saying finally, "What was it you wanted to talk to me about, Mrs. Winslow?"

Molly Winslow turned from the window and came to stand directly before her. Looking into her eyes, she said, "I wanted to ask you about Nathan . . ."

She paused and Laddie asked quickly, "Yes? What about him?"

"I wanted to ask you, Laddie—are you in love with him—as Daniel Greene is in love with you?"

The room grew still, the silence broken only by the sound of a soldier singing outside, and then Laddie fell into Molly's arms, crying as if her heart would break: "I don't know! I don't know! Oh, I'm so mixed up! Help me!"

Molly stood there holding the shaking body of the girl in her arms, praying, *God help us all!*

CHAPTER TWENTY-TWO

AT THE RED LION

★ ★ ★ ★

"When did you find out about me?"

Molly had waited, holding the weeping girl until finally the sobs had ceased. She gave Laddie a handkerchief and watched silently as the girl wiped her face, then said with a small smile, "When you left Virginia, Laddie."

"What?"

"I suspected it for a time—but when I made you hug me just before you left—that made me sure." She sighed and reached out to touch a tear-stained cheek. "Men are so blind!" she snorted with a crisp shake of her head. "See just what they expect to see! Oh, I know you put on around men, stomp and swing your arms and such. But I think when you were with me, you forgot your act. You remember when you helped me cook supper? Child, there's not a man in the world who could peel a potato or move around as daintily as you did! The thought came to me, and so I watched you. Then when you were leaving, I hugged you real tight." Her lips turned up, and there was a gleam in her eyes as she said, "I've not had much experience hugging men, but I *knew* it was no man I was hugging!"

"Oh, Mrs. Winslow, I'm so miserable!"

"Well, that Quaker, *he* knows you're not a man," Molly said. "He hasn't taken his eyes off you. And you've kept Nathan fooled—and now you're in love with him—and Friend Daniel

Greene is in love with you! Sounds like a real bad play or book, doesn't it? What's your name?"

"Julie Sampson." She looked up and said, "Can I tell you all of it?"

"Of course, Julie." Molly sat there, listening to the girl, and when all was told, she smiled and said, "I guess you've got two mothers running scared—Sister Greene and me."

"Oh, you don't have to worry! Nathan's nutty over that Howland woman! He's put his head in a noose *twice* for her—and she doesn't give a tuppence for him!"

"You don't know that."

"I *do*!" Laddie shook her head violently, and paced the floor like a caged animal. "Why, if she cared *anything* about him, she'd not ask him to stick his head into the lion's jaws, would she?"

"Women have a lot of power over men, child," Molly said thoughtfully. "If he loves this woman, he'll go to her, no matter what it costs."

"I wish she were *dead*!"

"You haven't answered my question," Molly said. "Are you in love with Nathan?"

"Why, how could I be? He doesn't even know I'm a girl!"

"I didn't ask you how *he* felt, Julie—I asked if you loved *him*."

"I—I don't know. I thought I did—but then I met Daniel—and he treats me like a woman—and he does care for me."

"I see." Molly looked long into the eyes of the girl, then said, "Nathan will have to know."

"No!"

"Yes, for your own sake, and for his."

"He'll hate me!"

"That may be—but he'll never love you, will he?—not until he knows you're there to be loved—that you're not a boy but a lovely woman."

Laddie began to tremble, and as she looked up, her enormous eyes and soft lips trembling, Molly thought, *Nathan is my son, but he must be the blindest man on earth! This lovely child—and he never saw!* But she said, "You did what you had to do, child, to escape your uncle. But you're not alone now. No matter what Nathan feels, Adam and I will help you—and besides, I think from what I saw of Friend Daniel Greene, it would take a pretty powerful man to shake him loose from you!"

Laddie shook her head, then moaned, "Oh, if Nathan only hadn't gone to Boston! When he got taken before, I nearly died!"

"We'll have to pray, Julie," Molly said. "Do you think God answers prayer?"

".Oh, I know He does!"

"Then we'll pray that he'll be safe—and that God will open his eyes. He's lost his way, Julie," she stated quietly. "God may have to put him flat on his back with no way to turn before he finds his way."

Nathan,
    I must see you. Please meet me at the old Red Lion Inn on the turnpike. I will be there tonight at seven. Don't come to the house. It's too dangerous.

Sitting outside the ancient inn that shed yellow bars of light from its windows, Nathan thought of the note. As he waited in the darkness, he pictured the words that were burned across his brain. There was no signature, but he knew the writing. He had brought along a brace of pistols and kept to the back roads to avoid patrols. After darkness fell, he rode to the inn, let a hostler take his horse, then kept to the shadows of the stable, watching the road.

It was not more than thirty minutes after seven when a closed carriage drew up, and Nathan's eyes picked out the driver—the same young man who had brought the message. He pulled the team to a stop, leaned down and said something, then nodded and got down. He hitched the team and walked at a leisurely pace into The Red Lion Inn.

For five minutes, Nathan stood there in the darkness, wary, suspecting a trap, but nothing changed and he moved to the window and saw the driver at a table, settled down with a stein of beer.

Cautiously he moved to the coach and peered inside. He could see nothing, so he put his hand on the pistol in his belt and whispered softly, "Abigail?"

"Nathan!" The door opened, and he quickly stepped up and practically fell into Abigail's arms! She clutched him, pulling his head down, and her soft lips met his in a long kiss.

"Abigail, what's the matter?" he asked urgently when she drew back. "I've had a bad time—thinking all kinds of things."

She took his hand and held it to her cheek, then kissed the back of it, saying, "That's sweet, Nathan! But does there have to be something *wrong*? Can't it be that I just long to be with you?"

He thought of the note, and realized that it actually said nothing about her being in trouble. "I guess I just assumed you needed me."

Her perfume was heady, and she turned toward him and put her arms around his neck. The rounded softness of her body disturbed him, and her breath was sweet as she whispered, "Nathan, when I heard you were off on a dangerous mission and might not come back, I almost lost my mind!" He wondered how she knew about the mission, but he was so overcome by her embrace that he could not follow the thought.

The dim light from a crescent moon turned the snow silver and the yellow light from the lanterns on the front of The Red Lion were reflected in her eyes, which he could now see faintly.

He looked at her face, and the touch of her hands on his face distracted him. He sat there holding her, and her perfume seemed to drug his senses. He whispered hoarsely, "Abigail—I've thought about you every day."

"And I've thought of you every day, too, sweet—and every night!" She pulled him closer, and her lips brushed his cheek as she whispered, "I know you must think I'm shameless, but I've been so afraid!"

"But—I thought you and Paul . . . ?"

"Oh, Nathan, you know women are vulnerable! Paul is an attractive man, and I enjoy his company—but I didn't dream you'd let that frighten you off."

He felt suddenly weak and drew back, and then he said dryly, "Well, I wasn't exactly *frightened* off, Abigail. I was dragged off by a troop of dragoons—almost to the gallows!"

"I know, sweet, I know! It must have been awful!"

He laughed and said, "Well, I've enjoyed a few things more than waiting to be hanged."

"I had a pass from General Gage to see you—but I think that friend of yours took it!"

"He certainly did!" Nathan remembered again how he had felt when Laddie had come to him in prison, and he said slowly, "He saved my life, Abigail."

"Oh, you wouldn't have been executed," she said quickly. "Father had it all arranged with the general to get you pardoned—but you escaped before we could get there."

"Sorry to spoil your plan," Nathan said with a smile. "But at the time it seemed a little frivolous to hang around until the execution."

"It's so terrible! Let's don't even *think* about it, dear!" She leaned against him, her soft body sending involuntary signals along his nerves. "You're not angry with me, are you?"

"No, of course not."

"I knew you wouldn't be—but I was afraid that you'd never come back. That's why I sent for you."

"Does anyone know you're here?"

"Just Justin, the driver—and he wouldn't tell anyone."

He sat there thinking; then he said, "It's a bad time for us, isn't it?"

"Oh, I get so tired of it all—but it can't last forever, can it, Nathan?"

"It can last longer than I'd like—and it can be unpleasant for you."

"Father says we ought to leave—to go to New York—but Paul's father says it would be just as bad for loyalists there."

"The only safe place would be England, Abigail—or maybe Canada. Father is worried about Uncle Charles. He told him to leave at once for Canada, but he said he was too old to leave his home."

"Oh, Nathan, Father isn't well, and I'm so afraid! I don't know anything about politics—and everyone is saying that if Washington comes in with his army, we'll all be slaughtered!"

He laughed and put his arm around her. She was trembling and her weakness, as much as her beauty, stirred him deep inside, and he said, "You won't be slaughtered, Abigail."

"Nathan, you'll take care of me?"

She lifted her face, and her eyes had a golden gleam, the reflection of the lantern light, and he could no more help kissing her than he could help living. Her lips were soft, but they moved under his hungrily, and her arms drew him frantically closer, until finally he drew back, saying roughly, "Abigail—don't push me too far."

"I love you, Nathan," she whispered. "I know I've been too bold—but I—I was afraid I'd lost you!"

He sat there and for an hour they talked, and finally she said, "I've got to get home before I'm missed." They had embraced several times, and she pushed at her hair, laughing, "Nathan, when will I see you again?"

"It will be hard to arrange," he said, then added, "I'll be here again in three nights—that's as soon as I can get away."

"Oh, darling!" she breathed, and lifted her face for a final kiss. "That's so far away!"

Nathan thought of the guns they'd brought and said quickly, "If there's an attack on the town, you must get away at once, you and your family."

"But—what if we can't get out of town?"

"I don't think there'll be any trouble. General Washington has built discipline into the troops."

"But—everyone says that we'll be attacked by the patriots!" she said.

"If the city falls, I'll be there as soon as the lines are open. Stay in the house, and I'll get an order from headquarters giving you some protection."

"Oh, Nathan, I knew you'd take care of me!" She gave herself to him in one final embrace, then said, "Go tell Justin I'm ready, will you, sweet?"

He stepped out, went to the inn, and caught the eye of the driver. As he stood up, Nathan walked quickly to the barn, and he heard the team gallop out of town as he took his horse from the hostler.

The roads as he came nearer Cambridge were closely watched, and he had to show his pass to three patrols. He thought of what he'd said to Abigail about leaving town, and thought, *Too late—they'll never get through!*

When he got back to town, he went to bed, but as the dawn came, he got up without having slept. He ate breakfast, then was greeted by his father, who found him drinking a last cup of coffee.

"Glad you're back," Adam said. He sat down and poured himself a cup of the strong brew. "None of my business, son, but did you get your business done?"

"Yes, sir. But if I hadn't had that pass you got for me, it would have been impossible. The roads are crawling with our guards." He looked around and saw through the window of the mess shack that men were everywhere, running and calling urgently to each other. "What's going on?"

Adam smiled at him, sipped his coffee, then said, "Washington and Knox—they've decided to use those guns you brought back."

"When?"

The question came so sharply that Adam blinked. Then he said, "Well, it'll take a little doing, Nathan. If the British *see* us fortifying those heights, they'll come out and fight. We'll have to do it without their knowing it."

"Don't see how."

"It's strange, son, but I think God has moved into this thing." A light touched his father's eyes, and he leaned forward and said in a lively tone, "A young engineer named Rufus Putnam was just passing by General Heath's quarters, and he had to wait for the general. There were some old books there, and he spied a book on field engineering. He noticed in the book a diagram and a description of something called a 'chandelier'—which is a piece of French equipment new to him. It's a sectional wooden framework, they tell me, designed to hold in place 'fascines,' which is French for large, tightly-bound bundles of sticks. And, son, when you join these chandeliers together, you get a barrier as effective as a trench. Young Putnam told Heath, who told Washington, and the order's out to make hundreds of these things."

"You think they'll work?"

Adam shrugged and leaned back, his eyes dim with memory. "In the French and Indian War, I saw British troops stopped by heavy brush and timber—the general was there and saw it, too. These things are a heap tougher than any brush you ever saw— and if the Redcoats charge them they'll be knocked down by our rifles!"

"It'll take a while, won't it, to build those things?"

"Not long as you might think. We've got a lot of men with nothing to do, and most of them are experts with an axe. Guess we'll be waiting for the right weather more than anything. Got to have a nice ground mist covering the base of Dorchester Heights, but with a full moon to light the top, so we can see what we're doing."

Nathan nodded, calculating days in his mind, then got up, saying, "How's Mother?"

"Worried about you." Adam grinned crookedly at him and said, "She and Laddie had quite a talk—mostly about you, I reckon. That boy gave you the hard side of his talk, didn't he?"

"Oh, he was just worried about me."

"I'd say so. But I guess Molly calmed him down—or maybe it was that Quaker preacher."

"He still here?"

"Oh, sure." Adam got up and took one final swig of his coffee. "Far as I can tell, he's settled in."

"For a man who doesn't believe in war, he's sure put himself in the middle of it."

"Isn't that a fact?" Adam looked out the window, straightened up and said, "The general said you and Laddie were to be in my company. But you know these boys—fact that you're a sergeant doesn't mean anything to them. You may have to pound a couple of them in the ground, just to show you've got a right to give orders."

"They're pretty tough, Captain," Nathan said with a grin. "Might be they'll pound me in the ground."

"Well, guess if one of them does that—*he'll* be the sergeant."

"Not likely. I'll use an axe handle on him!"

He worked all day with the company cutting saplings for the fascines, and after they had quit, he encountered Laddie. She was sitting outside Knox's tent working on a map that was pinned to a large table, and he was not surprised to see Daniel Greene bending over the same table, looking at something Laddie was pointing out.

"Hello, Laddie," he said. "You going into map-making, Friend Daniel?"

Greene flushed slightly, then shook his head. "Just trying to figure this thing out." He looked at the map, shook his head, and said, "Can't make much out of it."

Nathan went to stand between them, looking down from his great height at the map. "You draw this, Laddie?"

"Yes." Her tone was short, and he looked at her, noting that she was not smiling as usual.

"Something wrong?" he asked.

"No. Nothing's wrong."

He hesitated, then said, "Well, guess I'll get something to eat." He stood there staring at her, then said, "Now, you see I didn't get killed or anything."

"I'm glad of that," Laddie said steadily, then looked down at the map and cut him off, saying, "You see, Dan, if we can get these guns in place . . ."

Nathan walked away, and Daniel said quietly, "He's confused. Thee is not being fair to him."

She threw the stick she'd been using to the ground and said,

"Dan, I don't *care* what Nathan Winslow does! Let him kill himself over that woman if he wants to!"

"Thee is in love with him."

"That was before he started running around after her!"

Dan stared at her, and there was compassion in his brown eyes. "Julie, it's bad to deceive anybody—but the worst thing is to deceive thyself." He shook his head sadly and said, "I thought at first that Winslow was going to hurt thee—but I see now that he won't be the one—" He touched her arm gently and said quietly, "It'll be thee who will bring the grief!"

CHAPTER TWENTY-THREE

"I'LL DO WHAT I HAVE TO DO!"

★ ★ ★ ★

"This isn't an army—it's a theological seminary!" Henry Knox snapped impatiently.

The lights of Boston winked up like fireflies at the small group sitting around a cheerfully blazing campfire. For three weeks the plan to fortify Dorchester Heights had been delayed by weather, for though warmer breezes had come to melt the snow, Knox was forced to wait for a night when Boston itself would be beneath an umbrella of mist, while the heights would be clear enough to get the guns in place.

Adam had come most nights to sit with Nathan and Laddie as they waited, and Greene was usually there. Greene and Adam enjoyed talking about the Bible, and some of their finer points about the prophetic books grew heated. "Father," Nathan had grinned once when both men had lost their calm, "you and Dan get more worked up over the gray beard of that billy-goat in the book of Daniel than you do over shooting Redcoats!"

Colonel Knox had suddenly appeared, listened to the heated discussion, and made his disgusted remark. But he had sniffed the air like a hound on the scent. "This could be it," he remarked eagerly.

"Not enough mist to cover us," Adam commented. But he stood up and looked down the hill, adding, "Fog *is* rolling in, though . . ." He slapped his hands together impatiently, looked at

Knox, and asked, "What does the general say?"

Knox shrugged his heavy shoulders and grinned suddenly. "He's champing at the bit as usual." He laughed quietly and gave a sly look at Adam. "He ordered the chaplain to pray for mist on Boston. You think the Lord will hear the good chaplain, Captain Winslow?"

"I refuse to limit God," Adam answered with a smile. "If God can flood the earth, I suppose He can whip up a little mist."

Knox asked innocently, "But how does God settle on which prayer to answer? I mean—the British chaplain is praying for victory in this war, and our chaplain is asking God for the same thing. Now, He *can't* please both of them, can He?"

Adam knew full well that Knox loved to poke fun at such things, so he said, "You know that's a question no man can answer, Colonel. But I'll tell you one thing—General Washington is a praying man."

Knox suddenly flushed and said quickly, "You're right, Winslow—and I was wrong to speak in such a way. I know full well that if all the praying men in our army left, we would be lost. Matter of fact, I think this army comes about as close as any to the Model Army of Oliver Cromwell. The pastors all over are making it a holy war."

"Did you hear about Muhlenberg?" Nathan asked from where he sat propped up against a tree. "He was a Lutheran pastor from our state, over in the Shenandoah Valley. Right after Lexington he preached a red-hot sermon on the text, 'For everything there is a season, and a time for every matter under heaven.' Then at the end of his sermon, he threw off his pulpit robe and he was wearing the uniform of a colonel in the Continental Army."

"I've met him," Knox answered. "And there's that preacher from Chelsea, Philip Payson—captured two British supply wagons single-handed—and there's Major Craighead—he raised his own company and they say he alternates between fighting and preaching." He shot a sudden look at Dan, who was listening intently, and asked, "Friend Daniel, I talked to your uncle, General Greene, last week. He's anxious to see you. Said the two of you ought to get together, since you're both likely to be ex-Quakers for ignoring the rules."

Greene nodded his head, saying only, "I'd like to see him."

Then Nathan asked directly, "Are you going to get into this

war, Dan—I mean, sooner or later the fighting's going to start! We can't sit up on top of this blasted hill forever! What will you do then?"

"Haven't decided."

"Well, you'll have your chance soon." Knox stared down and said, "I'm thinking that fog is rolling in pretty thick—and if it stays still like this—and if it doesn't rain, but just stays damp—and if about twenty other things happen, we could move tomorrow or the day after. I'm going to bed. Sergeant Smith, you wake me up if that chaplain's prayers get answered."

"Yes, sir." Laddie watched Knox stalk away into the darkness, and Nathan got up and left the fire. Adam watched him go, and said quietly, "I hope he doesn't try to leave camp again." Twice in the last two weeks Nathan had managed to get free of duty and had disappeared, showing up the next morning looking hollow-eyed from lack of sleep. Laddie knew he was going to see Abigail, and was certain that Adam and Molly knew as much.

Adam got up, stretched, and said good night, then left the fire. It was late, but Laddie loved the sharp air, so she pulled her coat closer around her and sat there poking a stick at the fire. Finally she looked up and asked, "Have you heard from your mother?"

"Just today. Been waiting for a chance to give thee this." He reached into his pocket, extracted an envelope and passed it to her.

Laddie read her name on the front, broke the seal and held it up to the fire. As she read it her cheeks grew red, and finally she folded it up and put it in her pocket. She picked up the stick, poked the fire and watched the sparks swirl upward. Then she looked suddenly at him, and asked, "Do you know what she said, Dan?"

"No."

He had the Quaker habit of silence, which she had grown accustomed to. Most men would have asked at once what the letter said, but he sat there, a mild look on his square face, gazing at her across the fire. He was not like other men, she had discovered, and knew that his mother and his religion had melded him into a strange combination of strength and gentleness—a combination that she found most attractive.

"You haven't said a word about—about us," she said. "I guess you've changed your mind."

"No, I haven't." Again he sat there quietly, but he added after a time, "I don't change easily—but until *thee* has a change, I'll not be saying much about us."

"That's—that's sweet of you, Dan." She knew he was thinking of her feelings for Nathan, and she struggled to find something to say, but there was nothing. Finally she said, "Dan, do you think God is in this war—I mean, I hear all this talk about freedom and how it's God's will for us to fight for it. You never say anything."

"Haven't decided yet. But I'm pondering it." He shook his head and looked down at the dim lights of the city, saying quietly, "I think maybe that fog is getting thicker."

They sat there for an hour, talking quietly—and Laddie did not realize how much she had come to rely on being able to speak openly with someone. Finally, she said, "It's getting late. I'll see you in the morning, Dan. Tell your mother, when you write her, that I'll pray about—what she says."

She got up and left him, and for a long time Dan sat there watching the lights. Then he said aloud, "Well, Lord, I'll add my voice to that of the chaplain. Let it fog up so that the army can get this job done. I don't know what Thee has in mind for this country—but let me in on it, as soon as Thee finds it convenient."

The next morning Knox was up before dawn, pacing back and forth, and at noon he turned to Laddie and said, "Write this down, Laddie: 'General, we will fortify the hill as soon as possible. If you will give us the cover of a bombardment, it will be most helpful.' What's the date—March 2?" He signed the order and handed it to an orderly, saying, "Get this to His Excellency at once!"

All day long the camp hummed with activity, and all that night and the next what guns were available poured a steady stream of shot and shell down on Boston. Washington stayed up to count the shots and make sure that his limit of twenty-five shots was observed.

The next night was remarkably mild, and Boston was covered with a haze that made the top of Dorchester invisible. "All right," Knox snapped as dark fell, "Howe won't have his mind on us tonight, so get going!"

Nathan worked with the Virginians, and Adam was right beside him. He stopped to say, "We could have waited a year and not had a night this good! I reckon that chaplain's prayers are right forceful!"

Eight hundred men worked madly to place the pre-assembled chandeliers in position and load them with fascines—all of which were brought up the hill by three hundred amazingly quiet teams and drivers. Silently these men worked hour after hour in the moon-lit darkness. As dawn broke across the east, the last gun was rolled into place, and Knox said quietly, "Well, I've seen at least *one* miracle. To do a thing like this—*and nothing go wrong* . . . !" He took off his hat and added, "God has been with us."

General Howe was awakened abruptly by his aide, who was shaking him by the arm—an unprecedented action!—and saying in an agonized voice: "General—General! Wake up!"

Howe had spent part of the night gambling and part with Mrs. Loring, and his head ached from the prodigious amount of wine he had consumed. He struck out blindly at the aide, muttering angrily, "Get your bloody hands off me!"

But the aide pleaded, "Pardon me, sir, but you *must* come at once!"

"What the devil is it?" Howe demanded. He dragged himself out of bed and glared at the frightened aide; then he pulled himself together, knowing that it had to be serious for the lieutenant to behave so. "Is it an attack?"

"No, sir—"

"Well, let me get my pants on!" Howe dressed rapidly, then walked out of the bedroom where three of his staff officers were standing with ashen faces. "What's the matter?"

"Sir, look at that hill!"

Howe walked to the door and stared up at the heights; then he gasped, "Impossible!"

He looked up to see a fort on the hill where nothing had been the afternoon before. General Robertson came to stand beside him, and he said in an agitated voice, "General Howe, to do that in one night, the rebels must have had fifteen to twenty thousand men!"

Howe could not speak for a moment; then he said, "We must prepare for action, Gentlemen; the honor of the British Army demands an immediate attack on this rebel position." All morning he issued orders, and a plan emerged for two forces of two thousand men each to embark on the next tide. That afternoon files of infantry marched down to the longboats.

But at midnight a violent gale swept in from the south, making landings impossible. Windows were blown in, sheds overturned, and rail fences were actually blown away!

Howe had no choice but to cancel the mission, telling his generals the danger of the attack had been in his mind, but that he had thought the honor of his troops was of more concern. He ordered the evacuation of the city, and the boats were made ready.

The Boston Tories descended on Howe's headquarters. The most illustrious names of Massachusetts—Olivers, Saltonstalls, Mathers, Hutchinsons, Faneuels—gathered what few valuables they could carry to leave their homes—many never to see them again. Henry Knox's in-laws, the Fluckers, were among them.

Charles Winslow had stayed in town as this drama unfolded. He called Paul to his side and said with a pale face, "I won't leave this place."

"Well, if Uncle Adam will stand beside you, it may be all right. After all, he's part owner of the business." Paul grinned, and there was something cruel in his eyes as he added, "Maybe Adam's got enough honor for all of us, Father."

Charles turned pale, but did not respond. He asked instead, "What will Howland do? He's too sick to leave."

"I'll go see. He doesn't have a relative who's a patriot to stand between him and Sam Adams' Sons of Liberty." Then he paused and added, "Well, maybe he does at that." With this enigmatic word, he turned and left at once.

Charles left the city and went home, where his wife and his mother met him with fear in their eyes. Dorcas was weeping and clinging to him. "What will we do? What will happen to us, Charles?"

Charles Winslow did not answer her, but looked into the eyes of his mother. He said bitterly, "Well, Mother, you've hated my brother Adam all his life. You made life miserable for him when he was a child and despised him when he grew up."

"Charles—don't . . . !"

"But now this man—the best of the Winslows—is the only hope we have. If he doesn't help us—we're lost!"

Martha Winslow seemed to shrivel before his words, and she turned slowly and moved her arthritic joints painfully, leaving the room. Charles watched her, and his heart smote him. He shook his head and moved to go after her. "She's done no more than I have to Adam."

Anne clung to her mother, her freckles standing out against the pallor of her face. "Mother—will they kill us—the rebels?"

Dorcas held her tightly and whispered, "No! Your Uncle Adam

won't let them harm us!" And bitter tears flowed down her cheeks as she thought of the meanness she'd always shown toward Adam and his family.

When Paul entered the Howland mansion, he found Abigail alone in the parlor. Her face was serious, but she showed no fear. "Mother's with Father, Paul." She bit her lip, and added in a whisper, "I think he's dying."

Paul stared at her, then said, "I think you'd all better come with us. Adam won't let the rebels do anything to us."

"Father can't be moved," she said. "And if we do leave, they'll take everything."

He stared at her and she raised her head to meet his gaze. "We'll be all right, Paul. Don't worry about us."

"I see." He didn't move, but examined her carefully. Finally he said, "We're a great deal alike, you and I."

"Paul, we've been very close—"

"Well, *that's* a strange way of putting it!" he said angrily. *"We've been very close.* Can't you be more honest than that, Abigail?"

She flushed, but held her head imperiously higher, and there was a steely note in her voice as she said, "Paul, you just said that we're alike—and I agree. The world is coming to an end—our world. Yours is safe because Adam Winslow is going to look after you. My father's dying and my mother can't even look after herself—so I'll look out for us."

Paul stared at her, then shook his head. "I knew you weren't all sugar and spice—that image never fooled me for one instant, Abby—but I didn't look close enough. You're hard as flint."

"I'll do what I have to do," Abigail said quietly. Then she asked in a gentler tone, "So will you, Paul, won't you?"

He stared at her, then slowly nodded. "I suppose so—you know me as well as I know you." He moved his shoulders in some sort of weary gesture, then asked, "If it doesn't work out, come to me."

"It'll work out, Paul." Abigail smiled at him, and there was an adamantine light in her hazel eyes. She suddenly kissed him and clung to him fiercely, then pulled back and said, "Goodbye, Paul—at least for now!"

CHAPTER TWENTY-FOUR

OUT OF THE PAST

★ ★ ★ ★

Howe's army had not been defeated; it had been out-maneu-
vered by a larger force. This infuriated the British troops, and in
their final days in Boston they took their frustration out on the old
town. They broke into many houses, and military supplies that
could not be taken aboard the fleet were smashed and thrown into
the harbor.

Adam and Nathan spoke of the occupation of the city as the
final evacuation of the British took place. Adam had been watching
through a spy glass from a high point, and he suddenly snapped
it shut and said, "Putnam will go in first. I'm going in with him."

"The folks who've been faithful to the cause have taken an
awful whipping," Nathan commented. "If Charles didn't get his
family away, they'll probably be ridden out on a rail along with the
other Tories."

"He's not leaving with Howe," Adam stated. "I got a message
from him two days ago. I'm going in with Putnam to be sure nothing happens to them."

Nathan broke in quickly, "Father, I hate to ask favors—but I
need to go to the Howlands. They're worse off than the Winslows.
Saul Howland died day before yesterday. That leaves Abigail and
her mother alone."

Adam stared long at his tall son before saying, "I guess you
have to do this, Nathan. Your mother and I don't know this woman,

but you're a loyal boy, so we thought it'd be this way." He sorted out several ideas, then said, "One thing I can do, and that's get an official order placing the Howland estate under the protection of the army. The general says he wants law and order, and it'll just be a piece of paper—but maybe you can make it stick."

"Thank you, sir," Nathan said warmly. "It's what I wanted—but didn't dare ask."

Adam stared at him, doubt in his eyes. "Are you going to marry this woman, son?"

"Well, things have been so mixed up that we haven't talked about it . . ."

Adam wanted to warn him that it would be impossible to be loyal to the Continental Army with a wife who was a Tory, but he thought, *Nathan knows all that*, so he merely said, "I'll get the order and we can go in together with Putnam."

When the last Redcoat walked up the gangplank and Howe's fleet moved out of the harbor, Adam and Nathan were in the first unit that marched into the city. Doors and windows were packed with cheering crowds as they entered to the tune of *Yankee Doodle Dandy*. Back in Cambridge, Rev. Leonard gave a final church service for the siege of Boston, quoting from Ex. 14:25: ". . . And took off their chariot wheels, that they drave them heavily: so that the Egyptians said, Let us flee from the face of Israel; for the Lord fighteth for them against the Egyptians."

Adam said as Nathan left for the Howlands', "Be careful, Nathan. These folks have been hardly used, and they're liable to shoot first and argue later. You've got a piece of paper, but some of them have lost everything, and they see the Winslows and the Howlands as the enemy." He smiled and reached up to put his hand on Nathan's shoulder. "We've not been close until recently—and I'd hate for you to get killed over a house."

"I'll be careful." Nathan smiled and clapped his father on the shoulder. "You better take your own advice, Father!" He rode away, wondering at the way the war and the loss of Caleb had brought the two of them together.

Abigail and her mother were waiting for him. Mrs. Howland had aged ten years since the first time Nathan had met her. She was a tiny woman with smallish eyes that had been filled with pride—but now were so full of fear that it was hard for Nathan to look at her. Abigail said quickly, "You see, Mother? I told you that

Nathan would come. Now, you go upstairs and try to rest." A black woman stepped forward quickly, and Mrs. Howland went without protest, pausing only to whisper, "Thank you, Nathan!"

After her mother had gone, Abigail smiled and took Nathan's arm. Looking up into his face, she studied him, and finally said, "You'll never believe I care for you, will you, Nathan?"

"Why, of course . . . !"

She suddenly bit her lip and turned from him, her back straight. "No, you won't—because without you we would be lost. So you'll always ask yourself, *Does she really love me—or does she just need me?*"

He went to her, turned her around and looked into her eyes. "Abigail, you shouldn't talk like that. You need help right now, and I thank God that I can give it to you." She was trembling beneath his hands, and he took a deep breath and said, "I think we should get married as soon as possible. I know it's a bad time—with your father's death and all the trouble—but I want to take care of you!"

Abigail looked up at him, and there was an enigmatic light in her eyes. For a long moment she stood there, and he fully expected her to say no. Finally, however, she nodded slowly, whispering, "If that's what you want, Nathan." Then she raised her lips to him and he held her tightly.

Laddie came to Boston as part of Knox's staff on the eighteenth, along with Washington. The commander in chief made no dramatic speeches or gestures in taking over the city. When he attended services, the first to be held under the new flag of the Colonies— thirteen red and white stripes with the Union Jack in the corner— he asked Dr. Eliot, dean of the Boston clergy, to preach a sermon of devout thanksgiving, not of war. Dr. Eliot found his text in Isaiah, and George Washington of Virginia bowed his head to the words, "Look upon Zion, the city of our solemnities: Thine eyes shall see Jerusalem a quiet habitation, a tabernacle that shall not be taken down."

The next day, Knox called his staff together and put them to work. He was beaming with anticipation and said, "The Redcoats have made us a present of 250 cannon, Gentlemen! Thoughtful of them, by Harry! But we've got to train gunners for them—and fast!"

"You think we'll be going into action soon, Colonel Knox?" asked Lieutenant Harvester, a solid-bodied New Yorker.

"No doubt about it, Tom! Only question is—*where?* I'm no prophet, but I say it'll be New York. But what matters now is to get men trained." He gave orders rapidly, and sent the officers away, then turned to Laddie, saying, "I have a special job for you, Sergeant. We're going to be fighting this war for some time, I think, and all over this country. I want you to make my bookshop your headquarters, and before we leave this place, I want you to secure maps of every kind you can lay your hands on!"

"Yes, sir!"

"Go to every cartographer in Boston—go any place else you need to go. I'll see that you have leave and money—but I want a map for every place where we might engage the enemy, you understand? Here's the key to my shop. Mullins has kept it open, but here's a key for you. I'll be in and out, but you can fix up some kind of quarters for yourself."

"I'll do my best, Colonel," Laddie said, taking the key. "How long do you think we'll have?"

Knox shrugged his shoulders and said as he turned to leave, "That'll depend on how fast Howe and his brother, Richard Lord Howe, can get an army together and get back here! Maybe a month, more or less, is all we can count on, Smith—so get those maps quick!"

Laddie threw herself into the job, and as the days sped by she amassed a small mountain of maps and charts. She went to New York and brought back many more—so many that Mullins complained about the space she had usurped in Knox's store, but the owner had been highly pleased with what had been accomplished. When Laddie told him that the collection was fairly complete, he said, "Fine! Now you work on them—especially the New York area, because I'll eat my head if the Howe brothers don't show up there pretty soon! Washington thinks so, too. He's sending troops there every day. Better give me what you've got on that area right now."

During those first hectic days, Laddie had spent a great deal of her time alone. She had expected Daniel Greene to return to his home, but he made no move to do so. He had, she discovered, grown quite close to his uncle, General Greene, who evidently found his nephew to his liking. Daniel had brought the general by to meet Laddie, and she had found him to be a charming man. "Friend Daniel and I are in the same boat, Sergeant Smith," he said with a fond look at his nephew. "We Friends are a hard-headed lot—and the Lord practically sent the angel Gabriel to get me to join the army."

Laddie knew what hardships the general had undergone from his fellow Quakers, and she asked, "Are you making any progress toward converting Friend Daniel to your views, General Greene?"

"I think the Lord is doing a little along that line. My sister will disown me for making a soldier out of her boy, I suppose." Then he grew serious and said soberly, "It's never easy to find God, Sergeant, and when a thing like this revolution comes along—a man can get pulled to pieces trying to render unto Caesar what's his and unto God what's His!"

Laddie spent much time with Molly. The Winslows had rooms with a family living in town, but Adam was busy training his men, and Molly had little to do. She had dropped by Knox's bookstore, and the two of them had spent a pleasant hour. The visit was repeated, and often Laddie would spend the evening with the older woman.

But as Laddie came to love Molly more and more, a strange sort of constraint grew up between the two women concerning Nathan. His announcement that he was engaged to marry Abigail had shaken Laddie, though it had not been unexpected. As she spent more and more time with Molly, she saw that the engagement was a grief to Nathan's mother, and she wrote in her journal:

April 3, 1776

I feel so sorry for Molly and Adam! It breaks my heart to see the way they smile and never complain—when all the time they know that their only son is making a frightful mistake.

Why is he so blind? I have to bite my tongue to keep from screaming at him that Abigail Howland is *using* him—but he wouldn't believe me, of course.

But why do I get so furious? When I started keeping this journal, I vowed one thing—*to always tell the truth*. I've been saying that I hate Nathan because he's hurting his parents, and that's so—but it's not all of it. The truth is—I'm jealous of Abigail! Yes! Now I've put it down—and it seems ugly, but how many times have I thought of them together and hated them both?

God forgive me for such thoughts!

It cost Laddie dearly to write the words, but it brought some sort of relief, although not for long. Two days after she made the entry, Molly stopped by the bookstore late one afternoon to say, "Come along, Laddie. You're having supper with us." It was not the first time she had done so, and Laddie always enjoyed being with her and Adam—but this time when she walked into the private dining room at the inn and saw Abigail sitting there with Nathan, she wished fervently she had not come.

"Why, it's Sergeant Smith!" Abigail said gaily, and she told the story of Laddie's theft of the pass as they ate. Her narration was witty, and it made the whole thing into some sort of romantic comedy. She ended by saying with a condescending smile, "Of course, Father had already seen to it that Nathan was in no danger."

Laddie had stared suddenly at Nathan, who seemed embarrassed, but said only, "Laddie had no way of knowing that, Abigail."

"Oh, I'm sure of that—I like to see young men have a little romantic flair—even if it gets out of hand at times."

Adam and Molly said little, and it was a relief for Laddie to make her excuses and get away as soon as she could. But all night long she tossed and turned, anger rising in her like a red tide. She tried to pray but finally gave up the attempt, and when she got up at dawn, her eyes were red and her heart filled with bitterness.

She dressed and tried to work, but was too angry to think. Finally she decided to return a map for further revision to Jacob Goldman, a map-maker who had been of great assistance to her. She picked up the document and was fifty yards down the street when she heard someone call, "Laddie!" and turned to find Nathan hurrying to catch up with her.

He looked haggard, and as soon as he stood beside her, he said, "I've wanted to talk to you."

"I've got to take this map to Goldman." The sight of him stirred an anger in her breast, and she turned coldly and continued on her way.

He fell into step with her, saying, "Laddie, you weren't very kind to Abigail last night. After all, she's lost her father—and she's all alone except for her mother—and you hardly said ten words to her."

Laddie struggled to hold back the hot words that leaped to her lips, but did not succeed. "Oh, she's got more than her mother, I think. She's got *you*, Nathan Winslow!"

He stopped suddenly and forced her to halt by taking her arm. He said angrily, "What's the *matter* with you?"

"Oh, nothing's wrong with me! I just somehow get upset when good people like Adam and Molly Winslow have to stand by and watch their only son make an idiot out of himself!" The anger that she had struggled with made her face pale, and she whirled and half ran down the street. When she saw that he was beside her, his face stubborn, she said, "Leave me alone!"

"No, I won't. I'm going with you; then we'll go someplace and talk."

"I don't want to talk to you, Nathan!"

"That's too bad, because you're going to whether you like it or not!"

She was so angry that tears gathered in her eyes, and to keep him from seeing them, she walked down the street, ignoring him. He said nothing else, but when she got to Goldman's he went inside with her.

Goldman was in the back of the shop talking to a tall bearded man, but he looked up and said, "Ah, Sergeant Smith!" and hurried over, a small, bald-headed man with a nervous smile. "You need more maps, is it?"

"No, I want to talk to you about this one. It won't take but a minute."

Nathan lounged back against the wall, and Laddie spread the map out on a table. For several minutes she carried on a conversation with Goldman, the two of them disagreeing over several points. Finally, Goldman said, "All right, I agree that the elevations are probably incorrect. Leave it with me and I'll make the changes from the 1743 chart."

Laddie said, "I think that will be much better. I'll drop by tomorrow, Mr. Goldman."

She turned to go, but there was someone standing right behind her. It was the customer Goldman had been talking with, and saying, "Pardon me," she moved to go around him.

When she stepped to one side, his hand shot out and caught her by the arm. "What are you doing?" she cried; then she looked up at the man—and found herself looking into the face of Aaron Sampson!

He looked very different, for he had grown a full beard—but the eyes were the same, and there was a smile of triumph on his full lips. "Well, now, I knew I'd find you someday, Julie, but I didn't think it'd be like this! Now I know why you've been able to keep yourself hidden from me!"

"You—let me go!" she cried out, and tried to break away, but his fingers bit into her arms like steel.

"Not likely!" he laughed loudly, and began to pull her toward the door.

"What the devil are you doing? Let go of him!" Nathan had stepped forward and his blue eyes glared angrily at the big man.

"Get out of the way. This is none of your affair," Sampson growled.

Nathan reached out and grabbed a handful of Sampson's coat. "Take your hands off him or I'll break your neck!"

Sampson looked up at Nathan, and the impulse to fight was in him, but he shook his head, saying, "Sergeant, I won't fight you—I won't have to, because the law will see to it that you mind your own business."

Nathan said hotly, "I don't know what the devil you're talking about—and I don't give a hang! This is Sergeant Laddie Smith of Colonel Henry Knox's staff, and I'll tell you just one more time— if you don't take your hands off him, I'll break your neck!"

Sampson shook his head and said, "You're wrong. This is my ward, Miss Julie Sampson of Philadelphia."

Nathan stared at him. "You're insane! Come along, Laddie!"

Sampson said at once, "I see that you have been deceived by this girl, Sergeant. But I can prove what I say with no trouble."

Laddie was standing there, fear washing over her, so weak that she could barely stand. She had had nightmares much like this, but she knew that there would be no awakening from this scene. She looked at Nathan, who was red with anger, and then she heard Sampson say, "Julie ran away last winter, and I've spent a lot of money trying to find her." He pulled a paper out of his pocket, handed it to Nathan, saying, "I've put these in every major city in the country—but I see now why they brought no results. I never thought she might become a man!"

Nathan read the description, and when he raised his eyes and looked at Laddie, he said, "You've made a mistake, Sampson."

"That'll be simple to prove, as I said." He looked at Laddie and said with a sly look in his eyes, "All you have to do is take your coat and your shirt off. A young fellow wouldn't mind doing that, now would he? Of course—a young lady *would* object."

Nathan glared at him, then said, "He doesn't have to do *anything*! We're leaving here."

"You're in Knox's force?" Sampson said. "I'm sure the colonel would ask the sergeant to do this very simple thing—because if he doesn't, I'll be right there with civil law to get it done! But there's a simpler way."

"And what's that?"

"Why, just look at her, Sergeant!" Sampson said with a smile. "It's written all over her face!"

"Laddie . . . ?" Nathan started to speak, but then he looked full in the white face of Laddie, and stopped abruptly. He had not for one second considered that Sampson might be telling the truth, but as the silence ran on, he seemed suddenly to be outside of himself, looking down from somewhere on the scene—seeing the three of them in a frame—and the look of guilt on the face of the person he'd been calling Laddie Smith was unmistakable!

He swallowed and could only whisper, "Laddie . . . ?" And then he saw the dark eyes fill with tears.

"It's true, Nathan, but . . . !"

He did not grasp the rest of her words, but wheeled and plunged out of the shop. As he fled blindly down the street, he thought he heard a voice crying his name.

CHAPTER TWENTY-FIVE

JULIE GOES TO A BALL

★ ★ ★ ★

The story of a young woman masquerading as a soldier in the Continental Army spread like wildfire through Boston, and the soldiers themselves spawned ribald jokes. If Aaron Sampson had taken his ward away, it would have been easier for Nathan, but that didn't happen. As soon as Molly Winslow heard that Laddie had been discovered, she told Adam the whole story. The two of them had gone to Knox. He was thunderstruck by the affair, but after Molly gave him the extenuating circumstances, he had agreed to help. He had called Sampson to his office and told him that he would have to present legal proof of his relationship with the girl.

"But—I'll have to go to Philadelphia! The wench will run away again!" Sampson was livid with anger. He had been on the verge of leaving with Julie as a prisoner, and he glared at Knox.

"I'll have her detained. She's officially a member of my staff and under my authority. She'll be here when you get the evidence. That'll be all!" Knox snapped. He did not care for Sampson's looks, and after the man left, he stared at the small figure before him and shook his heavy head. "Well, by Harry! I never thought I'd be taken in by a snip of a girl!"

Julie looked up at him and saw that he was grieved, but not angry. "I'm so sorry, Colonel Knox," she whispered, and tears glittered in her eyes as she said, "Will you let him take me when he comes back?"

Knox was a gentle man, giant though he was, and he hated to hurt the girl anymore—but he had to tell her the truth. "I think the law will be on his side, Laddie—Miss Sampson, I mean." He came over and put his hand on her shoulder, adding, "Before he gets here your friends will think of some way to help you, I'm sure." Then he said briskly, "Now, I've talked this over with Mrs. Winslow, and since you have to stay somewhere, you can stay with her and Captain Winslow."

He had sent her to the Winslows, accompanied by Lieutenant Wilkins, who had given her a curious glance, but said only, "I hope things work out for you, miss." Molly had met her and when the door closed, she opened her arms and instantly Julie fell into them, the tears she had held back flowing freely. The older woman held the weeping girl, and finally said, "Well, that's done! Now we'll have some tea and talk."

Her matter-of-fact manner did as much as anything to calm Julie, and by the time Adam came in, she was able to greet him without a sign of distress. He took her hands, and there was a fondness in his dark eyes as he said gently, "This has been pretty bad, hasn't it?" Then his eyes twinkled and a smile touched his lips. "Going to be a little hard to get used to having a young woman around—Julie, is it? You must think all the Winslows are blind as bats, eh? Can't tell a young woman from a man!"

She knew he was trying to find some way to make her feel better, but the mention of Nathan disturbed her. "I don't think Nathan will ever forgive me, Captain Winslow."

"Nonsense! Of course he will," Adam said quickly. "He just needs a little time, child."

But three days went by, and while Julie grew to love the Winslows more than ever, Nathan did not come once to the house. Daniel, who was there every day, commented on it only once. "He's taking it pretty hard, Julie. Thinks the whole world sees him as a fool. But he'll come around—worse luck for me!"

But two more days went by, and Julie said sadly to Molly, "Nathan's never going to forgive me, and I—I love him so, Molly!"

"I know, Julie." Molly wanted to give some comfort, but doubt had filled her own heart, and there was nothing she could say.

But that evening before supper, Adam had come in and Molly saw at once that he was disturbed. "What's the matter?"

"Nathan—he's coming here tonight."

"How do you know, Adam?"

"Because I *ordered* him to come!"

"Oh, Adam, you shouldn't have done that!"

"I know it, Molly, but he's going to get himself in bad trouble if he doesn't pull out of this. I've tried to talk to him several times, but he just freezes up and says nothing. This morning one of the sergeants from the Maryland brigade made a remark about this thing—a dirty remark, and Nathan just about killed him! The man doesn't have a tooth left in the front of his head!—and it would have been all the same to Nathan if it had been an officer!" He shook his head and added, "He's acting like a child about this, Molly! He's got to act like a man—and like a Christian."

"And you think ordering him here will do that?"

"It can't be any worse than it is," he said grimly. "You see how hurt Julie is by the way he's acting."

Molly was disturbed by what Adam had done, but she said nothing to Julie, and when Nathan walked in that evening, she saw the girl's face turn pale as paper. But she had risen at once, and going to stand in front of him, she had said quietly, "Nathan, I've been wanting to tell you how sorry I am—for what I did to you."

Nathan stared down at her, searching her eyes to find something, and there was a combination of hurt and bitterness in his face. He said briefly, "I suppose it was something you had to do."

The coldness of his reply and the harsh light in his face struck her like a blow, and she bit her lip and said, "I'll never forget what you did for me, Nathan. I—I hope you'll be able to think of me a little more gently—after a while."

She had left the room, and Molly saw that Adam was as angry as she had ever seen him. Before he could speak, she said quickly, "Nathan, try to see it from her side—she was so alone, and you helped her as nobody else could. I've never seen a human being as grateful as she is to you."

"You knew about her, didn't you?"

"Well, yes—"

"And I found out that Daniel Greene and his mother knew. Why was *I* left out?"

"Oh, for heaven's sake, Nathan!" Adam exclaimed. "You sound like a spoiled brat, crying because you got left out! I've been so confounded proud of you—but now, I'm ashamed to see you filled with hate for a girl who's been through a terrible time!"

His words struck Nathan hard, for he treasured the approval of his father as much as anything in the world. But stubbornness pressed his lips together, and he said tightly, "I don't hate—her." Both of them saw how difficult it was for him to even mention the thing, and Molly knew the sensitive spirit that was in him. He was, to Adam, a man come to full strength, but she was aware that beneath the militant air, Nathan had a childlike quality.

The atmosphere was tense, and Nathan soon left, his head high and with a pallor under his tan. "Well, that wasn't exactly the best idea I ever had, was it, Molly?" Adam sighed, staring after him.

"I think you did the right thing," she said promptly, and came to put her arm around him. "He's so confused, Adam. But he's good at heart, so we'll just have to be patient until God gets him through this thing."

"There's not much time, though. Sampson could be back with those blasted legal papers any time." He sighed and turned to go look out into the darkness through the window. "I wish the Lord would do something quick."

"You know, I have an idea," Molly said slowly. "Maybe there's a way we can hurry things up." There was, he saw, a far-off light in her gray eyes; he had learned long ago that when his wife got such a look, things usually happened.

"Oh, Molly, I can't do it!" Julie wailed. She was standing in the middle of the floor staring at herself in the mirror. "Everybody will stare at me!"

"That's the idea, Julie—or part of it." Molly was on her knees working on the hem of the beautiful white dress that she and Julie had bought that afternoon. She stood up, stepped back, and gave the girl a critical look, then nodded. "You'll be the best-looking girl at the ball. But when—" A knock at the door interrupted her, and she said, "There's Friend Daniel. Now you mind what I told you."

"It'll never work!" Julie moaned, and she thought back to the day when Molly had come to her with the idea. *Nathan can't think of you as anything but a man, Julie—so we'll have to let him see you as a woman! There's a ball in three days, and Nathan will be there. We'll buy you the prettiest dress in Boston, pretty you up, and when Nathan sees you as a young woman, he'll just have to think differently!*

Julie, reluctant, had finally agreed, but now that the time had come, she stood there filled with apprehension as Molly admitted Daniel. "Why, Julie . . . !" Daniel came into the room, and stopped dead still as he caught sight of her, his eyes widening.

"Isn't she beautiful?" Molly beamed.

"Very." Daniel came closer, and Julie's color rose as he stared at her as if he'd never seen her before. Then he shook his head and smiled. "Well, I told thee, Mrs. Winslow, I feel pretty strange, a Friend going to a worldly ball." His eyes crinkled with humor and his smile broadened as he added, "But I reckon this young lady is going to need some protection—looking like that!"

"I don't want to go!"

"You have to," Molly said firmly, and began herding them toward the door. "I'd love to see Nathan when he gets his first glimpse of you in that dress! You'll have to tell me all about it when you get home."

Daniel had a carriage, and he helped her into it, then climbed in and took the lines. "We're going to be late."

"Dan, let's don't go to the ball!" she pleaded. "We can just drive around and talk."

He didn't answer for a time, waiting until they had passed along the wide streets lined with elms. Finally he glanced at her, huddled up and looking completely miserable. "To tell the truth, Julie, that's what I was going to try to talk thee into doing. Thee knows how I feel about thee, and it's a mark of grace that I'm willing to let Nathan see thee."

"He won't care, Daniel."

"Well, if he doesn't, you'll have faithful Friend Daniel Greene waiting for thee, Julie."

She didn't answer, and all too soon they pulled up in front of a huge mansion brightening the sky with a myriad of lights. Dan handed the lines to a servant, then helped her down. They passed up a walk as wide as a city street, then through a set of massive doors into a spacious foyer. Through a set of double doors on their right, they could see a large crowd, with music echoing around the two as they entered the room.

"Well, this is a little different from our Sabbath meeting, isn't it, Julie?" Dan said quietly, looking over the room with interest.

The brilliantly colored dresses of the women—red, green, blue—were highlighted by thousands of small candles set in the massive chandeliers overhead. Everyone seemed to be moving, some of them dancing and others going around the edges of the room, visiting the refreshment tables or engaging in conversation, and the hum of talk and laughter almost drowned out the small orchestra that played at the far end of the room. Many of the revelers were officers, and their buff-and-blue uniforms set them off from the civilians, who wore darker colors.

"Let's go over to the tables," Dan said. "Friends aren't much on dancing."

As Julie followed him through the crowd, she became aware that she was the target for many eyes. A woman dressed in a scarlet dress stared at her, then asked, loudly enough for her to hear, "Who is that?" Her escort, a tall major in the uniform of the 19th Maryland, leaned down and whispered in her ear, and the woman's eyes gleamed. "So—*that's* the one!" Then she had said something to a woman on her left, and the two of them had laughed.

By the time they reached the table, Dan had noted the sensation they were creating, and said, "Don't let it bother you. Some people aren't kind."

Julie stood there enduring the stares and the comments that were aimed at her, longing more than anything to run out of the room. Then suddenly someone stood before her, and she looked up to see Colonel Knox. He smiled down at her, then said, "My wife is a very jealous woman, Miss Sampson, so I'll probably pay for this—but I must have a dance with the loveliest woman in the room!"

Julie found herself dancing around the room before she had time to think. Knox, though large, was very light on his feet, and by the time the dance was over, Julie realized that he had asked her to dance in order to put his stamp of approval on her. "You've been so kind to me, Colonel," she whispered as he took her back to Daniel.

He gave her arm a squeeze and whispered, "You and that bunch of Christians will pray this thing out!" Then he was gone, but three officers jostled each other for her next dance, the winner being a smiling Virginian from Adam's company. He was followed by a tall captain from Glover's Marblehead fishermen, and then by a series of others.

Nathan and Abigail arrived late, but Daniel had been watching for them. He went across the room before they had a chance to speak to anyone else, saying, "Nathan, I haven't had the honor of meeting thy fiancee." He bowed as Nathan made the introductions, saying, "My congratulations to both of thee."

"Are you alone, Mr. Greene?" Abigail asked.

"No—but my partner has proved to be so popular that I'm quite left out." At that moment, Julie passed by not twenty feet away, floating on the arm of a youthful brigadier. "I believe thee knows her?"

Abigail straightened suddenly, her eyes narrowing, but it was Nathan that Dan was watching. His lips parted and his bright blue eyes recorded his incredulity. "That's *Laddie*?" he whispered, not conscious that he had used the familiar name.

"Not Laddie," Daniel corrected. "Miss Julie Sampson. Lovely, isn't she?"

The dress that Julie wore was pure white, with a voluminous skirt and a tight bodice that revealed her slim figure. Her hair was short but Molly had arranged it into a halo that framed her face with glossy black ringlets. She wore only one piece of jewelry, a gold locket with a green stone that glittered on her neck. Her skin was flawless, and Nathan, in shock, stared at the fully curved lips, the almond-shaped eyes, and the beautifully arched brows.

"I'm claiming your first dance, Miss Howland," Daniel said, and with a gleam in his brown eyes added innocently, "Nathan, I'm sure thee can get a dance with Miss Sampson if thee hurry." He moved so quickly that neither of them had time to react. "Now, Miss Howland . . ." he was saying as he took her hand and led her to the floor, "I'm just a poor parson, so you'll have to excuse my dancing . . . !"

Nathan stood there, tempted to follow Daniel and reclaim Abigail. The anger and bitterness he'd nourished for days over Julie's deception, however, had faded to some extent, and a sudden wave of curiosity ran through him. He quickly walked across the floor, stepped in front of a dandified young man who was pushing forward to claim the next dance, and said, "Will you dance with me, Miss Sampson?"

The sight of him towering above her touched Julie's nerves so sharply she could only nod and murmur, "Of course." The touch of his hand seemed to tingle, and as he guided her across the floor, there was a dreamlike quality about it.

He looked down at her, and thought suddenly, *Why, she's so small!* She was tall, but slim and fine-boned. Her head was down, and he stared at the classic lines of her face, the delicate features, marveling at her grace and beauty. Finally, she lifted her head and smiled at him with tremulous lips, whispering, "Do you hate me so much, Nathan?"

Her gentleness went straight through him like a knife, and he felt a rush of affection as the early times he'd had with her came flooding back. He started to speak, then noticed that they were the center of attention for many. "I have to talk to you," he said abruptly, and as they passed close to a pair of French doors, he led her off the floor. The doors opened to a low balcony that overlooked a large garden. The moon was bright overhead, and the muted sound of the music was almost ghostly on the air.

He paused, and looking down on her said, "I—I can't believe how terribly I've treated you—Julie." It was the first time he'd used her first name and it warmed her, as did his whole attitude.

"It wasn't your fault, Nathan. I know the things they've been saying—all the horrible jokes . . . !"

He shook his head and began to pace back and forth, his face twisted with shame. For several minutes he poured out on himself a litany of guilt, and she made no move to stop him. Finally he paused and she said, "Nathan—will you do me a favor?"

"Of course!"

She came to stand before him, putting out her hands. "Let's remember the good times, not these last few days!"

He took her hands, marveling that he'd never noticed how slender her fingers were. Her face was turned up to him, and he said, "That's good of you, Julie. I'd like that a lot. There were some good times, weren't there?"

Her lips parted and she said, "Oh, yes! You're the kindest man I've ever known! And—and I'll always love you!"

It was Nathan's turn to be shocked, and he thought he had misunderstood her. Bending down to put his face close to hers, he said, "I didn't hear you."

Julie knew that she was terribly wrong, but his gentleness had weakened her, and she slowly raised her hands and put them behind his neck, and pulling his head down, she whispered, "I said *I love you*!" And then she closed her eyes and kissed him full on the lips.

Nathan had never felt such a shock, and the touch of her soft lips was sweeter than anything he had dreamed existed. He held her, his arms going around her without thought, and the music that floated on the air seemed to brush against his mind.

"Well, Nathan? I see you and *Laddie* are getting along well!"

Nathan straightened up, whirled, and was appalled to see Abigail with Friend Daniel Greene standing at her side. She was furious, and he could not have uttered one word to save his soul.

Daniel had seen the kiss, and he knew something in his own soul of the bitter jealousy flashing out of Abigail's eyes. But years of developing Quaker-style patience came to his rescue, and as he looked at the three of them—he made himself smile. Putting a hand on Abigail's arm, he said, "Well, thee mustn't be too upset, Miss Howland. Nathan's mother tells me he was always an affectionate young fellow."

But Abigail did not smile. She grabbed Nathan's arm, snatched him away from Julie and practically dragged him off the balcony.

"Looks like Friend Nathan's in for a trip to the woodshed," Dan observed wryly. Then he said, "I've had about all the fun I can stand for one night. Is thee about ready to leave?"

"Yes!"

She followed him as he left the balcony, and when they pulled out of the driveway in the carriage, Daniel looked back at the house and shook his head, remarking, "Guess worldly pleasure's not all it's rumored to be. Always wondered about that."

CHAPTER TWENTY-SIX

A MATTER OF HONOR

★ ★ ★ ★

Day after day, units moved out of Cambridge and Boston, headed for New York, for Washington and his staff were convinced that Howe would strike there. Knox worked frantically training gunners to man the guns the British had left behind, and Adam kept the Virginia riflemen drilling constantly. "I expect we'll be leaving in a week, Molly," he said one night after supper.

"What will happen to Julie when we leave—if that scoundrel Sampson hasn't come by then?"

Adam shrugged and gave a disgusted grunt. "Don't know. I thought she might run away again. But don't guess she's got anywhere to run to." He stretched, then gave Molly a look of speculation. "I've had the idea that Quaker might marry her. That'd solve the problem."

"Yes—but I don't think she'd marry him."

"Good man." Then he gave her a closer look and demanded, "What's in your head? I know that look!"

"Oh—just thinking." She evaded his question, saying, "Charles wants us to come out tomorrow and have supper with them."

"Oh, Molly, I don't want to do that!"

"I know, Adam, but I think we should." She came over and sat down beside him. Taking his thick hand, she stroked it gently, tracing a long white scar in the shape of a fishhook that curled around his thumb. "I feel uncomfortable there, too, but we ought to go this time—for Charles's sake."

"I don't understand?"

"Why, he wants to thank you for saving his home—try to patch things up between you. He stopped by today while you were gone and asked. I tried to tell him we couldn't come, but he almost begged. I think maybe we ought to go this one time."

"Oh, blast!" he groaned. "I don't want any thanks . . . !" Then he threw up his hands and surrendered, as he usually did when she asked for something. "Well, we'll go—but get us away as soon as you can. Martha will be taking potshots at me as usual. Will Nathan come?"

"Yes, and Abigail—if she'll go. She and Nathan are having some sort of a fight. He won't say what—but Abigail is giving him a hard time. That's why he's been mooning around so much. She's dangling him, punishing him for something."

"He ought to whip her," Adam grinned. "Good beating every once in a while—that's what all wives need! But I guess he's too much in love to act sensibly."

Molly punched her husband playfully on the arm. "Better not let Nathan hear you say such things. He just might take you seriously!"

Julie, who was upstairs writing in her journal, felt the same way, but she dared not say it to Nathan. She wrote with a frown on her face, jabbing so viciously at the paper that she snapped the tip off her quill several times:

> I could pinch her silly head off! Or *his*! It's been nearly two weeks, and she's been absolutely *inhuman* to Nathan ever since she caught us kissing on the balcony.
> If he had any sense, he'd give her something to be jealous *about*! But he won't—he's so afraid he'll lose her.
> Well, the one good thing out of all of it is that I've gotten to see him almost every day. He goes to see Abigail. She either torments him for a little while and then sends him home, or else she won't see him at all.
> If I had a mind to do it, I could fix her! He's so sad, and I guess that one kiss really convinced him I was a girl! He's so gentle with me, and when he comes from her, humiliated, he's so vulnerable. He was telling me yesterday how bad he felt, and we were sitting close together on the couch. I really think if I'd given him *one* sign, he'd have kissed me again!

But I didn't. Even if that woman has driven him right into my arms (so to speak!), he'll never be any good to another woman—not the way she's got him bewitched!

And again, I looked all day for Aaron to come back. Ever since he left, every time a door opens, I tremble! It makes me almost ill to think of him—what he'll do when he has me back in Philadelphia!

God, help me! You're the Father of the fatherless!

She shut the journal, knelt and prayed for a long time, then left her room. Molly and Adam had already gone to bed, so she fixed a cup of tea and was sipping it when the door opened and Nathan came in. He had a heavy look on his face and there was gloom in his voice as he asked, "My folks already gone to bed?"

"Yes, they went early. Did you need to see them?"

He shrugged and turned to go. "It can wait until tomorrow."

"I just made some tea."

He came back and sat down, and the hot tea seemed to cheer him, but he seemed restless. "I'm not sleepy tonight. Hate to go to bed."

"Let's walk around the pond." The house that the Winslows had rented was on the outskirts of town, and the small pond that lay under the canopy of some huge chestnut trees had been a god-send to her. She had fished for the small perch that abounded in it, and in the late evenings had enjoyed it as she walked.

Nathan responded quickly. "If you're not sleepy, I'd like it."

The soft spring breeze had warmed the earth, bringing the peepers out, and they piped loudly, like ghostly sleigh bells until Nathan and Julie stepped onto the small beaten path that ringed the pond. The sudden silence made Julie laugh. "I think those frogs resent us. They think this pond is theirs, and we're trespassers."

"I guess so." Nathan looked up and saw the full moon and commented, "Look, Julie, there's some kind of a hazy ring around the moon—I wonder what it is?"

"I don't know much about the stars," she said. They moved on, and the pond was so still the reflection of the moon seemed solid as the reality. He reached down, picked up a stone and tossed it into the pond; it struck with a loud *plop*, and rapidly spreading circles broke up the image of the moon. As the tiny waves reached the shore, he murmured, "One little stone—and it changed the whole picture. Doesn't take much to mess things up, does it, Julie?"

She looked up at him quickly, knowing that he was thinking

of Abigail, and she hated what was happening to him. "Time changes things, Nathan." She motioned toward the pond. "See? The ripples are almost gone already, and it'll be like it was—smooth and clear."

"Life's not like that."

"No—because we're more than a pond," she agreed. There was a longing in her to say something that would take away the gloom that had come to mar his manner. Always he had been cheerful, even when things were bad, but he had lost that lightness of spirit. Finally she said, "Abigail will forgive you."

He stared at her, and shook his head. "She—she thinks that I've known all along that you were a girl. Says as close as the two of us were, I just *had* to know." His teeth gleamed in a quick smile, and he said ruefully, "I can see her point. Looking at you now, it seems downright impossible I didn't catch on!"

"Oh, I was clever," she said. "She'll get over it, Nathan."

"I guess so—" He stopped and turned to face her on the narrow path. He was so tall that she had to tilt her head to look up at him, and he put his hands on her shoulders and said, "Julie, I ought not to be bothering you with my troubles. You've got more than I have—and I'm worried about it. Maybe we ought to get a lawyer— you can't go back to Philadelphia with Sampson!"

She was totally conscious of his hands on her shoulders, but she let nothing show in her face. "It will be all right, Nathan."

"Well—" He dropped his hands suddenly as if they had been burned, and said awkwardly, "I—I guess we better get back."

"All right." They walked back, saying little, but when they got to the door, Julie spoke up. "Your uncle Charles came by today. He wants all of you to come to his house for dinner tomorrow—said for you to bring Abigail."

"Doubt if she'll come."

A streak of anger raced through Julie. "Tell her I'll be there— that'll make her come."

He shifted his shoulders uneasily, then said, "Might not be much fun for you. She's—upset with you."

Julie smiled as she turned to go in, amused by some thought. "She won't hurt me, Nathan. Good night."

Whether Abigail chose to attend the dinner at the Winslows because Julie would be there, Nathan was not certain. He looked across the table at Abigail, and thought he'd never seen anything more beautiful. She was wearing a blue silk dress that left her arms bare, and her rich brown hair was woven into a crown that sparkled with jewels. The dimples in her cheeks were often in evidence, for all evening she had been as charming as he had ever seen her.

She had kissed him when he came for her, the first time since the night of the ball, and on their way she had been animated as if nothing had happened between them. The change in her manner startled Nathan, making him somehow feel awkward. Her moods, he had discovered, were often like that, and he could not seem to adjust.

But the party is a success, he thought, looking around. Even Martha Winslow, his father's stepmother, seemed to be determined to keep things agreeable. Charles sat at one end of the table, with his wife on his right and Anne and Julie on his left. Nathan sat with his parents, and across from them Abigail sat between Paul and Martha.

They had eaten a sumptuous dinner, and the only thing that had marred the evening had been the fact that Paul was obviously drinking too much. He had been a little drunk even before the meal, and Nathan had noticed that he had eaten little but had emptied glass after glass of wine. His face was flushed, and there was an uncertainty in his speech and movement. Once his mother had said sharply, "Paul, you've had enough wine!" but he had paid no attention.

Charles Winslow had been less talkative than usual, but finally he cleared his throat and said in a voice that claimed attention, "I've been sitting here thinking how sad it is that our family has drifted so far apart. It's taken a war to get us all together at this table." He looked at Adam and spoke with a rueful shake of his head, "I'm no good at speeches, but this is one that I must make—"

He paused and looked awkward, then made a futile gesture with his hands. "Adam, I don't know how to put this, but you've saved the family—my family, anyway. God knows you had no reason to! We've not given you cause to love us." At this point his mother seemed to shrink, and Dorcas flushed and looked steadily down at the table. Charles seemed to struggle for words, found none, so he said in a whisper, "Thank you, Adam—for what you've done."

Adam was shifting uneasily in his chair, and he blurted out,

"Why, Charles, there's no need for all this! What sort of brother would I be if I didn't do what little I could for you? Let's say no more about it, if you please."

Charles smiled faintly and shook his head. "I know you didn't do it for thanks, Adam." His eyes lifted to the portrait of Miles Winslow, their father, on the wall, and he said, "I *look* like Father—but you've always *been* like him!"

The compliment took Adam aback, and he looked up at the painting. "He was a man, Charles, wasn't he? I wish we had more like him these days."

"Why, Captain Winslow, you shouldn't say that!" All eyes turned toward Abigail as she'd known they would. She gave Adam a smile and said, "I'm sure your father was a wonderful man—but you have a son who's going to do great things! The House of Winslow will be one of the great families in this new country!"

Nathan twisted uncomfortably in his chair as Abigail went on, and he said finally, "Oh, Abigail, I've done nothing. Everything I've done's been wrong!"

"That's not so!" Julie blurted out her thought, then tried to shrink into the chair. She had said not a word to anyone except Anne, feeling totally out of place.

Abigail stared at her, and she lost her smile for an instant, but quickly said, "I'm sure you must have high regard for Nathan, Miss Sampson." She paused and then added with a clipped edge to her words, "After all, it would be better I suppose for a woman who did what you did to have one man for a *friend*—than a whole squad!"

A shocked silence followed this taunt. They all realized that Abigail was accusing Julie of being a common woman—and Nathan of being a party to her behavior.

Abigail knew at once that she had gone too far, and tried quickly to modify the harsh charge. "I—I don't mean to imply . . ."

"We all know exactly what you mean, Abigail!" Paul stood up suddenly and there was a fine perspiration on his lip. His eyes were fixed on Abigail and his voice was harsh. He was usually so easygoing that the transformation was shocking.

"Paul, I'm sure Abigail meant nothing by the remark," Charles said quickly.

Paul stared at his father, then said in a quieter voice, "Father, you've told me many times lately that it was a sadness to you that after all Adam's done for you, there's nothing you can do for him, haven't you?"

"Why, yes, I have."

"Well, there's one thing we can do for him, and I propose to do it!"

"Paul! You're drunk!" Abigail said quickly.

"Yes, Abigail, I am drunk. And it's a shame that a man has to get drunk to do the right thing! But drunk or sober, my dear, we're going to have some truth tonight!"

"Paul, please don't do anything you'll regret." Abigail had been glaring at him angrily, but she suddenly grew gentle, and there was a softness in her tone.

"Regret?" he echoed, staring at her. He laughed harshly and said bitterly, "I've regretted just about everything I've ever done— but tonight I'm going to do the right thing." He settled back on his heels and stared at the Winslows. "Uncle Adam, as my father has said, you've saved our family—but he's wrong when he says there's nothing we can do for you—I'm going to save *your* family."

Adam and Molly had been mortified by the scene, and now Adam stared at his nephew. "Paul, I don't know what you're talking about."

"I'm talking, Uncle Adam, about Nathan."

"Nathan?"

"Oh, yes! And I'm talking about his intended bride, Miss Abigail Howland."

Nathan stood up suddenly, his eyes bright with anger. "Paul, shut your mouth!"

"No, I won't do that, Nathan," Paul said evenly, and then he got a strange look in his eye. "Honor—that's always been important to the Winslow men, hasn't it, Uncle Adam?"

"I hope so, Paul."

"Honor." Paul seemed to taste the word, then smiled sadly. "It's been just a word to me, I'm afraid. I've laughed at those who thought it was worth living for—or dying for. But lately, I've had to wonder if *I* wasn't the one who was wrong."

"Nathan, I want to go home!" Abigail uttered, her voice distraught, her face very pale.

"All right, Abigail. I'll take you," Nathan said.

He moved from his place, but Paul cried loudly, "Nathan, you've wondered who betrayed you when you went to Abigail?"

The question stopped Nathan in his tracks. Paul said evenly, "I turned you in."

"You!"

"Yes. I was in love with Abigail and you seemed to be winning her."

"Paul!" Charles's face seemed to be bloodless, and he cried out, "You betrayed your own flesh and blood?"

"Yes. But how did I know he was there?"

"I never told you that!" Abigail said loudly.

Paul reached into his pocket and pulled out several pieces of paper. "Nathan, you know Abigail's handwriting—here's the note she sent telling me you were coming to her house—and here's the one I got later that says our affair will have to stop—for a while—because she needs you to keep her from falling into the hands of the patriots."

Nathan took the notes, read one, then the other. He lifted his eyes, so filled with pain that Julie wanted to cry.

"I couldn't help it!" Abigail cried out, and then her face twisted and she ran out of the room sobbing.

Paul moved back and said with a hollow smile, "I'm sorry for you, Nathan, but not as sorry as I am for her—nor for me, because I love her. I know what she is—and I love her anyway. She would have ruined you, Nathan!" Then he turned and walked out of the room, and they heard the door slam as he left the house.

Nathan reached out and touched the notes to the tip of flame that rose from a candle, then put them into a silver dish. He watched the paper turn into blackened ash; then he looked at the silent group and said, "Uncle Charles, I hope you won't think too badly of Paul. When a man loves a woman—he's likely to do strange things, I guess." After a pause he asked quietly, "Are we ready to go home now?"

Adam and Molly came quickly to stand with him, and then he said, "Julie? Will you come with us?"

"Yes, Nathan, I'm ready," she whispered, and together they left the house.

CHAPTER TWENTY-SEVEN

THE FIERY TRIAL

★　★　★　★

The morning after the disaster at Charles's house, Adam sent Nathan on a mission to collect some cannon and powder from a post in Rhode Island. When Molly pressed him, he said, "I could have sent someone else—but Nathan needs to get away." He grimaced and clapped his hands together in an abrupt gesture, exclaiming, "Molly, when he realized last night what that girl had done, it was like he'd taken a bullet in the brain!"

"I know, Adam." Molly's eyes were tired, and she tried to smile. "I think it's just as well for him to go away for a while."

"He was so depressed I was afraid he'd desert. His enlistment is up in two weeks—by that time we'll be moving on to New York for sure."

When Molly told Julie later that day what Adam had done, she had said quietly, "It's best that way. He was hurting so!" The older woman gave her a compassionate look and thought in her heart, *And so are you, child!*

As the days passed, Julie said little, but the thought of Aaron's return was never completely out of her mind. She ate little and her cheerful smile was rarely seen. There was little work for her to do, so after cleaning the house she spent long hours beside the small pond, sitting under the canopy of tender gold-green leaves. For hours she would read the Bible, especially the Psalms; then she would walk around the pond, praying silently. Praying and thinking. Fear would strike her like a knife, but each time it did, she would seek God, and a peace would settle over her.

Except for Molly, she saw almost no one, which was a blessing, for the inward journey she was struggling with required all her attention. She wondered at times about Daniel Greene, for the gentle Quaker had disappeared. Once she had asked Adam, but he had said, "Well, he was getting pretty close to his uncle, General Greene. Nathanael's a wandering man—maybe he took the young fellow off on one of his scouting trips."

Privately Julie thought he'd gone back home, and was disappointed, but as she became more and more engaged in her search for God's will, she thought of him fondly, but not often. Molly was a blessing, for the dark-eyed woman had the blood of the Covenanters in her veins, and knew what waiting on God was. Sometimes Julie would sit for hours listening as Molly read in a soft, firm voice out of the Bible, and although she said little of meaning or interpretation, there would be those times when she would read a verse, then pause for a long moment with her eyes closed—and then she would smile at Julie and comment on the meaning so that the verse would suddenly come alive to the girl.

It came as a surprise to her when Paul Winslow came down the path as she was walking late one afternoon. He stopped in front of her, saying, "Sorry to intrude on you, Miss Sampson." Fatigue had dulled his neat features, making him look older, and his manner was subdued. "Perhaps you'd rather not talk to me—I should not blame you."

"Would you like to walk with me, Mr. Winslow?" she asked, and her gentle answer brightened his eyes.

"Thank you." He stepped beside her, and for several minutes he said nothing. She could see he was changed; he was struggling with his thoughts, attempting to say something that came hard for him.

"You feel badly about Nathan, don't you, Mr. Winslow?" she said quietly, sensing that it was this that had brought him.

He stared at her, then smiled and nodded. "You're a very discerning young woman!" He bit his lip nervously, and threw his hands out in a helpless gesture. "What can I say? Father won't speak to me—and he's absolutely right . . . !"

His conscience, Julie saw, had been cutting him to pieces, and the light spirit that had bubbled out of him was gone. She said little as they walked and he spoke of his life, for she saw that he was looking for someone to hear his confession.

Finally he paused and said in a hopeless voice, "I—I don't know why I came to you with all this. Actually, I'm not much of a man to speak of myself about such things. I—I guess I wanted to tell Nathan how sorry I am, and you caught it instead." He had been staring down at the ground. Now he lifted his head, looked into her eyes and said , "Well, I'll leave you to—"

"Don't go, Paul." She called him by his first name unconsciously, for there was something young and vulnerable in him as he stood there. "Let's talk some more." He brightened, and for over an hour they walked, and this time she shared with him her struggle to find peace. As he listened, the simple faith in her voice held him. She made little of the precarious state of her life, but he knew of it, and admired her quiet courage.

Finally he left, saying, "You've been a help, Julie." Then a trace of his old humor touched his eyes and turned his lips up in the first smile she'd seen since he'd arrived. "You know what I'm going to do for you?" He paused solemnly and said firmly, "I'm going—to let you pray for me!"

She smiled at him. "I haven't waited for your permission, Paul."

He blinked, nodded, then turned abruptly and left. Later that night she told Molly of the visit.

"He's lost his way," Molly said. "But Winslow men have a habit of getting pulled out of the miry pit." Then she shook her head, saying, "That girl! She could have had one good man—but it wasn't enough for her!"

"Molly," Julie asked suddenly, "Doesn't the Scripture say we are to pray for those who despitefully use us? Are you praying for Abigail?"

Molly said, "Yes—but it's not hard, Julie. She hasn't used me ill."

"But the way she treated Nathan—?"

"She would have harmed us all much more if she'd married him, Julie!" Then she smiled and said, "And you mustn't forget—she's a Winslow, too! Oh, the blood's thinned some—but her grandmother was Rachel Winslow—and *her* great-grandfather was Gilbert Winslow." She paused and said thoughtfully, "I think about those people a great deal—and it's hard to keep in mind that they weren't gods—just people like us. But Gilbert threw his life on the altar for God, and Rachel went to the brink of death at Salem out of a love for God—so I'm not giving up on Abigail!"

Julie leaned against the wall, hands behind her. The quiet days had thinned her face, hollowed her cheeks somewhat, and her eyes were clear and speculative. "I feel so strange, Molly. The world is falling apart—trouble everywhere. And all I've done for days is walk around a pond."

"There never has been a time, Julie," Molly answered with a nod, "that the world *wasn't* falling apart. Gilbert Winslow saw his world fall apart when half of the Firstcomers died that first winter at Plymouth. His son, Matthew, was in prison with John Bunyan in the shadow of the gallows. That's the kind of world we live in— and it won't ever change." Her lips were relaxed as she spoke, and she added thoughtfully, "As for walking around a pond—you've been doing more than that, child. You've been trying to find out who you are to God—and who He is to you. And that's the most important job in this little life we have!"

"That's right, isn't it?" A look of wonder came into Julie's eyes and she whispered, "That's what God's been saying to me all this time—'Trust me!' " She laughed shortly, adding, "I was expecting some sort of lightning bolt to strike me—maybe fall out—like Adam said He did when he got converted."

"He did!" Molly laughed. "It was at one of George Whitefield's meetings, and Adam had tried just about everything—was about ready to give up—and all of a sudden, he just folded up. He got up looking stunned—and he's been walking with God ever since. So for some it's falling down at a meeting—for others, God speaks in a still, small voice—perhaps when walking around a pond!"

Two days after this conversation, Julie answered a knock at the door, opening it to see Dan standing there dressed in the uniform of General Greene's company. She stared at him in astonishment, and he laughed before she could move, giving her a kiss on the cheek. "Well, here I am, Julie," he smiled ruefully. "See what thee has done to a poor humble Friend?"

"Daniel! I can't *believe* it!"

"Neither could Mother! But she's not going to disown me. I just came from home, and thee know what, Julie? She wasn't surprised—said the Lord had already told her about it." He laughed in embarrassment, adding, "I wish He'd told *me*!"

"How in the world—?"

"Oh, my uncle had gone through the same struggle, thee knows. And officially I'm a chaplain—but that doesn't seem to mean much! I think when the fighting starts, there'll be at least two fighting Quakers in General Greene's company!"

She pulled him inside, glad to see him, pushing him into a chair, and demanding the details. They drank a pot of tea as he spoke of the great change that had come to his thinking. The china cup looked small in his large hands, and he sometimes spoke quietly of the inner struggle that had shaken him—then his eyes flashed as he spoke of the new vision that had caught his spirit. He didn't call it a *vision*, yet it was so strong that it made his eyes glow as he spoke of the emerging nation.

"It's not just a little movement, Julie," he said finally. "God is up to something with this country! The old world is tired—and the church of the living God is bound in chains. But in this land, why, it can be a place where we can all seek God in any way we choose!"

Finally, he caught himself, laughed and said, "I sound like a recruiting sergeant, don't I? But that's not why I came, Julie, although since thee is a part of what's happened to me, I wanted to share it with thee."

"I'm glad you came. I've missed you, Dan."

He stared at her, then said simply, "Did thee, Julie? Well, that may mean something, but I guess thee knows how I feel. I know thee thinks thee are in love with Nathan—but I finally decided that I could either keep my mouth shut—or I could say what I've been thinking."

"Dan—!"

"Don't stop me now, Julie! I'm a plain man—always will be. Not at all romantic or exciting." He considered this, and it was characteristic of him that he was anxious to be fair, even at such a moment. "So—I want thee to marry me."

Julie stood very still, and he added, "Maybe I'll never have what thee had to give the other fellow. I'll never ask for that. I can't give thee what he could—but I can give thee my name—and my love."

The clock ticked loudly on the shelf, and tiny motes floated in the brilliant sunshine that fell through the windows in bars that seemed almost solid. Tears rose to Julie's eyes and she said, "I can't let you do that, Daniel. It wouldn't be fair."

He nodded and there was a faint regret in his eyes—but a stubborn set to his jaw. "I may not be romantic, Julie," he said, "but I'm hard to discourage. I'll not bother thee, but thee are pretty likely to find me underfoot for a spell."

"You'll be off at the war."

"Woman, thee are talking to the only living *nephew* of General Nathanael Greene!" His eyes twinkled and he said proudly, "Why, dear Uncle Nathanael practically *insisted* that I take a good leave! So here I am, Julie—and like I say, I'm a hard man to discourage."

Julie shook her head, but though she often asked him to leave during the next three days, he settled down in a room close by, ignoring her urgings. He said nothing more about marriage or about Nathan, and his presence, for all her protests, was a comfort to her.

On a Friday afternoon, Adam came in with bitter news. The moment he entered the room and said "Julie!" she knew what it was.

"My uncle is back, isn't he?"

"I'm afraid so."

Molly asked quickly, "Adam, isn't there anything we can do?"

"He's got the papers—and Judge Evans says that Julie will have to go with him." He came up and tried to smile, saying, "Child, this isn't the end. We'll get a lawyer—a good one!"

Julie looked at him and asked quietly, "When—will I have to go?"

"On Monday, I'm afraid. General Knox held him off until after the Sabbath."

"I'll be ready—and I'd like to write your mother a letter, Daniel."

She left the room, and Daniel suddenly slammed his hand down on the table. "Well, devil fly off! I'd like to sink that man in the depths of the sea with a blasted millstone tied around his neck!"

He stood there, shocked at the force of his anger, then wheeled and left the room. "I'm going to see if my uncle knows a good lawyer in Philadelphia."

Molly waited until the door slammed, then came to stand beside Adam. "I'm afraid for her," she whispered. "She's so young and helpless!"

"Well, God's not!" Adam said, and the muscles in his thick arms tensed. She knew that he, like Daniel, longed for some way to throw himself physically into the matter, but he finally said, "This is going to be hard on Nathan. I thought he'd be back before now—but I got word from a courier—they're just twenty miles out of Boston with the guns. Be in some time late tomorrow, or Sunday at the latest." Then he shrugged and said in a gloomy tone, "I don't look for him to be too happy, Molly. He was in bad shape when he left—and this news isn't going to help, is it?"

Molly's lips tightened. "Saints are made by being put through the fire. I've heard you say the same many times. This is our son's time to go through his fiery trial, Adam—and all we can do is pray!"

CHAPTER TWENTY-EIGHT

"AS LONG AS WE LIVE!"

★   ★   ★   ★

Sunday Julie went to services with the Winslows and Daniel Greene. Adam shifted all through the sermon, and as soon as they were outside, Molly asked, "What is the *matter* with you, Adam?"

"This business has got to me, Molly. Can't stand the thought of that poor girl going off in that man's hands!"

They went home after church, and although Molly had fixed a large meal, none of them felt like eating much. The afternoon dragged on, and when night fell, Adam said, "Something must have happened to Nathan. He should have been here long before this."

At ten o'clock, Julie said, "I want to thank you both for all you've done for me." There was a wistful light in her eyes, and she added, "No parents could have been better to me than you've been."

"Why, we've done nothing!" Molly said.

"Yes, you have—and I wanted to tell you tonight how much I've learned to love all of you." She hesitated, and they saw that she was close to tears. "I'm going to bed now—good night—and God bless you!"

She left quickly and Adam and Molly went to bed soon after, but there was little rest for them. All night long, Adam tossed and turned, and finally just as dawn was breaking, there was the sound of a horse galloping down the street. The rider pulled up, and when they heard the knocking at the door, Adam said, "That's Nathan!"

He got up, pulled his clothes on, and hurried downstairs to unlock the door. Nathan stepped in, his face tense. "Hello, Father. She's still here, isn't she?"

"Well, yes," Adam said. "But Sampson's taking her back to Philadelphia today. Why are you so late?"

"Spring rains washed a bridge out—we had to go a long way around to another bridge—and then the courier you sent couldn't find us."

Molly came down the stairs belting a robe on, and Nathan put his arms around her and kissed her. "I've missed you!"

She stood in his arms, looked up into his face. He was so tall that he made her feel like a child, but there was something different about him, and she asked quickly, "Nathan—what's happened to you?"

He grinned down at her, then shot a look at Adam. "I could never fool her, could I, Father?"

"Neither could I, son." He too was staring at Nathan, and saw that there was no sign of the tension and gloom that he'd worn two weeks earlier. "Well, even I can see something's different. You left here looking like death—but you're not that way now."

"It's not a very long story," Nathan said, but there was a glow in his blue eyes, and excitement ran through his voice. "You were right, Father, about how I left here. I was mad and feeling sorry for myself—and I came pretty close to just leaving for good."

"I figured that," Adam nodded.

"It was in my mind most of the time. I'd made such a mess of things! If my enlistment had been up, guess I'd have done it—but I didn't want to be a deserter on top of everything else—so I decided to wait till I was out of the army, then pull out." His face grew sober, and he walked over to the window. The gray dawn was breaking up, and tiny shards of rose began to show in the east. He seemed to have forgotten them, and neither Adam nor Molly moved.

Finally he turned, and they were shocked to see tears in his eyes. "It was last Sunday—April 19." He struggled to get control of himself, then finally said huskily, "One year after—after Caleb died."

Molly put her hand to her mouth and turned away, and Adam set his jaw—but neither of them spoke. They had never seen Nathan so moved. He had rarely let his emotions show, but now they looked into his eyes and saw that somehow during the brief time he'd been gone, something had stripped him of the wall he'd kept between his inner self and the world. *His eyes*, Molly thought suddenly, *are like windows.* Looking into them she saw her son as she had never seen him—and she knew that Adam was seeing the same thing.

"I didn't even know what the date was. We'd camped beside a river, and late that afternoon one of the men mentioned that it was a year since Lexington—and it hit me hard! I walked off and left them—walking along the bank of the river. It all came back— about Caleb, and all night I just walked and walked—and cried. I never cried much, you remember? Well, I made up for it, I guess."

"We've all done our crying, son," Adam said gently.

Nathan shook his head and then went on. "I finally just wore out and sat down under a tree. The mosquitoes were bad, but I felt so terrible I didn't even care! I sat there, so mad that I couldn't even think! And I was ashamed of making such a fool out of myself— over Abigail! That, on top of grieving over Caleb, just about made me want to drown myself."

He stopped suddenly and looked at them so strangely that Molly asked, "What is it, Nathan?"

He shook his head, and the words seemed hard for him. "Well, I've been trying to think of a way to tell you about what happened to me under that tree—but there's no way except to just come out with it." He sobered and there was such a look of wonder in his eyes that Molly wanted to reach out and hold him. "I've been looking for God so long—even tried to be a minister to please Him. Read a thousand books of theology—and then He had to get me out under a tree with the bugs about to eat me alive before He'd speak to me!"

"You found the Lord!" Molly exclaimed, her eyes bright.

"Not quite as dramatic as your conversion, Father," Nathan said. "I didn't fall down, or anything like that—but for about two hours God brought up just about everything I'd ever done—and by dawn I was just too tired to fight, so I just called on God and told Him that I wasn't worth anything, but that if there was anything in me that He wanted—why He was welcome to it!" Then Nathan laughed and said with a joy they'd never heard: "And that's when Jesus Christ came in and took over!"

"Nathan! That's wonderful!" They all turned to find Julie standing in the hall. She'd already been up and dressed when he'd come, and she'd stood there listening to him. Now she came forward and there was a light in her face as she said, "I'm so *glad*!"

He stood there looking at her with a peculiar expression on his face, but he said only, "I'm glad I got here in time, Julie."

"I'm going to fix some breakfast," Molly declared. "Julie, you start the coffee while I get dressed."

As Julie cooked, Nathan related the fine details of his experience, and soon his parents were back, drinking it all in. They ate a good breakfast, and were just finishing when there was a loud knock on the door.

Adam got up, hesitated, then went and opened it.

Julie's courage almost failed her when she saw the bulk of Aaron Sampson fill the opening, and his coarse voice broke out loudly, "All right, where's the gal?"

Julie went at once to her room, picked up a bag containing what few things she was taking back, and returned swiftly. She saw that Adam's face was red, and he was saying, "The coach for Philadelphia doesn't leave until ten—!"

Julie didn't want to cause trouble for these people she loved, so she quickly stepped around Adam. "I'm ready."

Sampson was angry, and he glared at Adam. "I've got the papers all proper. That general has given me the runaround—but I'll have no more of it!" He grabbed Julie by the arm and jerked her out of the door. The pain of his grip made her cry out, but he said, "None of that! You've cost me a mint, you baggage! But, I'll have it back on you."

He was dragging her along toward the carriage he'd arrived in when suddenly his wrist was seized and Julie was plucked away from him. Sampson went reeling forward, falling heavily on the ground from a shove in the middle of his back.

"Get out of here, Sampson!"

The burly man looked up to see Nathan staring at him. He scrambled to his feet and cursed, but there was something deadly in the gaze that met his, so he shouted, "I'll have the law on you!"

Nathan asked, "Do you need help to get in that carriage?"

Sampson was a strong man, but he had felt the power of the soldier's grip, so he backed away, screaming, "You'll be jailed for this—I swear it!"

280

He drove off, whipping the horses and cursing all the way, and when he was down the road, the silence that fell was broken by Julie. "Nathan, you shouldn't have done that. You'll get into trouble."

"You can't go with that man, Julie!"

"I have to."

They went back into the house, and there was much talk about what to do, but an hour before the coach was to leave, Adam said, "We'll have to go. Nathan—they'll send as many men as they need to take her."

The four of them climbed into the carriage, and all too soon they were downtown. "There's Daniel," Molly said as they pulled up to the inn. The coach for Philadelphia was waiting, and Aaron Sampson was standing there with a tall man, obviously some sort of official.

"There she is!" he shouted. "Now, you do your duty!"

The officer came over as Adam pulled up and got out. "I'm Sheriff Marks, and I've got to ask you to surrender that young woman without making any trouble," he said quietly. "I know how you must feel, but he's within his legal rights."

While Adam was talking with the sheriff, Nathan jumped from the carriage to help his mother and Julie down. Dan hurried up to say, "Why, Nathan, you're back!" But he did not wait for a reply. Turning to Julie, he said, "I've been talking to my uncle, and he's given me a letter to Mr. Franklin—a personal friend of his. He's asking Franklin to get a good lawyer and to take a personal interest!"

"Why, that's so good of the general, Dan," Julie said, but there was little hope in her voice. She well knew that once her uncle got her in his grip, he cared nothing for the threats of the law.

Molly started to speak, but Nathan said loudly, "Wait a minute!" They all turned, surprised. Adam and the sheriff abruptly stopped their conversation, while Aaron Sampson threw an angry, malevolent look at him. An elderly couple about to mount the carriage paused to stare at Nathan. The driver, coming out of the inn with a large mail pouch, gave him a surprised look, thinking he was being stopped.

Nathan had their attention, and for one brief instant they stood there, as if time had stopped. The only sound breaking the silence was the impatient stamping of the horses' hooves. Julie had been standing between Dan and Nathan, and when he spoke she looked up at him, and her heart, struggling with fear ever since her first glimpse of Aaron Sampson in the doorway, somehow lightened.

Nathan had said practically nothing on the way to town. He had let others do the talking, but there had been a grim perplexity on his wedge-shaped face. Now he seemed to have reached a decision. He set his feet firmly, and reached down and took a grip on Julie's arm, his chin thrusting forward as he said, "You're not taking her back with you, Sampson!"

The beefy face of Sampson grew red, and he yelled, "You just try and hold her, Winslow! I got the law on my side. Sheriff, you hear what he says? Do your duty, man!"

Sheriff Marks moved a few steps toward Nathan, took in the aggressive set of his face, but said in an authoritative voice, "Now, Mr. Winslow, you must be reasonable about this thing. I don't like it myself, but it's the law."

"The law gives him the right to take her back to his home because he's her guardian."

"That's right."

Nathan took a firmer grip on Julie's arm and said, "Well, I have no objection to that—but he's not going to be her guardian after this morning."

"What kind of nonsense is that?" Sampson snorted. He moved closer to Julie, then took one look at Nathan's face and said quickly, "You get that girl in that carriage, Sheriff!"

"No you don't!" Nathan said. "She won't be in his charge if she's a married woman." He felt Julie's body tense, but he didn't look at her. "That's law, isn't it? When a woman marries, her husband is responsible for her?"

Sheriff Marks looked confused. He raised a hand and scratched his neck, staring first at Nathan then at Julie. "Well, I'm no lawyer, Winslow—I just—"

Suddenly Nathan felt Julie pull away and, looking down, saw that her face was red with anger. Her eyes were snapping, and there was a tremor of indignation in her voice as she spoke to him. "And what makes you think I'd marry *you*, Nathan Winslow?"

He stared down at her stupidly, for in his own mind the idea of marrying her had seemed simple, but she drew her arms together to her sides, and her enormous eyes flashed fire as she looked up at him and said through set teeth, "You needn't stand there looking like a martyr! Oh, wouldn't that be a great marriage—for the next forty years every time I did something you didn't like, you'd get that look on your face: *I married her to save her—now see how she pays me back!*"

"Why, it won't be like that—!" Nathan protested.

"Besides," Julie ran on swiftly, "you needn't think you're so righteous—Daniel's already asked me to marry *him*!"

Nathan's face went blank, and then he pivoted his head around to stare at Daniel. "Why, you can't marry him!"

"Oh, why can't I?" Julie challenged, looking up at Nathan. "You think nobody would marry me except to get me out of trouble? No man would love me for myself?"

Daniel said quickly, "My offer still stands, Julie. I don't mind saying before everyone that I love thee. Marry me."

"She's not marrying you, Greene—she's marrying *me*!"

Greene's face flushed, and he moved around to face Nathan, his broad shoulders suddenly tense. Anger laced his mild voice as he said, "Thee don't love her, Winslow! I'll admit she's in love with thee"—Nathan's head went back and he shot a wild glance at Julie, but the Quaker went on relentlessly—"but she'll get over that in time."

Sampson raised his voice, protesting, "Sheriff, do your duty!" But the officer was caught up in the drama. Julie was suddenly aware that she was the focal point of attention. Even people passing by had stopped to stare.

The sudden flash of anger that had swept through her faded. She lowered her head, her eyes swimming with tears, and she wished that it would all be over. Then she felt a hand under her chin, and looked up to see Nathan's face. There was a strange look in his eyes. He stared at her, and she saw him only in a blur, for the tears spilled over and rolled down her cheeks. He asked, "Is that right, Julie—what Greene said? Do you love me?"

She blinked and saw the gentleness in him that she'd learned to love. His hands were on her cheeks, and as he held her face, memories swept through her. Finally she whispered, "Yes! I guess I always will, Nathan."

He was silent, and then he said, "I've been so mixed up, Julie. I told you about finding God on the riverbank—but I didn't tell you what else I found."

"What, Nathan?" she asked.

"After I got straight with the Lord, I found out I could think straight about other things—and all I could think about was you. I've been God's worst fool about women—but somehow I know there'll never be anyone for me—except you, Julie!"

She knew that the spectators were leaning forward avidly, but she didn't care. Everything around them vanished, and she saw only his face, heard only his voice. Then she whispered, "It's just pity, Nathan—you don't love me."

"I had to find out that not all people find God the same way," he said quietly. "And I'm finding out now that not all men find love the same way—but believe me or not, Julie, I know in my heart I'll always love you. I wish we had *time!*—but we don't, because I'll be leaving to go with Washington. But I'll come back, Julie—and I want to come back to you—if you'll have me!"

Julie suddenly smiled, her face illuminated with joy, and she held her arms up, saying quietly, "I'll have you—and you'll have me!"

He kissed her, ignoring Sampson's cries of rage, and when he stepped back, they heard him say, "It ain't legal, I tell you—I'm her guardian! There ain't no wedding—and I'm taking her with me."

Sheriff Marks said regretfully, "I think he's within his rights. Now if you were actually *married*, why that'd be different—but you'll not find a minister to marry you right now, and even if there was one willing, it'd take a few days to get the papers done." He shook his head, adding, "Have to ask you to go with this man, Miss Sampson."

Julie moved away from Nathan, but suddenly she heard Dan say, "I don't think it'll be any problem—getting thee married—if that's what thee wants, Julie."

"Why, Friend Daniel," Adam spoke up, "you heard what the sheriff said! It'd take a miracle to get them married."

Greene pulled a paper out of his inner pocket and held it up. "Here's a license from General Greene authorizing a civil marriage. Boston is technically under martial law, so all licenses must be is- sued or approved by military authorities."

"Whose name is on that paper?" Sampson demanded.

"Well, it's not filled in yet." He came to stand before Julie and Nathan, and there was sadness in his fine eyes but a faint smile on his face. "I thought thee might change your mind and have me at the last minute, Julie, so I had my uncle give this to me—meant to write *my* name on it, but—if thee are sure of this thing, all I have to do is fill in Nathan's."

"Oh, Dan—" Julie almost sobbed, "I—don't want to hurt you—but I love him so much!"

"And thee, Nathan?"

"Friend Daniel," Nathan said quietly, "I love her now—but it's just the beginning."

"Well—that's it!" Greene said.

"No, it ain't!" Sampson said, his face contorted with rage. "You got a paper—but you ain't got no preacher. Come on, get in that coach!" His thought, as Julie knew, was to get her away at once, and once they were in Philadelphia, he would force her to marry him.

"Oh, we've got a minister here." Greene smiled as they stared at him, then waved his hand. "Chaplain Daniel Greene, at thy service—fully authorized by the commander in chief of the Continental Army to perform all prescribed duties—sermons, buryings—and marryings!"

"Daniel! Can you marry us?" Julie gasped.

"Well, it's not what I had in my mind—or in my heart—but I see that it's the way God is moving."

Aaron Sampson's face was pale as paste, and he whispered, "Sheriff—can he do that?"

Sheriff Marks had a broad smile on his face. "I can't go against George Washington and the Continental Army, can I?"

Sampson glared at them and said, "I don't believe it! You'll wait till I'm gone and then back out somehow!"

Daniel saw that the man meant it, so he said briskly, "Captain Winslow, would thee and thy wife come and stand here by the bride and groom? The rest of thee can be witnesses."

There was a dreamlike quality about it all, and the crowd grew larger as the party arranged itself in the street beside the coach. Julie could not believe what was happening, but there was reality in the hard squeeze that Nathan gave her hand, and she took her place with him in front of Dan, with Molly standing beside her, Adam by Nathan.

The traffic on the street had stopped, and eager spectators crowded close to see what was happening, whispered excitedly, then pushed closer, forming a circle around the small group.

Greene looked around at the curious faces, then raised his

voice, saying, "I don't know all the right words, but I think I know what a marriage is. The Scripture says that one of the wonders of all this world is 'the way of a man with a maid.' Out of the millions of men and women on this globe, one man and one woman come together, and each of them finds something in the other that's stronger than death! So they become *one* and are no longer two separate beings."

He looked steadily into Nathan's eyes and asked, "Nathan, does thee love this woman?"

"Yes!"

"Will thee forsake all others and love only her as long as thee both shall live?"

"I—I will!"

Greene's voice trembled only slightly as he said, "Julie, does thee love this man?"

"Yes!"

"Will thee love only him as long as thee both shall live?"

Julie looked up into Nathan's eyes, saw the love that was in him, and she nodded and said, "As long as we live!"

Then Greene said the words that tied them: "I pronounce thee husband and wife!"

And as Nathan bent down and kissed her, she clung to him fiercely for one brief moment; then she pulled away and smiled. Sampson climbed into the coach, screaming curses, and the growing crowd swarmed around to stare. But Adam put his arms around Molly and, smiling at her with shining eyes, said, "They've got a war to go through, Molly, but they've got each other, and they've got God!"

Molly kissed him, and he tasted the salt of tears on her lips, but there was victory in her clear eyes. She looked at Nathan and Julie, and said quietly, "They'll make it, Adam."

And then they moved forward to welcome the newest member of the House of Winslow.

BESTSELLING HISTORICAL FICTION
For Every Reader!

The Acadian Saga Continues...

History comes to life in this captivating new story of an American woman in the Court of St. James, formed by the new writing team of T. Davis Bunn and his wife, Isabella.

With the War of 1812 raging, Erica Langston is left to deal with creditors circling her family business. Her only recourse is to travel to England to collect on outstanding debts, but her arrival leads her into the most unexpected predicaments and encounters.

The Solitary Envoy
by T. Davis and Isabella Bunn

Bestselling Author Tracie Peterson's Unforgettable New Saga

From her own Big Sky home, Tracie Peterson paints a one-of-a-kind portrait of 1860s Montana and the strong, spirited men and women who dared to call it home.

Dianne Chadwick is one of those homesteaders, but she has no idea what to expect—or even if she'll make it through the arduous wagon ride west. Protecting her is Cole Selby, a guide who acts as though his heart is as hard as the mountains. Can Dianne prove otherwise?

Land of My Heart by Tracie Peterson

◆BETHANYHOUSE

FROM *the* HEART *of the* PRAIRIE *to* YOUR HEART!

A BREATHTAKING NEW SERIES FROM A TWO-TIME CHRISTY AWARD FINALIST!

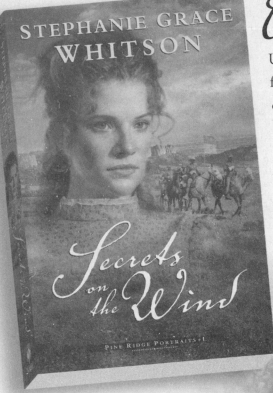

STEPHANIE GRACE WHITSON

Secrets on the Wind

PINE RIDGE PORTRAITS • 1

*O*n the desolate plains of frontier Nebraska, two U.S. soldiers discover a terrified woman in the cellar of a devastated farmstead. Laina Gray is taken to their post at Fort Robinson, where the best efforts to uncover the secrets of her trauma all fail. After living through her worst nightmare, is there any way she can learn to trust again?